Selected praise for *New York Times* bestselling author

KAT MARTIN

"Kat Martin is one of the best authors around!
She has an incredible gift for writing."
—*Literary Times*

"Kat Martin dishes up sizzling passion and true love,
then she serves it with savoir faire."
—*Los Angeles Daily News*

"*The Bride's Necklace* is a superb achievement."
—*A Romance Review*

"[A] delightful, sexy and highly satisfying read."
—*Romantic Times BOOKreviews* on *The Devil's Necklace*

"A stunning achievement for such a talented author!"
—*Literary Times* on *Bold Angel*

"Full of spirited romance and nefarious skullduggery
[and] one of Martin's trademark nail-biting endings."
—*Publishers Weekly* on *The Devil's Necklace*

"You'll be utterly captivated at Martin's
talent for creating a masterful, emotional
and unforgettable experience."
—*Romantic Times BOOKreviews* on
The Handmaiden's Necklace

KAT
MARTIN

Heart of Honor

MIRA®

ISBN-13: 978-0-7783-2383-9
ISBN-10: 0-7783-2383-8

HEART OF HONOR

www.MIRABooks.com

Printed in U.S.A.

To my mom, who recently passed away,
for all her years of love and support.
I miss you, Mom.

One

England, 1842

Leif shivered beneath the thin blanket that was all he had to warm his nearly naked body against the chill. It was not yet spring, the country roads muddy or still partly frozen. A weak sun appeared sporadically, sifting through the clouds, shining here and there for a few brief moments before disappearing again.

A sharp wind whipped the edge of the blanket and Leif pulled it closer around him. He had no idea where he was, only that he traveled through a rolling countryside marked by occasional villages, on uneven roads lined with low walls made of stone. He had been in this land for more than four passings of the moon, though mayhap he had lost track of time. All he knew for certain was that his small ship had been dashed against a rocky shore somewhere north of here, carrying his nine companions to a watery grave and leaving his own body broken and battered.

A shepherd had found him lying in the icy surf and had

taken him in, nursing him through a burning fever. Leif had been barely among the living when traders came, paid the shepherd in silver coin and dragged Leif away.

They wanted him because he looked different, because he *was* different than any of the men in this foreign land. He could not speak their language, nor understand a word of what they said, which seemed to amuse them and somehow enhance his worth. He was at least five inches taller than most of the men, his body far more muscular. Though some of them were blond, as he was, few wore beards, and none as long and shaggy as his. And their hair was cut short, while his grew past his shoulders.

Leif had been weak, unable to defend himself, when he had been lifted into the back of a wagon and driven from the shepherd's hut. As his strength began to return, the people who had taken him began to fear him, and his legs and arms were shackled with bands of heavy iron. He was shoved into a cage not nearly big enough for a man of his size, forced to crouch in the straw on the floor like an animal.

He was a prisoner in this hostile land, an oddity to be displayed to the people of the countryside, a cruel form of entertainment. They paid to see him, he knew. The fat man with a scar on his face who brought him food collected coins from the people who gathered around his cage. The man—Snively, he was called—beat and prodded him, goaded him into a violent temper, which seemed to please the crowd who had paid their money to see him.

Leif hated the man. He hated all of them.

Where he had lived, he was a free man, a man of rank among his people. His father had begged him not to leave the safety of his home, but Leif had been driven to see the world beyond his island. Since then, he had seen little outside his cage, and the hate and anger inside him gnawed like a hungry beast. Daily he prayed to the gods to help him escape, to give him strength until that time came. He promised himself it would happen, vowed he would make it so, and it was all that kept him sane.

But day after day, no chance came and the despair inside him deepened. He felt as if he were becoming the animal they drove him to be, and only in death would he ever find peace.

Leif fought the dark despair and clung to the faint hope that someday he would again be free.

Two

London, England
1842

"I tell you, girl, it is time you did your duty!" The Earl of Hampton's knotted, veined hand slammed down on the table.

Krista Hart jumped at the sound. "My duty? It is scarcely my *duty* to marry a man I cannot abide!" They were attending a ball at the Duke of Mansfield's town mansion. Through the library walls, she could hear the music of an eight-piece orchestra playing in the lavish mirrored ballroom upstairs.

"What is wrong with Lord Albert?" A tall, silver-haired man, slightly stooped—her grandfather—fixed his pale blue eyes on her. "He is young and not unattractive, the second son of the Marquess of Lindorf, a member of one of the most prominent families in England."

"Lord Albert is a complete and utter toad. The man is vain and prissy and full of himself. He is conceited and not particularly intelligent, and I am not the least bit interested in marrying him."

Her grandfather's wrinkled face turned red. "Is there a man in the whole of London who would please you, Krista? I am beginning to believe there is not. It is your responsibility to provide me with a grandson to secure the line—and time is slipping away!"

"I know my duty, Grandfather. I have been told often enough." With no direct male heirs, by special writ of the late king the Hampton title could pass through the female side of the family to the first male offspring. After her mother had died, it became Krista's sworn duty, her family believed, to provide that heir. "I am not disinclined to marriage. It is just—"

"Just that you are too busy running that confounded *gazette* of yours." He said the word with a vehemence that matched the ruddy hue of his face. "Your father indulged your mother in her silly desire to work like a commoner, and now he is indulging you. No decent woman of our social class holds a *job*, for God's sake. Or associates with the lower elements, as you do in order to produce your ridiculous magazine."

"*Heart to Heart* is not the least bit ridiculous. Our articles are educational as well as informative, and I am extremely proud of the work we do."

He made a harrumphing sound. "Your blasted gazette aside, it is time you thought of the future, time you assumed your responsibilities as my only surviving offspring and gave me the heir I need."

Krista walked toward him, the petticoats beneath the full skirt of her plum silk gown swishing against her legs as she approached where he stood next to the ornate table in the library. They'd had this conversation a number of times before—always with the same result—but she loved her grandfather and she didn't want to displease him.

Leaning over, she kissed his pale cheek. "I want a husband and family nearly as much as you want me to have them, Grandfather, but I refuse to marry a man like Lord Albert. I am certain that in time I will meet the right man."

And perhaps she already had. Last week she had made the acquaintance of a friend of her father's named Matthew Carlton. Matthew was an associate professor and the second son of the Earl of Lisemore, just the sort of man her family wanted her to wed, and Matthew had truly seemed interested in pursuing a relationship.

Still, she didn't dare mention that fact to her grandfather for fear he would begin to pressure her and perhaps even Matthew.

The earl looked her in the eye. "I don't want you to be unhappy. You understand that, don't you?"

"I know. In time, it will surely work out." At least that was what she hoped. But she was different from other women of her social class: unfashionably taller, more buxom—more independent. She didn't have a line of suitors waiting outside her door, and her grandfather knew it.

"Time," he scoffed, "is something an old man like me does not have."

She reached down and caught his thin hand. "That is not true. You are still quite robust—do not deny it." But as she looked at him, there was no doubt he was aging, and if she didn't marry and begin a family soon, the title might—as the earl so deeply feared—be lost to some distant cousin.

The old man sighed. "You try my patience, girl," he grumbled.

"I am sorry, Grandfather. I am doing the best I can."

Krista said no more and neither did he. Blowing him a kiss as she left the library, she made her way out the door toward the sound of gaiety in the ballroom, but she was no longer in the mood to dance and pretend to enjoy herself.

Still, she had promised her grandfather and the hour was yet early. Making her way through the house in search of her father and her best friend, Coralee Whitmore, who had accompanied her to the ball, she thought of Matthew Carlton and wondered at the possibilities.

Leif leaned back against the bars of his cage. In the distance, he could hear the odd, lyrical sounds of the machine that played music whenever the traveling company rolled into a village. The sun was out, warming him a little, but his cage was parked in a shady spot and an icy wind raised goose bumps over his bare skin. The only garment he wore was a spotted animal skin just large enough to cover his rod and the rest of his man parts. It did nothing to warm him.

He looked out through the bars of his cage. In the past few weeks, he had lost track of how long he had been confined. Again and again, he had attacked the men who guarded him, fought like a madman for his freedom, but shackled and chained as he was, he'd had no real chance to escape.

He reached down and plucked up a blade of straw from the damp mound covering the floor of his cage. He had wanted to see the world outside his homeland. He scoffed. He had seen any number of amazing things in this foreign land, seen animals unlike any he had known existed, seen houses larger than his entire village back home. There were people of different colors, of every shape and size. If he was not locked in this cage, he would be fascinated by the sights and places in this new and strange world, but instead, he remained a prisoner, locked up and treated like a beast.

In the days since he had been taken captive, he had been laughed at, jeered at, stoned and beaten. The people thought he was mad, and some days he believed it, too. Worse were the ones who pitied him. He had seen women cry at the cruelties he suffered. He did not want their pity, but it made him think that mayhap all of the people in this world were not like the ones who had stolen his freedom. Mayhap one day he would find someone willing to help him. If only he could speak to them, make them understand.

He said a silent prayer to the gods, as he did each day, begging them to help him.

Mayhap one day they would. It might even be today.

Leif clung to the thought as the crowd began to form around his cage.

Tonight the sky was clear, a full moon brightening the London streets. Leaning back against the velvet seat of the carriage, Krista listened to the clip-clop of the horses' iron shoes, grateful that the evening was coming to an end.

"Dear Lord, I hate these parties Grandfather is determined I attend." Since the night the two of them had argued in the Duke of Mansfield's library almost a month ago, Krista had dutifully been present at every soiree and house party to which she had received an invitation. Currently, she was on her way home from a musicale given by the Marquess of Camden.

Her grandfather wanted her to find a husband. She had an obligation to see it done.

A memory arose of Matthew Carlton and his pursuit of her these past few weeks, and she thought that her endeavors might actually be succeeding.

A dreamy sigh whispered through the carriage. "I think the party was marvelous." On the seat beside her, Coralee Whitmore, her best friend since their days together at Briarhill Academy, leaned back against the deep velvet squabs of the carriage. "If we didn't have so much work to do on the morrow, I could have danced until dawn."

Unlike Krista, who was very tall and blond, Coralee was petite, with dark-copper hair, green eyes and small, refined features. She loved dancing and parties and never seemed to grow tired of them. But the weekly gazette, *Heart to Heart,* that Krista and her father owned came first for them both, even if it meant leaving one of London's most fashionable balls just after midnight.

Though it seemed far longer, it was only six years ago that Krista's mother, Margaret Chapman Hart, had gone against her family's wishes and the unwritten rules governing a woman's place in society, and founded the magazine. Three years later, she had fallen ill and died, a long, protracted, painful death that left Krista shaken and grieving and her father even more grief-stricken than his daughter.

Krista had just turned eighteen the day she stood in the churchyard next to her mother's grave, her father weeping softly beside her. Knowing how important the paper was to her mother, Krista had taken over the operation of the gazette, which, she soon discovered, gave her a purpose and helped her to heal. She was determined to make *Heart to Heart* a success, and she would do whatever she had to in order to achieve that end.

A sound drifted toward them from the opposite side of the carriage and Krista smiled at her father's soft snore. Sir Paxton Hart was a retired professor of history, knighted by the Queen for his contributions to the study of arcane languages. Old Norse was his particular area of expertise, the language spoken by the early Scandinavian settlers. Viking lore was the professor's specialty, and since his wife's death, he had buried himself completely in his work.

"You can see how much Father enjoyed the evening," Krista

said to Corrie as she studied the lump he made on the seat, his head resting at an awkward angle against the red velvet. He was a tall, thin man with a straight, slightly too-long nose and brown hair turning to gray.

"Your father gets far more enjoyment from his studies."

Krista shifted on the seat, trying to ignore the corset stays biting into her waist beneath her pale-green, taffeta ball gown. "Father wouldn't have gone to the ball at all if he and Grandfather weren't so determined to find me a husband."

"And I assume the latest candidate is Matthew Carlton," Corrie teased. "You danced with him at least three times tonight. I gather he has asked your father for permission to court you."

Since they had first met more than a month ago, Matthew's interest in Krista had grown. Last week he had spoken to her father. Matthew was just the sort of man her family wanted her to marry. Aside from that, she liked him and she was flattered by his interest. Still, she needed time to get to know him. She told herself that allowing a man to court her was a long way from marrying him.

"You could do a good deal worse, you know," Corrie said as the carriage rolled along in the darkness, the lanterns inside giving the interior a soft yellow glow. "After all, the man is handsome and intelligent and—"

"Tall?" Krista interjected with a lift of a golden-blond eyebrow.

Corrie just laughed. "I wasn't going to say that."

But the truth was most men weren't interested in wedding a woman who was taller than they were. It simply wasn't the thing to do. "I was going to say he is also the son of an earl."

But social rank didn't matter to Krista. It was Corrie who thrived on society and the social whirl. She was a lady head to toe, the daughter of a viscount, raised with money and position. Coralee loved beautiful clothes, parties and outings to the opera and theater.

The only thing Corrie liked more was writing, and so, when Krista had taken over the gazette, she had convinced her friend to accept a job writing about the subjects she loved. Corrie had defied her family to take the position, and was currently in charge of the women's section, which constituted a goodly portion of the magazine.

The coach turned into a long gravel drive and pulled to a halt beneath the overhang in front of Corrie's house, an elegant, three-story stone structure in Grosvenor Square.

"I'll see you at the office tomorrow," she said as a footman helped her down the iron stairs. "And don't forget you promised to attend the circus with me on Sunday."

"I won't forget." Corrie wanted to write an article on the Circus Leopold for the women's section of the gazette and had asked Krista to accompany her to the Sunday performance. Since Krista hadn't been to a circus since she was a little girl, she thought it might be fun.

Corrie waved good-night as the footman escorted her up the wide granite steps to the massive front doors of the mansion, then returned to his place at the rear of the carriage. The coach rolled away and Krista's father stirred on the seat across from her, stretching his long legs out in front of him.

"Are we home yet?"

"Soon, Father. We're just round the corner." Like Coralee, Krista came from a family with money, at least on her mother's side. Margaret Chapman Hart had been born the daughter of an earl, and though she had married Paxton Hart, a near-penniless scholar, her status as a member of the aristocracy gave Krista entry into the highest ranks of society.

As far as Krista was concerned, it was more a burden than an asset.

They reached the house a few minutes later. The butler, Milton Giles, opened the door and, once they were inside, helped them remove their evening wraps: her father's silk-lined cloak and Krista's hooded cashmere cape.

"It's been a long night," she said. "I am going up to bed. I shall see you in the morning." Lifting her full silk skirt out of the way, she started to climb the curving staircase, then turned back. "Are you not coming, Father?"

"In a bit. I have an Old Norse text I've been studying. There is a passage in it I would like to review before I retire. I'll only be a moment."

Krista knew how long one of her father's "moments" could be. She started to argue, to remind him he needed his sleep, but she knew it would do no good. Her father was as passionate about his studies as Krista was about her ladies' magazine.

Thinking of the article she needed to finish in the morning before the gazette went to press, she continued climbing the stairs.

The three-story brick building that housed the offices of *Heart to Heart Weekly Ladies' Gazette* sat on a narrow street just off Piccadilly. The soul of the magazine, the heavy Stanhope printing press, one of the most modern presses of the day, sat on the ground floor next to a box that housed metal type, the letters, numbers and characters used to print the weekly publication.

Krista walked over to the wooden box. She had finished the article she had been writing for this week's edition, and except for one minor change, the gazette would be ready to go to press the next morning.

Along with Krista, her father and Corrie, the staff included Bessie Briggs, who did most of the typesetting; a printer named Gerald Bonner; his young apprentice, Freddie Wilkes; and a part-time helper who did whatever jobs were needed to get the paper out to its subscribers.

The crew was working late, as always on the night the gazette went to press. It was dark outside, the streets mostly empty, a brisk April wind blowing in off the Thames. Standing next to the press, Krista adjusted a section of metal type, then turned at the sound of footsteps on the cobbles outside the paned window at the front of the office. Glass shattered and one of the women screamed as a heavy brick sailed into the room, missing Krista's head by mere inches.

"Good heavens!" Corrie gasped.

The brick landed with a clatter and rolled several times across the wooden floor as Krista raced to the window.

"Can you see him?" Corrie rushed up beside her. "Can you tell who did it?"

Down the block, the glow of a streetlamp revealed a lad in coarse brown breeches running madly toward the corner. An instant later, he disappeared out of sight.

"It was only a boy," Krista said, turning away from the window, wiping ink from her hands with a rag. "He is already gone."

"Look! There's a note!" Minding the broken glass, Corrie knelt on the floor and retrieved a piece of paper from around the brick, fastened by a tightly tied bit of string.

"What does it say?" Krista walked up beside her.

Corrie smoothed the crumpled bit of paper. "'Stay out of men's business. If you don't, you will pay.'"

Krista sighed. "Someone must have paid the boy to do it." This wasn't the first warning *Heart to Heart* had received since she had initiated a change of format that included editorials and articles on education and social issues.

Last week, along with the usual fashion and domestic topics, there had been an article lauding Mr. Edwin Chadwick's Sanitary Conditions Report, which called for changes in the London sewer system and clean, piped water—necessary, he believed, for the prevention of disease.

The expensive proposal was highly unpopular with the water companies, local authorities and rate payers, who argued they could not afford to foot the bill.

"There will always be someone who disagrees with our position," Krista told Corrie as she plucked the scrap of paper from her friend's small hand.

"You're going to show that note to your father, aren't you?" Corrie cast her a look of warning, knowing how independent Krista was and how she hated to bother the professor with problems that related to the gazette. "Krista…?"

"All right, I'll show him." She glanced at the hole in the window letting in the chilly April air. "Have someone board that up and clean up the glass." She headed for the stairs, the note clutched in her hand. "I'll be back in a minute."

On the nights Krista worked late, her father insisted on accompanying her home. He had arrived at the office several hours ago and gone to work in his makeshift study upstairs. There was also a room for business meetings and one with a narrow chaise for napping if the hour grew late.

She knocked on his door, waited, knocked again. Finally giving up, she opened the door and walked into the high-ceilinged, book-lined room.

"I am sorry to bother you, Father, but—"

"Thought I heard someone." He removed the wire-rimmed spectacles he used for reading, and looked up from the stack of books sitting open on his desk. He was bone-thin and extremely tall. Krista had got her taller-than-average height from both her parents, but her blond hair, green eyes and more rounded, full-bosomed figure were a legacy of her fair-haired mother.

"Got involved in this translation," the professor explained. "Are we finished? Is it time to go home?"

"We aren't quite done, but we will be very soon." She crossed the room and handed him the note. "I thought I had better show you this. Someone tied this message to a brick and tossed it through the window. I guess they didn't much like my article on Mr. Chadwick's report."

"Apparently not." The professor looked up at her. "Are you certain you know what you are doing, dearest? Your mother had a number of strong opinions, but she rarely put them in print."

"True, but she wanted to. And times have changed in the past few years. Our readership has been growing steadily ever since we went to the new format."

"I suppose fighting for a good cause is worth a bit of risk. Just be careful you don't push things too far."

"I won't. One more article on the need for citywide water and disposal improvements and I am returning to our campaign for better working conditions in the mines and factories."

He chuckled. "As I recall, those articles stirred up a hornets' nest, as well."

Krista bit back a smile, knowing it was true. "Even so, I think our efforts are helping." She rounded the desk to look over his shoulder. "What are you working on?"

"I'm going over some tenth-century Icelandic tables that calculate the sun's midday height for each week of the year. They're remarkably accurate. Earlier I was reviewing a translation of the *Heimskringla* text."

The text was written in Old Norse, Krista saw, the language spoken in the Scandinavian settlements from around eight hundred until the last known Viking settlers disappeared from Greenland in the early fifteen hundreds. Her father even spoke the long-dead language.

She thought of the hours she had spent as a child in his study, listening to tales of the Vikings and even learning some of their language. She and her father had practiced together, and because she wanted to please him, she'd worked hard to perfect her skills. She was educated far more than most women, and along with her ideas of social reform, had, like her father, developed a certain fascination with Norse life and culture.

"You've a good deal of Viking blood in your veins," he would say when she bemoaned her height and the fact that most of the men of her acquaintance were shorter than she was. "Your mother could trace her family lineage back to the Danes. You should be proud of your heritage."

Mostly, Krista just wished her appearance wasn't quite so different from other women.

Her father shuffled some of the papers on his desk, closed the book he had been reading and looked up at her. "I hear you and Coralee are going to the circus on Sunday."

"Would you like to come with us?" she asked, surprised by his interest.

Her father chuckled. "Actually, I gave it some serious thought. I imagine you've heard about the main attraction. The man they call the Last Barbarian."

Krista laughed. "Yes, I gather he is part of the sideshow." Now she understood. "He is supposed to be a Viking." Anything Viking drew her father's interest. "They say he stands over seven feet tall and is covered head to foot with thick blond hair."

The professor smiled and shook his head. "It is all nonsense, of course, spouted to increase the size of the crowd. Still, it might be interesting. They say he is a terrifying brute, worth the price of admission just to get a glimpse of him in one of his towering rages. Undoubtedly some poor creature escaped from Bedlam. Mad as a hatter, I'll wager."

"Probably. But since you seem so interested, I promise I shall pay him a visit. He might make a good addition to Corrie's article."

Her father nodded. "In the meantime, try not to light a fire under the rest of London's male population."

Krista smiled. "I imagine my articles have just as many supporters as naysayers, Father. Perhaps even more."

"Perhaps. But most of them are in far less powerful positions."

That was true enough. It was men and women of the poor working classes who wanted improved conditions, not the wealthy manufacturers who would have to pay for them.

Krista left her father's office feeling a little uneasy at the notion. How far would men in power go to silence a voice that stood up for city sanitation and improving the awful conditions suffered by the working classes?

It didn't matter. Her course was set, and besides, the articles had increased the magazine's circulation by more than twenty percent. Though most men frowned on the notion that women wanted to be kept informed, it was becoming more and more clear that the female population wanted exactly that.

Heart to Heart would continue to move in that direction while also giving its readers the serialized fiction and society news they also enjoyed, Coralee's domain.

As Krista headed back downstairs to put the finishing touches on this week's edition, she found herself looking forward to the day she would spend with her friend at the circus.

Three

Sunday arrived and Coralee Whitmore appeared at Krista's front door exactly at the appointed time to pick her up for their outing to the circus. A brisk spring breeze cut through the air, while a weak sun shone down over the river where the circus had parked its wagons and set up its tents.

Krista wore a short pelisse over her mauve-and-black-striped silk day dress, while Corrie wore a gown of aqua silk edged with rose braid, and a matching rose silk bonnet.

"This is so exciting," Corrie said, filled as always with what seemed to be boundless energy. "I've never been to a circus before, have you?"

"Father brought me once when I was a little girl. It all seems different now."

But perhaps it was just this particular circus. The Circus Leopold was a traveling show that originated in the far north, at Newcastle-upon-Tyne. The troupe had made its way southwest though small towns and villages to Manchester, then traveled south through the countryside to Bristol, and eventually London.

Krista and Corrie wandered the grounds until it was time

for the early afternoon show to begin. They enjoyed the single ring performance, under a heavy canvas canopy, that mostly featured trained-animal acts. There were two dancing bears, costumed in little red satin skirts and matching hats, and some very charming monkeys that chattered away as they climbed the tent poles into the rafters. The young women watched foot jugglers, tumblers, a pair of gaily dressed clowns and three trick riders who did flips and jumps while standing on the backs of galloping horses.

The smell of sawdust filled the air, and the music of a calliope drifted across the open field, along with the shouts of barkers hawking their wares outside the main tent. It was an interesting way to spend an afternoon, but Krista was a little surprised at how run-down everything looked.

On close inspection, she found the brightly colored costumes faded, the big, dapple-gray horses old and swaybacked. Even the circus performers seemed to be weary people who had seen better days.

Still, the circus was a novelty in London and something to mark the coming of spring.

"I should like to interview the owner," Corrie said, determined to show the acts in a positive light. "His name is Nigel Leopold. Let's go see if he is in his wagon."

They set off in that direction, Corrie gazing around, making mental notes of everything she saw. She had an amazing memory for details, which was one of the reasons she was so good at her job.

"I really liked the bears," she said as they walked along. "They seemed to be smiling the whole time they danced."

Krista didn't mention that earlier, when she had passed by their cage, she had noticed the trainer tying their lips back with a thin piece of string.

She glanced at her surroundings and noticed a group of performers heading back to their wagons to prepare for the next performance. One of the trainers was leading five big gray horses away.

"There's something about this show," Krista said. "Everything just seems a bit...*ragged.*"

"Yes, I noticed that, too. I suppose so much traveling is hard on the horses and equipment."

"I suppose." But it bothered her that the animals all seemed so beaten down. The ponies' ribs showed through their thick winter coats and the bears hung their heads as if they hadn't the strength of will to lift them.

She and Corrie made their way through the throngs of people pouring out of the main tent, and noticed a group gathering in front of one of the brightly painted circus wagons. There were bars on the cage, Krista saw, and wondered what animal might be kept inside.

"Let's go see what it is," Corrie said, tugging her in that direction. Coralee was at least six inches shorter than Krista, and smaller boned. They were an odd pair, one short, one tall, one of them blond, the other with fiery copper hair, and yet they had long been best friends.

As tall as Krista was, even standing at the back of the crowd she could see that the creature in the cage wasn't an animal at all. The sign above the cage read The Last Barbarian, and beneath it Caution! Approach at Your Own Risk.

"It is him!" Corrie nearly shouted. "Come—let's get closer."

It was him, all right, the man Krista's father had mentioned. He was hunched over in the cage, which was too short to allow him to stand completely straight, and naked except for an animal-skin loincloth that hid his manly parts. He stood there shaking the bars like a madman—prodded, Krista saw, by a beefy man with a scar across his cheek, wielding a long pointed stick.

The man inside the cage was manacled hand and foot, ranting and raving, cursing, she was sure, though none of the gibberish he spouted made any sense.

But he was certainly not seven feet tall. Nor was he covered with thick blond hair. Still, he was taller than any man of her acquaintance, with long, shaggy blond hair that hung well past a set of massive shoulders and an unkempt beard that hung down over a chest banded with slabs of muscle. Thick muscles bulged in his thighs and arms, and his eyes...

Even from a distance, she could see the wildness there, the fierce hatred burning in the incredible blue depths, the color more intense than any she had ever seen before.

"God in heaven," Corrie said in awe. "We need to get closer."

Her gaze still fixed on the creature in the cage, Krista moved at Corrie's urging, and they weaved their way to the front of the crowd. Pity for the man tugged at Krista's heart, and part of her wished she had never spotted the cage.

Dear God, the worst sort of criminal deserved better treatment than they were giving the man in that cage.

The stick jabbed into Leif's ribs a second time and he let out a roar. He gripped the iron bars and shook them, knowing if he didn't the stick would find its mark again. There were scars on his legs and arms, scars on his back, scars on his wrists and ankles from the manacles he was forced to wear.

Part of him no longer noticed the pain. That part could barely summon the will to rise each morning and face another hellish day, no longer cared whether he lived or died.

It was the other part of him, the part with the fierce will to live, that kept him going another hour, another minute.

Kept him hoping that somehow he would find a means of escape.

Ignoring the roar of the crowd that had gathered in front of the cage, some of them pointing and laughing, others making jeering faces, he looked up at the tiny creature who slipped through the bars to join him. A *monkey,* they called it. Alfinn, he had named it, little elf—the only friend Leif had in this godforsaken world he had stumbled upon, and he valued that friendship greatly.

Leif spoke to the monkey as if it could actually understand him, making fun of the people who were making fun of him, though of course they didn't know what he was saying. One day, he told himself, he would find a way out of this cage, free of the manacles that rendered him impotent against his captors. One day, he would take the stick away from the fat Snively and run it through the man's wormy gut.

The monkey chattered, jumped up and down as Snively prodded Leif into a fit of rage again. The crowd roared and fell back from the cage. Some of the women cried out in fear.

He liked that they feared him.

It was the only power he held in a world where he was utterly powerless, his life no longer his own.

Little by little, the crowd began to disperse. They had seen what they came for, seen the wild man in the cage. When he looked out at them again, only two women remained. One was a redhead, smaller than average, and prettier, too, though she wasn't the sort who appealed to him, being too much like a child.

He remembered what it felt like to hold a woman, a real woman, one who could stir a man's blood.

The blonde was that way. Tall, voluptuous, ripe for a man's touch, with creamy skin and a mouth made for passion. His groin tightened. It was good to know that as much as they tried, his captors had not yet broken him. Good to know that he was still a man.

He grinned at the monkey. "Now there is a woman...a real woman," he said. "She could fire a man's blood with a single glance from those pretty green eyes."

Alfinn chattered as if he understood. The blonde said something to the woman beside her, then turned and started walking away. Leif watched as the breeze came up and blew her hat off her head. A cluster of thick golden curls rested on each of her shoulders, as shiny as the sun, only a deeper, richer shade. She bent to retrieve the hat, and even though the fullness of her garments disguised her feminine curves, he could tell that her waist was tiny and her bottom nicely rounded.

"See that, Alf. There is an arse built for a man's pleasure. If I was not in this cage, I would give her a ride she would not soon forget, a ride that would satisfy us both."

The grin slid from his face as the blonde whirled to face him. Her cheeks had turned flame-red and her green eyes snapped with fire. She strode toward him like a falcon swooping down on its prey, and Leif found himself stepping back from the bars of his cage.

"How dare you!"

For seconds, he stood there frozen, wondering how the woman could possibly have read his mind.

"You are a crude, vulgar beast! And to think I was feeling sorry for you—what a fool I was!" She glared at him, a look far more fierce than any he had hurled at the crowd. She turned and stomped back toward her friend before it occurred to him that she had spoken to him in the same language he had spoken to her.

"Wait!" he shouted after her. "Do not leave! Forgive me for

what I said. I knew not that you could understand me. I did not mean to insult you. I swear I would never insult a woman!"

The blonde's head went up but she just kept walking, her friend falling in beside her.

"Please, I beg you! I need your help." A lump formed in his throat. Every day he came closer to losing his mind; dimly, he wondered if mayhap it had finally happened. "By the gods, please come back. I am begging you." His voice broke. "You are my…only hope."

She stopped then, stood there with her back to him for several long seconds. Then she turned and started walking back toward the cage. He wasn't mad; she really had understood. Leif didn't realize there were tears in his eyes until he blinked and they ran into the heavy growth of beard on his cheeks.

He wiped them away before she could see.

"I am sorry," he said when she reached the front of the cage. "I know I insulted you, but that was not my intention. You speak my language. No one else understands. I am a prisoner here and in desperate need of your help."

She was frowning, he saw, no longer angry. "The language you are speaking…how did you learn it?" Her words were pronounced clearly, not perfectly, but well enough that he could understand her.

"It is the way we speak where I come from."

"That is not possible. No one has spoken Old Norse for more than three hundred years."

"On Draugr Island, this is the language we speak."

"Draugr Island? I have never heard of it."

His heart was beating. He knew one slip, one wrong move, and the woman would walk away, and with her his only chance for freedom. "I sailed from there six months ago. My ship was lost on the rocks in a place far north of here. I was badly injured when I washed up on the beach."

"You were shipwrecked?"

He nodded. "By the time I had healed enough to know what was happening, I had been captured and sold to the man who put me in this cage."

The blonde was biting her lip, which was plump and a rich shade of rose. It amazed him to feel a fresh shot of lust for her. Living like an animal as he had for the past six months, he would not have thought it possible.

"I am called Leif."

She looked down at his wrist, saw the faint trace of blood beginning to seep from the raw spot rubbed by the manacle.

"My father speaks your language much better than I do, Leif. He will be able to talk to you, help you get out of this cage."

Leif forced himself not to move toward her. He didn't want to do anything that might seem threatening. He couldn't afford to scare her away.

"You will come back then, and bring your father with you?"

"Yes."

"What is your name?"

"My name is Krista Hart."

"Do you vow this on your honor, Krista Hart?"

For a moment, she looked surprised. "Yes, I vow it on my honor."

He gave a faint nod of his head. As he watched her walk away, he suddenly felt exhausted. It was the feeling of hope, he knew. He had lost what little he had and now he didn't think he could survive if she didn't return.

He sat down in the cage, the little monkey, Alfinn, climbing up on his shoulder. Together they would wait for the man called Snively and his helpers to come. The men would take him into a larger cage, feed him, water him like an animal, spray him down with freezing water to keep him clean, then return him to the smaller cage for the next performance.

Leif's chest squeezed. Mayhap tomorrow she would come.

He thought of thick, golden-blond hair tied back in curls that framed a lovely face and lively green eyes, thought of a body fashioned by the gods, and prayed that she was more than just a beautiful woman.

Prayed that Krista Hart was a woman of honor.

Four

Krista rushed into her Mayfair town house, heading down the hall to her father's study. Since they had come straightaway from the circus, Coralee flew along in her wake.

Krista knocked, then shoved open the study door without waiting for permission. "Father! You won't believe—"

She stopped as Matthew Carlton rose from the chair in front of her father's desk. She hadn't expected to see him, though lately Matthew had been stopping by the house more and more often.

Her father also came to his feet. "What is it, my dear? Not more trouble with the gazette?"

She glanced at Matthew. He was openly courting her now, though Krista still wasn't sure how she truly felt about him. But Matthew was intelligent and a good conversationalist, and with his light-brown hair, hazel eyes and well-defined features, he was attractive. He would make a good husband, her father believed. And Matthew also believed they would suit each other very well.

Of course, there was every chance his interest was spurred by the size of Krista's very substantial dowry and the inheritance she had received from her mother.

"No, Father, this has nothing to do with *Heart to Heart*." She glanced again at Matthew, uncertain why she hesitated to speak in front of him. Coralee stood in the doorway, eager to hear what the professor would say when Krista told him about the man in the cage.

"I am sorry," Krista said, "but I need to speak to my father. In private."

"Of course." Matthew kept his expression bland, though it was clear he didn't like being dismissed. He was, after all, an associate professor and the second son of an earl. And he was becoming more and more proprietary where she was concerned.

He bowed his head politely. "If you will excuse me..."

"Perhaps Matthew and Miss Whitmore would care for some refreshment in the drawing room," her father suggested diplomatically.

"That would be nice." From the doorway, Corrie gave Matthew an airy smile as she floated into the study and took his arm. Casting Krista a *you-owe-me* glance, she led him off down the hall.

The moment the study door closed behind them, Krista launched into the tale of her adventure at the circus and the wild man she had seen in the cage.

"It was amazing, Father. The man speaks Old Norse. That is the reason no one understands what he is saying. I didn't figure it out myself, right away." She tried not to blush as she recalled the big man's bawdy remarks as she had bent over in front of the cage.

The professor removed his spectacles, his curiosity piqued. "Did he say how he learned the language?"

"That's just it. He says he is from a place called Draugr Is-land. He says everyone there speaks Norse."

The professor's eyes widened. "Draugr Island? Are you certain that is what he said?"

"Why, yes. Do you know it?"

"In Old Norse, *draugr* means ghost. There is a legend about Ghost Island. They say it is a place shrouded in fog, a rocky, fearsome bit of land, dangerous for an unwary sea captain and his ship. Most men say it doesn't actually exist."

"What is the legend about it?"

"Supposedly the ancient Vikings who settled in Greenland did not die off at the beginning of the sixteenth century as most scholars believe. When their numbers began to dwindle from disease and hostile weather, the people fled to the safety of an island somewhere north of the Orkneys."

"Draugr Island?"

He shrugged his thin shoulders. "No one really knows. But that is the legend."

Krista thought of the man in the cage. "There is a good chance, Father, it is far more than that."

She told him about the shipwreck and that the man had said he had been captured and sold into slavery. "It was pitiful. No one should be treated the way they do that poor fellow."

The professor rounded the desk, his brown eyes gleaming. "And you don't believe he was insane...someone who might have learned the language some other way and is making all of this up?"

"I have no idea what to believe. But I promised we would help him. I gave him my word."

"Then help him we shall." Her father walked over and opened the study door, waited for her to step out into the hall. "We'll make our excuses to Matthew and drop Coralee off at home on our way back to the circus."

Krista felt a rush of relief. She had given her word. She was determined to keep it.

Leif was back in his cage for the late-afternoon performance. The fat man, Snively, didn't even have to prod him to get him to shout and rage at the crowd. All Leif had to do was imagine that the woman he had spoken to would break her vow and not return. All he had to think of was living out his days crouched on the floor of an iron-barred cage, and the frustration inside him bubbled over into fury.

The usual crowd gathered. The little monkey, Alfinn, appeared, somehow sensing his need for companionship during these times. Leif raised his manacled fist and banged it against the bars, and one of the men in the crowd tossed a stone in his direction. Several others followed, the sharp sting of the rocks sending Leif's fury up another notch.

Snively was grinning, thrilled by his performance, which only made his anger more fierce. He was raging, calling them names not fit for a decent man's ears, when he caught a glimpse of shiny blond hair at the back of the crowd.

His heart kicked into gear, slamming like a hammer against the inside of his chest. She had come. There was no mistaking the tall blond woman who stood above the rest, the smooth skin and bright green eyes. He bit down on the next words he might have hurled at the crowd. He had offended the woman once. He would not do it again.

Silently, he watched her move toward him, followed by an even taller, very thin man wearing one of the silly-looking high hats the men here seemed to favor. Leif made himself wait patiently for the pair to arrive, when he wanted to shout with glee, his hopes soaring again.

Just then Snively stepped in front of the cage, blocking the man and woman's approach. Leif could tell he was warning them away from the danger.

The thin man just smiled. He began speaking to Snively, but Leif couldn't tell what he was saying. All the while, the woman watched Leif, her expression growing more and more grim. Then the fat man said something and started walking away. Leif imagined he was going to get his master, and a chill went through him. The man called Leopold was even crueler than the fat man, Snively.

Leif fixed his attention on the pair in front of the cage.

"My name is Paxton Hart," the thin man said, and Leif understood every word.

"I am Leif of Draugr. That is where I come from."

"My daughter has told me some of your story. I would like to hear the rest."

Leif glanced back toward the wagon where Leopold would likely be found, but saw no one coming. Quickly, he told the man, Pax-ton Hart, the story of leaving Draugr Island with nine other men, the shipwreck and how he had been badly injured and washed ashore. That the other men had all been killed, and that while he was unconscious, healing in the barn owned by a local shepherd, he had been bound and sold.

"I was a free man, but now I am a slave. I am hoping you will be able to help me."

"There are no slaves in England," Pax-ton said. "Here no man can own another." He turned to the woman who said she was his daughter, and spoke words Leif couldn't understand. Leif looked up at the sound of footsteps and saw Leopold approach. As much as he tried to control it, his insides quivered.

"Are you the man who owns the circus?" the professor asked. The man was black-haired, perhaps in his forties. He made an exaggerated bow and came up with an oily smile. "Nigel Leopold, at your service. And you would be…?"

"Professor Paxton Hart."

"*Sir* Paxton Hart," Krista added, hoping it might somehow help them.

"Pleasure meeting you, Sir Paxton." Leopold flashed another phony smile and Krista felt an instant dislike for the man.

"Mr. Leopold," she said. "You're holding a man against his will. He claims that you abducted him. That makes you guilty of a terrible crime." She pointed toward the cage. "Release him at once."

Leopold just laughed. "The fellow escaped from Bedlam. I am doing him a favor, but if you wish to see him returned—"

"There is nothing wrong with his sanity," her father said. "He merely speaks a different language."

"Gibberish—that is what he speaks. Mad as Mrs. Crane's daughter. Here, at least he earns his keep. We feed him three meals a day and give him a dry place to sleep."

"He isn't an animal," Krista said. "He doesn't deserve to be treated like one."

"The man is mad. As I said, I am doing him a favor."

Her father studied the circus owner with a frown. "I believe I understand the problem. How much do you want for his release?" Leif was a unique attraction. The Last Barbarian drew large, very profitable crowds. Leopold would not want to lose him, and buying his freedom would not be cheap.

"Trust me, my friend, you can't afford the cost," Leopold said.

Krista glanced at the blond man in shackles crouching in a cage that was far too small for him. Though the day was fairly warm, a sharp breeze blew, and with so little clothing he had to be cold. For an instant, their gazes met and held, and there was such despair, such a tortured look in his eyes that her stomach squeezed with pity for him. There was no way she was leaving any human being locked in that cage, no matter how much it cost.

Her father rattled off a more than fair sum of money, but Leopold just smiled and shook his head. "'Fraid not, gov'nor. Like I said, here he earns his keep."

"Then I suppose we shall have to take another tack," Krista said. "First, let me remind you that my father has been knighted by the queen. Second, my name is Krista *Chapman* Hart. My grandfather, Thomas Herald Chapman, is the Earl of Hampton."

Leopold's thin black eyebrows shot up, though he quickly smoothed his features.

"That said," Krista continued, "the man in the cage has accused you of a crime. My father and I both speak his language and we will be more than happy to testify in a court of law that you have abducted him illegally and are keeping him here against his will, that you have forced him into slavery for your own selfish purposes. We will make it abundantly clear to the authorities, Mr. Leopold, that *you* are the man who should be locked behind bars."

Leopold's face turned a vivid shade of red. "You can't threaten me!"

"My daughter has made no threat," the professor said. "She had merely stated a set of facts. If you wish to refute them, it will be your word against ours."

A greedy circus owner against a knight of the realm and a member of the aristocracy. Krista almost smiled.

"The choice is yours," the professor continued. "Either you accept a reasonable amount of money as repayment for your investment in Mr. Draugr's *care* these past six months, or you face the wrath of the authorities. Which will it be?"

Leopold sputtered and cursed. One of his hands tightened

into a fist he raised in Krista's direction. In the cage behind her, she heard Leif threatening to cut out Leopold's tongue if he laid a hand on either one of them.

Again she might have smiled, but when she turned toward the cage, she saw the man's big, manacled hands wrapped around the bars as if he meant to pull them out with pure brute strength, and his eyes, the most intense blue she had ever seen, promised vengeance.

Dear God, what would they do with the man once they set him free? They couldn't simply abandon him. And of course, her father would be determined to study him.

What if he really was as dangerous as the circus owner claimed?

"Mr. Leopold…?" her father pressed.

"All right, all right. You win. Give me the damnable money. Take the bloody bastard and good riddance, and none of you better show your faces around here again."

The professor cleared his throat. "I'm afraid I don't carry that quantity of money on my person. We shall have to wait here for my daughter to return with the coin."

Leopold swore an oath and stalked away.

Krista took her cue and hurried back to the carriage. Half an hour later, she returned to the circus grounds with a bag of gold sovereigns. Her father delivered them to Mr. Leopold's wagon, then walked back to the cage with the heavyset man she had seen before, the man with the scar on his cheek.

With a muttered curse, the man shoved the rusty iron key into the lock and opened the door to set Leif of Draugr Island free.

Krista stood by as the cage door swung open and the big blond giant climbed down the wooden stairs. When he stretched to his full height, she saw that he was at least six inches taller than she.

It was amazing. For the first time in her life, she actually felt petite.

He stood quietly in front of her father as the heavyset man, Snively, she recalled, knelt to unfasten the manacles around his ankles, then removed them from his wrists. As soon as he was free, Leif grabbed the man by the front of his shirt with a growl and lifted him clear off the ground, shaking the fellow so hard Krista was afraid he would break the man's neck.

"Leif! Stop it! If you hurt him, they will put you back in a cage for sure!" she cried in Old Norse.

His eyes swung to hers and she could read the turbulence there. For a moment, he continued to hold the man up off the ground. Then her words seemed to penetrate his rage and he tossed the beefy man away as if he were a sack of garbage.

"My friend," the professor said to Leif. "You must learn to control that magnificent temper of yours if you are going to live among civilized people."

"I *am* controlling my temper," Leif said. "If I were not, the son of a whore would be dead."

Krista bit back a grin.

"I think it is a good time for us to leave," her father announced.

"I do not leave without my things." Leif glared at Snively, who hauled himself up out of the dirt. "Tell him I want my sword and the rest of my property they stole from me." He flicked a glance at the tiny monkey that clung to the bars of the cage. "And tell him Alfinn goes with me."

"Alfinn?" Krista repeated.

He pointed to the small animal, not much bigger than his hand. "Alf is the only friend I have had for the last six months. I will not leave him here."

Krista sighed. "I will see what I can do." She translated the blond man's words and pointed toward the monkey, and Snively grumbled something she didn't quite hear.

Leif took a threatening step toward him and Snively held up his hands and retreated. "Tell the bloke he can have the damn monkey. Tell 'im I'll go get his things."

Leif reached for Alfinn, who scrambled up his arm and sat down on his shoulder, looking ridiculously pleased. Krista had to admit the little fellow was cute, though she had no idea what they were going to do with him.

For that matter, she had no idea what they were going to do with Leif, either.

A few minutes later, the beefy man returned. He laid Leif's heavy sword, encased in a thick leather sheath, on the ground, along with a carved staghorn pendant and an armband that apparently also belonged to him.

"Tell 'im 'is clothes was torn to pieces on the rocks."

Krista nodded, translated for Leif and the man hurried away. Her father started walking and Leif, after collecting his few possessions, fell into step behind him. Krista ignored the people staring at them as they walked past: two men, one of them nearly naked, and a woman as tall as an average man. The threesome stopped when they reached the carriage and their waiting coachman.

"Well, Father, what do you suggest we do now?"

"What? Oh, yes...yes, we do need to speak about that." He looked up at the huge blond man. "You have nowhere to go, Leif of Draugr. That much is clear. You may stay with us until you have time to sort things out."

Though she knew this was coming, Krista inwardly groaned.

Leif seemed to ponder the notion. "I will need a ship to return to my home." He gazed at the busy London streets. "This place you live… What is it called?"

"London," the professor told him.

"In Draugr, for many years the young men dreamed of seeing faraway places…places our ancestors spoke of in sagas. But there was no more wood, no way to make a sailing vessel like those built by our forefathers, great Viking warriors of their day. Then a ship crashed onto the rocks along the north end of the island and we finally had the chance we had been seeking."

His eyes strayed toward Krista, so blue and intense she felt as if they touched her. He spoke once more to her father. "I left the island to discover the world…to learn all that I could. So far, I have known only cruelty, but I believe good may be found here, as well. Now more than ever, I need to learn all that I can. Will you teach me?"

The professor fairly beamed. "We will make a trade, you and I. I will teach you—if you will teach me!"

The blond man's face broke into a wide smile, revealing a flash of white teeth through his heavy beard. It transformed his features, made him look young, and his eyes even bluer against his sun-browned skin.

He stood there nearly naked, and for the first time Krista saw him as a man. He had the body of a Viking warrior, an amazingly masculine physique that sent a funny little shiver down her spine.

Her father must have noticed the direction of her gaze, for he opened the carriage door and removed a blanket from beneath the seat. He draped it over Leif's powerful shoulders, the monkey scrambling out of the way for an instant, then returning to its perch.

"I am sure you've had enough of people staring at you."

Leif merely nodded. Clutching the blanket around him, he waited while Krista climbed into the carriage and settled herself inside.

The professor entered next and Leif followed, filling the interior with his massive frame. As the vehicle lurched into motion, Krista found herself studying his face, the high cheekbones and incredible blue eyes.

She couldn't help wondering how old he was and what he might look like without all that long hair and scraggly blond beard.

Five

❧❧❧

"I am not quite certain where to go from here," the professor said to Krista, once the three of them stood in the entry of the town house.

"He needs some clothes." Krista tried not to stare at the powerful legs revealed beneath the blanket he clutched around his massive shoulders. "He needs to shave and he needs a haircut."

"Yes, yes, of course." Her father repeated the words to Leif, whose jaw subtly tightened. "If you wish to live here, you will have to learn our ways," the professor told him. "Is that your wish?"

Leif glanced from her father to her and nodded. "I am here. I have no other choice."

Surveying his surroundings, he looked up at the light dancing through the crystal prisms on the chandelier above his head, then down at the black-and-white marble floor beneath his bare feet. The place was fashionable and elegant, Margaret Hart's finest handiwork. The drawing rooms, morning room and guest rooms were all done in light, airy colors and delicate wallpapers. The men's rooms—the study, library and billiard room—were paneled in dark wood and filled with heavy, ornate furniture.

Leif studied his elegant surroundings and Krista could see the amazement on his face. He walked over and picked up a cut-crystal lamp. "This is for light?"

"Yes," she said. "It burns oil."

"We use candles and torches. This is a good idea."

She bit back a smile. He wandered away from them, into the drawing room, sat down on the rose velvet settee. He moved up and down, testing the springs, then looked over to where she stood next to her father in the doorway.

"No furs? We use wolf pelts to keep warm."

Wolf pelts! She pointed to the marble-manteled fireplace. "We burn coal," she said.

She watched him moving around the room, lifting one item after another, a cloisonné vase, a small painted portrait of her mother, a silver candlestick that held a beeswax candle. Her father gave him a few moments to get comfortable in the house, then moved toward him.

"I'll show you around in a bit," he said. "Point out some of the things you have probably never seen and might find interesting."

Leif just nodded, his eyes moving ceaselessly over the items in the house.

"In the meantime, why don't we go upstairs and I'll ring for my valet?" The professor's glance moved over Leif's long hair and heavy beard. "We'll need to do a bit of work. Let us see if Henry is up to the challenge." He smiled at Krista. "If you will excuse us, my dear."

She nodded. "While you're at it, I'll see what I can do about finding him something to wear."

The professor's gray-flecked brown eyebrows went up. "That could certainly pose a problem."

"I'll think of something." Krista left her father to his task and made her way out to the stables. The coachman was a large man, not as big as Leif, but perhaps his clothes would do until they could have some made.

"Skinner!" she called out, and the big, burly man appeared. "I have a favor to ask. If you agree, you will be well compensated."

The coachman listened to her offer and grinned.

Twenty minutes later, she returned to the house carrying a pair of brown trousers and a full-sleeved, homespun shirt. They would probably be a snug fit, but better than what Leif was wearing now—which was nearly nothing at all.

Krista gave the men enough time to finish what had to be a Herculean task, then headed upstairs, the clothes draped over her arm, a pair of Skinner's boots clutched in one hand. She started down the hall toward her father's bedroom, then froze where she stood as the door to the bathing room swung open and she caught sight of Leif standing in the center, naked except for the small, white linen towel tied round his trim hips.

He shook his head like a big wet dog, flinging drops of water all over the bathing room and clear out into the hall. Krista's eyes locked with his and her breath caught.

With his hair cropped short and his face clean-shaven, Leif of Draugr was unbelievably handsome. High cheekbones, a straight nose and well-formed lips…a jaw that was lean and hard… And when he smiled, he had very white teeth.

With a will of its own, her gaze moved down his body. Now that his bushy blond beard was gone, his chest was completely exposed. It was heavily muscled and lightly furred with golden-blond hair.

Her eyes dropped lower, over the only part of him decently covered. The towel moved, jerked and began to rise, and her eyes widened in shock. Her gaze flew back to his face and she saw the corner of his mouth edge up.

"I hope you are pleased with what you see, lady. You can see how much you please me."

Krista whirled away, her face flaming. She could hear the little monkey chattering as if he were laughing. Barely holding on to her temper, she stormed off down the hall, banged on her father's bedroom door and walked in.

Seated in front of his dresser reading a book, the professor pulled off the silver spectacles curled round his ears. "What is it, dearling?"

"That…that *man*," she sputtered. "You have to do something about him."

"I am doing my best, dearest. Henry gave him a shave and cut his hair. He bathed himself quite thoroughly. I thought he looked rather a good deal better."

He looked better, all right. Leif of Draugr was handsome as sin and built like a Viking god, the finest specimen of man Krista had ever seen. She held out the clothes. "He is still very nearly naked and he is…he is…"

"Yes?"

What could she say? That it was extremely clear the path of the man's thoughts where she was concerned? Then again, perhaps she wasn't being fair. After all, the poor fellow had been locked in a cage for the past six months and he was, it was clear, a very virile man.

"Never mind." She pressed the clothes into her father's arms. "They'll be a little tight, but at least he will be decent."

Her father nodded. "I'll take them to him straightaway."

She watched her father's thin figure walk down the hall and disappear into the bathing room. He returned a few minutes later.

"He is getting dressed. I'm sure he is hungry. I asked him to join us for supper. Have Cook set an extra place, will you, my dear?"

Krista tried to imagine the huge man sitting down with them at table. The man was a barbarian. He came from a culture that was supposed to have disappeared more than three hundred years ago. Though she found the Vikings fascinating, they were wild, crude, primitive people.

Krista inwardly groaned. She just wished she could think of a way to send Leif of Draugr home.

Leif finished toweling his hair, enjoying the feel of his close-cut blond locks and smooth, hairless cheeks. In his world, men wore long hair and beards. But in the months since his capture, he had grown to hate his unruly mop and scraggly face hair.

Mayhap this place, London, had a few worthwhile customs.

He pulled on the clothes Pax-ton Hart had handed him. The breeches—*trousers,* they were called—were too short and fit so tightly he thought they might split right down the seam. His manhood bulged at the front, pressing into the fabric so hard it was painful.

At home, men wore comfortable, loose-fitting breeches beneath their kirtles, the long robes that came to below their knees. For summer the tunics were shorter, leaving their legs completely bare except for their knee-high boots.

Leif pulled on the white, woven garment, a *shirt,* Pax-ton had said. Pax-ton was a *professor.* That was what they called a mentor here. In Leif's world, there were no formal places of learning. Information was passed down from generation to generation: how to grow crops, how to raise sheep and goats and cattle, how to harvest fish and seals from the sea, how to fight to protect your family. It was, he had always thought, a good way to live.

Still, there was a written language on Draugr, and much of their history was scribed so that each generation would remember. In this new world, information was written in what the professor called a *book*.

"I have a very large room filled with books," the man had said with pride. "Once you learn to speak English, once you learn to read, the entire world will be open to you."

Just then tiny Alfinn appeared, prowling the bathing chamber, inspecting the tub and sink. Leif turned and caught a glimpse of himself in the reflecting glass, saw how the white shirt stretched over his shoulders, pulling at the seams. And his arms were a little too long for the full, gathered sleeves.

Still, he was covered, his dignity restored to him.

He felt the beginning of a smile. He had learned during his months of captivity that women here were prudish and pretended to know little of men. But their eyes often betrayed them, revealing their curiosity, or thoughts of a more prurient nature.

Even the blonde had been curious. She had liked his appearance, too. Liked the way his body looked without clothing. He figured he would like to see her that way, too, though he didn't think the professor would approve.

Even on Draugr, a father protected his daughter's virtue. A young woman's virginity was meant for her husband. Still, there were women who enjoyed an evening of pleasure as much as a man, and if there was money enough, a man could afford to keep several concubines in his household as well as a wife.

Before he had left Draugr, Leif had considered taking a woman to wife, and there were any number of females who would have been willing. But he'd been determined to see the world outside his island, and when the chance arose, he had taken it. He had suffered for it, but there were bad men everywhere, and the kindness shown by the professor and his daughter renewed his hope that his journey would not be in vain.

Turning away from the glass, he left the monkey in the bathing room with a promise to return with food, and made his way downstairs, the tight trousers rubbing his manhood and making him think of the blonde. He tried to shove the thought away, but then he saw her, standing next to the professor.

She was wearing a gown of smooth, finely woven cloth the same bright green as her eyes. The top fitted closely over her voluptuous breasts, and her waist was smaller than that of any of the women on the island. The bottom half of the gown was full and flared out over her hips in a tantalizing manner.

Though in some odd fashion the clothing appealed to him, it appeared to be even more uncomfortable than the men's garments here. Still, he liked the slight glimpse of creamy flesh he caught where the top dipped into a vee. Nice, round breasts, he could tell, and his trousers became even tighter.

"Good evening, Pro-fes-sor," he said, using the English word. "Lady." He didn't know the English for that, but he imagined he would learn it very soon.

"The proper way to address me is 'Miss Hart.'"

"Miss…Hart," he repeated, having only a little trouble saying the words. He had been listening to the language of the people in this country for more than six months. From the start he had known his chances for freedom would improve if he could master some of the sounds, learn some of the words. Now that he was free, it was even more important.

"We will begin working on your speaking lessons tomorrow," the professor told him. "For tonight, we will converse

only in your language. You must be hungry, Leif. Why don't
we all go in to dinner?"

His stomach growled in answer, and he nodded. He prayed
these people ate something more substantial than the gruel he
had been living on for the past six months.

Krista watched Leif of Draugr walk ahead of her into the
dining room. Though a woman was respected in Viking society, she came second to a man. The thought did not sit well.
Leif of Draugr had a lot to learn if he intended to make his
way in the civilized world.

Krista started to correct him, tell him that here a lady entered
in front of a gentleman, then remembered her father had said
that for tonight there would be no lessons. She supposed the
Norseman deserved an evening to simply enjoy his freedom.

They sat down at the table, her father at the head, Leif to
his right. He looked a little surprised to see her sit down in the
chair across from him.

"I imagine you are hungry," she said, determined to put him
at ease.

"I could eat the hindquarters of a sheep," he said with a grin
that formed a dimple in his cheek. Dear God, there ought to
be a law against one man looking so good. It wasn't fair to the
rest of the male population. Still, his crude remark reminded
her he was nothing more than a pretty face, and she had never
been interested in that sort of man.

Her father cleared his throat, warning her not to correct
Leif's manners, and started asking him questions. They spoke
rapidly, and Krista missed some of the conversation, but
thought she heard that Leif was unmarried and had no children, the eldest son of the chieftain of the island.

"I have known twenty-seven summers," he said. "And like

many of our men, I was restless to see what lay beyond my island."

Krista drew her napkin across her lap. "You said the ship you built sank somewhere north of here."

He nodded and followed her example. "My father feared something like that might happen. As his eldest son, I am meant to rule in his place when his time on earth is over. He forbade me to go, but I would not listen."

It was clear how much this bothered him. He had a duty to his father, his clan, it seemed, and unless he could return, he could not fulfill it.

A pair of servants arrived just then with platters of meat and vegetables, and the conversation ended. Leif watched the professor, who carefully showed him how to take a serving of roast lamb from the platter being held out to him. Leif took a hefty portion, then another, then helped himself to enough boiled mackerel to fill his plate to the limit.

The moment he set the plate on the table, he picked up his knife, stuck it into a hunk of meat and shoved the meat into his mouth.

Krista's eyes widened as he grinned in pleasure and wiped away a trickle of grease with the back of his hand.

"This is very good," he said.

She opened her mouth to tell him that here people ate with a fork and did not take so much food in one bite, but her father shook his head.

"Tomorrow we begin," he said to her softly in English.

Leif took a big gulp of the red wine in his crystal goblet and froze. His eyes found hers and she saw that the taste was completely foreign to him and not one that pleased him. He looked down at the floor, and she could see he was thinking of spitting it out.

Krista quickly shook her head. "Here we do not spit."

Leif eyed her a moment more, then swallowed as if drinking a mouthful of poison. "What is that?" he asked, his lips curled in disgust.

"Wine," her father answered. "Your people usually drink ale, as I recall. I gather it doesn't please you."

The Norseman made a face and Krista bit back a grin.

"It is an acquired taste," her father explained.

Leif finished his food in short order. Krista had eaten only half her meal when she looked over to find his plate empty.

"I think Leif would like a little more," she said to her father, careful to speak in Norse, as they had agreed. His gaze dropped to the big man's plate, which was scraped completely clean. Krista motioned for one of the servants to bring another platter of meat and a few more vegetables.

Leif ignored the carrots, turnips and potatoes, and she remembered that except for a few wild onions and a couple of varieties of seaweed, Vikings mostly ate fish, meat and dairy.

Dessert followed the meal, and Leif looked down warily at the custard pudding covered with a paste of sugared almonds one of the servants set in front of him.

"You don't have to eat it," she said. "Not unless you want to."

Leif looked wildly relieved. He shoved back his chair. "I promised Alfinn I would bring him some food." He reached down for the platter of turnips and carrots, got up and started toward the dining room door. It was clear he wasn't used to asking permission.

"Monkeys don't generally stay in the house," she called after him. "Perhaps Alfinn would be happier out in the stables."

"Sta-bles?" he asked, turning to face her.

"Where the horses are kept."

He nodded. "Alf is used to being around other animals. I

think he would like that." Leif disappeared, and while he was gone, Krista finished her delicious custard. When the meal was over, Leif still had not returned.

The professor rose worriedly from his chair. "I had better go see what has happened to him."

"I had one of the guest rooms prepared," Krista said. "He should be more than comfortable there."

"I'll bring him inside and show him his quarters."

But when her father returned, he was alone. "He was sleeping out in the stable. He has made himself a bed on the straw in one of the stalls. I wasn't sure I should wake him."

After what he had suffered the past six months, it bothered her to think of him sleeping another night in the straw. "Perhaps he didn't understand. I'll go explain, tell him he doesn't have to live like an animal anymore."

Her father nodded. He was tired, she knew. So was she. Tomorrow was Monday and she needed to start working on her editorial for this week's edition. One more article on the benefits of city sanitation and she could return to even more pressing issues.

A vote was coming up on a proposal that would ban women, young girls and boys from working underground in the mines. Though the act had sprung mostly from concern about public morals after it was discovered women and children often stripped nearly naked to tolerate the heat, she believed the law was a good one.

Making her way out the door, Krista headed for the stables, still uncertain what to do about Leif.

Leif slept deeply. He dreamed of home, as he often did, thinking of the life he had left behind. In truth, he never should have left the island. His friends would still be alive and he would not be trying to make his way in a hostile world completely foreign to him. Still, now that he was free, he had begun to see the world he had once hoped to discover, and leaving Draugr grew more difficult to regret.

Then again, had he remained, he would not be aching with need for a woman, dreaming of soft, feminine curves and full breasts, of golden hair that could make a man hard just to think of touching it.

A voice floated toward him in the darkness, drifted into his dreams. He remembered then that Inga had come to his bed tonight and he had taken her until both of them were wildly sated. He was half-awake now, hard again, and ready for more. When she touched his shoulder, shook him a little, he knew she must be ready, as well.

He reached for her, pulled her down in the pile of straw and rolled her beneath him, then began to massage a plump, round breast as he kissed the side of her neck.

"You were always a woman of passion, Inga, but tonight—"

Her shriek of outrage nearly burst his ears. Leif jerked away from her, fully awake now, blinking owlishly and remembering that he was no longer on Draugr, but in a place called London.

"How dare you!"

He was in London, not Draugr, and the ripe breasts he had been caressing belonged to the voluptuous blonde.

"I was dreaming. I thought you were someone else."

"Someone else!" she screeched. "Someone else!" She straightened and looked down her very nice nose at him. Even angry, she was beautiful, with the finely carved features of a Norsewoman, the graceful neck and full lips. "This is the third time you've insulted me, Leif of Draugr. You will apologize right now or you will leave this house and not return!"

His jaw hardened. He had nowhere to go. He needed these people's help and yet he would not be commanded by a woman, no matter how comely she was.

"I am not sorry I touched you. Only that you did not wish me to. For that I apologize, lady."

He was still wearing the uncomfortable trousers that molded his hips and legs like skin. But he had unbuttoned the front and now he was afraid she would see what she had done to him. He came up out of the straw, turned away from her a moment and struggled to rebutton the trousers.

In the dim light of a lantern hanging on the wall, he could see that her face was flushed, the pins gone from her hair. The heavy mass tumbled in thick, golden curls around her shoulders, and bits of straw stuck out here and there.

His groin tightened even more. He couldn't remember a woman who had stirred such rampant lust in him. He swore a soft curse.

"I heard that," she said, "and you will refrain from swearing in this household."

"You give orders like a man, lady. Is that another of your customs?"

Her cheeks flushed. For an instant she glanced away. She was used to giving orders, but deep down, he was pleased to see, she was still a woman.

"I came out here to tell you there is no need for you to sleep in the barn. A room has been prepared for your use in the house."

He glanced over at the tiny monkey, who was looking at him with fear in his shiny dark eyes. "What about Alfinn? He will think I have abandoned him."

The woman looked at the monkey. "Monkeys don't belong in the house."

Alfinn gave a forlorn, pitiful cry, a trick he had learned to get treats from the crowd.

The woman sighed. "All right, you can bring him with you, but you are the one who will have to clean up his messes."

Leif grinned. "Alf is a very clean monkey."

She rolled her eyes and started walking back toward the house, and Leif fell in behind her. Her cumbersome female garments mostly hid her curves, but her bottom swayed nicely beneath the heavy fabric.

By the gods, he would have to watch himself where Krista Hart was concerned. He had long been without a woman and this one pleased him greatly. He was used to taking his enjoyment from whatever woman he desired. They welcomed his advances and always had.

Not this time. Although he was now a free man, he would have to forgo his pleasure. He thought of her outrage when he had unwittingly caressed her breasts. He was glad his weapon had not been nearby. If she had found his sword, she surely would have plunged it into his heart.

Leif grunted. Unlike Inga, it didn't seem likely the blonde would invite him into her bed.

Six

~~~~~~~~~~

She was running late. Krista rarely overslept, and wouldn't have this morning except that she had been so furious after her encounter in the stables last night that she'd had trouble falling asleep. Leif Draugr was a big, crude, overgrown lout without the least sensibilities. Why, the liberties he had taken! No man had ever touched her the way he had. No man had ever dared to cup her breasts, let alone caress them as if he knew exactly how sensitive they were. She had known he would be trouble, but she never would have guessed how much.

Krista made her way down the hall, refusing to think of him as she hurried toward the bathing room, opened the door and walked in. Shock widened her eyes at the sight of the big brute lounging in the copper tub, his legs drawn up against his chest, water barely covering his manly parts.

"Good morning, lady."

Krista whirled away from him, her face burning. Unconsciously, she pulled her quilted robe a little tighter around her. "What are you doing in here?" Her eyes remained closed but she couldn't block the image of broad shoulders banded with muscle, and arms that looked as solid as steel.

"I am bathing," he said, as if it was his right to usurp her usual time in the marble-floored chamber converted from one of the bedrooms her mother had designed. "I thought it was the custom here to bathe. In my country we cleanse with steam or in one of the hot volcanic pools, but I suppose this will have to do."

She ground her teeth but kept her back to him. A memory returned of those moments beneath him in the stables, the feel of his big hard body pressing her into the straw, the heat of his mouth on the side of her neck. A faint shiver ran through her.

Krista took a deep breath. "Why is it every time I see you, you are at least half-naked?"

He started to reply, but she simply marched out the door, slammed it as hard as she could and stomped back to her bedroom.

By the time he was gone and she'd had her turn in the bathing room, she was running even later and furious about it. Dear God, was it only yesterday that the house had seemed a quiet place of refuge? Now it was filled with the presence of a big, overbearing hulk of a man, and she had no idea what to do about it.

Her maid, Priscilla Dobbs, helped her dress and coif her hair, then Krista hurried for the stairs, grabbing the ribbons of her felt bonnet on her way to the door. The carriage waited in front. She plucked her woolen cloak off the ornately carved coatrack in the entry, urged even faster by the sound of her father's prized pair of matched chestnuts stomping, jangling their harness in their eagerness to get under way.

The butler, long-time family retainer Milton Giles, silver-haired and always extremely proper, pulled open the door and stepped back to let her pass. "Have a good day, miss."

"Thank you, Giles."

She started forward, anxious to reach the office, but just as she stepped through the door, Matthew Carlton appeared in her path, having just reached the top of the front porch stairs.

"Krista! I was hoping I would find you here." He smiled. "I stopped by your office. They said you hadn't come in yet. I thought perhaps I might catch you before you left for work."

Krista bit back a sigh of frustration. "I'm sorry, Matthew. I am running extremely late this morning. Is there something you need?"

"I suppose you could say that. Viscount Wimby and his wife, Diana, have extended an invitation tonight to join them for a performance of the *Unearthly Bride* at Her Majesty's Theatre. I realize it is extremely short notice, but I was hoping you might accompany me."

She needed to catch up on work. She had this week's editorial to write, which reminded her she must speak to Corrie about her article on the circus. Krista wanted to be sure her friend left out any reference to the wild man in the cage. Corrie didn't yet know the man was living in her best friend's house—at least for the present. Once she did, she would realize how important it was to protect his privacy.

"I appreciate the invitation, Matthew, I truly do, but I have a great deal to do and—"

"And what? It seems there is always something you have to do that takes precedence over me."

"That isn't true. I have simply been busy. A rather unexpected…*guest*…has arrived and it has thrown my schedule off a bit."

She looked up just then and inwardly groaned. Leif was descending the stairs in his ridiculously too-tight shirt and trousers, his fierce blue gaze drilling into Matthew.

Matthew stared equally hard at Leif. "Who…is…*that?*" His

eyes nearly popped from their sockets. "Surely that is *not* your house guest."

Krista didn't like his tone, and apparently, neither did Leif. Though he couldn't understand a word, his jaw subtly tightened.

"It's a very long story, Matthew. Right now, I don't have time to explain."

Matthew looked at the tall blond man, incredibly handsome even in his ill-fitting clothes, and overwhelmingly male. "If you imagine any possible future for the two of us, you will take the time to explain."

Surely he couldn't be jealous. Leif might be handsome, but he was also insufferably crude and completely barbaric, certainly no threat to a gentleman like Matthew.

She fixed a smile on her face. "All right, we'll go to the opera, as you wish. I'll explain everything tonight."

"I would like an explanation now. I believe I am entitled to one."

Thankfully, her father appeared in the hallway just then. "I thought I heard voices...."

Krista sighed with relief. "Father, Matthew has some questions about our...houseguest. Would you mind taking a moment to explain?"

Leif stepped off the bottom stair. "Who is this man?" he asked her, as if he had a right to know. He spoke in very rapid Norse, which should have made it hard to understand, but his tone made his meaning extremely clear.

"He is a friend," she told him, and saw Matthew's eyebrows creep up at the language they were speaking.

Her father spoke in English to Matthew. "His name is Leif Draugr. He is Norse. That is the language he is speaking. I shall be happy to explain, but in return, I will expect your discretion in the matter. This is a golden opportunity, Matthew, a chance to study a culture long believed dead."

Matthew turned a shrewd look on Leif, who was glaring at him as if he were the fat man with the stick outside his cage.

"You have my word," Matthew said, obviously intrigued. "Whatever we discuss will be kept strictly between the two of us."

Her father nodded, turned to Leif. "You will have to pardon me, Leif. I need a word with my colleague. As soon as I am finished, we can begin your lessons." He turned his attention to Krista. "It is obvious our guest needs appropriate clothing. If you wouldn't mind, I would appreciate your help in the matter."

She flicked a glance at Leif. He did look ridiculously out of place. Not only was he wearing the clothes of a servant, they didn't begin to fit his large frame.

"I could pick you up at the office this afternoon," her father said, "if you could find a bit of time."

Inwardly, she sighed. Her mother had always helped her father with his wardrobe, which cut of garment suited his thin frame best, which fabrics went together. Krista had taken over the task and was fairly good at it. She could assist the big Norseman far better than the professor could.

"All right, I'll go with you. I should have things under control by this afternoon."

"Around two o'clock, then?"

She nodded, worked up a smile for Matthew. "Now if you gentlemen will excuse me...."

Matthew and her father both made faint bows. She said nothing to Leif, but she could feel his eyes on her as she walked out the door. Ignoring an odd little flutter in the pit of her stomach, she headed down the front steps to her carriage.

* * *

Work at the gazette continued as it always did. Lately she had been looking for a cheaper source of paper, and she spent the morning reviewing different bids. Immersed in the job, Krista didn't notice the time. She was sitting at her desk, poring over the notes she had made for the article she needed to finish, when her father walked into the office.

"Oh, dear. I am sorry, Father. I completely lost track of time." She removed the apron tied over the skirt of her dove-gray gown, which was trimmed with scarlet braid and one of her favorites. "Just let me get my bonnet and I'll be right with you."

He nodded, waited patiently while she went upstairs to check her appearance in the mirror in the retiring room and grab her scarlet-trimmed bonnet and cloak. Setting the bonnet over the blond curls nestled against her shoulders, she tied the ribbons beneath her chin, then returned downstairs.

"Leif is waiting in the carriage," the professor said.

And rather impatiently, she discovered when she climbed into the coach and took a seat across from him.

"You are late, lady."

A trickle of annoyance slipped through her. "Women are supposed to be late. That is to be expected. Besides, how would you know? You don't have a…a…" she didn't know the word in Old Norse for *clock,* so just said, "a way to tell time."

He leaned over and looked out the window, pointed up at the yellow orb shining over the city. "The movement of the sun tells me all I need know." He pinned her with a glare. "And you, lady, are late."

Krista opened her mouth to tell him he was lucky she had agreed to come at all, but her father gave her one of his looks. "Remember, dearest," he said, speaking English, "things are different where Leif comes from."

"Yes, well, Leif is in London now, not on Draugr Island." She flicked the blond man a glance. "He has to learn to accept the way things are here."

Leif grunted as if he knew what she had said.

Krista ignored him, just settled back against the seat and stared out the window, silently suffering the jounce of an occasional pothole as the carriage made its way through the heavy London traffic. Still, she could sense him there in the carriage. She seemed to be attuned to his every movement, seemed to feel the heat of his eyes as they roamed over her. She had never been so aware of a man before. She found it strangely unnerving.

They reached her father's favorite tailor's shop, Stephen Ward and Company on Regent Street, and made their way inside the building. Mr. Ward had earlier been sent a note informing him of their arrival, and he appeared at the front counter himself.

"Welcome, Sir Paxton…Miss Hart. As always it is our pleasure to serve you." He was a small man, with black hair parted in the middle and a thin mustache. Only the faintest lift of a single black eyebrow betrayed his surprise at the sight of Leif's tall figure in his too-small clothes.

"This is Mr. Draugr, a friend of ours from Norway," her father smoothly explained. "His baggage was stolen when he arrived at the dock, and as you can see, he is in dire need of a wardrobe."

"Yes…I do see that, indeed." The man turned, clapped his hands, and two of his young male apprentices, one tall and gangly with very pale skin, the other shorter, with sandy hair and blue eyes, appeared in the receiving room.

"I believe we have quite a job ahead of us," the tailor said to them. He turned, smiled at the professor. "Have no fear, Sir Paxton. Stephen Ward is up to the job."

He guided the group through a curtain that led into the luxuriously furnished back room of the establishment, and pointed toward a dais at one end. "If Mr. Draugr will step up on the platform, we will get started with the necessary measurements."

Leif looked at the professor, who translated Mr. Ward's wishes, then climbed up on the dais.

Stephen Ward approached the platform, pausing for a moment to inspect Leif's impressive, broad-shouldered frame. "My, he is quite a specimen." There was blatant appreciation in the man's dark eyes.

Krista allowed herself the same inspection and couldn't say she blamed him. In the vee at the front of Leif's full-sleeved shirt, muscles bunched every time he moved. His waist was narrow, his abdomen flat, his legs long and muscular. For an instant, her glance strayed to the heavy bulge at the front of his too-tight breeches before she jerked her eyes back to his face.

A corner of Leif's mouth faintly curved. "If you wish these new clothes to fit, lady, you should not stare at that particular place."

Her face flamed. Sweet God, the way he spoke to her! At one-and-twenty, Krista had heard enough women's gossip to be aware of a man's anatomy. She knew that as big as he was, and from what the tight-fitting trousers revealed, Leif Draugr must be very well endowed. The married women would titter about it. Krista tried not to imagine what the man's very large masculinity would mean to a woman, but her mind strayed there anyway.

Worst of all, Leif seemed to sense her interest, even approve. "It is good for a woman to know what pleases her."

Silently, she ground her teeth, biting back the rude remark

that lingered on the tip of her tongue. She squared her shoulders. "Time is running short," she said to Mr. Ward. "Shall we get on with it? I have a good deal to do back at my place of business."

"Of course," said Stephen Ward. "Just let me take a few quick measurements and then we will decide on what styles might suit your friend. From there we can choose the fabric and colors that will be best for him. Once we are finished, you can take him next door to Menkin's Millinery for whatever hats he may need, then down the block to Beasley and Hewitt for boots and shoes."

The shopkeeper rolled his dark eyes. "I daresay Mr. Draugr is a very lucky man. Just think, by the end of the day he will be the proud owner of an entirely new wardrobe."

An entirely new wardrobe, Krista thought sullenly—and she and her father would be footing the bill. The least Leif could do was show a bit of gratitude.

Instead, he grumbled and growled through the entire fitting, complaining about the uncomfortable tightness and the scratchiness of the fabric.

"On Draugr, men's garments are made to be comfortable," he told her father, then fixed his blue eyes on Krista. "And the women's clothes here are even worse. How can you work in such confining garments? I would think they would cut off the blood to your head."

Krista paused in her task of sorting through dozens of fabrics and styles, and tossed him a glare. "This is the way civilized women dress. It is the…the…" She didn't know the Norse word for fashion, wasn't sure there was one. "…the proper way to dress. Most men find the way we look attractive."

She refused to admit he had a point, that she particularly hated wearing the ridiculously uncomfortable whalebone corset that cinched in her waist and forced her body into the fashionable hourglass style of the day.

Leif's eyes ran over her from head to foot, took in her small waist, paused for a moment on her bosom, then returned to her face.

He made a slight inclination of his head. "I concede the point, lady. But I believe your beauty has little to do with clothing. In fact, you would be far more attractive without any clothes at all."

Her eyes widened. She couldn't believe he had said that, and right in front of her father! And the way he was looking at her... No man of her acquaintance would ever dare to do so.

Her father cleared his throat and spoke to Stephen Ward. "As my daughter has said, she has a great deal left to do this afternoon. If we might hurry this along a bit..."

"Yes, yes, of course." The tailor rushed to complete the fitting, his apprentices lending a hand.

"Mr. Draugr will need the garments very quickly," Krista told him. "For your trouble, we will be happy to pay whatever price you deem fair."

Ward's small eyes gleamed at the prospect. "Yes, well, I can certainly see the urgency. We can have the garments ready for the initial fitting three days hence. The outfits should be completed by the end of the week."

"Very good," her father said, looking extremely pleased. "We shall return three days hence."

They left the shop, stopped by the hatters, then the bootmaker's down the block. They were finished at last and back in the carriage, Leif lounging like a big, sultry lion in the velvet seat across from her. The coach returned her to the narrow brick building that housed the offices of *Heart to Heart* and her father escorted her inside.

"What time shall I expect you home?"

"Matthew has asked me to attend the opera with him tonight. I'll need time to get ready. I hope to be home by six."

The professor nodded, but somehow seemed distracted, perhaps even worried, and she wondered if it might have something to do with the hot looks that had passed her way from Leif Draugr's side of the carriage.

Seven

Her Majesty's Theater in Haymarket was lavish, with crystal chandeliers, red velvet draperies and gilded sconces along walls covered in red-flocked paper. A sea of elegantly dressed ladies and gentlemen filled the seats, the crowd rising now in the pit below the boxes as the performance came to a close.

For the occasion, Krista had chosen a gown of amethyst silk, the bodice riding low on the shoulders, with rows of gold lace that swept across the front and displayed a modest glimpse of her bosom. The full skirt, cut in a deep vee front and back, was the height of fashion, the gathered overskirt of matching lace tied up with amethyst bows.

The opera drew to a close, the orchestra music fading as the curtain came down. The crowd applauded loudly, and seated next to Krista and Matthew in the viscount's very elegant box, Lord Wimby shouted, "Bravo!"

An older man with iron-gray hair and a ruddy complexion, his lordship was there with his much younger wife, Diana, the two of them acting as chaperones for the evening, since Krista and Matthew were as yet unwed.

Matthew rose from his chair and helped Krista to her feet.

His hand found her waist, settled there, and he urged her toward the red velvet curtain that closed off the box.

"Michael Balfe was wonderful, Matthew," she said of the composer. "Thank you for inviting me."

He smiled. "The pleasure was mine, I promise you."

"Matthew usually prefers to spend his evenings doing something a bit more exciting," Diana said, flashing him a smile Krista couldn't quite read.

"His father and I try to encourage him to the finer pleasures in life," Lord Wimby said. "We shall expect you to be a good influence, as well." His eyes twinkled at his reference to them as a couple. Krista was still trying to think of her and Matthew that way.

As they moved out into the hallway, Diana spread her black feathered fan and stirred the air in front of her face. "The opera was splendid, wasn't it? I do so love music. I could listen for hours. There is nothing I find more entertaining."

Gowned in dark-blue-and-black-striped silk, her auburn hair swept into a cluster of curls on each side of her face, Diana Cormack, Viscountess Wimby, was an extremely beautiful woman.

"You love music," her husband agreed with a soft smile just for her, "but you also quite enjoy the theater." It was obvious the man was enamored of his younger wife, a widow he had married just last year.

"You're right, darling." Her blue gaze lit for a moment on Matthew. "I should have said there was *almost* nothing I would rather do."

They left the box and made their way downstairs to the line of carriages pulling up in front. It didn't take long for the viscount's fancy, four-horse coach to arrive, and soon they were bowling along the busy streets, returning Krista to her town house.

Still, it was nearly midnight by the time she arrived at her residence in St. George Street and Matthew escorted her up to the door. Since the servants had all retired, she used her key to gain entry, then turned to bid him good-night.

Matthew surprised her by pulling her close and pressing a soft kiss on her cheek. "Thank you for a lovely evening, Krista. We'll have to do this again very soon. I'll stop by in a day or two so that we may discuss it."

Krista merely nodded. She wished she knew how she felt about Matthew Carlton. Each time they were together, she became less certain. Perhaps time would bring the answer. She closed the front door and turned toward the stairs, then spotted the glow of a lamp down the hall, shining through the open door of her father's study. Presuming he was either working late or had forgotten to blow out the lamp when he went to bed, she headed in that direction.

As she stepped inside the study, she saw that it wasn't her father, but Leif's blond head bent over the mahogany table in the corner, and her feet came to a sudden halt.

He was holding a pencil in one hand, gripping it as if it might escape, working to copy the shape of the letters her father had written down for him. She must have made some sound, for he set the pencil aside, shoved back his chair and rose to his feet.

"So…you are finally home."

Her chin inched up. Why did the man always manage to annoy her? "The hours I keep are hardly your concern," she said, though the Norse words she chose were far plainer.

He tipped his head toward the window. "This *friend* of yours…you stay out with him until late into the night?" A lantern burned beside the front door and she realized he must have seen her with Matthew.

"We went to a…a—" she how no idea what word might best describe an opera "—a place where music was played, and we were not alone."

"You say he is a friend, but I think he is more."

She ignored the remark. Matthew had merely kissed her cheek, hardly enough to deserve recriminations, and certainly not from Leif. Instead, she walked behind the table to look at what he had been studying. She saw the letters he had written again and again, improving with each of his efforts.

"Father is teaching you to write the alphabet. Once you know the letters you can learn to read. Do you know what that word means?"

He nodded. "In ancient times, our people used sagas to record those things they wanted to pass from generation to generation. Then the priests came. They taught my people the written word and about your Christian God."

"So you are a Christian?"

He shrugged those powerful shoulders. "On Draugr, we have our own religion. It is a mixture of your Christianity and our belief in the ancient Viking gods."

"I see." She wanted to ask him more about the place he had come from, but the hour was late and she saw that Leif was watching her, his gaze burning into her in that way that so unnerved her.

"It is getting on past midnight," she said. "I think it is time we both went up to bed."

His blue eyes sharpened. "Aye, lady, if that is your wish. I would like that above all things."

She wasn't prepared for the quick movement that propelled her into his arms. She gasped as his mouth came down over hers. For an instant, she was too shocked to push him away. Then the heat of his kiss, the brush of his tongue sliding over her lips, urging her to open for him, sparked a wave of heat that turned her mind completely to mush.

Her stomach tightened and warmth floated out through her limbs. His lips felt soft yet firm as they moved over hers, and her eyes slid closed. Her heartbeat quickened, his hard body pressing into hers made her nipples tighten beneath the bodice of her gown, and her bones seemed to melt into his.

Then his hands moved lower, down over her hips until he cupped her bottom through the layers of her gown, and her eyes flew open.

Dear sweet God! For the first time, she realized exactly what Leif was about—that she had somehow erred in translating her simple wish to retire, and he believed she was inviting him into her bed.

She started to struggle, pressed her palms against his granite-hard chest and tried to push him away. With obvious reluctance, Leif ended the kiss an instant before her father walked into the study.

She was breathing a little too hard and so was he, and she could feel warm color washing into her cheeks. Her father glanced from one of them to the other and his eyebrows slowly lifted.

"I came to check on Leif," he said to Krista, "to tell him it was time for him to go to bed."

Her color deepened. "Yes, well, I was trying to tell him that same thing." She kept her gaze carefully fixed on her father. "Unfortunately, I said it wrong and Leif misunderstood."

The professor's eyebrows climbed even higher as her meaning grew clear.

"It—it really wasn't his fault," she said. "I mistranslated the words and he got the wrong impression."

The professor flicked a glance at Leif, who stood there stoically, not understanding a word. "I see."

"You said yourself things are different where he comes from." Why she was defending him she couldn't begin to say. Perhaps it was only fair, since, in truth, she had returned his kiss, at least for a time, and found it not the least unpleasant. The thought made her face heat up again.

Dear Lord, she was being courted by Matthew Carlton, considering the possibility of sharing a life with him. What on earth was wrong with her?

"I would like to know what you are saying to your father." Leif's gaze pinned her where she stood.

"I told him what happened, that you misunderstood what I was trying to say."

"That is correct," the professor agreed, speaking Leif's language now. "My daughter was merely trying to suggest that you and she retire upstairs for the night."

The glitter of heat returned to Leif's eyes. "That is what she said. It is the custom here, then, for a man to share his daughter with a guest?"

"No!" they said in unison.

Her father cleared his throat. "What we both meant to say was that the hour is getting late and you need to get some sleep. That is *all* we were trying to say."

His face fell. Then he straightened, making him look even taller than he usually did. "I am sorry, Professor. I meant no insult to you or your daughter."

"I'm certain you didn't, Leif."

"I will admit that I would like to have her in my bed. Any man can see she is a woman of great beauty and strong passions. Once I have learned your language and customs and am able to make my own way, mayhap I will make you an offer for her."

Krista bit back a gasp and her father made an odd choking sound. He seemed to be groping for words. "Y-yes, well, we both appreciate your interest, Leif, but I think Krista may already have plans of her own."

"She is your daughter. It is up to you to decide what is best for her. But now is not the time. I have nothing to offer and no way to provide for her. When the time is right, mayhap we will talk again."

Her father looked to her for help, but Krista couldn't think of a single thing to say. "I'm sorry," he said, "I don't believe time will alter things."

Leif's jaw firmed. "We will see," he said simply.

Krista fixed her attention on the professor and forced herself to smile. "Come, Father. As you say, it is time for all of us to get some rest." She took his arm and guided him toward the door. "Good night, Leif," she said, her smile still carefully in place, and disappeared out the door.

Krista couldn't sleep. Good heavens, was the man completely mad? Make an offer for her! Ten cows, perhaps, or maybe twelve sheep? That was what a Viking warrior did when he wanted a wife. Indeed!

Still, he had called her a woman of great beauty and strong passions. She had never thought of herself as either of those things, and it made her feel strangely feminine, womanly in a way she never had before.

As she lay in bed, unconsciously her fingers came up to her lips. Leif might be a barbarian, but he certainly knew how to kiss. Perhaps that was it. The man was wild, primitive. Perhaps his untamed desires aroused something wild and primitive in her.

Whatever the reason, she had discovered something about herself tonight, discovered that she was indeed a woman, one with the same physical desires as other women. It was a revelation worth the outrageous kiss, though *that,* she vowed, was never going to happen again.

The week slipped into the next. Krista rarely saw Leif, who was ensconced from early morning until late into the evening in the study with her father. They even took their meals there, declining to join her, probably her father's attempt to spare her from Leif's lack of table manners.

Still, it was obvious the professor was beginning to think a great deal of him.

"The lad is amazing," he said proudly one morning as she prepared to leave for work. "I have never known a more determined pupil. He is smart as a whip and his memory for words is astounding. In the course of a day, he manages to do all the work I set out for him, and master an entire new list of vocabulary words."

Krista could see how hard Leif worked. He remained in the study long after the household had retired for the night, and was already at his studies by the time she came down in the morning. He was fastidiously clean, but now he finished in the bathing room long before she was even out of bed.

During the week, the professor twice accompanied Leif back to Stephen Ward and Company for fittings on his wardrobe. As promised, the clothes were delivered late in the afternoon of the following Monday. As soon as they arrived, Leif went up to his room to put them on; Henry, her father's valet, hurrying to assist him.

She didn't see Leif again for more than an hour. Matthew Carlton had dropped by on the way to his early evening fencing lesson, and Krista was en route to the drawing room to greet him when she spotted Leif and her father's little valet walking down the stairs, Henry preening at the job he had done on the man he considered the professor's protégé.

Krista halted at the sight. For a long moment, she just stood there staring.

Dressed in a pair of dove-gray trousers, a light-blue waistcoat embroidered in dark-blue silk and a navy-blue frock coat, he moved with surprising grace for a man of his size. His hair was freshly combed, a rich golden color, his face lightly suntanned, bringing out the blue of his eyes. He was the son of a Viking chieftain, and in that moment he looked every inch a man of aristocratic blood.

Then he tugged on the wide white stock stiffened with whalebone that encircled his powerful neck, gave a soft curse, and the illusion swiftly faded. He was Leif of Draugr, an illiterate barbarian, she reminded herself. The attraction she told herself she didn't feel was merely a reaction to his startling good looks.

Still, when he stopped in front of her, when she found herself looking up into those blue, blue eyes, her heart gave an odd leap and started beating like rain on a roof.

"Do the garments please you, lady?"

She swallowed. "You look very…very…"

A corner of his mouth edged up. "You are pleased with my appearance. I can see it in your eyes. I had hoped that you would be."

The man had no lack of conceit—that was for certain. "I think you look very…nice in your new clothes." So nice, in fact, that she couldn't stop staring. Which she continued to do even as Matthew and her father walked out of the drawing room.

Matthew took one look at Leif and started frowning. Her father's gaze traveled from Matthew to her, followed her gaze to Leif, and he began to frown, as well.

Leif and Matthew seemed to be sizing each other up. There was something territorial in both men's expression, each warning the other to stay away from the prize, which in this case seemed to be her. Leif stepped toward her and she quickly edged away.

She managed to muster a smile. "Matthew, you remember Mr. Draugr?"

Matthew seemed to be fighting for control. "How could I possibly forget?"

Leif's jaw firmed. He hadn't a clue what they were saying, but the look of disdain on Matthew's face apparently said enough.

Her father cleared his throat. "Matthew dropped by to pay his respects, my dear. Why don't the two of you go back to the drawing room and I'll have Giles bring you some nice hot tea."

Krista forced herself to smile. "That sounds like a very good notion." Anything to escape the tension building between the men.

But Matthew shook his head. "I'm afraid I can't stay long enough for tea. My fencing instructor is a highly impatient man. I just stopped by to extend an invitation. My father is hosting a small dinner party on Saturday next, and he has asked if you and the professor might be able to attend."

The Earl of Lisemore was an extremely powerful man and one used to having his wishes obeyed. If she was seriously interested in Matthew, she had no choice but to accept the invitation.

Besides, she wanted to get to know the man who courted her. To do that, she needed to make at least some effort in that direction. "Father?"

"That is very kind of the earl," the professor said. "Of course we would both be delighted to attend."

"Fine. I'll send my coach round to pick you up...say, seven o'clock Saturday night?"

Her father nodded.

"In the meantime, I would like a word with you in private, Professor Hart."

Her father glanced at Leif and wearily nodded. "Let's go into my study, shall we? If you will excuse us, my dear?" He excused himself to Leif, whose jaw seemed to tighten even more, and the two men disappeared down the hall.

"I do not like that man," Leif said.

"You don't even know him."

"I know he wants you. He tries to hide it. I do not understand why."

She had no idea whether or not Matthew desired her. Now that Leif had mentioned it, it bothered her that she hadn't the slightest clue.

"Matthew is courting me," she said, hoping she had translated the words in a way Leif would understand. "It is the custom here when a man is interested in a woman."

"He has offered to pay the bride price your father set?"

"We are only getting to know each other. It is not yet time to speak of marriage."

He grunted. "He is weak. You are a woman of strong needs. He is not the man for you."

"Whether he is the right choice for me or not is none of your concern. Now, if you will excuse me…" She turned and started walking, then felt Leif's hand close around her upper arm, stopping her progress and turning her to face him.

"You need a man of strength, Krista Hart, a man who knows how to handle you. You need a man like me."

She pulled free of his hold. "You are arrogant and conceited, Leif Draugr, and the last sort of man I need!" She started walking again, and though he didn't try to stop her, she heard his faint rumble of laughter as she started up the stairs.

Of all the nerve!

On the floor below, the study door opened and she heard her father speaking to Matthew as they walked down the hall. Krista ignored them. She was tired of men and their constant manipulations. Her father, her grandfather. Even Matthew. Leif might be audacious and far too bold, but at least he spoke his thoughts frankly.

As she opened the door to her bedroom, she wondered what Matthew had wanted to speak to her father about—then decided she really didn't care.

He was a man and she was tired of men in general. Krista firmly closed her bedroom door.

Another day dawned. With a single dark glance, Leif sent the little valet, Henry, scurrying from the bedroom. He'd had a lesson yesterday on how to dress himself. There was nothing wrong with his brain. He was perfectly capable of putting on the outlandish clothing men wore in this place.

He smiled. Now, if Krista Hart wanted to assist him… He went hard just thinking of her soft pale fingers moving over his body, buttoning the front of his pleated white shirt, moving down to help him fasten his trousers.

His arousal strengthened. Mayhap if she were here to help him, he wouldn't mind putting on the ridiculously uncomfortable garments quite so much.

He held up the white cotton drawers men wore, then tossed them away. He would wear the shirt and snug-fitting trousers, and the *waist-coat*, it was called, and also the burgundy *jacket*, but not the confining garments men here wore underneath. There was a limit to his tolerance and he had reached it.

He pulled on the shirt and closed the fastenings, then reached for the trousers. The clothes were uncomfortable, yet they fit him well enough, he supposed, and he had no choice but to wear them. He had to get along here, to make his way in this alien land he had stumbled upon. In truth, he planned to do far more than that.

He had defied his father in leaving the island, certain he would soon return. He had duties, responsibilities, and he never meant to shirk them. But a force beyond his control had driven him to see the world outside his home. For a while after his capture, he had believed he was wrong, that his death would be the only result of his leaving. But now he was free and a new world stretched before him. His adventure had finally begun and he meant to make the most of it.

And he was rapidly learning. The gods had blessed him in providing the professor as his teacher. Leif would learn all he needed to know to survive in this foreign world. And in time—he was determined—he would prosper.

He would earn the money to buy himself a ship to carry him back to his homeland. When that happened, he would not arrive as a pauper, a failure, but as a man who had flourished in this place called Eng-land.

He would make his father proud, make him see that his son had been right to leave.

He turned at the sound of a knock on his door. It had better not be that little son of a weasel, Henry. He had tried to tell the man he needed no more help putting on his clothes, but the man hadn't understood, and Leif had finally tossed him out of the room on his skinny little arse.

He opened the door, but it was Krista who stood there, not Henry. She looked pretty today, as she always did, with her enticing womanly curves and shiny golden hair.

"My father wishes to see us in the study."

He nodded, picked up the burgundy jacket the professor

had told him it was customary to wear, and followed her out into the hall. He walked beside her down the staircase, pleased by her height, apparently uncommon in most of the women of this land, and thought how well her soft curves would fit with his larger, more solid frame.

"What is it the professor wishes?" he asked, just to keep his mind from straying in that direction.

"I'm afraid I don't know."

She seemed a little nervous and he wondered why. It occurred to him that mayhap the professor had decided it was time for him to leave, but Leif didn't think so. Pax-ton seemed a man of his word, and they had bargained to learn from each other. Leif thought the man was equally pleased with the teaching he himself received.

Still, when he walked into the room called a *study*, taking Krista's hand to guide her in behind him, he saw the professor frown. For the first time he worried what he would do if he was wrong and Pax-ton Hart had decided he must leave. Leif wasn't ready for that yet. He needed more time, needed to learn more of the country's language and customs before he could set off on his own.

As he moved toward a chair across from the professor, he wondered what fate the gods had in store for him this time.

Krista walked behind Leif, who led her into the study, still sure it was his right to walk in front. He let go of her hand, but the heat of his touch remained. As they approached the desk, her father rose from his chair and motioned for each of them to take a seat across from him.

"I have asked you both here for a reason." The professor spoke Old Norse and seemed to be carefully choosing his words. "I have given this matter a great deal of thought, and yesterday Matthew Carlton's remarks on the subject gave me even more food for thought."

Though she and Leif were seated, her father remained standing, his expression a little too grave. "It is becoming more and more apparent that Leif's presence here in our home is disrupting the household."

Krista's breath caught. Surely he wasn't going to make the man leave. Leif wouldn't be able to survive out there on his own. No one would understand him. He had no money, no place to stay. He would wind up in one of those horrible institutions.

"Surely you can't mean for Leif to leave," she said to her father in English.

"Hear me out, dearest. Though Leif is learning very rapidly, he is not yet ready for life here in the city. As soon as arrangements can be made, I am taking him to Heartland." It was the family estate in Kent. "There, we will be undisturbed by the dictates of society. I will be able to give Leif my complete attention and be able to study him in return."

Krista felt a sweeping relief.

"What is he saying?" Leif asked, a worried look on his face.

"Father is taking you out of the city, to a place where you will be able to study and learn without being disturbed."

"It is for the best, Leif," the professor said to him. "You will like it at Heartland and you will have all the time you need to study and learn."

"You are worried about your daughter. You know that I desire her."

Krista's cheeks grew warm. "We don't speak that way here, Leif," she said to him softly. "Those sorts of thoughts are kept to oneself."

"The way your friend Mat-thew does? I will not pretend I do not want you."

Krista looked away from the intensity of his gaze, her heart beating oddly.

"It's all right, Leif," her father said gently. "You have been honest in your interest in my daughter. I can find no fault in that. Still, I believe this is the right thing to do. If you wish to learn, you will travel with me to Heartland."

Leif said nothing for several moments, then he nodded. "Mayhap you are right. There is much to distract me here. I will go with you. There are many things for me to learn and I am blessed by the gods that you have agreed to teach me." His gaze moved to Krista. "When I have learned what is needed, I will return."

There was something in those blue eyes, something that made soft heat curl in her stomach. It was ridiculous. The man had no money, no future. He couldn't read or write or even speak English. Still, there was something about him….

"Father is right," she said to Leif, suddenly grateful the decision had been made. "It will be far easier for you to learn once you are out in the country. And I think that you will like it. The air is clear and the grass is green. Perhaps it will seem more like your home."

And she could get her own life back to normal, as it hadn't been since the day she had seen Leif of Draugr Island at the circus.

Finished imparting his news, her father excused her from the study, and she rose to leave while the men prepared to continue the day's work. Krista escaped out into the hall and closed the door, feeling as if a weight had been lifted off her shoulders. Leif would be gone. Her life would be hers once more.

For the first time in days, she was able to focus her mind on work.

Eight

The weeks slid past, April turning to May, summer approaching, the afternoons growing warm and then hot as June slipped into July. Subscriptions to the gazette were increasing each week and the money was pouring in.

In the months since Leif and her father had left the city, *Heart to Heart* had become the most successful ladies' magazine in London. With Coralee's help, Krista had worked hard to build up readership, and her efforts had truly paid off.

And the long hours she spent at work kept her from missing her father. She was used to his companionship and advice. Even the presence of her aunt Abigail, who had volunteered to act as chaperone while the professor worked with his pupil in the country, couldn't fill the void of his absence.

Krista told herself she didn't miss Leif Draugr in the least. The man was outrageous. He was rude and outspoken and without the slightest manners. He lived in a far different world, one he would eventually return to, and the fact that she could still recall the heat of his kisses only made her more determined to forget him.

Still, she eagerly awaited the arrival of her father's letters, which always praised Leif's uncommon aptitude for learning and extolled his many virtues. She recalled a portion of the first she had received.

The man is amazingly intelligent, far beyond what I had originally imagined. He has already begun to read and has an incredible ear for language. He seems to enjoy it here in the country. He says his island home has the same fresh air, but there the breeze is tinged with the scent of the sea. It is rocky there, I gather, more like Scotland, and colder, of course. It is clear he likes it here in the country.

Each letter relayed Leif's progress, and her father was learning about Leif's culture, as well.

From what Leif has told me, I am convinced his people emigrated from Greenland to Draugr in the early sixteenth century. On the island, they have their own language and religion—a mix of Norse beliefs tinged with Christianity—and apparently the people on Draugr are completely self-sufficient. I am writing a paper on the subject, though Leif has made me promise not to divulge his identity or the location of his homeland.

Every letter turned Krista's thoughts to Leif, and for days afterward, she wondered about him. She missed the sound of male voices in the house and told herself it was simply that she missed her father.

Fortunately, Aunt Abby kept her from getting bored. She was Krista's mother's sister, Lady Abigail Chapman Brooks, the widow of a once-prominent London barrister. Aunt Abby now lived in a lovely country manor house in Oxfordshire, but came to London for the Season every year. She was forty-eight years old, with silver streaks in her once-blond hair and a lithe figure that still drew longing glances from men.

Aunt Abby was vivacious and charming, a sparkling presence who lived life to the fullest, which was perhaps good for Krista, since her aunt forced her into the social whirl she generally avoided.

"But we *must* go to Lord Stafford's ball, darling," Aunt Abby said of the occasion coming up at week's end. "It is going to be *the* party of the Season."

No matter how many lame excuses Krista managed to come up with, her aunt always seemed to persuade her.

"And remember, Matthew Carlton will likely be attending."

"I suppose he will be. He usually enjoys those sorts of affairs."

One of her aunt's silver-blond eyebrows went up. "You don't sound particularly enthused. Considering the man is one of the most eligible bachelors in London, I should think you would feel fortunate to be the woman who has captured his interest."

She *was* fortunate, she supposed. Matthew had the qualities every woman wanted in a man. He was kind, considerate, intelligent. And the soirees, balls and house parties her aunt insisted she attend gave Krista the chance she had been seeking to get to know him.

With her father away, Matthew was even more attentive than he usually was, and as July faded into August, she spent more and more evenings in his company, chaperoned by her aunt, of course. Earlier tonight, she and Aunt Abby had attended a melodrama with Matthew and his older brother, Phillip, Baron Argyle, and his wife, Gretchen, enjoying the production from their father's opulent box at the Theatre Royal in Drury Lane.

Though the play had been well-done, Krista was tired from the lengthy performance, her dark-blue silk gown a little wrinkled, her curls beginning to droop against her bare shoulders. Matthew looked none the worse for wear, and when they arrived at her town house, he surprised her by asking if he might come in for a brandy.

Aunt Abby, tireless as always, immediately agreed. "Of course you may come in. I should have invited you myself. We would love to have your company all to ourselves."

They sat in the drawing room for a while, making polite conversation, while Krista worked to stifle a yawn behind her hand. Then Matthew suggested the two of them go out on the terrace for a breath of fresh air. As they stepped through the French doors, she caught a glimpse of Aunt Abby peering through the curtains, very properly playing the role of chaperone, though Krista and Matthew both pretended not to see.

"I enjoyed the evening, Matthew," she said, fighting another yawn. "Thank you for inviting me."

A light breeze ruffled his thick brown hair. He gave her a warm, soft smile. "I hope to share a lifetime of evenings with you, Krista."

She glanced away. Lately, Matthew had hinted more and more at marriage, and she told herself that was exactly what she wanted. It was time she settled down. Her grandfather had known for some time that Matthew was courting her, and he was pushing hard for the match. She owed it to him and to her family, owed it to herself.

She knew she was too tall to attract most men, and far too independent. There was no line of suitors standing outside her door. If things didn't work out with Matthew, she might wind up a spinster and she certainly didn't want that. She wanted children as much as any woman, and apparently Matthew wanted a family, as well.

She managed to smile at him, saw the subtle shift in his expression, the determined look that came into his eyes, but had no idea what it meant. Shock held her immobile when Matthew went down on bended knee in front of her on the terrace and took hold of her white-gloved hand.

"You must know how I feel about you, Krista. You must know that I care for you deeply. We're good together, you and I. We can make a wonderful life together. Marry me, Krista. Make me the happiest man in London."

Her hand trembled in his. Standing there in front of him, she told herself that the time had come at last. She might have wished for a week or two to consider his offer, but she knew she had already held him at bay as long as she dared. She didn't think she was in love with him, and he had never said those words to her, but they had a great deal in common and she liked him. Marriages were often based on far less.

Krista swallowed, gave him an uncertain smile. "I would be honored to become your wife, Matthew."

He rose to his feet, lifted her hand to his lips and kissed the back. "You won't be sorry, darling, I promise you. We're going to be very happy." He took her in his arms and kissed her, and Krista prayed to feel at least some of the fire she had felt the night Leif Draugr had kissed her. Instead, there was merely a pleasant, warm sensation that seemed closer to affection than love.

"We'll need to tell our families."

She nodded. "I'll write to my father on the morrow."

Matthew beamed. "I'll speak to Mother and Father, tell them the news. I know how excited they're going to be." He smiled. "You've made me a very happy man, Krista." Matthew kissed her again, more gently this time.

They walked back into the house and relayed the news to Aunt Abby, whose eyes twinkled conspiratorially when she glanced at Matthew. Krista's fiancé was smiling. Aunt Abby was happy.

Krista couldn't help wondering why she didn't feel happier herself.

The deed was done. Her decision was made. By this time next year, Krista would be a married woman.

First thing the following morning, she penned a letter to her father relaying the news, and two days later, received a note from him in reply, giving her and Matthew his blessing and heartiest congratulations. She knew she should tell her grandfather—and she would, she told herself. Sometime very soon.

But a date for the wedding had not yet been discussed, and she and Matthew agreed that their engagement should not be officially announced until her father returned from the country. As the days crept past, Krista discovered she was glad for the delay. Since the night she had accepted Matthew's proposal, she had been besieged by doubts.

And lately, to add to her uncertainties, the problems at *Heart to Heart* had begun to grow worse.

Standing next to Coralee beside the heavy Stanhope printing press, she thought of the number of threatening notes she had received since her father's departure—seven, including the one she had found in her mailbox that morning and now held in her hand.

"So what does this one say?" Corrie asked, trying to read the note over Krista's shoulder.

She handed the slip of paper to her friend. "It is pretty much the same as the last one."

Corrie read the note aloud. "'You have had your last warning. Now you will reap the trouble you have sown.'" She looked up, moving a cluster of dark-copper curls beside her ear. "I don't think the handwriting is the same as on the last one."

Krista walked into her office and over to her desk. Opening the left-hand drawer, she pulled out the small stack of notes she had received in the past several weeks.

The message on top read, *Spawn of the devil. Cease your meddling or suffer the consequences.* It was the last one to have been delivered, pinned to *Heart to Heart's* front door.

Krista shuffled through the stack. "All of the handwriting seems to be different. It appears we have an army of dissenters out there."

"Or at least that is what they wish us to think."

"The handwriting is different, but several of the warnings seemed to be connected." She handed the notes to Corrie.

Two were in protest of the articles Krista had written in regard to needed improvements in the city sewage and water systems, controversial because of the expense. Several others dealt with the editorial campaign she had started after her father left, favoring a bill called the Mines Act. The bill, if passed, would prohibit all females, and boys under the age of ten, from working underground in the mines. Since children played a large role in the work force, it was highly unpopular with mine owners.

In fact, a man named Lawrence Burton, the primary shareholder in the Consolidated Mining Company, had been particularly outspoken in the matter, but of course, he wasn't the only one.

Coralee looked down at the message received just that morning. "None of these notes are good, but somehow this one sounds more ominous than the others."

Krista smiled. "Oh, I don't know… 'Spawn of the devil' certainly had a nasty ring to it."

Her friend laughed. "It is past time we called in the authorities, Krista. We need to send these notes to the police. Perhaps they can discover who is behind the threats."

"So far that is all they have been, and as you say, the handwriting isn't even the same, which means they must have come from different people. I can't imagine where the authorities would begin to look for the guilty parties."

"Still, I think you should consider it."

Krista made no reply. She had enough problems without bringing in the police.

Or at least that was what she thought as she left the gazette that night for home.

In the morning, when she found the back rooms of *Heart to Heart* nothing more than a heap of smoldering soot and blackened ash, she realized she had made a mistake.

Krista arrived early that morning in front of the three-story brick building that housed the offices of *Heart to Heart*. On her way, she had had Mr. Skinner, the coachman, stop in Grosvenor Square to pick up Coralee, which she had been doing on occasion of late.

Krista was saying something to her friend when she spotted the bright-red fire wagon pulled by a pair of big gray draft horses sitting in the alley behind the building. Throwing open the carriage door before the conveyance had completely rolled to a stop, she quickly descended the stairs and rushed toward the scene.

Corrie followed close on her heels. "Good heavens!"

The fire was mostly out, Krista could see, remnants of white smoke trailing upward where a team of firemen doused the back rooms of the office with a heavy stream of water. But the damage was fairly extensive. She prayed it hadn't got into the main portion of the building where the printing press sat.

"Ye'll have ta stay back, miss," said a burly man with thick red hair who seemed to be in charge. "Fer yer own safety."

"My name is Krista Hart. This is my place of business. Can you tell me what happened?"

He looked over at the smoke drifting out of a broken window. "Fire started at the back of the buildin'. Didn't get into the main section, though."

"Thank God. How did it start?"

"Near as we can tell, looks like someone tossed somethin' through the window in the back door."

Her eyes widened. "You mean this wasn't an accident?"

"No, miss. Fact is, if ol' Mrs. Murphy hadn't spotted the blaze, your whole buildin' woulda gone up, maybe the whole durned block."

Mrs. Murphy lived with her ailing husband above Murphy's Family Grocery just a few doors down the street. Krista shivered to think of the property, perhaps even lives that might have been lost, if the fire had not been so quickly discovered.

Beside her, Corrie surveyed the blackened brick walls and broken glass strew over the alley. "Well, I guess it is now more than merely a threat."

Krista sighed. "I was wrong. I should have gone to the authorities as you said."

"It is not too late for that. And you need to tell your father. There is no way you can keep this a secret."

She nodded. She would send the professor a note. She didn't want him to worry, but there was simply no way around it.

"Who do you think it was?" Corrie asked.

"I have no idea. Perhaps the police will have some notion."

"It is possible, but they are very busy. Perhaps we should hire someone ourselves to look into the matter."

"That is a very good idea. In the letter I send to Father, I shall ask him if he knows anyone who might be competent to handle the job."

Krista watched the firemen roll up their hoses and carry them back to the fire wagon. The police would be there soon and there would be questions to answer.

Corrie cast her a look. "Send the letter today, Krista."

Krista blinked against the stinging smoke. "Yes, I believe I had better."

Leif strode into the stables at Heartland, a big stone building that smelled of dust and fresh cut hay. Perched on his shoulder, the tiny monkey, Alfinn, screeched merrily, glad to be back in his favorite place. As they walked into the shadowy interior, the monkey leaped away, landing on the top rail of one of the stalls and climbing up into the rafters.

"Behave yourself, Alf," Leif warned, and the monkey chattered a noisy reply, content with his surroundings and the stable boy, Jamie Suthers, who had mostly taken over his care.

"He's full o' mischief this mornin'," said the lanky, dark-haired boy with obvious affection.

"He's enjoying himself. He likes you, Jamie." Leif waved at the youth, happy that Alf had found another friend, and headed back to the house, making his way inside, then down the marble-floored hall and into the high-ceilinged library the professor used for a study.

After months of long days spent in the comfortable wood-paneled, book-lined room, he felt more at ease in here than in any other room of the big, elegant country house.

Leif thought about those first few weeks after his arrival. Heartland was a place fit for a king. Built of beautiful golden stone, standing four stories high and protected by a roof of heavy black slate, the house sat on a knoll surrounded by vast fields of rolling green. The lawns and gardens were perfectly groomed, and a stream, rich with fish, rippled alongside the house.

The interior was more magnificent than anything he, with his limited view of the world, could ever have imagined, with even more lavish furnishings than the professor's house in the city. The bed Leif slept in was even wider than the one in London, the mattress not just made of feathers, but the soft down feathers of a goose.

The professor had told him there were hundreds of houses far more elegant than Heartland, but to Leif it didn't matter, for he loved the place from the moment he saw it and he couldn't imagine why the wealthiest of men would ever want anything more.

He sat down in an ornately carved wooden chair that reminded him of the high-backed chair his father, as chieftain, sat in up on the dais in their longhouse back home. This chair was only one of six that surrounded a beautiful carved wooden table in the middle of the library. A stack of books the professor thought Leif might find interesting sat on the table in front of him. Cracking open the one on top, he settled in to read.

He didn't have much time, he knew. Soon Professor Hart would arrive with a new list of words and meanings, and they would start his lessons again. The hours were long and tiring, but he was doing very well, the professor said, and Leif believed the outcome would be worth it.

He remembered those first exhausting weeks in the country. The professor had begun his studies with what he called a *battledore,* a heavy paper board that folded into three parts. Once Leif had learned the alphabet and could write it to the professor's high standards, he began to learn to pen whole words. He was a very quick student and he studied hard, and the professor seemed pleased. Leif learned to read from a *primer,* then read books designed for slightly older children. He was reading everything now, learning more and more words and the correct way to say them.

After four months of intensive study, he felt confident in his progress, knew that he had done far better than the professor had expected.

The man appeared just then in the door of the library, tall and a little frail, his brown hair thinning and beginning to turn gray. Leif frowned as he noticed the man's face looked strained, and the paper he carried shook a little in his hand.

Leif rose to his feet. "What is it, Professor?" They spoke only English now, had for more than a month. Leif found the words flowing more and more easily off his tongue.

"Something has happened. There's been trouble at the gazette. I must return to the city."

"What sort of trouble?" He knew about newspapers now, and magazines, knew that the professor and his daughter owned what was called a *gazette,* a weekly paper, theirs printed for women. He was eager to see the machine that accomplished such a task.

"Apparently, she has received more threatening messages. She got a few before we left, but they seemed more a prank—a joke," Pax-ton explained. "I never really took them seriously."

"The ladies didn't like what she was printing in her mag-a-zine?"

The professor shook his head. "It wasn't the ladies. She has been writing articles that call for social reform…better water systems in the city, shorter working hours for children and women, that sort of thing. Apparently, she has made some enemies, men who don't want things to change. Yesterday someone set the office on fire."

Leif felt a shot of alarm. "She was not injured, your daughter?"

"No, Krista is fine, but she is worried. The police have no clue as to who might be responsible, and she is afraid someone is going to get hurt. I am afraid that someone might be her. I must return at once."

"I am going with you," Leif said.

The professor cast him a glance. "I had hoped we would have a bit more time. At least a few more weeks. We have yet to get into the social graces, the things you need to know to move about in polite society. I thought those things would best be learned after you had mastered our language. Of course, you have done a fine job of that." He smiled. "And if you are in town, perhaps my daughter will be willing to teach you. She is far better at that sort of thing than I am."

"Mayhap—perhaps, then, this is for the best. We will go back and make certain that your Krista is safe, and in return, she will teach me more of what I need to learn."

The professor hesitated only a moment, then nodded. "Yes…now that I consider it, it is good you are going. My daughter values her independence. She won't want anyone watching over her, but after the fire, I believe it is necessary. With the two of us to look after her, perhaps we can keep her safe."

"Your daughter will be safe, Professor. This, I vow to you."

Nine

◦◦◦

"Are you certain you should go, Krista?" Aunt Abby followed Krista nervously toward the front door. This was the third morning since the fire, and each day the lecture was the same. "As I said before, I think you should stay at home, at least for a while. Give the police a little time to look into the matter of the fire and who might have started it."

Krista leaned down and kissed her aunt's powdered cheek. "The gazette goes out in the morning. It takes the entire staff to get it ready for distribution, and with the dispatch room burned to a crisp, we'll have to set up tables on the second floor to use for the assembly. That means we'll have to carry the sections up and the finished bundles down, which will make the task even harder."

She grabbed her straw bonnet off the top of the coat tree, but ignored her cloak. It was mid-August, the weather warm, the air often hot and still.

Her aunt wrung her pale, slender hands. "I wish your father were here. I'm sure he would forbid you to leave the house until all of this has been settled."

Krista didn't think he would go quite that far, but with the problems at *Heart to Heart,* she was glad he remained in the country. Her father would only worry, and she didn't want that.

"I promised you I would be careful, and I have been."

Since she had not yet received his reply to her letter, and speaking to the police had done no good, she had hired an investigator that Coralee's father, Viscount Selkirk, had suggested. His name was Randolph Petersen—Dolph, his business card said—and as soon as he had agreed to take the assignment, he had insisted she employ a night watchman to guard the offices of *Heart to Heart* when no one was there. Mr. Petersen was on the job and she believed in time he would discover the identity of her nemesis and the police would arrest him.

Until then, Krista had a magazine to run.

She headed out the door and hurried down the front steps to her waiting carriage, only to see a second carriage parked behind it. The door swung open and Matthew Carlton descended the iron stairs, a scowl on his face.

"I heard what happened at the gazette," he announced. "Everyone in town is talking about it. Why didn't you tell me? Did you believe I wouldn't hear about it sooner or later? People have been whispering, wondering why I was the last to know. Didn't you think I should be told? Did you imagine I wouldn't be concerned?"

Krista toyed with a fold of her apricot dimity skirt. "I didn't want to worry you."

"Well, I *am* worried, and I don't think you ought to be anywhere near *Heart to Heart* until the police have arrested the man who set fire to your building."

Krista sighed. This was exactly the reason she hadn't told Matthew in the first place. She knew he wouldn't want her to continue working there, and since they were newly engaged—and unofficially, at that—she didn't want to displease him.

"We need to get the paper out, Matthew. It takes a very large effort. As I am the publisher, I have to be there to help."

He tilted his head back and looked down his nose at her. "Once we are married, you will have other things to keep you occupied besides your silly paper."

Her spine stiffened. "There is nothing silly about *Heart to Heart.* I thought you understood. I told you the magazine was important to me, and you said you thought we were doing valuable work. You said you admired my independent spirit."

His angry look softened. "I'm sorry, darling. Of course I understand. It's only that I am worried. I couldn't bear it if something happened to you."

He seemed sincere. She should be grateful for his concern. "I've hired an investigator, Matthew. And a guard to watch the building at night. No more notes have arrived since the fire. There is nothing to worry about."

He sighed. "I hope you are right." Taking her hand, he helped her climb into the carriage. "I spoke to my father last night. He thinks we should set a date for the wedding."

Krista shook her head. "Not until the professor returns. That is what we agreed. I imagine he'll be back in a couple of weeks, a month at most."

Matthew didn't argue, but he didn't look pleased. Even unsmiling he was handsome, with the sunlight glinting off his light brown hair and his features so refined. He could have had his pick of London's most fashionable young ladies and yet he had chosen her.

She again tried not to wonder if the size of her dowry had motivated his interest.

Matthew closed the door as Krista settled herself in the seat. She leaned toward him out the window. "I presume we are still going to dinner at Lord Wimby's Saturday night."

"Of course," he said. "I'll pick you and your aunt up at eight."

"All right, I'll see you then." Krista waved farewell as the carriage rolled away, then slumped back against the seat. What was it about Matthew that always kept her on edge? She wasn't sure why, but she could never seem to relax in his company. Surely, in time, that would change.

The morning passed without incident. At the end of the day, she was still thinking about Matthew and her unsettled feelings where he was concerned when she left the office and the carriage rolled toward home. Dusk had begun to fall, outlining the city skyline in a soft purple glow.

They had assembled the gazette for distribution on the morrow, and the day had been a long one. She was tired to the bone and worried about the magazine and whether there might be more trouble. With her mind miles away, she climbed the front porch steps.

Giles pulled open the heavy front door, as usual, and bowed to her. Krista froze at the sight of the big blond giant who thundered down the curving staircase.

"You are home." Leif Draugr looked down at her from the third step, his words spoken in nearly perfect English. "Your father and I were just coming to get you."

Krista said nothing. She had forgotten the devastating effect the man had on her, how impossibly handsome he was, how tall, how utterly brawny and male.

"We just got to town," he added, his slight Norse accent softening the words in a way that made them sound somehow seductive. "After your message arrived, your father was very worried."

Telling herself not to stare, ignoring the sliver of heat that slipped into her stomach, she nervously moistened her lips.

Leif's gaze strayed to her mouth and his incredible eyes turned the scorching shade of blue she remembered.

"I have thought of you often, Krista Hart."

She swallowed, finally found her voice. "You have… You have learned a great deal in the months you've been gone."

He smiled. "I have worked hard, but I have much more to learn. Your father says that you might teach me."

The words sobered her. "Teach you? What could I possibly—"

"There you are!" The professor appeared before she had time to finish. "Dearling…it has been so very long."

She ran toward him, felt his thin arms closing around her. "I've missed you, Father. It wasn't the same here without you."

"I cannot tell you how good it is to see you." He hugged her tighter and she hugged him back.

With a swish of rose silk skirts, Aunt Abby joined the small group in the entry. "I thought I heard voices." She smiled at Krista. "I am glad you are safely home, my dear. I had begun to worry. Then your father and Mr. Draugr arrived. They were just on their way to Piccadilly to fetch you."

"So you've met Mr. Draugr?"

She had never seen her aunt smile quite so brightly. "Why, yes. You told me a little about him, but you forgot to mention how handsome he is."

Krista had tried to forget that herself.

She looked at Leif, saw that he was grinning at the praise. It was clear his ego had grown along with his education.

"Your aunt is a very beautiful woman," he said. "It is easy to see the re-sem…re-sem—"

"Resemblance," the professor interjected.

"It is easy to see the resemblance between the two of you."

Krista couldn't hold back her smile. So the man could be charming. She never would have guessed.

"I didn't expect you home for several more weeks," she said to her father.

"Yes, well, after your note arrived, both of us were worried."

Leif was worried about her? Surely her father was merely being polite. "Well, you are home at last and I cannot say I am sorry."

Leif's eyes darkened. "So you thought of me, too."

Color rose in her cheeks. She hadn't thought of him at all. Or at least she had tried very hard not to. "I was speaking to my father."

But it was obvious Leif didn't believe her. The man hadn't changed. He was still completely outrageous.

"You've had a long day," her father said. "I imagine you must be tired. Why don't you go upstairs and refresh yourself? At supper, we can catch up on all that has happened in the months we've been gone."

She *was* tired. And she needed a moment to compose herself. "Yes, I think that is a very good notion. As you say, the day has been a long one." Grateful for the respite, she turned toward the stairs. "If you will all please excuse me…"

As she passed the entry hall table, she caught a glimpse of her reflection in the gilded mirror, her blond curls drooping, an ink smudge darkening her cheek. She looked a fright, yet Leif didn't seem to notice. She couldn't help thinking of Matthew. He said he understood how important the gazette was to her, but she knew if he had seen her as she was tonight, he would have disapproved.

Leaving the men behind, she lifted her skirts and started up the staircase. Krista could feel Leif's eyes on her all the way to the top.

She couldn't help wondering if her father had told him she was now engaged to be married, and if he understood that meant she was now out of his reach. As she headed down the hall, she glanced over the railing to where he stood. The hot look he gave her made his thoughts more than clear.

He wanted her. That much had not changed.

She ignored the breathless feeling in her chest. Surely, once he understood…

Then again, for all his newfound education, the man was still a barbarian. Perhaps, even if he knew, it wouldn't end his desire for her.

The thought made her stomach contract.

Ten

＊＊＊

Krista dressed for supper that night in the same dark-blue silk gown she had worn the night Matthew had proposed. She wasn't quite sure why. Perhaps to remind herself that she would soon be announcing her engagement.

She found her father and Leif in the study, poring over a stack of books. They had changed into evening clothes as well, Leif dressed now in a black frock coat, silver waistcoat and gray trousers. She remembered choosing the material for the garments that day at Stephen Ward, but she couldn't have guessed how good Leif would look in them.

Her father rose when she walked into the room. Leif flicked him a glance and imitated the movement, rising to his full height beside him.

"You look lovely, my dear," the professor said.

Leif's gaze ran over her, returned to her bosom, displayed modestly but stylishly by the gown. A slow smile spread over his lips. "Even Freya would be jealous of your beauty," he said.

Krista blushed. Freya was the Viking goddess of sex, more beautiful than any of the other female deities. She was wildly passionate and completely insatiable. Krista wasn't sure the comparison was actually a compliment, though clearly Leif believed it was.

"Thank you." On the chair back next to him, she spotted the tiny monkey, Alfinn, and couldn't help a smile. "I see you brought your friend back with you."

"He would have been bored in the country," Leif said, sounding surprisingly urbane.

Krista cast Leif a glance. "Yes, I'm sure he would have been. Life in the city, even for a monkey, is so much more exciting."

A corner of Leif's mouth edged up, but he made no further comment. The monkey was his friend. Where he went, Alf went. It was as simple as that.

They were still in the study when Aunt Abby arrived, having changed into a gown of gold brocade edged with flounces of dark green taffeta across the bodice and around the hem. "Good evening, everyone."

"Good evening, Abigail," her father said. "You know Mr. Draugr, but I don't believe you have yet met Alfinn."

Aunt Abby's pale eyebrows rose at the sight of the tiny monkey. "Oh, my. Isn't he cute? Wherever did you get him?"

Leif's jaw subtly tightened. Krista could see that the days he had spent as a captive still bothered him.

"Alf is a friend of Mr. Draugr's," her father said diplomatically.

The tiny monkey tilted his head, giving Aunt Abby one of his long, endearing stares, and she smiled. "Well, isn't he just a treasure." She leaned over and stroked her gloved hand over his small furry head, and Alf leaned into her palm.

"Treasure or not," the professor said, "it is getting on toward time for supper. Jamie will be looking for Alf. Leif, you had better take him back out to the stables."

"Jamie?" Krista asked.

"Alf made a friend at Heartland," Leif said.

"The Suthers boy," the professor explained. "You remember him, worked out in the stable? Boy's an orphan, you recall. Grew rather attached to the monkey. I thought he could be useful here and also keep an eye on Alf."

The monkey jumped from the back of the chair onto the study table then and crossed over to where Krista stood. He stuck out a tiny hand and she reached toward it, let him take hold of her finger. He had the biggest, darkest eyes, and they seemed to have a way of looking into you.

"I think Alf is very good at making friends," she said.

"He likes you," said Leif. "You saved him that day and he remembers."

She looked up at the tall Norseman. There was something in his eyes that said, *You saved me, as well, and I also remember.*

She turned away from him, her heart beating far too quickly, and smiled at her father. "I am completely famished. How about everyone else?"

"Fam-ished?" Leif said from behind her. "What is this word?"

"It means hungry," the professor said.

"Fam-ished," Leif repeated several times as Alfinn climbed up on his arm and they headed for the door on their way to the stables. Every time he said it, his pronunciation improved.

He was an amazing man, Krista thought, just as her father had said, and handsome as sin. She looked down at the dark-blue silk gown she wore and firmly fixed Matthew Carlton's image in her head.

In celebration of the men's homecoming, Cook had prepared an extravagant meal of roasted ribs of beef, baked halibut in oyster sauce and venison pasties. Leif consumed a goodly portion, even eating small amounts of potatoes and carrots, which Krista was certain didn't really appeal to him.

He seemed to particularly enjoy the fish, and she asked him if the ocean provided a large part of his diet back home.

Leif swallowed a bite of halibut and nodded. "On Draugr, we mostly eat the sheep, cattle and goats we raise for food, but there are also deer on the island, which we hunt for meat and hides. We eat fish and the sea animals you English call seals. Every few years, a creature you call a walrus washes ashore. We make use of its meat and tusks."

His manners had improved, Krista noticed, as he waited for a servant to refill his plate with another helping of meat. But he still seemed to think it was a man's place to walk in front of a woman. Though he no longer bolted his food, he still used only his knife and spoon.

Krista caught a glimpse of Aunt Abby, who was watching him with fascination. If she noticed his lack of sophistication at table, it didn't seem to bother her.

Abby smiled in his direction. "You have quite an appetite, Mr. Draugr."

Leif nodded. For an instant, his glance strayed to Krista. "I have always been a man of strong appetites."

Aunt Abby's gaze followed his and her eyes widened. Faint color crept into her cheeks. "Yes, well…I can imagine."

The professor cleared his throat. "What Mr. Draugr meant was a man of his size must eat heartily to keep up his strength."

Indeed, Krista thought. He looked as strong as an ox, even in his perfectly tailored black coat and gray trousers, in which, she grudgingly admitted, he cut a very dashing figure.

Determined to direct the conversation back on a proper course, she took a sip of her wine, then set the goblet back down on the table. "You said your island has no wood. Without boats, I would think catching fish would be a problem."

"We have boats—small boats made of reeds. But they are

not big enough for sailing any distance. In olden times, there were forests on the island and the men built ships, but over the years, the people used up the wood and the ships became old and rotted."

"You said a foreign ship crashed onto the rocks. Is that how you were able to construct the boat that brought you here?"

"The boat broke up, but most of the timbers were still good. Some of the men survived, Englishmen, and they were eager to return to their homes." He ignored the wine and instead took a drink of the ale her father had provided him. "We had drawings of the ships our warriors sailed in ancient times, and that is the sort we built. There were those of us who had prayed to the gods for years for an opportunity to discover the world outside our island. Finally our chance came."

"Do you have family there, Mr. Draugr?" Aunt Abby asked.

"Aye. My father is there, my sister, Runa, and my brothers, Olav, Thorolf and Eirik. My father didn't want me to leave. I am the eldest, the son whose duty it is to take his place when he journeys to the Otherworld. It is a responsibly I cannot ignore and the reason I must return."

His jaw was set with iron determination. It was obvious Leif Draugr was not a man who took his responsibilities lightly.

They talked a bit more about life on the island, the months he had spent at Heartland and how much he had learned.

"You are quite an amazing young man, Mr. Draugr," Aunt Abby said. "I cannot think how difficult it must be to assimilate an entirely new culture in so brief a time."

"Assimil-ate?"

"Absorb," Krista said, and he nodded.

Her father smiled. "Leif worked extremely hard in the time we were gone. You can't imagine the number of books he has read, and he continues to expand his education every day. Now, however, it is time he learned to move about in society. In this regard, I am hoping the two of you will be able to help him."

A light went on in Krista's head. So this was what Leif had been talking about.

Aunt Abby's eyes twinkled. "My, that sounds like a great deal of fun. I'm sure Mr. Draugr will be a very apt pupil."

"I don't know how much help I would be," Krista countered, searching for a means of escape. "I am scarcely an expert on the social graces. And I am kept quite busy with the gazette."

"You are home in the evenings and at week's end," her father said. "Surely helping someone make a fresh start in a completely foreign country isn't asking too much."

She felt guilty. Her father and aunt were right. Leif had studied hard. He deserved this chance to better himself. She just hoped she was up to the task.

She pasted on a smile. "You are right. I would be happy to help Aunt Abby teach Mr. Draugr whatever it is he needs to learn."

"Oh, I won't be able to help," Abby said. "It is past time I returned to my home in the country. I have obligations there, you know, though I shall be very sorry to miss out."

"But you said—"

"I said it would be fun, and it will be. Imagine the joy of teaching Mr. Draugr to waltz. And he'll need to know how to make a proper introduction and how to escort a lady. You will have to take him to the opera and the theater, of course, and perhaps he should learn how to ride a horse. A man should be a proper horseman, and you could help him, Krista. You are a very proficient rider."

"Leif rides very well," the professor said. "He rode a good bit at Heartland."

"We have horses on Draugr," Leif explained. "They were brought to the island by my ancestors."

"Krista is also an excellent rider," the professor said proudly. "And I am sure she will be a very competent teacher of the social graces."

Inwardly, Krista groaned. She thought of the items her aunt had listed and knew there were countless more things Leif would have to learn. At least riding lessons weren't necessary. She managed a polite response. "I'll be happy to help in any way I can."

"Capital!" Her father beamed. "Then it is settled. Oh, and there is just one more thing."

She eyed him warily. "What is that?"

"Leif has expressed a desire to pay his own way." A conspiratorial glance passed between the men. "He doesn't wish to be a burden. He has asked for a job and so, as owner of *Heart to Heart,* I have hired him to work for the gazette."

"You what?"

"I don't see any reason for you to object. Surely you can use a big, strapping fellow like Leif to help you around the office."

Krista held on to her temper. She wasn't a fool. After the fire, her father was worried. He wanted a watchdog, someone to act as her protector. Though she actually ran the day-to-day operations of the paper, her father was officially the owner. He usually left employment decisions to her, as publisher, but he had the right to hire whomever he wished.

"We are fully staffed, Father. I don't see what use—"

"I am sure you will think of something."

She gritted her teeth. Leif wanted to work. Well, she would put him to work, all right.

Krista took a sip of her wine, eyeing the big blond man over the rim of her glass. She would see that Leif Draugr regretted the day he had ever heard the name *Heart to Heart.*

* * *

The weather turned hot that Friday, the air thick and muggy, only a faint breeze moving the leaves outside the windows. As Krista left her bedroom and headed for the door, she spotted Leif waiting for her at the bottom of the stairs.

"Good morning," he said.

"Good morning. I gather you still wish to go to work with…" Her words trailed off as she noticed the heavy sword he clutched in his hand. The weapon in its leather sheath was the one he had retrieved the day he'd left the circus. "What on earth are you planning to do with that?"

"You have had trouble." He drew the sword partly out of its scabbard. "This is good for trouble."

She shook her head. "People here haven't used swords like that for several hundred years, Leif. Men use guns now, pistols and muskets."

He shoved the sword back into its scabbard, causing a metallic ring. "Your father showed me those things. We used them to hunt birds at Heartland."

"Well, then, you can see how ridiculous it is for you to take something so outdated as—"

"I will take my sword." With that he started for the door, paused a moment to look back over his shoulder. "Do you come with me?"

"I…" She took a step, then stopped. "Not quite yet. Since you and Father have assigned me the task of teaching you proper etiquette, we might as well start right now. In England, it is the custom for a gentleman to allow a lady to precede him. That means from now on I walk in front of you, Leif, not behind."

He frowned. "A man walks *behind* a woman? Why would he do that? A man is stronger and he is her protector. He should lead the way in case there is danger."

"One rarely encounters danger when entering a drawing room, so there is no need for a man to walk in front. It is a gesture of respect to allow the lady to enter first."

His frown deepened. "Do you have a book on this thing you call et-i-quette?"

"Yes, and reading it is a very good notion. You can study as we go along. I shall fetch the book for you tonight when we return home."

They left the house—Krista walking in front, Leif behind, carrying his ridiculous sword. It appeared to be the sort men might have used in medieval times, like a Scottish claymore, the handle of ornately carved bone—an impressive weapon, no matter that it was outdated.

When they reached the carriage, she gave him another brief lesson, explaining how a man helped a lady inside, then climbed in and seated himself across from her. Ignoring the warmth of his big hand at her waist as he guided her up the iron stairs, she seated herself, fluffing the skirt of her pale blue day dress around her legs. Leif climbed aboard, so big he filled the seat across from her. And yet, dressed as he was in his expensively tailored clothes, he didn't look the least out of place in the carriage.

As the vehicle lurched into motion, rolling along the crowded streets toward Piccadilly, she noticed Leif's gaze strayed often out the window, and realized he was keeping an eye out for trouble.

"Was there fighting on your island?" she asked, suddenly curious why he might have need of a sword.

"There are several different clans on Draugr. One of them covets our land, which is less rocky and far more fertile than theirs. They raid our homes and take our women, steal our cattle. We defend ourselves when there is a need."

Of course there would be fighting. They were men, weren't they? "Father says your people are completely self-sufficient. If you don't trade, how do you get the iron for your weapons?"

"There is enough bog iron in the mountains to serve our needs, enough to make swords, lance points and axes, cooking pots and farming tools."

Krista didn't say more, but she couldn't help noticing how easily he carried the sword, as if the weapon were a part of him. He knew well how to use it, she would wager. Krista shivered. On the surface, Leif might look civilized, but underneath his gentleman's clothes, he was a warrior—a Viking. That had not changed.

The carriage made its way along Piccadilly, turned the corner onto a side street and dropped them off in front of the brick building that housed *Heart to Heart.* Krista led Leif inside and straight to her office.

She pointed to his sword. "You may store that in here, if you please." She pulled open the door of an upright chest against the wall that held office supplies.

"I would rather keep it with me."

"You may leave it in here, or take it upstairs. You certainly cannot carry it about the office. You will frighten the employees witless."

"Wit-less?"

"It means half-mad. Now put up the sword."

He grumbled something she couldn't quite hear, but leaned the sheathed sword against the inside wall of the upright chest and closed the door.

"Now I will show you round the office and introduce you to our staff, then you can start to work." Yesterday, they had assembled the gazette and tied it into bundles. Today those bundles needed to be loaded into wagons, which would deliver the magazine to distribution points in the city.

It was the perfect job for Leif, among other tasks she had in mind for him.

"I would like to see how your papers are made," he said as they left her small office, so she took him over to the heavy Stanhope press.

"It was invented by the Earl of Stanhope," she said. "It is the first printing machine ever designed that was fashioned completely of iron."

"How does it work?"

She showed him the box of metal type with the letters and numbers they used to print each edition of the gazette, then turned to the heavy cast-iron press. "The machine uses a system of compound levers to increase the pressure applied to the paper. This model has been improved since the first ones came out. We can print up to two hundred sheets an hour."

Leif was studying the press, examining the heavy piece of equipment from different angles, when Coralee walked up beside them.

"Corrie, this is Leif Draugr. I believe you may remember him."

Leif turned toward her just then and Corrie's mouth fell open. She stood there staring, her gaze locked on his impossibly handsome face. Her glance moved lower, over the width of his shoulders, assessing his flat stomach and the length of his long legs.

"This can't be… It cannot possibly be…"

"Leif, this is Miss Coralee Whitmore. She is managing editor of the women's section of the gazette."

"What is an *editor*?"

"It means she oversees a certain portion of the paper, which articles are written, that sort of thing."

"I am pleased to meet you, Miss Whitmore."

Corrie just stood there, craning her neck to look up at him. "I—I cannot believe it."

"It is difficult, I admit, but it is he nonetheless, I assure you."

"Good heavens."

"Exactly so."

Corrie cast Krista an accusatory glance that said, *You never told me he was absolutely gorgeous!*

Krista ignored her. "Mr. Draugr is going to be working with us for a while, Coralee. As soon as he has met the rest of the staff, I'm going to put him to work helping Freddie load the bundles."

Her friend's gaze returned to his powerful physique. "Yes… I'm sure Mr. Draugr would be very good at that."

Krista walked past her, continuing to show Leif the office and its staff, introducing him as a friend of her father's from Norway. Bessie Briggs, the typesetter, looked as if her eyes might pop from their sockets. Gerald Bonner, the printer, looked small and effeminate standing next to him, and Freddie Wilkes, Gerald's young apprentice, a boy of fourteen with sandy brown hair, stared up at him in awe.

"Pleased to meet ye, gov'nor," the young man said.

Leif frowned. "Gov-nor? What is this you call me?"

A hint of fear crept into the young boy's eyes. "It don't mean nothin' bad. Honest."

"It is slang," Krista explained. "A colloquial—a local expression. Just a casual greeting."

Leif nodded. "Pleased to meet you, as well, gov'nor."

Krista rolled her eyes, thinking of the job that lay ahead of her. Turning a Viking into a gentleman seemed an impossible task.

As they made their way toward the back of the building, Leif paused. "Much has been destroyed," he said of the soot-

and-water-damaged back rooms ravaged by the fire. All of the furniture was blackened and burned, and there were soggy, half-charred bundles of magazines strewn about the floor. "When I finish loading your gazette, I will clean up in here."

Her eyes widened. It was the awful job she had meant to give him, punishment for intruding into her world. That he would volunteer for such a filthy task made her feel shrewish and small. It confirmed things about his character she had already begun to suspect.

"It is kind of you to offer, Leif, but—"

"Someone must do it and this I know how to do."

"Thank you," she said softly.

He reached out and touched her cheek. "Do not worry, Krista Hart. You do not think you need a man, but I will prove that you do."

She opened her mouth to tell him he was wrong, that she didn't need a man in the least. Well, at least not for everything, but certainly there were some things she couldn't accomplish by herself. Having a family was one of them, but for that she would soon have a husband.

An image of Matthew Carlton arose. She needed to make sure Leif understood, but he turned away before she could form the words, and he and Freddie set to work loading the finished bundles.

Pulling off his jacket and waistcoat, Leif tossed them over the back of a chair, untied his stock and removed his cravat. He unfastened the top button on his shirt and began carrying stacks of printed papers to the waiting wagons.

Krista went to work in her office, but it wasn't long before he appeared in her doorway.

"We are finished with the loading. I will start to work in the back."

They had loaded the wagons in record time, even though he and Freddie had to carry the bundles through the front door instead of the rear. For the next several hours, she could hear Leif carrying out the debris that filled the back rooms of the office.

"Mr. Draugr is quite a hard worker," Corrie said as Krista walked out of her office to check on his progress.

"So it would seem."

Just then the back room door opened and Leif appeared, shirtless, using his expensively tailored shirt to mop the sweat and soot from his face and chest. "I am almost finished," he said. "I was hoping you might have a drink of water."

Krista's eyes fixed on his sweat-slick chest.

"Oh, my," Corrie said, her gaze going there, as well.

His face was streaked with dirt. His arms glistened with sweat, outlining his powerful biceps, and Krista could see his navel, exposed above the waistline of his trousers, which rode low on his hips.

She swallowed. "Leif, you cannot...you cannot remove your clothing in public. It is simply not done in our world."

"It is hot in there and I have only removed my shirt."

"Yes, I realize what you're doing is very hard work, but...but—"

He grinned. "You are yet a maiden. The day will come when you will not be embarrassed by the sight of a man's bare chest." He unfolded the wrinkled, soot-stained garment, shook it out and pulled it over his head. "I am sorry if I offended you."

"You didn't...didn't offend me." She lifted her chin. "It is simply my job to teach you manners, and that is what I am trying to do."

His gaze moved down her body. "There are things I wish to teach you, as well, Krista Hart. If it is the will of the gods, mayhap—perhaps one day it will be so."

Krista couldn't breathe. He wanted to teach her things, and she knew well enough what those things were. Worst of all, for a single insane moment, she wanted to learn them more than anything on this earth.

But sometime in the next several weeks, her engagement would be announced. She was marrying Matthew Carlton. He was the right man for her, the sort her family approved of, the sort who would make a good husband and father. She had to tell Leif, make him understand. She had to convince him to leave her alone.

She had to convince herself that she wanted him to.

Krista worked in her office the rest of the afternoon, and the moment they returned to the town house, went straight upstairs to her bedroom. Later that night, when she joined Leif and her father for supper, the Norseman was once more clean and properly clothed. But she would never forget the sight he had made, standing in the middle of her office half-naked and covered with sweat.

Her pulse leaped at the thought.

And tomorrow was Saturday. She would be working with him all day, teaching him manners and deportment. Dear God, how would she survive it?

Eleven

Leif went in search of Krista on Saturday morning. He had been up for hours, going over the books she had given him last night after supper on the subject of manners. He was well into *The Gentleman's Book of Etiquette,* though he still was not quite sure how to pronounce the last word.

He sighed as he walked down the hall. The book was dull and boring, nothing at all like the fascinating books the professor had given him on subjects like the heavens, which were filled, he had learned, with planets as well as stars. He had read about great steam-powered boats and mechanized factories that wove cloth into the fabric used to make clothes. One day he hoped to see such incredible things.

He glanced down at the volume in his hand, a book stuffed full of silly rules. How to make a proper bow on first being introduced. How to escort a lady in to supper. There was a section on carriage manners, one on how to behave with people of various ranks: inferiors, equals or superiors.

Bah, it was all ridiculous. A man was judged by how valiantly he fought, whether he was honorable or not, whether he was wise or foolish. Those were the things that mattered.

At least they mattered to him.

But whenever he began to think what a waste of time it was to learn the meaningless customs practiced in this place called England, he remembered the awful months he had spent in captivity, living in a cage like an animal. He would never forget the terrible humiliation, the cruelties he had suffered, how living that way had made him feel—as if he were less than a man.

If he wanted to survive in this place, he had to fit in, had to learn the ways of the people of this land. He had to find a way to earn money if he was ever going to get back home.

The thought made his chest ache. He and his father had parted in anger. Ragnaar hadn't understood that Leif had no choice but to leave. He was driven to see what lay outside the confines of their island. It was the will of the gods, Leif believed, that had drawn him from his home and brought him to this place.

And what a place it had turned out to be! More fascinating than anything he could have imagined, more challenging, more intriguing. If he stayed a hundred years, he could not glean all of the knowledge this place held. He would stay if he could, but instead he had to leave. He had to return to his homeland, had to fulfill his promise to his father. He had to assume the duties he had been born to.

And yet Leif believed the gods had led him here for a reason, and during the months he had been at Heartland, and the days following his return to London, he had discovered what that purpose was.

The thought made him smile. Returning to the life he had led before would not be so bad, he told himself, for when he went back, he would be taking home a bride. He had met the woman the gods had sent to be his mate in this strange place called London.

Leif had never known anyone like her, this woman, Krista Hart. Proud. Intelligent. Independent. A woman who earned her own way in this difficult world run mostly by men, one who commanded the respect of the people who worked for her, who was as smart as a man and mayhap even more determined. Tall and blond, she was as comely as a goddess, as shapely as Freya herself.

Her image appeared in his head and his body clenched with fierce desire. He was hard an instant later, his need for her nearly overwhelming. During his time at Heartland, he had thought of her often, had awakened in the night, his thick rod painfully stiff and throbbing.

In the stable at Heartland, he had taken one of the milkmaids who had offered herself to him, and after so many months without a woman, the act had been a blessed relief. But even as he buried himself between the maid's pale thighs, he'd thought of Krista Hart and yearned for her. When he took his pleasure, he remained unsatisfied, and he knew then that no other woman would be able to slake the lust he felt for Krista.

She had been chosen for him by the gods, Leif believed, and he wouldn't leave this land without her.

He thought of their wedding night and how he would plant his seed deep inside her, thought of the strong sons she would give him, and his rod stiffened painfully. The back of his neck grew damp with sweat and his stomach muscles tightened. He had never felt this unrelenting lust for a woman.

And though she was yet a maiden and did not understand the feelings he stirred within her, Leif believed Krista felt that same fierce desire for him. He would teach her, he vowed. He would awaken her passions and heat her blood until she could think of no other man save him.

He scoffed at the attention paid to her by her suitor, Matthew Carlton. The man was a weakling, not strong enough for a woman like Krista. In time, Leif would make her see that.

Still, the day had not yet come that he could approach her father. Leif respected the professor greatly and he thought the man had developed a certain respect for him. In time, Pax-ton would see that Leif was the right man for his daughter.

In the meantime, he had more to learn, had yet to find a way to earn the money he needed to pay the bride price and buy a ship that would carry him and his future wife home.

As he padded down the hall in search of her, Leif looked down at the book on manners he carried in his hand. He would learn whatever he needed to, would do whatever he must. He would study the book—and listen to the teachings of the woman he meant to claim as his mate.

Leif smiled again. That part, he had begun to believe, he might actually enjoy.

Aunt Abby left for the country Saturday morning. She had a beau, Krista was sure—one of the local gentry—though her aunt had never mentioned the man to her. Earlier that same morning Krista had received a message from Matthew Carlton saying that something important had come up and he wouldn't be able to escort her to Lord Wimby's dinner party that night. Matthew hoped she would forgive him.

Sweet Lord, Krista had forgotten all about it. He hoped she would forgive him? All she felt was relief.

But Saturday had arrived and Krista had promised her father she would teach Leif Draugr proper manners and deportment. No matter how difficult the task proved to be, that was what she intended to do.

To that end, she dressed in a simple yellow gauze day dress

with roses embroidered round the hem of the full gathered skirt, and left the safety of her bedroom. The morning was slipping away. There was no way to put off the task any longer.

Heading down the stairs, she spotted Leif striding along the hall in her direction, long legs carrying him with purpose. A copy of *The Gentleman's Book of Etiquette* was clutched in his hand, one of several volumes she had purloined from the study last night, including *A Gentleman's Guide to Proper Attire,* and a volume called *The Unsuitable Suitor,* which dealt with masculine-feminine relationships, courtship and marriage—a book she thought might prove exceedingly useful.

Leif halted in front of her. "I was afraid you had forgotten."

If only she could. "I haven't forgotten. I just…I thought I would give you some time to look through the books."

"I am reading this one." He held it up, and she noted he had made a very good start. She wondered how late he had stayed up last night poring over the pages.

"There is much to learn," he said. "I do not understand why you need so many rules."

"I'm afraid I can't tell you the answer, only that the rules developed over hundreds of years."

He glanced down at the leather-bound volume, then looked at her. "Where should we begin?"

Krista tried not to get caught in the depths of those crystal blue eyes. "I have been thinking about that. Follow me." Turning away, she started for the dining room, Leif's heavy footfalls pounding on the marble floor behind her. She walked into the room and over to the long mahogany table, which was already set with china and silver for the evening meal.

"How far have you got in the book?"

"I am reading the section on paying calls in society." He cracked open the volume to the spot his finger had been marking. "'Morning calls—so designated on account of their being made before luncheon—are, strictly speaking, afternoon calls, as they should only be made between the hours of three and six o'clock.'" He looked up at her and grinned, showing the tiny dimple in his cheek. "Very useful information."

Krista rolled her eyes. "I'm sure it is, but for now, since you have very few acquaintances in London on whom you might pay a call, let us turn to something a bit more practical." She stood near one of the twelve carved, high-back chairs. "Pretend we are here for supper. After the man escorts the woman into the dining room, he pulls out her chair and helps her into her seat. Let's try it, shall we?"

He offered his arm as she had shown him before, and they took the last remaining steps to the table. Leif pulled out one of the chairs and Krista sat down, fluffing her skirt around her feet.

"Now sit down beside me. Keep in mind, you might be seated anywhere at the table, depending upon your rank. At a formal supper, there would be a place card with your name on it."

Leif nodded, seated himself very properly.

"All right, now we are going to learn correct table manners."

A hint of rose appeared in his cheeks. "You wish me to use this thing called a *fork*." He was embarrassed. She had never seen him that way before and thought it rather charming.

"Using a fork is the way people eat in this country. You have eaten like a Viking long enough."

"I am a Viking," he said.

"Yes, but that is beside the point. You are here now. Using a fork is the proper way to proceed."

"I have tried. I cannot seem to master the bloody thing."

Her eyes widened. "Wh-what did you say?"

"I said I cannot seem to master the bloody—"

"I heard you the first time."

"Then why did you—"

"Because a gentleman does not speak that way. At least not in front of a lady. Who taught you that word?"

"I heard one of the milkmaids say it."

"A milkmaid said that?"

His flush deepened and suddenly Krista had a suspicion she knew why.

"She was talking to a cow. I liked the sound of the word."

"Did you also like the milkmaid?" Krista asked mildly, though she was feeling an odd sort of pique.

Leif looked straight into her face. "She took care of my needs, that is all. It was you I wanted, even as I lay between the milkmaid's legs."

Krista opened her mouth, but not a single word came out. She moistened her lips, which suddenly felt dry as cotton. "Leif, you mustn't…mustn't… A man doesn't say those things to a lady."

"Why not, if they are true?"

"It just… It simply isn't the proper thing to do."

"Does it say so in the book?"

Sweet God! "I doubt it very much. You will simply have to trust me in this."

He smiled, a flash of white in his handsome face that made her breath catch. "I trust you, Krista Hart," he said softly, his eyes locked with hers. "In time, I pray you will learn to trust me."

Something fluttered in her stomach. It was strange, but in some ways she already did. He was honest to a fault, and she felt safe with him as she never had with another man. Leif would not harm her. She thought of the sword he carried when he accompanied her to the office. He would protect her at any cost, perhaps even with his life.

Her mind zipped back to the milkmaid, and a vision appeared of them lying together, Leif making passionate love to her. Jealousy mingled with an erotic image that made Krista's pulse leap. Sweet God in heaven! Of all the men in London, why did she have to be attracted to this one?

"All right, let's get back to the business at hand," she said brusquely, taking a firm grip on a situation that seemed to be spiraling out of control. "I will show you the proper way to use a fork." Picking up the largest of the silver forks on the left of the place setting in front of him, she placed it in his big hand.

"You use your right hand for most things, do you not?"

He nodded. "But I can wield a sword with both."

"Why am I not surprised?"

He frowned, clearly not understanding.

"Never mind." Rising from her chair, she moved behind him, leaned over his shoulder and took hold of his hand. It was large, strong, masculine, and warm to the touch. She ignored the little tremor that ran through her. Separating his fingers, she rested the fork in the correct position, then wrapped her fingers over his. Leif looked down at their joined hands, turned in the seat and pulled her onto his lap.

"Leif!"

"You make my blood run hot, Krista Hart." She tried to get up but he held her there, her bottom nestled against his hard thighs. "Can you not feel what you do to me?"

Good heavens! Even through the layers of her skirt and petticoats she could feel the thick, hard length of him. The man was huge! Her face turned scarlet. "Let me go this instant, Leif Draugr!"

He released her and she jumped to her feet, her whole body trembling. "You have to stop this, Leif. You cannot behave this way. It simply is not done!"

He frowned. "You truly do not wish to know that I desire you? A woman should be compli—compli—"

"Complimented?"

"A woman should be compli-mented by a man's desire. You are a very beautiful woman. Many men here must want you, but they do not say it. I tell you this so that you will know how beautiful you are."

Krista took a shaky breath and walked away from the table, careful to keep her back to him. She was breathing a little too fast, her palms slightly damp, and yet she felt an odd sort of power at his words. Perhaps Leif was right. Perhaps a woman needed to know she was desirable to a man.

Still, she couldn't let him know how much his words affected her. She steadied herself and slowly turned to face him. "Do you truly wish to learn or are you simply enjoying yourself at my expense?"

Her question seemed to sober him. "I must learn these things you have agreed to teach me."

"Then there will be no more talk of desire. You will behave as the gentleman I am trying to teach you to be. Is that understood?"

He nodded briefly. "As you wish."

"Now…place the fork in your hand as I have shown you."

He did as she told him.

"Take the fork and pretend you are picking up a bite of meat—and that is another thing. Since you are so *bloody* good at using your infernal knife, you should be able to use it to cut your meat into smaller pieces. Once you have done that, you can use the fork to pick up each piece."

He seemed to be trying not to smile. "Not only do I desire you, Krista Hart, I like you. I will do as you wish, *honning*."

"What did you just call me?"

"*Honning*. It means—"

"I know very well what it means, and don't you dare call me that!" *Honning* meant honey, but in Norse it would not have been used as a term of endearment—the language had few such words. She thought that Leif had learned the translation and twisted the usage to serve his own purpose. "Save it for your milkmaid!"

He did smile, then. "You are jealous. I like that in a woman."

"One more word and I am leaving and I won't be coming back."

Leif turned away from her and looked down at his plate. He didn't say another word—thank God—until they had finished with the lesson.

By the time they left the dining room, his table manners were impeccable. Of course, he hadn't yet actually used the fork with food.

"Let's go into the drawing room," Krista suggested. "We can work on introductions. We will see how you do with that and decide where to go from there."

Remembering that a woman entered first, he followed her into the drawing room, and she began to instruct him on the proper phrases and greetings. By the end of the morning, he could bow more gracefully than her father, who'd had forty years of practice, and when Krista rested her hand on the sleeve of his coat, pretending he was escorting her into a ballroom, she had to remind herself exactly who he was.

After a brief stop for luncheon—Leif using his fork superbly—they returned to the drawing room and a lesson on afternoon tea.

"Women are more inclined to take tea, but the occasion certainly might arise and you should know what to do."

"Show me," he commanded.

After a bit of practice and only a single mishap where the teacup—fortunately empty—landed upside down on the Persian carpet, he could handle the dainty porcelain cup with the smoothness of a dancing master.

And his memory was amazing. Whatever information she gave him he could repeat back to her nearly word for word. She had never seen a man more determined to learn. Krista couldn't help wondering what drove him. Then, recalling the months he had spent locked up in a cage, she thought that perhaps she knew.

By midafternoon, it was clear that if Leif continued to work as hard as he had been, he could master the tasks she set for him and eventually be able to move about in society. He was growing more confident, which made him even more appealing, and the atmosphere between them began to change.

Krista tried to ignore the tension building inside her. But Leif was a handsome, virile man, and when he placed his hand at her waist to help her climb a set of stairs, when he took her arm to escort her over to the sofa, the affect of his nearness began to take its toll.

He swept her a perfect bow, his eyes on her face, and her heart kicked up as it had before. When he pretended she was a countess, calling her "my lady" in his deep, seductive voice, a soft shiver ran down her spine. When he caught her hand and brought it to his lips, her heart seemed to stop beating.

"Where…where did you learn that?"

"I saw a drawing in one of your books."

"Well, it would…would only be something you'd do under special circumstances. It would probably be best if you forgot all about it."

A faint smile curved his lips. "You liked it. I could tell by the pink in your cheeks."

Her face went warmer still. "I didn't like it. I was just sur-prised, is all."

He moved closer, his eyes still on her face. "How surprised would you be, Krista Hart, if I kissed you?"

"Leif, you mustn't—"

But it was already too late. His mouth covered hers, the kiss as hot and fierce as the time before, melting her insides, mak-ing her heart thrum wildly. For an instant, she kissed him back, caught up in the pleasure, the deep erotic sensations that pulled at the womanly place deep within her she had only begun to know.

She might have gone right on kissing him if Leif hadn't groaned.

Her eyes flew open. Planting her hands on his chest, she firmly shoved him away. "That was…that was not a gentle-manly thing to do."

Leif ran a finger along her cheek. "I will pretend to be a gen-tleman for as long as it suits my purpose, but I am no gentle-man, in truth. I am but a man and I want you. As I can tell that you want me."

He reached for her again, but she jerked free of his hold.

"You are wrong, Leif! I don't want you. You took me by sur-prise, that is all. Besides, I am already spoken for. I am prom-ised to another man." There. She had finally said it, as she should have done long before now.

Leif frowned. "Your father set a bride price? Why did he not tell me?"

"He didn't set a bride price. Here, no price is paid for a bride. While you and my father were at Heartland, I spent a good deal of time in company with Matthew Carlton. He asked me to marry him and I accepted."

"And to this your father agreed?"

"Yes. He should have told you. I don't know why he did not."

Leif walked away, over to the window that looked down onto the garden. "May—perhaps he thought it would not matter to me anymore." He turned to face her, his expression intense. "You have given your word? You have vowed to wed this man?"

She thought about lying, telling him that it was a matter of honor that she marry Matthew Carlton. Leif was the sort of man who understood honor. He would accept the fact and leave her alone. But she couldn't make herself say the words.

"Not…not precisely. An engagement is a time for people to decide for certain if they are suited to each other. In a couple of weeks, we will make a formal announcement, and then some months after that, we will be married."

He started back toward her, moving silently across the carpet. "But you will marry him only if it is certain that the two of you are suited."

"Yes, but you see, Leif, Matthew and I are very well suited. We have the same goals, the same friends, the same interests. Those are the things that are important in a marriage."

Leif reached out and touched her cheek. "You are wrong, Krista. This is what is important between a man and woman." For an instant his gaze held hers and she couldn't look away. Then he drew her back into his arms and very thoroughly kissed her.

Krista told herself to fight him, to make this foolishness end. She tried to break free, but he wouldn't let go, just kept kissing her and kissing her, his lips teasing and nibbling until her mouth softened under his and she was clinging to his shoulders. He coaxed her lips apart, then slid his tongue inside, and a sweeping pleasure washed through her. Little flutters of heat slid into her belly and melted through her limbs.

Dear God, it was the middle of the afternoon and she was

kissing a man who wasn't her fiancé, kissing him and kissing him, and she couldn't seem to stop.

Leif ended the kiss long before she wanted him to, leaving her dizzy and disoriented, barely able to stay on her feet.

"You will see, Krista. There is more to finding a mate than having the same *interests.* This I will show you."

Wildly shaking her head, she backed away from him. "You cannot, Leif. We're from two different worlds. It could never work between us—you know that as well as I do. This cannot…cannot ever happen again."

Leif ignored her as if she hadn't spoken. "Tomorrow you will teach me this thing you call dancing."

Krista swallowed. *Dancing.* But that was nearly as seductive as kissing! "I don't think… Perhaps I can find someone else to teach you."

He moved nearer, took hold of her hand, turned it over and pressed his mouth against her palm. "Do not be frightened, Krista Hart. I am not going to hurt you. This I vow." His jaw hardened. "No man will ever dare to hurt you."

Krista just looked up at him.

She tried to conjure Matthew Carlton's face, but his image refused to appear.

Twelve

It was Sunday. Leif surprised Krista by asking to accompany her and her father to church. As yet, he'd spent little time outside the house, had spent it instead learning the English language and customs.

Once inside the church, he sat on the wooden pew stoically, surveying the stained glass windows and magnificent stone arches, listening to the vicar's words—learning, she was sure. He seemed to have a bottomless thirst for knowledge.

After the service, her father introduced him to the vicar, who seemed pleased at his attendance. "Please do come back, young man. We would love to have you join our flock."

Krista had a hard time imagining the big blond Viking as a member of Vicar Jensen's *flock,* but with Leif one never knew. As they left the church, he paused at the bottom of the steps and looked up at the bell tower.

"In my homeland, it is said that even before we moved to Draugr, there were priests who lived among us. They taught the people about the Christian God and convinced them to give up their slaves." He looked down at her and she caught a hint of darkness in his eyes. "I am glad. I know what it is like for a man to live as a slave."

Krista gently touched his arm. "I'm sorry that happened to you, Leif."

He shrugged his shoulders. "It was the will of the gods."

"Mine or yours?"

"I do not think it matters."

Perhaps it didn't. Perhaps, in the end, doing what was right was all that mattered.

"Leif says that today you are teaching him to dance," her father said, obviously pleased as they made their way back to the carriage and settled inside.

"Actually, I think his lessons will have to wait. With Aunt Abby gone, there is no one to play the pianoforte. I could play, but then he'll have no one to dance with. I'm afraid we'll have to postpone the lessons." *Thank God.* No dancing with Leif. No feeling his arms around her. No looking into those disturbing blue eyes.

Her father just smiled. "I thought that might be the case. I spoke to Mr. Pendergast, your old piano instructor. I told him we could once more use his expertise. He will be here to play for you at two this afternoon."

Krista inwardly groaned. She had been certain she had found the perfect excuse.

Leif leaned toward her. "Do not look so worried, *honning.* I will try not to step on your pretty feet."

She ignored a little sweep of pleasure at his use of the endearment. "I told you not to call me that."

Leif just smiled.

She flicked a glance at her father to see if he had heard, but his head was tilted back against the squabs, his eyes drifting closed in the afternoon heat.

"I thought you didn't know what dancing was," she said softly to Leif.

"You gave me books to read. It says in dancing, two people move their feet together in rhythm to the playing of music."

"Yes, well, that is rather a simplification, as you will soon see."

The carriage pulled to a halt in front of the house, jarring her father awake. Once inside, he left to spend the afternoon in his study, slipping into his favorite room and quietly closing the door.

They had a little extra time before Mr. Pendergast was scheduled to arrive. Krista went into the drawing room, removed her straw bonnet and white cotton gloves, then turned to see Leif standing in the doorway watching her.

"I have tried to memorize the steps in the book," he said, "but the drawings are difficult to understand. If you would show me, perhaps it would help."

Krista started toward him like a woman on her way to the gallows. In dancing, partners had to touch. Touching Leif was like touching fire. She wished the country dances had not become so passé. But couples dancing was the vogue these days, the waltz the most popular of all.

"I suppose since you have been learning the steps, we might as well get started. The quadrille is most difficult and not something a person should do in public until he becomes fairly proficient. Currently, the waltz is the dance most in favor, and it is relatively simple, though it does require a certain amount of finesse."

"*Fin-esse.* This means to move without awkwardness, does it not?"

"Yes." She looked him over, wondering how in the world a man of his size was going to move gracefully on the dance floor. Then again, he always seemed to have an innate sort of grace about him, no matter what he did.

"We'll practice the steps of the dance a bit. Then when Mr. Pendergast arrives, you will be able to see how the steps fit together with the music."

Leif moved in front of her and made a very proper bow.

"How did you know—"

"It is in the book."

Disarmed by his smile, she took a place beside him. "Now, watch my feet." He looked down at her kidskin slippers. Krista counted the steps as she moved in time to a beat she heard only in her head. "One—two, three. One—two, three. One—two, three. There is a sort of rhythm to it. You'll hear it once music is being played. Then you turn—very gracefully—moving your partner around with you. You try it. Count the steps as you move."

He concentrated hard. "One—two, three. One—two, three. One—two, three."

Krista sighed. "You need music. None of this makes any sense without it." She started toward the pianoforte, thinking to play a few bars, then heard a familiar voice in the doorway.

"You are just getting started. It appears my timing is perfect."

"Mr. Pendergast! It is so good to see you. Please, do come in."

The piano instructor moved toward them, a fine-boned, elegant little man with silver hair and pale, delicate features. Krista introduced him to Leif, and the music teacher eyed him with a bit of curiosity.

"Mr. Draugr is a friend of father's from out of the country," Krista explained. "He is not familiar with some of our customs." That was putting it mildly.

"Well, a man must know how to dance, my friend," the

music teacher said. "And I believe you may have found your-self the perfect partner."

Not that she was a particularly good dancer. It was simply that they were of a size. Leif would have far more trouble learning should he be partnered with Corrie or some other woman of petite stature.

Leif smiled down at Krista. "I think you may be right, Mr. Pendergast. I am sure Miss Hart will partner me very well."

He had called her "Miss Hart," using the proper form of address. She could scarcely believe it. And yet there was some-thing in the way he said it that made her wary.

"Take your places," Mr. Pendergast instructed.

Krista took her position facing Leif. When he made no move to touch her, she steeled herself and reached for his hand. "The gentleman places his palm against the lady's waist."

He settled his hand against the silk of her pale blue gown, and the heat of it seemed to burn right through her clothes. "Is this right?"

"Yes…"

He moved his hand back and forth across her middle. "What is this stiff thing you are wearing beneath your clothes?"

Krista flushed. "It's a corset," she whispered. "Not a subject for discussion in the drawing room."

"What is it for?"

"To make my waist look smaller. Now concentrate on what we are doing."

"I wondered about that—why your waist was so much smaller than those of the women where I come from."

"Leif, please."

He straightened, settled his hand in the position she had shown him.

"Now the man takes the woman's hand in his," she said.

Leif caught her hand, laced their fingers together. "Like this?"

Krista shook her head. "No. You just sort of collect her hand—rather like this." She showed him the proper technique and he imitated the movement, enveloping her fingers in his. "That...that is correct."

They were standing toe to toe, his wide palm at her waist, his other hand gently cradling hers. "Raise your arm a little," she instructed. "That is better."

Mr. Pendergast ran his fingers gracefully over the keyboard in a flurry of notes, then began a popular Viennese waltz. Krista started counting in rhythm, until Leif began to hear the beat, as well. "Count for me."

He did as she told him. "One—two, three. One—two, three."

"Now all you do is move your feet in the pattern I showed you, to the same rhythm."

"I must try it first by myself." He smiled at her. "I do not wish to step on your feet." Pretending she was still in his arms, he moved around the drawing room. It took less time than she'd expected for him to catch on. He returned and pulled her into his arms, swept her into the dance.

Krista gasped as one of his big feet landed on the toe of her slipper and sent a jolt of pain up her leg.

Leif instantly halted. "I am sorry. I did not mean to hurt you."

She managed a smile. "It takes a bit of practice. Why don't we try it again?"

He did far better this time, and after an hour of gliding around the room, had the movements fairly well mastered. Leif was smiling, pleased with himself, growing more confident with every sweeping turn. "I like this thing called dancing. I did not think I would."

"Yes, well, it can be quite a lot of fun." For some people, at any rate. Until today, Krista had always felt big and ungainly on the dance floor. Not with Leif. Now that he knew the steps, he made her feel as if she were floating.

"I like holding you in my arms," Leif said beneath the sound of the music. "I like the way we fit together. When we make love, you will see why this is good."

Krista's feet stopped moving. She tried to step out of his hold, but he wouldn't let her go.

"You were doing very well," Mr. Pendergast said from his seat at the piano. "Why did you stop?"

Because dancing with Leif was driving her mad. Last night, Krista had dreamed of him, imagined his scorching kisses, his hands moving over her body. She had dreamed of him caressing her breasts as he had done that night in the barn, remembered how her nipples had hardened and begun to distend. Even now she wanted him to touch her, ached to touch him.

"I am sorry, Mr. Pendergast, but suddenly I am not feeling very well. I am afraid we will have to continue Mr. Draugr's lessons some other day."

Pendergast came to his feet. "Of course, dear lady." He closed the lid of the pianoforte. "I'm sorry you are feeling unwell, my dear." Picking up the leather satchel that held his sheets of music, he bade Leif farewell and left the drawing room.

Krista started for the door behind him, but Leif caught her arm. "I know what is wrong with you, *honning*. We share the same illness. I promise you, when the time is right, I will make both of us well again."

Krista ignored the heat in those hot blue eyes and walked past him out the door.

"This is silly. There've been no more notes, nothing untoward has happened. There is no need for you to go with me."

"I am going," Leif said simply.

Krista rolled her eyes. "Men!"

She thought of speaking to her father, but knew it would do no good. For a while, after her mother had died, her father had argued against her going about without a chaperone. But times were changing and, like her mother, Krista was a very modern woman.

Lately things had changed once more. Since the fire, the professor insisted Leif travel with her. Her father didn't know the biggest threat Krista faced was the big handsome Viking who was determined to have her in his bed.

She amended that. The biggest threat was that she *wanted* to be in his bed. Or at least wanted to discover what it might be like if he made love to her.

She banished that embarrassing thought and let her head fall back against the velvet squabs of the carriage. Leif sat across from her, his heavy sword resting beneath the seat within easy reach should he need it.

The hum of the carriage wheels lulled her. Her eyes drifted closed. She hadn't slept well last night. Twice she had awakened from an erotic dream of Leif, her body drenched in perspiration. She knew only the basics involved in making love, only what she had read in the book she and Coralee had found in the basement of the dormitory at Briarhill Academy.

When they had read the words, she and Corrie had been aghast at the thought of a man connecting his male anatomy to the female part of a woman.

Now Krista dreamed of how it might feel to be connected that way to Leif, to feel his heavy weight on top of her, pressing her down in the mattress, his muscular chest rubbing sensuously against her breasts, his mouth moving hotly over hers.

The carriage hit a pothole and she opened her eyes with a

start. Leif sat across from her, his gaze on her face. "You are beautiful when you are sleeping."

No man spoke to her the way he did. No man had ever told her she was beautiful, not even her fiancé.

Krista glanced away. She said nothing as the carriage rolled along, and once they reached the office, she put Leif to work as far away from her as possible. He never questioned her authority, never complained about whatever task she set for him.

Over the weekend, she had continued his lessons on manners and decorum, and as usual, he had been a very rapid learner, committing to memory each instruction she gave him, perfecting his skills more easily than she could have imagined. His competence was evident here, as well. By the end of the day, she realized how useful he had made himself around the office. In the few days he had worked there he had managed to earn the employees' respect and make a place for himself among them.

"Leif is a very hard worker," Corrie said. "I like him, Krista."

Krista turned away, her chest suddenly tight. "I like him, too, Corrie. I like him far too much."

Her friend eyed her uncertainly. "I realize the man is incredibly handsome, but surely—"

"I'm attracted to him, Corrie. I can scarcely think when I am around him."

"Oh, dear." Corrie's gaze found the object of their discussion over in the corner, lifting some heavy boxes that Freddie wasn't big enough to move. "What about Matthew Carlton?"

Krista shook her head. "I'm going to marry him. I have no choice. My family needs an heir and I am the only person who can give them one. Besides, I want a husband and family of my own, and Matthew and I are very well suited."

"Perhaps you and Leif—"

"He's going back, Corrie. Leif is the eldest son. He is destined to be chieftain of his clan. He has duties to his people, just as I have duties here."

"I can't believe he intends to leave. He watches you as if you already belong to him."

Krista glanced to where Leif stood, saw his gaze move over her a moment before he went back to work. "Leif is very protective. It is simply his nature, I think. And there is the fact that I am the one who got him out of that cage. Perhaps he feels he owes me a debt of some kind."

"Perhaps…" Corrie said, but it was clear she thought Leif's feelings went far beyond payment of a debt.

Krista told herself whatever feelings she held for Leif were unimportant. Besides, he was leaving and she was staying. It was as simple as that.

Krista was tired at day's end. Thoughts of Leif and her ridiculous attraction to him left her irritable and out of sorts. When he removed his sword from the upright chest in her office and walked ahead of her toward the door, she snapped at him, though she hadn't really meant to. "How many times have I told you that a woman precedes a man? I can't believe you have already forgotten."

His eyes darkened. "And I told you that a man walks in front of a woman in case there is danger. There is danger here for you, Krista. Whether you wish to believe it or not."

With that he jerked open the door and stepped out onto the porch. He disappeared for a moment, checking the area around the building to be sure it was safe, then returned. Drawing her a little too rapidly down the steps, he then lifted her off her feet as if she weighed nothing at all, and dropped her onto the seat of the carriage.

Leif climbed in behind her and hurled himself into the opposite seat. He was angry and she really didn't blame him. It was scarcely his fault her thoughts were so unruly where he was concerned. True, he preyed on the attraction he knew she felt for him, but he was a man—a Viking, no less—and he wanted her. He had made his desire perfectly clear.

By the time they were halfway home, darkness had settled over the city. They were rolling along the street when the carriage made an unexpected turn. Krista started to lean out the window to see why the coachman had changed direction, but Leif pulled her back inside.

"What is wrong?" he asked.

"We don't usually go through this part of town."

Turning, he blew out the brass coach lamp, leaving the interior in darkness. She heard the sound of his blade sliding out of its leather sheath, and realized he had drawn his sword.

"I'm sure it is nothing." She leaned over once more, determined to look out the window. Surely once she knew which way the coach was traveling—

Leif pushed her back down in the seat. "You will obey me in this, Krista. Do not get up again." There was steel in his voice. If she hadn't known him as she did, she might have been frightened. Even now, her heart was thumping faster.

"I am certain we are not—"

"Silence, lady!" His jaw looked as hard as granite in the dim light and Krista's mouth snapped shut. He had never spoken to her this way and it was clear he meant for her to heed his words.

Leif's eyes searched the darkness outside the window and the muscles in his shoulders tightened. A little shiver ran down her spine at the fearsome sight he made. This man was no gentleman, no matter his facade. He was a Viking through and through, and he was ready for any sort of danger.

Surely there was a simple explanation, she thought, then felt the jolt of the brakes as the carriage rolled to a halt. She started to call out to the coachman, ask why he had stopped, but Leif's dark look warned her not to.

Her heartbeat quickened even more. Across the street, light filtered out through the dirty windows of a seedy tavern. The sound of a woman's high-pitched laughter drifted on the warm night air, followed by the gruff sound of men's voices just outside the carriage.

Her stomach tightened. In the shadowy darkness, she saw Leif's hand tighten around the hilt of his sword. Then the door jerked open and the barrel of a pistol appeared.

"Get down here. Both of ye. Now!"

Leif's gaze found hers. There was cold fury in his eyes and bloodlust in the hard lines of his face. "Ladies first," he said softly.

Pulse drumming almost painfully, Krista descended the narrow iron stairs. A big, heavyset man with a thick black beard waited at the bottom, also brandishing a weapon.

"Now you, bucko!" the first man shouted into the carriage.

Leif leaned forward, his head and shoulders appearing through the open carriage door. He took a single step down the stairs, then his arm shot out, the heavy sword flashing in the light from the tavern, slashing upward as he leaped from the coach. The first henchmen shrieked in pain and his pistol flew into the darkness. Krista bit back a scream as blood spattered over her gown and darkened the legs of Leif's gray trousers.

"Bloody bastard!" the man shouted. "'E's cut off two o' me fingers!"

Shoving Krista out of harm's way, Leif whirled toward the second man, sword raised for another cutting blow.

Shaking all over, scarcely able to breathe, she watched the two opponents. Using the flat of his sword, Leif knocked the second henchman's pistol away with an ease that made her shiver, and planted his blade at the base of the big man's throat.

Footsteps pounded as the first man shot down the alley and disappeared into the darkness. Krista looked up at the driver's seat, but their coachman was nowhere to be seen.

Leif fixed his attention on the man beneath his blade, backing him up, step by step, until he was flattened against the side of the carriage.

"Who hired you?"

The big man shook his head. "Don't…don't know 'is name."

Leif pressed the iron tip of the blade beneath his bearded chin.

"I don't know 'is name! I swear it, gov'nor!" He was breathing hard, his body shaking with fear. "Me and Willie got a message over there at the White Horse Tavern. Said a carriage would be pullin' into the alley across the street. We was to stop the coach and deliver a message. Paid us real good to do it."

"What message?" Leif asked darkly.

"Said to tell the woman she was gonna be real sorry if she didn't stop printin' those articles in her paper."

"What else?"

The man cut his eyes away.

"What else?" Leif pressed the sword tip deeper, until a trickle of blood appeared.

The henchman swallowed. "Said…said we should teach the litt'l tart a lesson."

"Go on."

"Said we could each have us a taste o' her before we let her go."

Leif made a growling sound low in his throat. He tossed

down his sword and jerked the man up by the front of his shirt. "I will teach *you* a lesson." He drove his fist deep into the big man's stomach, doubling him over, then punched him hard in the face. Blow after blow rained down until Krista was certain he would kill him.

"Leif, stop! You must stop, please!"

Another vicious blow fell, knocking the man's head back, sending him crashing into the side of a building in the alley. Leif dragged him up and struck him again.

"Leif, please! You can't just keep hitting him! Stop it right now!"

He drew back his arm another time, then seemed to collect himself as her words began to sink in.

"Please, Leif. You have to stop."

His fist shook as he stepped away, leaving the man in a bloody heap at his feet. "Get in the coach," he said.

She cast a last glance at her surroundings, worried the other man might return, then started up the stairs. "What about the coachman?"

"He was one of them. I will drive you home."

"Do you know how?"

"I can drive a wagon. I will get us there."

"But—"

"Get inside, lady! Do as I say!"

Krista swallowed, but didn't argue. This was a far different man than the one who had danced with her in the drawing room. She shivered as she settled herself on the red velvet seat, and a few minutes later the carriage lurched into motion.

She thought of Leif and the men he had brought down with frightening ease. If she had ever doubted the stories she had read about Vikings, she didn't now.

* * *

Paxton Hart paced the entry. One of the grooms had come to him only moments ago, worried that the carriage had not yet arrived home from *Heart to Heart*.

"Mr. Skinner sent me," the young man said. "He took ill, ye see, a disease of the bowels, just before time to fetch yer daughter home from work. The new man took the coach, sir. Mr. Skinner—he's beginnin' ta worry somethin' mighta' happened."

"Yes, well, I am beginning to worry, myself. Perhaps a wheel has broken or some other problem has occurred."

"Yes, sir. Shall I rig out the other carriage, sir?"

"Perhaps you had better. As soon as it is ready, have it brought round front and—"

Footsteps on the front porch stairs cut off his words. The butler hurried to open the door, and when it swung wide, Leif and Krista appeared in the opening.

"Good heavens!" said Giles.

"Indeed!" Paxton moved forward. "Quickly. Let's get them inside." Both Leif's and Krista's clothing was stained with blood and the pins had come loose from his daughter's hair, leaving it to trail in golden ringlets around her shoulders. "What has happened? Shall I fetch a doctor?"

"There is no need for that," Krista said. "I am sorry to worry you, Father, but you see there was a slight…slight altercation."

"Your daughter's carriage was attacked," Leif said. "She is lucky she escaped unharmed." His voice was harder than Paxton had ever heard it, and his jaw looked like iron.

"You were right to send Leif, Father," Krista admitted. "If he hadn't been with me…" She looked down at the blood spattered over her skirt, and the color leached from her cheeks. "I don't know what might have happened."

She swayed a little and Leif scooped her up in his arms.

"Take her upstairs," Paxton said. "I'll ring for her maid."

"I am fine," Krista told them, but she turned her head into Leif's powerful chest and slid her arms around his neck. "I was wrong," she said to him softly. "I am sorry."

"It is all right. I was there to protect you. That is all that matters." Leif kissed the top of Krista's head and a tightness squeezed Paxton's chest. He had known from the first time he had seen them together the risk he was taking. It was the reason he had insisted on removing Leif to Heartland.

Since their return to London, he had watched the attraction between the pair grow. He was afraid Krista was falling in love with the handsome blond Norseman, and that could only lead to disaster. As much as Paxton admired and respected the man, he knew that in time Leif would be returning to his far north island home. He was determined in that regard, and Paxton had never met a man of stronger will.

Krista's life was here in London. The people she loved, the business she had built into such a successful enterprise, her passionate ideals, those were what mattered most to her. They were the things that made her happy. Whatever her feelings for Leif, it could never work between them.

Paxton was worried about his daughter and the man he had invited into their home and yet he trusted Leif to protect her as he trusted no one else.

As he watched the big man carry her up the stairs, Paxton prayed Krista would be wise enough to protect her heart.

Thirteen

Krista rose early. She wanted to speak to Leif, to thank him for the way he had come to her rescue last night.

She found him in the breakfast room, a small, sunny parlor at the back of the town house. He was carefully dipping his fork into a plate of eggs and ham, eating with relish, if a bit slower than usual. Perched on the back of the chair beside him, tiny Alfinn looked up at her with big, brown, soulful eyes. Leif dipped a piece of bread into the pool of honey on his plate and handed it to the monkey.

"I see you have company this morning."

At the sound of her voice, Leif spotted her in the doorway and smiled. "You are up early." He stayed seated a moment, then recalled he was supposed to rise when a woman entered the room, and shot to his feet.

"I wanted to talk to you," she said.

As she walked toward the table, Alfinn reached a tiny hand out to her and she stopped a moment to pet him. Leif pushed back his chair, rounded the table and very properly seated her across from him.

"Would you like something to eat?" He indicated the silver chafing dishes on the sideboard, but Krista shook her head.

"I rarely eat much in the mornings." Just then one of the servants appeared with a cup of hot chocolate and several small biscuits, her usual morning fare. Leif gave Alfinn a slice of orange off his plate and the monkey ate it very daintily.

"I thought my father might be in here," Krista said, "though I should have known he would already be locked away with his work."

"Your father had a meeting with one of his professor friends. I do not think he plans to be gone very long." The servant slipped back out the door and closed it quietly behind him. "We are private here," Leif added. "What is it you wished to say?"

Krista smoothed her napkin over the full skirt of her rose dimity morning dress. "I just… I wanted to thank you for what you did last night. You risked your life to protect me, Leif. You could have shot, perhaps even killed. What you did…it was amazing and, well, as I said, I just wanted to thank you."

"It is a man's duty to protect a woman."

"I suppose that may be so where you come from. Still, it was a very brave thing to do."

He looked at her, studied her face, seem to read her thoughts. "There is more you wish to say. What is it?"

She released a breath. "I just… I wish I had been more courageous. I'm sure the women where you live would not have simply stood there and done nothing, the way I did. They would have helped you in some way."

A corner of his mouth edged up. "I am a warrior. I do not need a woman to help me fight."

"No, you did a very fine job all by yourself. Perhaps if I hadn't been so completely taken by surprise… In truth, I never believed I was in any real danger until it was too late." She managed to smile. "At least I didn't scream or fall over in a swoon."

His lips widened into a grin. It made him look young and devastatingly handsome. "You were very brave—for an Englishwoman."

Both of them laughed. Alfinn joined in, screeching merrily, and Krista was surprised at the relief she felt. She had worried that she had somehow disappointed Leif. It was foolish, perhaps, but she was glad that he still looked at her with the same warmth in his eyes.

She took several sips of her chocolate and ate one of the biscuits, then voices in the entry caught her attention. Leif rose from his chair as her father and Matthew Carlton walked into the breakfast room. Matthew's features were set and there was a determined look in his eyes. Her father's expression was equally grim, but his features seemed tinged with regret.

Krista's heartbeat quickened. "Is something wrong, Father?" She rose to her feet in turn.

"I am afraid so, dearest."

As if by magic, one of the footmen arrived to carry little Alfinn back out to the stables. The monkey leaped onto the young man's arm and the pair disappeared out the door.

"Last night after supper," her father continued once they were alone, "I received a note from Matthew requesting a meeting this morning." Matthew had been in the country, she knew, his father taken ill with an ague.

She turned in his direction. "I hope the earl is all right."

"My father is fine. This has nothing to do with my family. It has to do with you and me and the future we have been planning."

"I'm afraid I don't understand," Krista murmured. Across from her, Leif stood tense and unmoving. "If this concerns only the two of us, Matthew, perhaps it would be better discussed in private."

"I'm afraid this also concerns your house guest, Mr. Draugr. You see, as your fiancé, I highly protest his presence in your home."

"But he is here at my father's invitation."

"Which your father and I discussed at length this morning. It has also been brought to my attention that Mr. Draugr has been accompanying you about town in your carriage—without a chaperone. This is highly improper, Krista, and I want it stopped—now!"

She glanced quickly at her father, silently beseeching him for help, but saw no aid in the grim look on his face.

"Mr. Draugr has been acting as my protector," she said. "As you know, I have received a number of threatening messages. Last night, Leif…Mr. Draugr…saved my life."

"Yes, your father told me the tale of your rescue during our discussion this morning."

"So you see, it is necessary that Mr. Draugr—"

"I will be happy to provide any protection you might need. In the meantime, I want Draugr out of this house by the end of the day or our engagement is over."

"You can't mean that, Matthew."

"The choice is yours, Krista. We can build a life together as we have planned, or you can throw it all away for a few months in the company of your barbarian—the professor's guinea pig."

Krista bit back a gasp as Leif surged forward and grabbed Matthew by the front of his shirt.

"Leif, no!" she cried out.

"Let him go, Leif," her father commanded. "This is not the way for a gentleman to behave."

Leif held on to Matthew's shirt a moment more, then released him. "I will not take your insults, Carlton. Gentleman or no."

Matthew smoothed the wrinkles from the front of his crisp white shirt. "Are you challenging me, Draugr? Dueling, my friend, has been outlawed for years." Matthew arched a brow. "However, there is no law against a fencing match between two acquaintances." His mouth tightened. "We won't need any protective armor, of course, being such *old friends.*"

"No!" Krista nearly shouted. "Leif doesn't know how to fence. Are you trying to kill him?"

"Of course not. But you've been teaching him a number of different things. Perhaps a lesson on what happens when a man poaches on another man's territory might be useful."

The professor looked worried. "I don't think this is a good idea, Matthew. The man has never used a fencing sword before. The contest would hardly be fair."

"I will fight him," Leif said, a muscle working in his jaw.

Krista caught his arm. "Leif, you can't do that. You don't know how to fence. The swords they use are nothing like the blade you used last night."

"I will fight him with whatever weapon he chooses."

Matthew smiled. "You see—he wants the match. How does tomorrow sound? Say ten o'clock in the morning?"

Leif gave a stiff nod of his head and Krista's heart twisted in fear. "Leif, please. You can't do this."

He cast her the same look of warning he had given her last night.

"Then it's settled," Matthew said. "I'll even provide him with a sword."

Krista looked into Leif's face and knew he was determined in this. He would fight and nothing she could say would stop him. Her chin went up. "He can use my great-grandfather's sword."

Matthew bowed. "As you wish. Oh, and there is one more thing. If I win the match, Leif Draugr leaves this house, and you and I set a date for our wedding—which will take place very soon."

The air seemed to stall in Krista's lungs. Leif would not back down, but Matthew had just given her a way to end this deadly game before either of the men got hurt. "You don't have to fight him, Matthew. Leif can return to Heartland, as you wish, and you and I can set a date for the wedding."

Leif's blue eyes darkened in fury. "I will fight," he said to Matthew. "And if *I* win, your engagement to Krista is over."

The room fell silent. Krista could count every beat of her heart.

Matthew Carlton smiled. "Agreed. Tomorrow, then, ten o'clock." He made a slight bow to Krista, turned and walked out of the breakfast room. In the entry, she heard Giles open and close the front door.

Krista looked up at the Norseman and her eyes filled with tears. "Dear God, Leif, what have you done?"

The weather turned gray and cloudy, darkening the sky outside the windows of the drawing room. Krista watched Leif pull her great-grandfather's fencing sword from its scabbard, one of a pair used for dueling. The other nestled on a bed of dark blue velvet in the carved wooden case.

"They belonged to my mother's grandfather, the fourth Earl of Hampton," she said. "He was a big man, blond like you, Leif. He claimed to be of Viking descent."

Leif nodded. "Then Tyr has blessed me." He was the god of war, she knew, the bravest of all the gods. Leif tested the sword, flexing it one way and then another. "The weapon is well made. I am honored to use it. If the gods remain with me, it will serve my purpose well."

Krista swallowed against the lump in her throat. There was no way Leif could possibly win a match against Matthew, a man who prided himself on his skill as a master swordsman. Only Leif didn't seem to know that.

She turned to her father. "Is there nothing we can do to stop this, Father?"

He only shook his head. "It has gone too far, I fear. It is now a matter of honor." He sighed. "This is all my fault. I should have known Matthew would disapprove of Leif staying here in the house with you."

"It isn't your fault. We were simply helping a man who needed our help very badly."

"Still, Matthew is going to be your husband. I should have taken his feelings into consideration." Paxton reached over and grasped her hand, gave it a gentle squeeze. "Whatever happens, Matthew is not a murderer. I do not believe he intends to do any real harm to our friend."

Krista wished she was more convinced. Her chest constricted. Unless a miracle occurred, even if Leif remained unharmed, when the match was over he would be forced to leave the house. A date would be set for her wedding to Matthew Carlton, and soon she would become his wife.

She looked over at Leif, who practiced with the sword, whipping the thin blade back and forth through the air. It would take a miracle for him to win, and yet she found herself praying that miracle would occur.

Praying that Leif would somehow win and set her free.

The thought was more than a little sobering.

Krista shook her head. It wasn't going to happen. The best

she could hope for was that Matthew would take pity on Leif and not hurt him too badly.

The following morning, Krista confronted the men as they left the house. "I'm going with you, Father."

The day was dark and damp, a late summer drizzle blowing in off the Thames. Krista had risen early. She wasn't about to let Leif face Matthew Carlton while she waited dutifully at home.

"A duel is scarcely the place for a woman," her father said, "and whatever this match pretends to be, a duel is what it is. Now go back inside and wait until our return."

Leif looked down at her, his eyes so blue it made her chest ache. "Do as your father says, *honning*."

"I am going. If you two won't take me, then I shall get there on my own. If Leif… If either of the men should be injured, I intend to be there to help tend his wounds. I am going, and there is no way you can stop me."

Leif reached out and cupped her cheek. "So fierce, my little Valkyrie." He looked over at her father, who gave a resigned sigh.

"When her mind is made up," the professor said, "there is simply no stopping her."

Leif smiled. "Come, then, if you must. Your friend Matthew will need some of your tending."

Her eyes widened. Surely he didn't believe he could actually win! True, he had stayed up well past midnight, poring over the books on fencing she and her father had collected for him from the library. But knowing how to swing a sword and developing a skill that required years of practice were two far different things.

They boarded the coach. Their driver, Mr. Skinner, had recovered from his untimely bout of illness—the work, no doubt, of the men who had attacked the carriage. He snapped the reins and pulled the team out into the tree-lined street. It didn't take long to reach Matthew's town house, also located in the fashionable Mayfair district.

The small group headed up the brick path toward the front door and the butler pulled it open before they reached the top of the stairs.

"Professor Carlton has been expecting you. He awaits your presence upstairs in the ballroom."

Walking ahead of her father and Leif, Krista climbed the curving staircase to the third floor. Inside her chest, her heart fluttered like a trapped bird. She said a silent prayer that neither of the men would be hurt, then said an extra prayer for Leif.

Matthew was waiting when they entered the elegant marble-floored ballroom, flexing his sword, watching his perfectly executed movements in the gilded mirrors that lined the walls, moving with a graceful ease that made Krista's insides churn.

He frowned when he saw her walk into the room. "Krista. What are you doing here? This is men's business. Have your driver return you home at once."

"I am staying, Matthew."

His lips curled into a sneer. "Why? Because you're worried about your Viking?"

"Because I am worried for both of you. I beg you to end this madness before one of you is seriously injured."

He shrugged. Matthew wasn't as tall or as powerfully built as Leif, but he wasn't a small man, either, and his skill with a sword more than made up for any physical advantage Leif might have. "If your friend concedes to my demands, I will be happy to end this here and now."

"It is ten o'clock," Leif said, interrupting him. "Let us get on with it."

Matthew looked pleased. He turned to the professor. "I

would advise you to remove your daughter. This may not be pleasant to watch."

Her father's worried gaze found hers. "Krista?"

"I am staying, Father."

Matthew frowned. "Then I shall not be held responsible for any upset to your female sensibilities." He walked over to where Leif stood, her great-grandfather Herald Chapman's fencing sword gripped in one of his big hands.

Both men wore snug-fitting trousers and a full-sleeved shirt. Matthew wore boots of fine Spanish leather, while Leif wore black, knee-high Hessians.

"If you are agreed," Matthew said to Leif, "we fence until first blood is drawn."

"We fence until one of us yields," Leif countered, making Krista hiss in a breath.

"Agreed," Matthew said with obvious relish. "The rules are simple—"

"There are no rules," Leif said, and Matthew's brown eyebrows went up.

"Are you certain that is your wish?"

"Very certain," Leif declared.

"Leif, no!" Krista pleaded, afraid he would refuse to concede even if it was clear he was losing, and worried that Matthew might wind up hurting him very badly.

"Professor, if you cannot control your daughter, I suggest the two of you leave."

"Perhaps that would be best, dearest," her father said.

"I am sorry, Father. I won't say anything more."

The men squared off, their blades crossed in the air, each of them standing in profile to provide a smaller target, something Leif had no doubt learned from one of her father's books. Krista's heart pounded as steel rang against steel. Leif parried the first of Matthew's vicious blows, then Matthew lunged forward and an instant later, the sleeve of Leif's shirt blossomed with bright red blood.

Krista stifled a cry.

She felt her father's hand at the small of her back. "Steady, dearling."

"He won't yield, Father. He'll die before he'll do that."

The professor looked grim but said nothing more. The combatants moved back and forth across the ballroom, and Krista gasped in horror when Matthew's blade sank into the fleshy part of Leif's thigh.

"Make them stop, Father—I beg you."

"I wish I knew how, dearest."

"Do you yield?" Matthew asked, his blade circling, circling, poised for another crippling blow.

Leif answered by bringing his own sword down hard on Matthew's blade, forcing him to parry and take several steps backward. Leif followed, his blade slashing left and right, raining down blow after blow that Matthew easily deflected. Krista thought she caught the hint of a smile on her fiancé's face as he raised his sword, knocked the tip of Leif's blade harmlessly out of the way, and lunged toward Leif's torso.

She squeezed her eyes shut and clamped her lips together to hold back a scream. When she looked again, a smear of red slashed across the shirt over Leif's rib cage.

Though again and again he avoided Matthew's punishing blows, her heart ached with fear for him. Leif knew nothing of proper form, nothing of advancing and retreating, thrusting and parrying, and yet as he moved to defend himself, to advance on his opponent, he somehow looked graceful. He was a warrior, no matter the weapon, but he was no match for Matthew's skill. There was every chance Leif might die, and Krista's heart squeezed so hard she could scarcely breathe.

For the first time, she realized how much she had come to care for him, how much he truly meant to her. She clung to her father's arm, watching the men in terror as Leif fell back beneath Matthew's sword again and again.

Then suddenly he lunged forward, bringing his blade up in the same manner he had that night outside the carriage. Catching the hilt of Matthew's sword, he wrenched it out of Matthew's grip and sent the weapon careening away. She watched in amazement as Leif's wrist came up and he used the butt of his own sword to deliver a powerful blow to Matthew's jaw, one that sent him crashing into the wall. The blade flashed again and Leif pressed the tip against his opponent's chest, above his heart.

"Do you yield?" Leif asked.

"You broke the rules."

"There were no rules."

And even if there were, Leif had managed by some trick of fate—or perhaps the intervention of his Viking gods—to separate Matthew from his weapon.

"Do you yield your claim on this woman, Mat-thew Carlton?"

Matthew looked ready to kill. "I yield," he growled.

Leif lifted the tip of his blade and Matthew came away from the wall, his face set in tight lines of fury. He walked straight toward her.

"Is this what you want, Krista? Whatever happened here, it is you who has the final say."

Tell him you still want to marry him. Do your duty. Make your grandfather happy. Take care of your family's needs.

"Perhaps…" She moistened her lips. "Perhaps for now this is for the best."

A muscle jerked in Matthew's cheek. He said nothing more, just turned and stalked away.

The professor stopped him just as he reached the door. "I realize how you must feel, Matthew. My daughter is an extremely independent woman. Perhaps she is simply not ready to accept the notion of marriage, though I am sure in time that will change." He flicked a glance at Leif. "In the meanwhile, no matter how great your dislike of Mr. Draugr, I expect you to keep your silence where his background is concerned."

Matthew's features darkened. "Draugr's origins are of no importance to me. I don't intend to repeat what was said to me in confidence."

The professor reached out and squeezed his shoulder. "I'm sorry, son."

Matthew ignored the remark. He disappeared through the ballroom door just as Leif walked up beside Krista. Her eyes blurred with tears at the sight of the blood spreading over the gathered sleeve of his white shirt, the crimson stain seeping through the leg of his trousers. The patch of blood over his ribs had widened and she realized he was hurt even more badly than she had feared.

"Hurry, Father. We need to get him home and have his wounds taken care of."

Leif reached out and touched her cheek. "You are free of your vow, Krista Hart." He looked at her father. "It is not yet time, but soon we will speak of the future."

The professor made no reply, just urged Leif toward the door. Krista let him lean against her along the way, shouldering his heavy weight more easily than a smaller woman would have. All the while she kept thinking, *I am free of Matthew Carlton.* She should have been angry at Leif for the trouble he had caused, furious at her own foolishness in allowing her fiancé to walk away. Instead she felt as if a great burden had been lifted from her shoulders.

At the bottom of the stairs, she asked the butler to bring her towels and a roll of bandages, then used them to wrap Leif's wounds to slow the bleeding until they could get him back to the house. They made their way out to the carriage, and she helped him climb inside, wishing his face didn't look quite so pale.

He tilted his head back against the squabs and she realized he was hurting far more than he let on. Her hand trembled as she reached out to touch him, felt his fingers tighten over hers. *Dear God, let him be all right*, she prayed, fighting to hold back tears.

She had been frightened the night of the attack on her carriage. She was far more frightened now. She vowed she would not let him know.

The ache in her chest expanded. She was free, her engagement ended, but she could not have the man she truly wanted, the man she had only just realized she would choose as her husband. They came from two different worlds, had two very different futures ahead of them. No matter how much Leif had sacrificed to gain her freedom, she could never marry him.

Surely he understood, she told herself. He had never actually spoken of a future together. He planned to leave England—he had made that more than clear—and she could not return with him to his home.

Krista drew in a steadying breath. Whatever the future held, it was still some time away, and at present she just wanted Leif well again. She prayed to his gods as well as her own that he would be all right.

Fourteen

Every minute in the carriage seemed an hour, though the town house was mere blocks away. Krista and her father helped Leif inside and an ashen-faced Giles raced off down the hall, shouting for help from the other servants. A few minutes later, Mr. Skinner and two of the grooms appeared. Draping Leif's muscular arms over their shoulders, they helped him climb the stairs.

Krista snapped out more orders, sent one of the grooms to fetch a physician, and called for her maid, Priscilla Dobbs, to bring the household medical supplies, as well as cloths, warm water and fresh bandages. By the time she reached Leif's room, she found Henry helping him undress, trying, along with her father and Mr. Skinner, to get him into bed.

Standing unnoticed in the doorway, Krista felt her eyes widen as the little valet stripped off Leif's trousers and she saw that he wore not a stitch of clothing underneath. She turned away, her face heating up, giving the men time to get him settled beneath the covers. But the image of his broad back, long, powerful legs and round, muscular buttocks remained etched into her brain.

Though Leif did his best to fit in, he ignored the dictates of society whenever it suited him. Apparently wearing men's small clothes didn't suit him at all, and it occurred to her, as it had in the ballroom, how thin was the veneer of civility that Leif Draugr wore. Still, he affected her as no other man had, and seeing him weak and pale from loss of blood made her heart twist painfully inside her.

She took a steadying breath, clutched the wooden box that held the household medical supplies, and started toward the bed. The men backed away, giving her room to work.

"Call if you need any help," her father said as she set the box on the table.

Krista mustered a faint, tremulous smile. "You got him into bed. Big as he is, that was the difficult part."

The door closed softly behind the men and Krista turned to Leif, who lay back against the pillow, his eyes open and watching her.

"You've lost a lot of blood," she said, "but the bleeding seems to have slowed and the doctor will be here very soon."

"I am fine, *honning*." He amazed her by reaching up and capturing her face gently between his palms. He drew her toward him, pulled her mouth down to his for a kiss. It was insane. The man was injured. And yet the long, deep, very thorough kiss turned her insides furnace-hot and her brain to mush. She was trembling by the time he released her.

"You—you are wounded, Leif Draugr. You need to conserve your strength."

"With your tending, I will be well soon enough." His blue eyes searched her face, and she could read the desire he made no effort to hide. "The gods have smiled on me this day. You are free and soon I will show you some of the things I have wished to teach you."

Krista's breath caught. She didn't ask what those things were. Already he had taught her more about passion than she ever could have learned from a book. As she turned away from him, her nipples felt stiff and sensitive beneath the bodice of her dress, and a slight ache pulsed in her core. With Matthew out of her life, at least she no longer felt guilty for the things Leif made her feel.

Still, she was an unmarried woman and her conduct with Leif was highly improper.

Krista sighed as she opened the box that held the medicinal supplies. She knew the sort of things Leif wished to teach her. And no matter how wrong it might be, she badly wished to learn them.

Days passed. The first of September arrived, the evenings growing longer, the air crisp and cooler. Leif's wounds were healing. Krista could tell he was feeling better by his foul temper and black, restless mood.

"It is time I was up and moving," he grumbled late in the morning when she went into his room to change the dressings on his wounds.

"You need your rest—the doctor said so."

"You coddle me like an infant, lady."

"And you are acting like one. Now here, eat your lunch. Cook has prepared a very nice tray." She started to set the tray down beside the bed, but he tossed back the covers and swung his long legs over the side of the feather mattress. "I am tired of lying abed. I will eat downstairs with you."

His private parts were covered, but little else. There were faint scars on his thighs that matched the scars she had seen on his back and shoulders, remnants of the days he had spent in captivity, but they were rapidly fading. Krista tried to look away from all of the hard male flesh and thick slabs of muscle, but it seemed impossible to do.

"I like the way you look at me, *honning*. Like a she wolf eager for her mate."

Her face flamed. "That is completely untrue, Leif Draugr, and a very ungentlemanly thing to say."

He shook his head. "I am only sorry that I cannot yet fulfill your wishes. In time I promise I will take care of your womanly needs."

Her eyes widened. "Of all the nerve!"

He walked toward her, pulling the sheet off the bed as he moved, wrapping it around his flat belly and tucking it at the top so it rode low on his hips. "Do you deny that you desire me?"

"I don't—don't…"

"You cannot say it because it would be a lie. You are no liar, Krista."

She felt his big hands encircling her waist as he drew her closer, and then he was kissing her and her eyes were closing, her hands sliding up around his thick neck. His tongue dipped into her mouth and she made a little sighing sound at the wave of pleasure moving through her.

Oh, she desired him, all right. She only wished that he could not tell.

Leif drew her closer and her body seemed to melt into his. His chest was wide and ridged. Rows of muscle rippled down his abdomen, tightening as he moved to kiss an earlobe, then press his lips against the side of her neck. He claimed her mouth again and sweet sensation tore through her. Beneath the sheet, she felt the long, heavy length of him, and her heartbeat quickened, began to pulse oddly inside her breast.

Krista told herself she was afraid of what might happen if she didn't stop him, but she wasn't truly afraid, and she only pressed closer, wishing the sheet would disappear, along with her cumbersome gown and petticoats. Wished that their bodies touched skin to skin, heat to heat.

She didn't realize Leif had unbuttoned the bodice of her gown until the front gaped open and he bent his head to kiss the plump mounds rising above the top of her corset. Krista bit back a whimper at the hot, moist heat of his lips against her skin, the warmth tugging low in her belly.

A lock of short blond hair fell across his forehead as he left a trail of kisses over her heated skin. When his tongue slipped beneath the lace of her chemise to lap at the hardened tip of her breast, she gasped at the rush of desire that tore through her. Swaying against him, she gripped his shoulders while he laved and tasted, suckled and tugged until her nipples ached with need.

She knew it was wrong, knew she should stop him. Leif was not her husband and never would be, but she couldn't seem to find the will. "Leif…"

"I am right here, *honning*." A rush of cool air rippled over her skin when he drew away. She stood immobile as he kissed her deeply one last time, then reached behind her and began to rebutton her mint-green gown.

Krista reached up to touch her kiss-swollen lips. "Dear God in heaven."

Leif ran a finger along her cheek. "You are a woman of powerful needs, Krista Hart." He smiled wickedly. "I promise to keep you well tended."

Her cheeks burned hotter than they had before. "Leif, you cannot… We cannot… This just cannot happen."

He ignored her. "I am hungry." He cast her a burning glance. "For now I will settle for food. Call your father's man, Henry. Tell him I wish to bathe and dress. I will join you downstairs."

She didn't argue, just latched on to the excuse to leave, and hurried out of the room. Recalling the strength of his arousal beneath the sheet, she thought that perhaps he was right about getting out of bed. He certainly seemed healthy enough to her!

Krista hurried down the hall, angry at Leif for taking liberties, even more angry at herself for allowing it to happen. Silently she cursed Leif Draugr for the indecent power he seemed to hold over her.

Krista sighed. At least he was up and about, and she could finally go back to work. She had been in and out of *Heart to Heart* several times this week, accompanied each time by her father, their big beefy coachman, Mr. Skinner, and at least two footmen, but she had been too worried about Leif to stay there overly long.

She returned to her room to pen a few more lines of the article she was writing for this week's gazette, "Workers Remain United," which dealt with the strikes going on against mines, mills and factories in protest of wage cuts and deplorable working conditions.

She was well into the piece, explaining the workers' desperation, how their endless frustration had boiled over into acts of violence, when she glanced at the ormolu clock on the mantel and saw that it was indeed time for luncheon. Setting pen and paper aside, she left the bedroom and made her way downstairs, heading for the drawing room where it would be served.

She paused at the sound of men's voices coming from her father's study. Krista turned down the hall, then stopped when she reached the open doorway. Seated at a round mahogany table in the corner, Dolph Petersen, the investigator she had hired, sat across from her father and Leif.

"Krista," her father called out, rising to his feet. "I was just about to send for you. Mr. Petersen has brought us some very good news. Come in, dearling."

She walked into the study, careful not to glare in Leif's direction, afraid the memory of his scorching kisses, the heat of his mouth on her breast, would somehow show on her face.

Petersen rose to his feet and Leif moved to stand up, as well.

"Please, gentlemen, there is no need for formality." She smiled at the investigator. "Mr. Petersen, it is good to see you. My father says you bring news." She sat down in the fourth chair at the table, Leif very properly seating her. Still, she didn't look at him, just kept her gaze carefully fixed on the investigator, a tall, lean, dark-haired man perhaps in his late thirties.

"We've apprehended the villain responsible for the attack on your carriage," Petersen said. He was attractive, but not in the usual sense, his features harsher, his skin sun-browned and weathered, a man whose toughness showed in the lines of his face.

"How did you find him?" she asked.

"I spoke to the owner of the White Horse Tavern. With a little friendly *persuasion,* he recalled the name of the man who'd left the money and instructions for the attack on your carriage that night."

She flicked a glance at her father, then spoke once more to Petersen. "Who was it?"

"A man named Harley Jacobs. He's one of the overseers at Consolidated Mining—at least he was."

"Apparently Mr. Jacobs didn't agree with your series of articles in favor of the Mines and Collieries Act," the professor added. The law banned children and women from working below ground in the mines. Krista liked to think that her articles had in some way helped to finally get the act passed.

"You'll be happy to know Mr. Jacobs is currently occupying a cell at Newgate Prison," Petersen said. "I imagine he'll be there quite some time."

Krista shuddered to think of it. She had read articles about the terrible conditions at the prison, but over the last few years, work done by a female reformist named Elizabeth Fry had considerably improved the prisoners' lot.

And Jacobs certainly deserved whatever punishment he received.

"Do you think he is the man who set the fire at *Heart to Heart?*"

"Jacobs denies it, but I think there's a very good chance."

"Well, I am certainly relieved by your news," Krista said.

Petersen smiled. "I'm sure you are." When he looked at her his dark-brown eyes seemed to warm with appreciation. It was rare that a man saw past her unnatural height, saw her as an attractive woman rather than an oddity, and she decided that she liked Dolph Petersen.

"Even with Jacobs out of the way," he added, "I think you should retain your night watchman, just to be certain no more problems arise."

"Of course, if you think we should."

He rose from his chair, and everyone else stood up, as well. "If you have future use of me, you know where to find me."

"Thank you, Mr. Petersen, for helping us as you have."

"The pleasure was mine, Miss Hart." Petersen bowed over her hand, his lips not quite brushing the back. A few feet away, Leif's gaze narrowed. "As I said, if you need me, you know where I am."

Krista watched Dolph Petersen leave the room, and felt a sweep of relief that the man behind the attack was now behind bars. "Well, it looks as if I can safely return to work."

"So it does," her father said. "Still, at least for a little while longer, I think it best that Leif accompany you."

"But—"

"Come, *honning*, you know you enjoy my company." Leif reached out and touched her cheek, and she saw her father frown.

"I will keep you safe," Leif continued, "but in return, I ask a favor."

Krista arched a brow. "What sort of favor?"

"Now that this man Jacobs has been caught, it is safe for you to go out in the evenings."

Though she hadn't given it much thought, she *had* been staying home a great deal. Since her engagement to Matthew, her grandfather had not pressed her to go out in society. Then Matthew had been away in the country, and though Coralee had invited her to several posh functions, Krista had declined, having no real desire to attend.

"Go on," she said to Leif.

"I need to earn money. I have taken far too much from you and your father already. It is time I paid my way."

"You're being paid for the work you do at the gazette."

"That is true, but I need enough for a ship. I must find a way to buy one so that I can return to my home."

"What are you suggesting, Leif?"

"There is a thing in your country called *gambling*. I have been reading about it. It appears there is money to be made if a man knows well enough the game. I am particularly interested in this amusement you call cards."

"Gambling is a good way to lose money, Leif, not earn it."

"Do you know how to play, then?"

"I don't gamble, but I play a little whist."

"On Draugr we wager on any number of things, from tests of strength and skill to the racing of island horses. But I do not believe it is the same. There is a certain knowledge involved in your gaming. I have been practicing the skills I have read—how to remember the cards that have been dealt, how to figure the odds of which card will fall next. I would like to try this game, but I need you and your father to go with me."

He did have a powerful memory. She had never seen anything like it. Still, winning at gambling would not be easy, even for a man with a memory like Leif's.

"I would need you to loan me some money," he continued, "but only enough for one night. If I fail, I will work more hours, enough to repay my debt."

He was good at most anything he tried, so why not this? "That sounds fair enough."

"There is a place called Crockford's. I have read they have gaming tables there."

Krista glanced to her father, asking the unspoken question, *Is he ready to go out in society?*

"Are you certain you want to do this, Leif?" the professor asked. "Your manners will be put to the test, your speech, everything you've spent these past months learning. Do you think you are well enough prepared?"

"I will never be entirely a gentleman. Surely you must know this. But I will manage well enough. Will you grant me this favor I ask?"

"After all the hard work you've done to educate yourself, I think you deserve this chance." Krista smiled. "Besides, I have never been to Crockford's. It might be fun."

With only a little help from Henry in selecting the proper garments, Leif dressed for the evening in a black frock coat, burgundy waistcoat and black trousers. He used the bristle brush to comb back his short blond hair, then turned to the mirror and straightened his white silk cravat.

He checked his appearance, thinking how different he looked from the shaggy, unkempt man who'd been locked in a cage. His jaw tightened. Mayhap the day would come that he would find justice against the men who had locked him away, though in truth, it no longer mattered. He had found what he had come for, seen and learned things that his people would find hard to believe.

He started for the door, glancing at his reflection one last time, thinking that he was actually growing used to the way he looked in the ridiculous English garments. His mind strayed to Krista and the clothes women here were forced to wear, the heavy gathered skirts and revealing bodices, though he much enjoyed the occasional glimpses of her pale, creamy skin and the plump mounds he had but briefly tasted.

His rod went instantly hard. He had been some months without a woman, but Krista was a woman worth waiting for. Adjusting himself inside his trousers, ignoring the faint, relentless throbbing, he started for the door, trying not to think of Krista and how much longer it would be before he could make love to her.

Still, her image haunted him, and as he imagined her dressing for the evening, a curious notion struck. He had read thousands of words, studied hundreds of pictures etched in books, but he had yet to see this thing women wore called a corset.

Instead of heading downstairs as he had intended, he walked down the hall to the bedroom that belonged to Krista. If he knocked, she would never let him in, so he simply turned the silver knob and pushed open the door. He expected to hear a gasp from her little maid, Priscilla Dobbs, but instead, Krista stood there completely alone.

Leif grinned. And she was only half-dressed, as he had hoped, and wearing the oddest assortment of clothing he could imagine.

"Leif! What are you doing in here? Get out of my room immediately."

He simply walked toward her. "I came to see this thing you wear beneath your clothes."

Her pretty face began to glow. She was beautiful, he thought, all smooth skin and high, full breasts, her golden hair curling in ringlets that fell onto her shoulders. Her eyes were the color of a meadow in spring, a rich, deep green that sparkled when she was angry, as she was now.

"A man is not supposed to see what is beneath a woman's clothing—not unless she is his wife—and you, sir, are behaving very badly. You will leave this instant."

His gaze ran over the thin white cotton garments that covered her hips and bottom. Some sort of drawers, he figured, the female version of the ones he refused to wear. And a contraption that thrust up her breasts and bit into her waist, the *corset* she had mentioned, the top of which he had glimpsed the day he had kissed her magnificent breasts.

"Get out of here, Leif Draugr—before Priscilla returns and finds you in here."

"Turn around," he commanded, standing right in front of her. "I wish to see how this device that squeezes you works."

She clamped her full lips together, then blew out a breath. "You are insufferable!" With a frustrated sigh, she turned her back to him. "It laces from behind. The tighter someone pulls the laces, the smaller my waist appears."

"What makes it so stiff?"

"It is made of whalebone. They are huge fish the size of a house that live in the sea."

"I have seen them in the water near Draugr."

"Some corsets use metal stays."

"It looks like it hurts."

"You get used to it."

Used to it? It was a contraption of torture unlike anything he could imagine.

He turned her around to face him. "What is the garment you wear over it?"

"It is a corset cover and a gentleman is not supposed to see it."

Mentally, he untied the tiny pink bows that closed the garment in front, and stripped it away. He imagined dragging the thin cotton drawers down over her hips, leaving the soft blond curls of her womanhood exposed. His mouth began to water as he imagined kissing her there, tasting her.

Just yesterday, he had found three dusty novels on a partly hidden shelf of the library. On Draugr, he had never lacked for bedmates, but never had he given much thought to a woman's pleasure. His partners had been satisfied with his lusty kisses and bold caresses, the feel of his heavy rod moving inside them.

Now he understood there were many more ways to please a woman, ways that also increased a man's pleasure. He had already finished *On the Altar of Venus,* written, like the others, by a man called Anonymous, though Leif didn't really know how to pronounce the name. By the time he finished *Miss Boots' Confessions,* and *The Pearl of Passion,* he would be a master in the art of making love.

His rod stiffened, began to press painfully against the fly of his evening trousers. He looked down at Krista, wondered if what he was thinking was there in his eyes. Reaching out, he slid a finger between the soft, plump swells of her breasts, pushed together by the bones of a whale. He felt her tremble and wished he could jerk open the laces and toss the painful contraption away.

Instead, he slid an arm around her waist and pulled her against his chest.

"Leif, please, you cannot just walk into a lady's boudoir and—"

He cut off her words with a kiss. She smelled of flowers. He wondered at the name. For an instant she stiffened and tried to pull away, but he just kept kissing her, sliding his hands into her hair, taking her mouth one way and then another until she softened in his arms. Coaxing her lips apart, he slid his tongue inside to taste her sweetness, moved his hands down to cup her bottom. The thin drawers were all that covered her there and he could feel the warmth of her skin through the light cotton fabric.

"Where is your maid?" he whispered against her ear.

"I—I sent her on an errand, but—"

He ended her speech with another scorching kiss, his hands roaming over her bottom, squeezing gently, testing the fullness, liking the way she filled his hands.

Krista moaned softly. He could feel her trembling as he lifted her against his hardness, let her feel how much he wanted her. He heard her little soft mew of pleasure, and slid his hand between the rounded globes of her buttocks, touching her more intimately, heightening her arousal. There was an odd split in the fabric of the drawers, and he realized in an instant its purpose.

It would serve his own purpose far better, he thought, sliding his fingers inside, pleased by the dampness he felt in the plump petals of her sex. Krista stiffened in shock, but he only tightened his hold.

"I will give you pleasure, Krista," he whispered against her ear. "Greater than you ever dreamed."

She made a faint sound in her throat as he claimed her

mouth again, kissed her deeply and began to gently stroke her. She was wet and trembling, and the knowledge made him harden even more. He wanted to bring her to fulfillment, wanted to slake her desire and bury himself so deeply she would never think of another man.

Instead, he eased away.

Krista looked up at him with wide, green, uncertain eyes. "I never thought… I didn't know that…that…it would feel so…"

"Good?" Leif suggested.

She flushed.

"When the time is right, I will show you how good it can be." He stepped back, fighting to bring his own urgent need under control.

His gaze ran over her body. "This thing you call a corset. I do not like you wearing it. Once you are mine, I will forbid it."

Her pretty mouth rounded in surprise. "Leif, please—you mustn't say things like that. I—I know I should have stopped you. It is highly improper for a woman to allow a man to take…take those sorts of liberties. I can only imagine what you must think, but—"

"There is nothing wrong with what we do. Soon you will be mine and you will no longer feel guilty."

Krista shook her head, moving the mass of heavy golden hair on her shoulders. "That can't happen, Leif—you know it as well as I do. I can't ever be yours and you can't ever be mine. In time, you will be returning to Draugr and I will be staying right here. Nothing can change that. Not for either one of us."

"You are wrong, Krista. You have been mine since the day you freed me from that cage. The gods sent you to me and that is what is not going to change."

A squeak in the doorway announced that Priscilla Dobbs

had arrived. Her eyes went even wider than Krista's. "Oh, dear. I—I'm sorry, miss, I didn't realize that you…that you…"

Krista cast Leif a dark glance. She managed to smile at her maid. "It's all right, Priscilla. Mr. Draugr walked into the wrong room, *by accident*." She grabbed her robe with a shaky hand and pulled it on over her garments of torture. "He was just leaving."

Leif took his cue. He had pushed her far enough this night. "My apologies, Miss Hart," he said in his best imitation of an English gentleman, making her a very proper bow. "I don't know how I could have mistaken the room."

Her mouth looked tight as he closed the door and walked off down the hall. He thought of what she had said, that she could never be his, words she had said before. He hadn't believed her then and he didn't now. She might be beautiful and intelligent, and he might admire her greatly, but she was only a woman, with little say in the matter.

First, he needed money. Then he would speak to her father. He believed the professor would accept his suit. Paxton Hart was a brilliant man and Leif believed he had long ago accepted the fact that one day his daughter would become Leif's bride.

Leif thought of the books he was reading and smiled to himself. Krista was his, whether she believed it or not. Out of respect to her and her father, he had taken few liberties, but remembering her words of denial, he knew that would have to change.

His rod pulsed as he remembered the feel of her body opening to him, responding to the touch of his hand. Already she desired him. He would use the knowledge he found in these latest books to heighten that desire. She was his and he would have her. He would make her ache for him, make her beg him to take her. Once he had buried himself deep inside her, she would belong to him.

She would be his, body and soul.

It surprised him to realize how much he wanted that to happen.

Fifteen

It took far longer to finish dressing than Krista intended. Returning to the bathing room, she dipped a cloth into the basin of water and used it to cool her flushed skin. She washed away Leif's scent—not the perfume of a fancy gentlemen's cologne, but the uncomplicated, far more intoxicating fragrance of soap and virile man.

Even as she went back to her bedroom and Priscilla used the heated iron to style her hair, then helped her into her gown, Krista thought of Leif and the wicked, delicious things he had done to her body. Her eyes slid closed at a memory of his mouth on her breasts, his big hand stroking between her legs.

Dear God in heaven, she had never felt anything like it!

Time and again she had allowed him liberties she knew she should not, allowed him to kiss her, touch her, when she knew it was wrong. Even when she had been pledged to Matthew Carlton, she'd found herself unable to resist the potent drug of Leif's masculinity.

But she was no longer affianced to Matthew, no longer owed him the loyalty, the chastity, she should have reserved for him and had not. Her life was her own once more, and though her grandfather would soon begin to press her again to fulfill her duty, marry and produce an heir, for the moment she was free.

She thought of the months she had spent in company with Matthew. Never once had he made her feel the desire Leif did. Never once had she known passion when he kissed her. Eventually, she would be forced to wed, but she didn't believe she would ever know true passion again. There was no other man like Leif and none who would be able to make her feel the way he did.

Krista sighed as she picked up her shot-silver reticule and drifted out of the bedroom. She could never have Leif, the man she truly wanted. She understood that, was resigned to it. He would be returning to his home, while her home was here in London.

Would it really be so bad, just for this brief moment in time, to experience life as she would never be able to again? Would it truly be such a sin to enjoy a bit of forbidden fruit?

She descended the curving staircase, her mind spinning with thoughts of him. Her footsteps began to slow as she spotted him in his black evening clothes, waiting for her at the bottom of the stairs. With his golden hair, finely carved features and stunning blue eyes, he was so handsome it made her heart clench.

He looked up at her and smiled. "You are beautiful, *honning*...." The words, spoken in that deep, seductive voice, made her stomach contract. His gaze swept over her, and the heat there said he was remembering the intimate way he had touched her, the way her body had responded.

Warm color washed into her cheeks. "You shouldn't call me that, Leif. At least not in public. It is far too intimate. People will think—"

"That you are mine."

"I told you—"

"Come. Your father awaits us in the carriage."

Krista said no more. Whatever Leif thought, in the end it would not matter. When the time came, he would recognize the truth for what it was.

But that time was some distance away, and a little voice said, *What would it hurt to pretend you were his just for a while? How would it feel to belong to a potent, utterly masculine man like Leif?*

The thought stayed with her as the two of them left the house.

Crockford's, Curzon Street, Mayfair, had been established more than a decade earlier by a man named William Crockford, a fishmonger who won a sizable fortune one night at the hazard table. With its Venetian glass chandeliers and gold-leaf marquetry ceilings, it was known as the most exclusive gaming establishment in London. Having never been to such a place, Krista grew more and more excited as the carriage drew near.

In a gown of turquoise silk overlaid with silver tulle, the décolletage lowered to show more of her bosom in accordance with the evening ahead, she walked in on Leif's arm, her father beside them, acting as chaperone. Though the professor had frowned when he had seen the changes she'd had Priscilla make in her dress, it was hardly indecent. Krista was, after all, one and twenty, a modern woman who owned her own business, and she deemed the gown entirely appropriate for the occasion.

Escorting her inside as if he was actually the gentleman he appeared, devastatingly handsome in his fashionable black evening clothes, Leif led them past the hazard tables, pausing at the refreshment counter long enough for each of them to obtain a drink. Leif ordered an ale, though it was hardly fashionable, while Krista and her father chose champagne.

"I believe I see a friend," the professor said. "If you two will excuse me a moment…"

"Of course, Father," she murmured. Krista and Leif wandered a bit, passing elegantly garbed patrons, men in embroidered waistcoats and white silk cravats, women in gowns of taffeta and brocaded silk carrying painted or feathered fans, wearing jeweled headbands or feathers in their hair.

Proceeding toward the green baize tables at the rear of the main salon, they made their way to the area where the card games were played. Being the tallest couple in the room, Leif and Krista began to attract attention. Heads swiveled in their direction, and Krista watched as one pair of feminine eyes after another studied Leif, followed by smiles of blatant appreciation.

As Krista sipped her champagne, she was surprised to discover how much those come-hither glances bothered her, though Leif seemed not to notice. Instead, his gaze strayed again and again to her bosom, where the shadowy valley between her breasts was revealed as it never had been before.

"I like this gown you wear," he whispered, his warm breath fanning the nape of her neck. "But so does every other man in the room. They dream of your pretty breasts, but they can only guess how soft and full they are. Soon I will know the feel of them in my hands."

Her knees wobbled beneath the skirt of her turquoise silk gown. "F-for heaven sake, Leif, you have to stop saying things like that. It isn't proper to speak to a lady in such a manner." *To say nothing of what those words did to her insides.*

He arched a golden eyebrow. "This is another of your rules?"

She flipped open her feathered fan and waved it back and

forth to cool her heated face. "One you are sorely in need of learning."

"I will try to remember…" he looked pointedly at the plump swells rising above her bodice "…if you will."

Her stomach tightened. How could she possibly forget? The man was a veritable bundle of masculinity. She just prayed he could control himself long enough to get through the evening.

They strolled the room for a time, giving Leif a chance to accustom himself to the sights and sounds, the way people moved and spoke. Across the room, she noticed her father in conversation with Phillip Carlton, Lord Argyle, Matthew's older brother, and wondered if the professor was trying to smooth over his daughter's broken engagement and somehow salvage her slightly tarnished reputation.

Determined not to dwell on the notion tonight, she turned back to Leif and noticed something she had missed before. Always when she went out in society, her unusual height made her feel ungainly and unattractive. But now she stood next to a gentleman far taller than she, a blond, blue-eyed man who was, in truth, the handsomest man in the room.

The fact seemed to alter the situation, and instead of being the object of speculation and pity, she began to receive the same appreciative glances from the men that Leif was receiving from the women.

"They are jealous," he said. "The fools did not recognize the prize they could have had. Now they see they are too late."

Krista wasn't quite sure what to say. It did seem as if the men were casting her far different glances than she had ever received before. She felt a little curl of warmth that, in escorting her tonight, in behaving with such a possessive air, Leif had given her this gift.

"Well, this is certainly a surprise." Diana Cormack, Viscountess Wimby, strolled up on the arm of a handsome, black-haired man who seemed to be her escort.

"Viscountess," Krista said, dropping into a curtsy. "It is a pleasure to see you again."

"You, as well, my dear." She flicked a glance at the man accompanying her. "This is Marcus Lamb, a close acquaintance of my husband's. We're here with Lord and Lady Paisley. As a favor to Arthur, Marcus was kind enough to offer his escort for the evening."

"A pleasure, Miss Hart." The gentleman bowed formally over her hand.

"May I present Leif Draugr, a close friend of my father's who is here visiting from Norway."

Diana's keen blue eyes skimmed over Leif's powerful body and her mouth curved into a provocative smile. "Well, it is certainly clear why you suddenly decided that you and Matthew would not suit."

Krista flushed.

"Krista is a woman of strong passions," Leif said. "She requires a man who can take care of her needs. Carlton is not the man for her."

Diana's eyes widened. She opened her mouth to say something, then snapped it closed again. Krista wished the floor would simply open up and swallow her.

She forced herself to smile. "I—I'm sorry, my lady. Leif is unfamiliar with our customs. Sometimes he misunderstands the meaning of certain words or speaks more bluntly than he should."

Diana's gaze swept over him, taking in the breadth of his shoulders, the thickness of his chest, his long legs and powerful thighs.

Her smile was almost feral. "I like a man who speaks his mind. I shall talk to Arthur. Perhaps you and Mr. Draugr would care to join us for a night at the opera."

Krista could scarcely believe she was hearing correctly.

Leif just smiled, a flash of white so potently male it made something flutter in her stomach. "I have never seen an opera. I have read some of the stories, though. I think I would like to see such a thing."

Diana's pretty lips curved again. She was dressed in the height of fashion, her black-and-gold evening gown cut so low her breasts threatened to spill out of the bodice. "As I said, I'll speak to Arthur."

Leif's gaze moved over the tempting swells of flesh, but he didn't seem unduly impressed. His attention returned to Krista and she felt an unexpected sweep of relief. Just then, she spotted her father returning, and could have kissed him for his timely arrival. Introductions were made, then Diana and her companion left to return to their party, who were busy tossing dice at the hazard tables.

"It is time I played," Leif said, his gaze going to the back of the room. Krista had already given him the money he needed to try his luck—or skill, as the case might be. It was a relatively modest sum, considering Leif's intention to win enough to buy himself a ship.

A ship. Krista looked up at him and her chest squeezed. Once he owned a sailing vessel—and she was certain he would find a way to get one—he would leave.

She found herself praying with all her heart that Leif would lose.

Leif did not win.
Unfortunately, he did not lose, either.

Sitting behind the desk in her office, Krista yawned. The hour had been late when they returned home from Crockford's last night. Though he had played for some time, had lost some and won some, Leif had ended the evening within a few gold sovereigns of where he had started.

And he had been exuberant with hope.

"I see now what I did wrong," he had said as the carriage rolled through the dark streets. "There is more to the game than counting cards and figuring the odds of what will fall next. I do not know the word for it—a way of trying to guess what your opponents will do. It can make a difference in how much you win or lose."

He had been playing loo against five other men, a high-stakes game that had been known to beggar even very wealthy gentlemen.

"From what little I know," Krista told him, "you watch their expressions. If you can learn to read their faces, you can guess what they might have in their hands."

"That is what I thought."

"One thing is certain, Leif. If it were easy, everyone would win."

He nodded. "I am going back tonight by myself. Tonight I will only watch. Tomorrow night, I will play again."

"Even if you're very good at all the different aspects of the game, you still may not win. Skill at gambling is always tempered by luck."

He seemed resigned to that, though it didn't discourage him, and even in the faint light of the brass lantern inside the carriage, she could tell his mind was whirling, examining what he would need to do in order to be successful.

As Krista sat at her desk recalling the events of last night, she sighed. Leif was relentless in whatever he pursued—including her. She had to admit it felt good, for once, to be the object of a man's determined pursuit.

"You are smiling." Dressed simply but elegantly in a day dress of printed apricot muslin, Coralee Whitmore walked through the door of Krista's office, which was most always left open. "If I didn't know you better, I would believe you were thinking very wicked thoughts."

Krista laughed. "Not at precisely this moment, though lately some of the things we read in that book we found in the basement at Briarhill have begun to return to my mind."

Coralee's eyes widened. "Good grief!"

"I have a feeling we may have been wrong, Corrie. Making love might not be quite so terrible as we imagined."

Corrie laughed. "Perhaps not." She handed a slip of paper across the desk. "This arrived for you just a few moments ago."

Krista's head came up. "Another threatening note?"

"I don't think so. They rarely come with your name penned with a flourish on very expensive stationery."

Krista popped the wax seal on the message and began to read. "This is from Cutter Harding. He is the owner of Harding Textiles. The man is requesting a meeting. The note says he wants me to hear his side of the issue in regard to the strikes." She tapped the paper. "He wants to know if I might be available to come out to the factory and observe conditions there for myself."

"That sounds reasonable."

Krista looked up from the paper and smiled. "I am beginning to believe *Heart to Heart* is doing some very good work, Coralee. First the overseer from Consolidated Mining hires someone to scare me out of supporting the Mines and Collieries Act. Now the owner of one of the country's largest textile manufacturing firms thinks our magazine has enough influence to warrant a personal tour of his factory. I can only believe that all our hard work is actually doing some good."

"It is mostly your hard work," Corrie said. "I just write the society column."

"You are in charge of the entire women's section, not just the society column. In truth, you help me run this place, and I couldn't do it without you."

Corrie seemed pleased at her words, which were utterly true. "So what about Mr. Harding?"

"I'll agree to go, of course. I am extremely interested in seeing his factory." She smiled. "Besides, if he expects me to hear his ideas, then he shall be obliged to hear mine."

The meeting was set for the end of the week. Krista planned to travel by carriage to the small town of Beresford-on-Quay, where the factory was located. Along with her big beefy coachman, Mr. Skinner, Leif had insisted on coming, and though she put up a token protest, secretly she was relieved.

Especially so after what happened last night. Sometime after midnight, the offices of the *London Beacon,* a widely read weekly newspaper, had burned to the ground. A fireman had been seriously injured trying to put out the blaze, and one of the employees, an old man who slept in a room upstairs, had died of smoke inhalation.

The fire had undoubtedly been set. The *Beacon* was even more vocal in its reform ideas than *Heart to Heart.* The newspaper had a far wider readership, its subscribers mostly men, while the gazette appealed mostly to women, but its destruction had put Krista's already heightened senses on alert.

The newspaper business had become a dangerous game, as she had already learned. Harley Jacobs had been apprehended for his part in the assault on her and Leif, but apparently the danger remained.

It was a bit of a ride to the textile factory in Beresford-on-Quay, but Leif would be traveling with her, and she could think of no more capable man. If trouble arose, she would be glad to have him along. This time she intended to err on the side of caution.

Meanwhile, every night since the evening she and her father had accompanied him to Crockford's, Leif had returned to play cards. He had not come home until the early hours of the morning, when she heard his heavy footfalls climbing the stairs. He caught only a few hours' sleep, then hauled himself out of bed and accompanied her to work.

Today was no different. He was exhausted, she knew, but he had been winning. He was good, she realized. *Very* good. Given his astonishing memory and fierce determination, she understood why he would be. And he wasn't about to quit until he had the money he needed.

The notion made a knot form in her stomach.

It was Thursday, late afternoon. Today was the day the gazette was printed, assembled and tied into bundles, which would be loaded into carts on the morrow for distribution on Saturday. Coralee would oversee the job while she and Leif left in the morning to travel to Beresford-on-Quay for their scheduled appointment with Cutter Harding. Her father hadn't much liked the notion, of course, since she would be spending time with Leif without a chaperone.

"This is work, Father," she had told him, "not a holiday in the country. Besides, we'll be back by nightfall."

He had grumbled, but reluctantly agreed. Having been married to the woman who had founded the gazette, he understood that running a business required a great deal of independence and a certain amount of bending society's rules.

Rising from behind her desk, Krista walked into the main part of the office, passing the heavy Stanhope press, which thumped loudly as it printed the pages for this week's magazine. Coralee sat at her desk a few feet away, her copper hair glinting as she bent over a sheet of paper, already at work on next week's column.

Krista continued toward the back room of the office, operational again after the fire, thanks to Leif, who worked there now, helping Freddie move some heavy boxes into the storage room.

Krista surveyed their progress, noticing how much taller Leif was than the dark-haired boy. "Looks like you two are just about finished."

"This is the last box," Leif said, easily hefting it as he tried to stifle a yawn. Despite the late hours he had been keeping, he continued to work extremely hard, and he never complained, never tried to shirk whatever job she gave him.

"All right, now that you are done, come with me." Turning, she started walking, and a few seconds later heard his heavy footfalls behind her.

"Where are we going?" he asked.

"Upstairs."

He didn't say more. She figured he was so tired he didn't care. When they reached the second floor, she walked down the hall and pulled open the door to the employees' lounge, tipping her head to indicate he should go inside.

He walked into the room, then stood there watching her through heavy-lidded eyes.

"Take off your shoes."

His head came up. For the first time, he showed a hint of interest. "Why?"

"Just do as I say. I am your employer, in case you have forgotten."

His mouth curved as if he found the notion amusing. "I have not forgotten." Seating himself on the edge of the chaise, he removed his shoes and carefully set them aside.

"Now your jacket."

He looked up at her and his eyes darkened. He shrugged out of his coat and handed it to her, and she draped it over the back of a chair. In deference to the heavy lifting he often did, he wasn't wearing a waistcoat, and she couldn't help thinking how good he looked in his full-sleeved, white linen shirt and simple black trousers.

"Now lie down on the chaise."

Leif grinned. "If this is another of your lessons, *honning*, I think I am going to like it."

Krista rolled her eyes. She walked over and pulled the shade on the window, darkening the room, then returned to where Leif waited with a look of anticipation.

"I didn't bring you up here to seduce you. I merely wish you to get some rest. You are practically asleep on your feet. If you intend to stay out until the wee hours of the morning, from now on you will sleep for at least two hours each afternoon."

Leif shook his head. "I have a job to do."

"Yes, you do. And your most important task is to protect me. That is the reason you were sent down here in the first place. In order to do that, you need to be at least half-alert. Now do as I say."

He smiled. "I will lie down if you will lie down with me."

Krista made a sound of frustration in her throat. "The object is for you to rest. I doubt you would be thinking of sleep if I lay down beside you."

He chuckled as she walked to the door. "Go to sleep," she said softly. "I'll wake you in a couple of hours."

But his eyes were already closing, his head relaxing against the cushion at the end of the chaise, his long legs protruding over the end as he drifted into slumber. For several moments, she just stood in the doorway watching him. His massive chest rose and fell in a deep easy rhythm, and his eyelashes lay against the high bones in his cheeks, a darker shade than his golden-blond hair.

Quietly, she closed the door, feeling an odd pang in her chest. Every night his winnings increased. Unless his skill evaporated or his luck turned very bad, it wouldn't be long before he had the money he needed to leave.

He would go and she would stay.

For the first time, Krista realized how much it was going to hurt when he was gone.

Sixteen

~~~

The journey to Beresford-on-Quay took longer than Krista expected. It had rained in the night, leaving the road rutted and covered with deep puddles of mud. Dark clouds loomed overhead, bunching and shifting, hinting that last night's storm might return. Outside the carriage window, rolling green fields crisscrossed with low stone walls stretched out into the distance, and a narrow road wound to the top of a far-off hill where a manor house surveyed the landscape below.

Krista smiled, enjoying the view. As the coach passed through villages along the route, children played ball in the streets. A tinker's wagon rolling along in front of them pulled over so that they might pass. As the hours stretched on, Leif suggested a game of cards, and Krista laughed as he beat her quite soundly again and again.

"You're very good at this," she said as his king trumped her jack and he raked in another stack of make-believe winnings. "It would seem all your study is paying off."

"I need to win," he said simply. "This is the chance I have been seeking."

Krista smoothed a wrinkle from the skirt of her dove-gray

traveling suit, then toyed with the black frogs marching up the front of the jacket. "Is buying a ship really so important, Leif? Would it be so terrible if you remained in London?"

His intense blue eyes fixed on her face. "I would stay if I could. There is much to learn here. Every day offers more knowledge. In a lifetime I could not learn it all. But I cannot stay. I made a vow to my father."

"What sort of vow?"

He stared out the window. "When the men decided to use the shipwrecked timbers to build a boat, my father and I argued. He forbade me to leave, but I told him I must go. That I had to see what lies beyond our world. He begged me to stay, but I could not. I pledged to him on my honor that I would return. I said that I would come back, that I would not forsake my duties as eldest son. No matter what happens, this I must do."

Krista nodded. Inside her chest, her heart was squeezing painfully. She knew about honor and duty. She had duties of her own. Since her mother's death, her father had not been the same man he once was. He needed her and she had done her best to take care of him.

And she had important work to do at the gazette. *Heart to Heart* was gaining influence in the community, reaching people, helping to make important changes.

Most crucial of all, her grandfather desperately needed an heir, a grandson to assume the Hampton title and fortune. Since his wife had borne him no sons, by special writ of the king, an heir could come from the female side of the family. With her mother gone, the task had fallen to Krista. If she didn't marry and bear a legitimate son, the title would go to a distant cousin. Her family—Aunt Abby, her father, Krista's children—and even Krista herself, would suffer.

She looked over at Leif, watched him studying the cards in

his hand, and for an instant, she allowed herself to imagine what it might be like if he were her husband. Imagine how it would be if he gave her the child her family needed, a beautiful, golden-haired boy, as strong as his father.

But Leif could not stay, and she could never be happy in some distant, primitive world so different from her own. Her place—her life—was here in England.

Whatever her future, she would not be sharing it with him.

They arrived in Beresford-on-Quay late in the afternoon, two hours later than Krista had intended. The textile factory, a huge three-story brick building, sat on a bluff overlooking the river, its location necessary to run the massive power wheels that ran the heavy machinery inside.

"I think it would be best if you waited out here," Krista told Leif. "I think Mr. Harding would prefer—"

"No."

"This is business, Leif. I am scarcely in danger. I don't imagine Mr. Harding would have invited me here in order to do murder."

"If you go, so do I."

She blew out a breath. "You are the most irritating man."

Leif just grinned.

Clamping down on her temper, Krista entered the long, narrow building through the door below the big red-painted sign *Harding Textiles.* She was directed to Cutter Harding who was at work in his office, his head bent over a stack of paperwork on his desk. His secretary, a young man in his twenties working at a desk in the front part of the office, intercepted her before she could reach him.

"May I help you?"

"My name is Krista Hart. This is my associate, Mr. Draugr. We had an earlier appointment with Mr. Harding, but the roads were a bit more difficult than we expected and so we are, unfortunately, late for our meeting."

Across the room, Cutter Harding rose from his desk and started toward them, a man in his late forties with thick blond hair and a slight limp in his stride. "Miss Hart...I thought that perhaps you had changed your mind."

"Not a'tall, Mr. Harding. As I said, the roads gave us a bit more trouble than we expected. This is my associate, Mr. Draugr."

"A pleasure to meet you both." The glance Harding gave Leif said he knew very well why Leif was there, and the one Leif gave him in return warned what would happen if all was not as it seemed.

"Well, come along then. It is certainly not too late for me to show you around. Once you have toured the factory, you will see that much of what you and your reformer friends believe is simply not true."

"I hope that is so."

Harding led them out of his office, and for the next half hour they toured the main floor of the factory. The huge wheel that provided power for the mill dominated the space, making an annoying racket, but the machine was a necessary part of the milling process.

"Sorry about the noise," Harding said. "Gotta have power to run the place, which means the big wheel's gotta turn."

There was nothing to be done, she supposed. The clatter was only compounded by row after row of spinning machines—spinning jennys, they were called—that sat on the wide-planked oak floor. Though the air was smoky and workers occupied every square inch of space, she saw no children under the working age of nine, which was the current law, and the huge room was relatively clean.

"What is upstairs?" she asked when the tour was finished.

"Just storage," Harding said.

"And below?"

"A similar sort of operation, but I'm afraid I won't have time to show you. I'm already late for an appointment. As I said, I thought you had changed your mind."

"That is quite all right. I've seen what I came to see. Working in a factory is not the most pleasant sort of job, but neither does it seem you are breaking any laws or treating your employees unkindly."

"Hardly. These people are paid a fair wage and you don't hear any of them complaining."

No, the men and women she had spoken to had nothing bad to say about Mr. Harding or the place that employed them. Of course, since he was standing there, Krista hadn't expected they would.

Harding had just started leading them back to the office when a door at the opposite end of the spinning room burst open and a little boy came running up from downstairs. His clothes were worn and ragged, his dark hair shaggy and unkempt, and there were tears in his big, dark eyes. He raced toward the exit and might have made good his escape except that Leif reached down and scooped the child up in his arms.

"Lemme go, ye 'orseson! I didn't mean to break the bloody spool, and I ain't takin' another beatin' for it. I don't care 'ow bad me da needs the work."

"Easy, lad," Leif soothed, gently pinning the little boy's flailing arms and holding the child against his chest. "No one is going to hurt you."

"I said lemme go!"

Krista turned her furious gaze on Cutter Harding. "What is going on here, Mr. Harding? This child is no more than six years old. It is illegal for him to be working in a place like this."

"Turnbull!" Harding roared, and a stout man with a thick mustache came running. "Take this child back downstairs to his father."

"You haven't answered my question, Mr. Harding."

Turnbull reached up for the child and the little boy started sobbing. He clung to Leif's neck and wouldn't let go, and Leif's powerful arms tightened protectively around him.

"I'll take him down to his father," Leif said.

"Ye can't do that," said Turnbull. "Only employees allowed downstairs."

"Oh, really?" Krista cast a glance at Harding. "Perhaps we should all return the child to his father." With a nod at Leif, she marched off toward the stairs, Cutter Harding swearing softly as he and Leif fell in behind her.

By the time little Rodney Schofield had been returned to his father—with a promise extracted by Leif that the boy would not be punished—Krista had discovered what Cutter Harding hadn't meant for her to see. The bottom floor of the factory had only a few high windows and those were dim with a heavy layer of dirt. The room was smoky and full of lint and dust so thick she could barely breathe.

Here, great looms wove the yarn from the spinning machines above into woolen cloth, and every inch of floor space not occupied by a machine was cluttered by humanity. Each worker had only room enough to do his or her job, and the stench of sweaty bodies was nearly overwhelming.

Worse yet, at least thirty of the more than a hundred workers were children, many of them far less than nine years old.

"You are breaking the law, Mr. Harding. Obviously, you do not care."

"This is a factory, Miss Harding. We need workers to piece together the strands that break, or take out the empty yarn spools and set full ones in the empty cores. Children are the only ones small enough to fit into those spaces."

"You are despicable." She started to walk away, but Harding caught her arm.

"Manufacturing is a man's business, Miss Hart. You're a woman. I was a fool to bring you out here. I should have known you wouldn't understand."

"I understand enough, Mr. Harding. Now please release my arm."

Leif took a threatening step toward him and Harding let her go. The man's jaw looked tight as he turned and stalked away.

Krista felt Leif's hand at her waist as they left the factory. He said nothing as he led her outside to their waiting carriage and helped her climb in, then seated himself next to her instead of taking his usual place on the opposite side of the coach.

"There is always sadness in life," he said gently, "no matter where you live. I am sorry you had to see this."

Krista shook her head, fighting to hold back tears. "No wonder workers are striking all over the country. I cannot imagine laboring under such miserable conditions." She took a shaky breath. "I have to go to the authorities, tell them that Harding is breaking the child labor law. I have to help those children."

Leif reached over and captured her hand. Stripping away her dusty white glove, he brought her trembling fingers to his lips and kissed each one. "You will write your articles and you will help them."

Krista swallowed against the lump in her throat. She was glad Leif had been with her today, glad he was here with her now. She thought of the gentle way he had held the boy, and the lump in her throat grew tighter. She was becoming more and more dependent on him, she realized. She had always prized her independence, but somehow it seemed all right to let down her guard when Leif was there.

She turned to look at him, sitting on the carriage seat beside her, still holding her hand. It was odd. She had thought of him as the man she would choose to marry, even imagined having a child with him.

Never once, not until this very moment, had she realized that she was in love with him.

The carriage rolled toward London.

As darkness continued to fall, Leif became more and more worried.

"The hour grows late," he said. "There are footpads and high-way-men on the road, and the storm could break at any time. It would be better to stop for the night, wait until morning to finish our journey."

Sitting beside him, Krista shook her head. "I have to get back, Leif. My father will be worried."

She was concerned about the professor, as she always was, and Leif knew enough about the rules of society to know how improper it would be for her to spend the night with him alone.

Silently he cursed. He wanted to take Krista to wife, and to that end, he had made a certain amount of progress. He was good at the card games he had learned—very good. He had studied the art of betting and learned how to wisely wager his coin. He had learned to read the other players' faces, to know which had the greatest skill, which bet recklessly and who could afford to lose the most.

If he was careful, soon he would have enough for his ship, and then he could speak to her father, see the marriage arranged. Once they were wed, Krista would no longer be worried about propriety and he would keep her well content in his bed.

The thought stirred the blood in his loins. Wicked images arose of her lush form spread beneath him, the feel of her full breasts pressing into his chest, her body moving in rhythm with his own. His arousal strengthened, became almost painful.

He wanted her as he never had another woman, and soon he would have her.

And yet in the back of his mind the notion lurked that she might continue to refuse him. By Thor, he needed to make her his, claim her as his mate and prove that he was the man for her. With the help of the gods, he would find a way to make that happen.

Forcing his mind back to the threat that might lie in the darkness outside, Leif stared into the night. He wished he had ignored Krista's protests and insisted they stay somewhere safe until dawn.

They had traveled the muddy road for another hour when he heard a loud grinding sound, then the crack and snap of heavy wood rending in two. The carriage lurched wildly to the left, tossing Krista out of her seat. Leif caught her and dragged her back to safety in his lap.

Her cheeks turned a little pink as she resettled herself beside him. "Thank you."

He wanted to tell her he enjoyed holding her, but only nodded his head, reached over and turned the knob on the carriage door, pushing it open.

"What has happened, Mr. Skinner?" he called up to the driver.

The brawny coachman climbed down from the driver's box. "Bloody axel…er, the axel's broke, sir."

"Stay here," Leif commanded Krista, descending the iron stairs to the ground next to the coachman. Leif surveyed the wooded area around them, the rolling fields he could barely make out in the dim rays of a moon mostly hidden by clouds. His sword lay under the seat, but this time he had also brought a pistol, a three-barreled pepperbox he had won in a card game last night. And he carried a knife in his boot.

Still, he didn't like being caught out on the road at this late hour. Krista had made an enemy this day in the man named Cutter Harding, though Leif didn't believe Harding had had enough time to take any sort of action against her.

"How long will it take to fix it?" Leif asked.

"Can't get it done till mornin'. Got to take the wheel to a smithy. But we just passed an inn back there. Shouldn't be too far a walk."

Leif nodded. He remembered seeing the inn, the Swan and Sword. Turning, he helped Krista down from the carriage.

"We must spend the night at the inn," he told her. "There is no longer a choice."

"Yes, I heard what Mr. Skinner said."

He and the coachman unharnessed the pair of matched bay horses and led the animals off toward the inn. Declining to ride, Krista carried the small traveling satchel she had brought with her. Because she hadn't been expecting to spend the night, Leif didn't think there was much inside.

They reached the inn within the hour. Krista had worn sturdy shoes instead of her soft kid slippers, which meant he didn't have to carry her. He almost smiled. Not that he would have minded.

The inn was actually a tavern with rooms to let upstairs, not the sort of place he would have chosen for a lady. But at least they would have a roof over their heads.

"I'll see to the horses," Skinner said, taking the lead rope from Leif. "I can make meself a pallet out in the barn and take care of the wheel first thing in the mornin'."

"Thank you, Mr. Skinner," Krista said.

Parting company with the coachman, ignoring the gusty wind and the first drops of rain, Leif led Krista toward the front door of the tavern, an old, drafty stone building with wide-planked wooden floors. Heavy oak beams, dark with soot from the big open fireplace, lined the low ceiling of the taproom. A group of rowdy patrons, obviously more than half-drunk, sat around a long wooden table in the corner.

As Leif and Krista walked up to the tavern keep, a fat man with thick, wooly sideburns and an apron tied around his heavy girth, she took charge.

"We need lodging for the night," she said. "Our coachman will be sleeping in the stable. He needs food, and our horses need hay and grain."

"I'll have the boy see to your man and horses." The tavern keep's gaze ran over Krista's tall, womanly figure, and a lecherous smile curled his lips. "How many rooms?"

Leif stiffened at the way the man's small pig eyes mentally stripped away her clothes. "Two," he answered, though he would get little use of his own, since he would have to stay awake to make sure no one bothered her. "The lady will need a room of her own."

The fat man's lewd smile remained. "Well, now, that's a problem. Only got one room left for the night. Got a big bed, though. Plenty o' room for ye both."

Leif looked at Krista, who returned his gaze with uncertainty. "We'll take the room," she said.

The fat man chuckled. "Figured ye would."

Leif clamped down on an urge to hit him.

Krista managed a smile. "We'll have to make do. We don't have any other choice."

No, there was no choice at all, not with the storm closing

in and no way to travel. They would be sharing a room, spending the night alone together, and in that moment Leif realized the gift he had just received. He had asked the gods for their help in making Krista his. He believed his prayer had just been answered.

"Have ye et?" the tavern keep asked.

"We've been on the road," Krista answered. "We were hoping you might have something left in the kitchen."

"I'll have the girl fetch ye up a tray and light the fire. Be extra for that." He handed Leif a big iron key. "Room's upstairs, down to the end of the hall."

Leif reached into the inside pocket of his frock coat to pay the bill. As he pulled out the bag of coins he carried, he saw Krista open her reticule.

He tossed her a hard look of warning. "Do not even think to pay."

She glanced up at him. "I was only—"

"I will be the man this night."

Her golden eyebrows lifted. "Fine," she said a bit tartly, and turned and started walking toward the stairs.

Key in hand, Leif caught up with her before she reached the landing. She walked ahead of him down the hall, but when she reached the door, she found the room unlocked.

"Stay here," Leif commanded, stepping silently inside to make certain it was safe. He found a plump-breasted serving maid already setting a tray of cold meat, bread and cheese down on a rough-hewn table in the corner. She had lit a lamp and started a small coal fire in the hearth. In the soft glow of the lamp, he could see she was young and fair-haired.

She turned when she saw him, her eyebrows lifting as her gaze traveled the length of his body. "Well, ain't ye a fine-lookin' sort." She walked toward him, her hips swaying in an invitation as old as time. "Ye need some company, 'andsome, me name's Betty Rose. Ain't never had me a man a' yer size. If yer yard be as big as the rest of ye, I'll only charge ye half the usual price."

Before Leif could refuse her offer, Krista walked into the room. "He already has company for the evening, and I'm not charging him anything."

The woman's face turned red. Realizing her error, she hurriedly backed away. "Sorry, missus." Turning, she fled from the room and quietly closed the door.

Leif walked over and used the iron key to lock it. He turned to Krista, who was angry, he saw—not the beginning he had in mind.

"Since there is only one bed," she said, "I guess you will have to sleep on the floor. Unless, of course, you intend to spend the night with Betty Rose."

Leif strode toward her. He tossed the key onto the dresser and settled his hands at her waist. "I do not wish to sleep with the wench. The bed I wish to sleep in is yours."

Krista's pretty green eyes went wide. "What…what are you talking about? Just because we are sharing a room—"

"I did not plan this, Krista, nor did you. The gods have spoken this night. Can you not see? These things that have happened…they have led us to this place, this room, this bed, where I will claim you."

Her full skirts flared as she whirled way from him, but Leif caught her arm. "Do not be frightened. I will do my best not to hurt you, but know this, Krista—tonight I intend to have you."

She swallowed, her big green eyes fixed on his face. "Surely you…you don't intend to force me."

Leif drew her closer, until her lush breasts pillowed against his chest. "Tell me you do not want this—that you do not want me—and I will stop. If you cannot say those words, then tonight you are mine, Krista Hart."

Seventeen

A distant bolt of lightning flashed outside the window, but the thunder was too far away to hear. Krista stood mesmerized as Leif bent his head and claimed her mouth. Soft, firm lips moved over hers, gently at first, tasting her, letting her taste him. She felt surrounded by the essence of him, the strength of his powerful body, the clean scent of soap and man. The kiss grew deeper, more thorough, turned hot and fierce, his tongue delving in, stroking the inside of her mouth, taking what he wanted, demanding more.

He was determined in this, she realized, and yet in her heart, she knew she could stop him.

Tell him you don't want him. Say the words before it is too late.

But already her fingers were digging into his powerful shoulders, her body catching fire. She tried to force out the words, but the lie would not come. She wanted him. Wanted to know what it felt like to be possessed by him. Dear God, she had never wanted anything so badly.

The kiss went on and on, softening for an instant, then turning wildly savage once more. He ravaged her lips, took her deeply with his tongue, nibbled the corners of her mouth, then claimed her lips again. She felt his hands working the frogs that closed the jacket of her traveling suit, then he slid the coat off her shoulders. He reached behind her to work the buttons on the bodice of her gown, eased it down off her shoulders, along with the straps of her chemise.

Her arms and shoulders were bare above the top of her corset. Leif kissed the side of her neck, nipped and tasted the sensitive spot beneath her ear, kissed his way down to the tops of her breasts. He pulled the tabs on her layers of petticoats, shoved them, one by one, down over her hips, and drew her out of the circle of fabric that puddled at her feet.

She thought he would pause, say something about the corset he so hated, but his entire concentration was fixed on getting her out of her clothes. Turning her around, he pulled the bow on the tight laces that held the stiff whalebone garment together, and they loosened. She didn't realize he had a knife until she felt the glide of the blade beneath her corset strings, then a rush of cool air against her skin as the corset fell away. She had time for one deep, lung-filling breath before his mouth closed over hers again.

Her chemise came off and Krista clung to his shoulders as he filled his hands with her breasts. Her nipples were so sensitive, so tight and hard, swelling and burning against his palms, and he seemed to know exactly how to touch them, how to make her insides quiver with every brush of his fingers against the hardened tips. She was wearing only her stockings, garters and shoes when he kissed her once more, then knelt in front of her.

"It is time these came off." Swiftly, he removed the shoes, then the stockings, one by one, his big hands brushing over her calves, taking his time, sliding upward to stroke the inside of her thighs. Each touch, each gentle caress, sent a sliver of heat into her stomach, and an ache rose up in her core.

"Leif…" She trembled, swayed against him, and he returned to his feet. She stood in front of him naked, and when she looked into his face, she saw rampant desire burning in the depths of his eyes.

"You are beautiful," he said, "like a goddess."

And as he lifted her into his arms and carried her over to the bed, she felt like one, felt how much he desired her, sensed his powerful need of her.

It didn't take him nearly so long to remove his own clothes. In the faint light of the candle burning on the table and the glow of the coal fire in the hearth, she watched him, fascinated as each part of his magnificent body came into view. His chest was deep and wide, ridged with slabs of muscle and covered with a light furring of golden hair. His stomach was flat, and muscles formed a ladder that disappeared into the waistband of his trousers.

Those came off last, the garment sliding down his long legs, his gaze following hers to the thick length of his manhood.

"This is the part of me that I will use to claim you." He was big and hard, his shaft jutting forward from its nest of coarse blond curls. She trembled, swallowed as he moved toward the bed, unashamed of his nakedness. She should have been frightened, but all she felt was a wild yearning to touch him, to run her hands over his skin, to feel the bands of muscle that flexed and tightened whenever he moved.

Leif came down on the bed beside her and started kissing her again. A big hand cupped her breast, began to mold and shape it, then his mouth followed his hand, and the pressure of his white teeth tugging at her nipple sent a tremor of heat running through her.

Krista moaned.

Leif's eyes darkened. "The taste of you fires my blood. I

need to be inside you, Krista. I need to feel you moving beneath me."

She shivered, her eyes fixed on his face. His big hand sifted through the soft curls above her sex and he palmed her, separated the soft folds of her flesh and began to gently stroke her. Heat and need burned through her, and a yearning so strong she cried out his name.

"Tell me you want this. Say that you want me as I want you."

Her body trembled. She swallowed and told him the truth. "I want you. Oh, Leif, I want you so much."

He parted her legs with his knee and came up over her. His engorged sex probed for entrance, and for a moment she was uncertain. "What…what if there is a child?"

"There are ways…. It is not yet time for that to happen." He began to ease himself inside her, moving slowly, doing his best not to hurt her.

"You're so big…I am not sure…."

"Trust me, *honning*. Your body was made for mine. Let me take care of you."

They were words she couldn't resist. She had always been the strong one, even more so since her mother died. She had never had anyone take care of her…not until Leif.

She relaxed as he kissed her. Long, deep, drugging kisses that made her tremble. Slow, passionate kisses that had her squirming beneath him. Little by little, he eased himself farther inside, but when he reached the barrier of her innocence, he paused.

"You are yet a maid, but now that will change." He rocked forward, positioning himself more fully. "In the name of the gods, I claim you. You are mine, Krista Hart." And then he surged forward, driving his heavy shaft deep into her womb, tearing the thin membrane that proclaimed her a maiden.

Krista cried out against a swift flash of pain, her body arching upward, trying to free itself from the heavy length of him inside her.

"Do not move," Leif whispered. "I do not wish to hurt you again and I do not know how much longer I can last."

She trembled beneath him. She could feel the unfamiliar weight of him inside her, stretching her to accommodate his inordinate size and length. Her nipples rubbed against his chest as he held himself above her, and even the slightest movement sent a fresh rush of heat burning through her. Little by little, the pain receded, and in its place a sweet fire began to build, seemed to hover just out of reach.

Krista moved. She couldn't help herself.

Leif swore something she couldn't understand, and his massive body surged forward, driving him deeper still. His hips flexed and his rigid length pumped in and out. The last of the pain disappeared beneath an onslaught of staggering heat, and her body arched again, sheathing him completely and urging him on. Caught up in the fierce sensations, Krista met each of his powerful thrusts and gave herself up to the delicious tightening that was building in her core.

Leif's jaw clenched but he did not stop, just drove into her again and again until she couldn't bear the pleasure a moment more. Something sweet and wild blossomed inside her, opened and spread through her limbs. Tiny stars burst behind her eyes and the taste of honey rose on her tongue. Powerful waves of pleasure shook her and she bit down on her lip to keep from crying out. She felt Leif's muscles tighten, felt the last of his control slipping away the instant before he withdrew himself from her body and spilled his seed harmlessly on the mattress beside her.

Long seconds passed. Her heart was thumping, beating

madly. Leif cuddled her against him and she could feel his pulse hammering in rhythm with her own. Her body felt limp and sated, yet faint tremors of pleasure still hummed through her.

Leif turned onto his side to look into her face. He traced a finger along her cheek. "Do you yet doubt that you are mine, Krista?"

She only shook her head. In that moment, her body still pulsing with pleasure, she had not the slightest doubt.

Nestled spoon fashion, held against Leif's powerful chest, Krista gazed into the low flames of the coal fire burning in the grate. Tonight she had made love with a man who wasn't her husband, could never be her husband, and yet nothing had ever felt so right, so completely perfect.

"I did not hurt you too badly?" Leif asked softly.

She turned her head so that she could see his face. "No, you didn't hurt me, only a little, and only for a moment." She smiled softly. "I have nothing to compare it with, but I have a feeling you are as good at making love as you are at playing cards."

She felt the rumble of his chest. "I am glad I pleased you."

"I'm not sure why but…there was something in the way you touched me…as if you knew exactly the right place…exactly what I would like. I wouldn't have thought a Viking would concern himself so much with a woman's pleasure."

"I have learned much since I came here."

Her gaze sharpened on his. "Don't you dare tell me you learned that from the milkmaid."

He laughed, such a hearty rumble of amusement she knew it was not so.

"All right, smarty, how did you know?"

"The same way I learned to play cards. I read it in a book."

Her eyes widened. "Certainly not one from our library."

"I found them on a back shelf, all written by a man named Any-mous, though I do not think I am saying it right."

"Any-mous?" She laughed. "I think you mean *anonymous*."

"Aye, that sounds more like it. *The Pearl of Passion* had some particularly interesting parts." He rolled her onto her back and came up over her, softly kissed her lips. "Shall I show you?"

She felt breathless, almost dizzy. "I don't think I am ready for anything new quite yet. I am having trouble enough accepting what we've just done."

"You are right. For now, you need only get used to the feel of me inside you." So saying, he kissed her. Krista's breath caught as he parted her legs and slid himself deeply inside, far more easily this time and with much less discomfort.

"Your body fits mine perfectly."

It certainly seemed so. And when he started to move, she knew for certain he was right.

A dawn sun brightened the room, rousing Krista from a deep, dreamy sleep. Worried about repairs on the carriage, Leif had already gone. They departed the inn two hours later, when Mr. Skinner returned from the closest village, Marley-in-Wood, with the repaired carriage wheel. He had ridden one of the horses and led the other, and tied the heavy iron-banded wheel on to the spare horse's back.

With Leif to lift the carriage, it didn't take long to reset the wheel, and soon they were on their way home. It was quiet inside the coach most of the way. Krista wasn't sure what Leif was thinking, but in the bright light of day, the events of last night seemed almost a dream. Even though they had made love again before he left this morning, none of it seemed real.

Or perhaps she simply wished to pretend.

It wasn't easy. As she rode along in the carriage, her body ached in places it had never ached before, and a soft pulse of remembered pleasure throbbed in her core whenever she dared a glimpse at Leif. She wondered at his thoughts, knew she should bring up the subject of what had occurred between them, but couldn't find the courage.

One thing was certain. Leif believed she belonged to him, and in a way he was right. There would never be another man who suited her as well as he did, never be a man who could make her feel the passion he made her feel.

Or the love.

Still, whatever her feelings for Leif or his for her, nothing had changed.

He still intended to leave.

And she could not go with him.

She ignored a sudden tightness in her chest.

On the opposite side of the carriage, Leif shifted. "I will gamble tonight," he said, ending the lengthy silence. "If I keep winning as I have been, soon I will have the money I need."

Her heart squeezed. He would have his money and he would leave. "Ships are very expensive, Leif."

"I do not need a big one, just large enough to get me safely home. But I have been thinking…."

"Yes?"

"The people of England spend money on goods from many different places. I am thinking that once I have a ship, I could estab—estab—"

"Establish?"

"Aye. Estab-lish a trading route between Draugr and England."

"What would you trade?"

"Some of our people are very fine craftsmen. They weave intricate patterns in finely woven woolens, carve ornate brooches and hair combs from the shells of the tortoise, make pendants from the ivory of animals' teeth. They also craft fine staghorn pendants and knife handles. I think the people here would pay a very good price for such things."

"Yes, perhaps they would." A tremor of excitement slipped through her. "If you did that, you could stay here in England, Leif. You could stay in London and build up your business. You would have to sail home on occasion, of course, to collect more merchandise, but—"

"My home must be there. I have a duty to my father and my clan. One day I will be chieftain."

She slumped back against the seat, her heart pinching painfully. Leif reached out and caught her hand. "Do not look so sad. As you say, once I have a ship we can come back here and visit. You will be able to see your father and your friends, and in time you will make friends in your new home."

Krista looked over at Leif. She had known this conversation would have to come, but she had hoped to postpone it, to bask a little longer in the glow of their lovemaking.

"I know you would like for me to go with you, and you will never know how much that means to me. But I can't go, Leif. My home is here in England. What happened between us last night didn't change that."

His golden eyebrows crashed together like clouds gathering for a storm. "Everything has changed. Last night you gifted me with your virgin's blood. You are mine now, as the gods have decreed. I will speak to your father and you will return with me to Draugr as my wife."

Krista shook her head. "I can't go. I have a business to run. My father needs me and so does my family. I have responsibilities here just as you have there. I tried to tell you that—I tried to make you see."

His jaw hardened. "I see but one thing. If you do not mean to wed with me, then you have played the whore. Why, Krista? Why would you give yourself to me and then refuse to wed me?"

"Because I wanted you! Just as you said you wanted me!"

"Do you want me still?" His eyes locked with hers, so blue and intense her heart twisted hard inside her. "The truth, Krista."

"God help me, yes!"

"Then there will be no more discussion. I claimed you as my wife when I spread you beneath me and drove myself into your maiden's body. My wife is what you shall be."

Her temper heated. She wanted him, yes. In truth, she was in love with him. It didn't matter.

"You don't own me, Leif Draugr, no matter what your gods have to say. And I won't marry you! I cannot!"

Leif said nothing more, but a muscle tightened in his jaw. Crossing his arms over his massive chest, he turned away from her to stare out the window. Krista silently fumed. She was in love with the big, overbearing brute. Even now, just looking at him made her body clench with desire for him.

A lump rose in her throat.

She loved him, but she could not marry him.

Dear God, what was she going to do?

Another hour passed before they finally reached her town house. The storm last night had left the road even muddier and more difficult to travel, and the return to London took longer than it usually did.

Krista found her father waiting for them in the drawing room, worriedly pacing the Persian carpet. He turned at her approach. "Krista! Dearling, thank heaven you are safe!"

She hurried toward him, went into his arms. Leif walked in behind her, still angry, she knew. After what they had done last night, he expected her to marry him. She prayed he wouldn't say anything to her father.

"I'm so sorry," she said now. "I knew you would be worried. The wheel broke on our carriage and we had to stay overnight at an inn so that Mr. Skinner could have it fixed this morning. We left as soon as we could."

"I confess I was worried sick. After what happened that night in the alley, then that awful fire at the *Beacon*…"

"Yes, I know. We tried to get home, then the wheel broke and there was simply no choice but to stay."

No choice. She tried not to remember the trouble those words had caused last night. She looked up to see Leif's intense blue eyes boring into her, and knew he was thinking that, too.

Krista forced herself to smile. "At any rate, we are safely returned and none the worse for wear." Except that she was no longer a virgin and she couldn't tell if Leif would rather strangle her or tear off her clothes and make love to her again.

Her pulse leaped at the thought, and inwardly she groaned. What a mess she had made of things. She wished her friend Coralee were there. Perhaps between the two of them, they could figure out what to do.

"So how did your meeting with Mr. Harding turn out?" her father asked, guiding her toward the sofa in the drawing room.

"It was quite a disaster, I'm afraid."

"Is that so? Why don't I ring for tea and you and Leif can tell me all about it."

"Aye, Krista," Leif interjected from the doorway. "Why don't we do that? You can tell your father what happened with Harding and I can tell him what happened on our way home."

Krista's whole body tightened. *Surely he wouldn't.* But when she looked up at him, the hard line of his jaw said that he would, indeed. She bit her lip, which had started to tremble, and silently beseeched him to keep his silence. He must have read her plea and granted mercy, for he released a long-suffering sigh.

"I will have to miss the tea. I need to practice awhile. I am going back to Crockford's tonight."

Krista watched him walk away, but it wasn't until he disappeared that her heartbeat returned to normal.

Leif gambled that night and the next, and every night that week. When an invitation arrived from Lord and Lady Wimby to a house party at the viscount's exclusive town mansion, he pressed Krista to accept.

"Lady Wimby is a very big gambler," he said. "There is always gaming at her parties."

Krista didn't have to ask how he knew. He was becoming a player of some renown, and his size and astonishing good looks made him all too popular with the ladies. She tried not to be jealous when invitations began flooding in.

"Women love him," Coralee confided one afternoon while they were at work. "Not much of a surprise, I suppose, when you look at him."

Krista ignored a trickle of jealousy. "Are you speaking of the women who gamble at Crockford's?"

"Well, yes. The place is a favorite of the fashionable elite. Sooner or later, most everyone goes there. The ladies say he's an Original."

"That is certainly an understatement. One never knows what Leif will say, only that it will probably be tne very blu... truth."

"Leif is a Viking. People may not know, but the women

seem to sense that he is different. He is virile and lusty and he makes no bones about it. They call him 'a rare, manly man.'"

Krista rolled her eyes, but of course it was the truth. She remembered his scorching kisses, the moist heat of his mouth on her breasts, his hands stroking boldly between her legs.

"You are blushing," Corrie said, one of her russet eyebrows arching up. "I am afraid to guess why that might be."

"Yes, well, it would be better if you didn't try."

"Krista…"

"I am going back to work. I need to finish the article I am writing about Cutter Harding and the conditions at his factory, and I believe you also have a bit of work to do."

Coralee just smiled. "I will humor you for a while, but remember it is my job to ferret out interesting bits of information. And I have a feeling this information is extremely interesting, indeed."

Refusing to rise to the bait, Krista turned and set off for her office, determined to finish the article on the deplorable working conditions at the textile factory. She had already reported Harding's child labor abuses to the authorities, but she wasn't sure how much good it had done. The gazette was her best means of helping the workers' plight.

Krista sat down at her desk and tried to organize her thoughts, but her mind strayed instead toward week's end. Corrie had agreed to accompany Leif, Krista and her father to Lord Wimby's house party on Saturday night.

Krista knew Leif intended to gamble.

She prayed he wouldn't win enough money to buy his blasted ship.

Eighteen

The mansion overflowed with guests. Great urns of roses and chrysanthemums decorated the entry and drawing rooms, the ballroom upstairs and the gaming room down the hall. Diana Cormack, Viscountess Wimby, surveyed her surroundings and smiled, pleased the affair was progressing so splendidly.

As soon as she and Arthur had finished greeting their guests, Diana made her way down the hall to the card room, where she preferred to spend most of the evening. She stood there now, beneath the molded ceiling next to a potted palm, drinking champagne with her best friend, Caroline Burrows, Countess of Brentford, watching a small group conversing near the card tables.

She opened her black feathered fan, a perfect compliment to her black feathered headdress and gold, black-trimmed gown.

"You are staring," Caroline said.

"I can't help it. The man is utterly magnificent." Her gaze ran over the big blond giant with the stunning blue eyes in his perfectly fitted black evening clothes. He played cards as he seemed to do everything else, with intense concentration. Diana had rarely won against him, had, in fact, lost twenty thousand pounds to him in deep play at Crockford's last night.

She smiled. It was almost worth it, just to sit at the table and feel those blue eyes occasionally drifting over her breasts. It was clear he read her unspoken invitation, also clear he didn't intend to accept it. "What I wouldn't give…"

Caroline smiled. "Yes, well, odds are it isn't going to happen." Caro and Diana were of an age, both married to much older men. While Diana was dark-haired and full busted, Caroline was blond, blue-eyed and slender. Both were discreet in taking lovers, yet only their husbands seemed unaware of their occasional forays outside the marriage bed. "I don't believe I have ever seen a man quite so…so…"

"Extraordinarily male?"

Caro laughed. "Exactly. Aside from that, no one seems to know much about him." Her gaze ran over his magnificent physique, handsome face and amazing blue eyes. "He is rather a mysterious sort."

"The only thing I know is that he is a friend of Sir Paxton's, from Norway. There is actually a rumor going round that he is some kind of Scandinavian prince."

"Well, he certainly looks like one." A feline smile curved Caro's lips. She leaned closer. "Gossip also has it Leticia Morgan made a very good try at getting him into her bed."

Diana's dark eyebrows went up. "Knowing Leticia, I am not surprised."

"I heard she approached him at Crockford's, told him her husband was spending the next few weeks in the country and invited him back to her house."

"What happened?"

"Apparently, he said something to the effect that it was

clear she was in need of a good, hard swiving, but at present he was otherwise occupied."

"Oh, dear God." Both women giggled like schoolgirls. Diana took a sip of her champagne, trying to cool the heat in her cheeks. "He said he was occupied?"

"He did, indeed."

"Occupied with whom, I wonder."

"The man simply oozes virility. I cannot imagine him denying himself female comfort when it is so readily available to him."

Diana ran a finger around the rim of her champagne glass. "He seems to have very few acquaintances. I've rarely seen him with anyone but Professor Hart and his daughter."

Caroline's blond eyebrows went up. Her expression turned shrewd. "Now that you mention it, he and Miss Hart do make rather a stunning pair."

Diana pondered that. "Krista was always a very pretty young woman. I assumed it was her looks that attracted Matthew—beyond her very substantial dowry, of course—but personally, I thought her too tall and a bit too robust to be truly appealing. As I look at her next to Draugr, she seems… Well, she looks quite beautiful."

"Perhaps Matthew saw what the rest of us missed. She's really quite stunning, isn't she?" Caroline studied the group that included Leif Draugr, Coralee Whitmore, Krista and her father. "You don't suppose…?"

"As you say, the man is so potently male it is difficult to believe he denies himself." She smiled. "Time will tell, I daresay. The truth always has a way of leaking out."

They watched Leif excuse himself, cross the room and take a seat at one of the gaming tables. A few hands were played, and minutes later, Lord Elgin tossed in his cards and rose to leave.

Caroline set her empty champagne glass on a passing waiter's silver tray. "It seems another seat has opened up. I believe I shall join the game."

Diana watched her friend walk away. "Good luck," she called after her. The countess wasn't nearly as good a player as Diana, even worse when she was distracted by a handsome face. Caro's husband had even more money than Diana's, however, and her friend didn't mind spending it in whatever manner she pleased.

Diana laughed to think how many thousands of pounds Leif Draugr might take home with him tonight.

Krista watched Leif's single-minded play, watched his stack of winnings pile up in front of him.

"Leif is one of the best players I've ever seen," her father said with a touch of pride. "He has the most incredible memory. It is invaluable in games of chance like the ones he has been playing."

"He is certainly very good," Corrie agreed.

Krista made no reply. She didn't want to think of the endless stream of money Leif kept winning, didn't want him to win enough to buy his infernal ship.

A shadow fell over the group as one of the guests walked up to join them. "I see your friend has yet to leave town."

Krista turned, recognizing the familiar male voice as belonging to Matthew Carlton. Her gaze settled on the tall man she hadn't seen since the day of his duel with Leif.

"Matthew, my boy!" her father said, beaming at the arrival of one of his favorite young men. "It is good to see you!"

"You, as well, Professor." Matthew's dark gaze swung to her and Coralee. "Krista. Miss Whitmore."

Corrie nodded and made an appropriate reply.

Krista forced herself to smile. "It's nice to see you, Matthew."

"You look lovely tonight, Krista." The words surprised her.

He had never been much on compliments before. She wondered at the change. "Thank you."

"I read your article on Harding Textiles. It was very well written, though you have certainly made an enemy in Cutter Harding."

"The truth is the truth, no matter how you might wish to disguise it."

"As I said, it was very well done."

"Thank you," she said again, and Matthew smiled. She had never thought him particularly charming, but as he made conversation with Corrie and her father, charm practically oozed from his pores. He took her hand, urged her a few steps away. Reluctantly, she followed.

"It's been too long, darling. I've missed you, Krista. I was rather hoping you might have missed me."

She eased her hand from his and carefully worded her reply. "We were friends, Matthew. I miss our friendship."

"There was a time we were more than just friends. We were engaged to marry, Krista."

"I know, Matthew, but—"

"Are you in love with him?"

The question took her by surprise and her cheeks warmed. "I don't...don't know what you mean."

"You know exactly what I mean."

She took a steadying breath, let it out slowly. "He is going home, Matthew. It is only a matter of time. Whatever I feel for him, I won't be going with him."

"Are you certain?"

"Quite certain."

Matthew seemed to relax. "Then, for the present, I shall indulge your infatuation and hope that in time you will once again see reason."

She wasn't sure quite what to say. "It is difficult to predict the future, Matthew." But she didn't really dissuade him. She would have to wed. Yesterday, she had received a letter from her grandfather. News of her broken engagement had finally reached the earl and he was furious. So angry, in fact, he was planning to travel to London from his country estate in Kent. He intended to "set down the law," his letter said. She would "do her duty or else."

She had no idea what measures he planned to take, but it really didn't matter. She had a responsibility to her family, and sooner or later she would have to see it done.

And the hard truth was, once Leif was gone, she didn't really care which man she married. Their union would merely be an alliance, a loveless match for the benefit of both parties. She was no longer a virgin, but the size of her dowry should compensate for that.

Matthew Carlton was still interested…

He took her hand, brought her gloved fingers to his lips. "We'll talk again, soon."

"There is no need for talk," said a deep voice from behind her. "Krista is not for you."

Matthew's features tightened. "I guess we will have to wait and see."

"Leif, please," Krista murmured, hoping to prevent a scene.

Leif cast her a look that could have frozen stones.

Matthew bowed deeply. "I'm afraid you will have to excuse me. Of a sudden, the air grows close in here." Turning away from them, he headed for the door of the drawing room, and she returned her attention to Leif.

"That was hardly necessary. The man was only making conversation."

"You are mine," Leif said. "If you cannot remember, I will make it clear to every man in the room."

Her eyes widened. "You…you are being ridiculous. Matthew was merely being polite."

The edge of Leif's mouth barely curved. "I will be polite to you when we get home. All you need do is leave your door unlocked."

Her face went crimson. Worse yet, her pulse kicked into gear. A sliver of heat tugged low in her belly and her nipples tightened inside her gown.

"Do not say such things," she whispered. "I cannot do that and you know it."

His look turned to one of amusement. "More's the pity."

Krista bit back a laugh, easing some of the tension between them. "Good heavens, you're sounding more British every day."

He only smiled.

He was still smiling when he returned to the gaming table. By the end of the evening, he had set a new record among the fashionable elite for winnings in a single night.

By morning, when he set off for the harbor to investigate the purchase of a ship, Krista knew he was about to break her heart.

Leif was no longer welcome at Crockford's. The customers were beginning to complain of their losses, and he was quietly asked not to return. He played at several other places, including an even more elegant gaming club called 50 St. James. Last night he'd accepted an invitation to a private card party at the home of Alexander Cain, a gambler whose past was nearly as mysterious as Leif's own.

Alex Cain was one of the best players in London, a fact confirmed by Leif's meager winnings that night. The play had been close and deep, and by the time Leif left Cain's town house, he felt blessed that his modest fortune remained mostly intact.

One good thing had come of the evening. He and Cain had developed a certain respect for each other. Like Leif, the man kept his personal life private, but Cain was also a very shrewd businessman, and one of his more successful endeavors was a partnership with wealthy shipping owner Dylan Villard, in a company called Continental Shipping.

"I hear you're in the market for a ship," Cain said to Leif casually as the men sat in his study, drinking brandy and smoking cigars—a vice Leif had recently discovered he enjoyed on occasion.

"I intend to do some trading," Leif said. "I need a vessel that is easy to handle, one that requires a very small crew. In time, I hope to expand, but for now, that is what I'm looking for."

"Let me talk to Dylan, see if he might know something suitable that could be for sale."

"I will need to hire a captain and crew, men willing to be gone for at least a year. Men who know how to hold their tongues."

Cain swirled the brandy in his glass. "Interesting…" He was taller than most Englishmen, with brown hair and intelligent green eyes. "But then, Draugr, you strike me as a very interesting man."

Leif just smiled. He liked Alex Cain. So did the women, Leif knew, though Cain seemed to have little use for them outside of his bed. Alex Cain was a man with his own set of secrets, and yet Leif sensed that he could be trusted.

Within the week, Cain had set up appointments to look at three different ships: a brigantine, a refitted sailing packet that had once carried passengers along the coast and a sixty-foot, square-topsail schooner.

The schooner suited Leif perfectly.

It was a beautiful ship, nothing at all like the vessel he and the men of Draugr had built from sea-washed timbers, but sleek and well-crafted, with a pair of fine spruce masts. Here vessels had names, and this one was called the *Lily Belle*. As a surprise to Leif, Cain changed the name to *Sea Dragon*, which he had painted on the stern in red letters.

When Leif read the words, his eyes widened. "How did you know?"

"Know what?" Cain asked, his shrewd eyes probing.

Realizing his error, Leif just shrugged. It was only a co-incidence, he realized. Alex Cain had no way of knowing that in Draugr, he was called Leif the Dragon-hearted, a named earned by his ferociousness in battle. "*Sea Dragon.* It pleases me."

Cain just smiled. "I thought it might. Somehow it just seemed more appropriate."

They were becoming friends, and even though Leif would soon be leaving, it felt good to think he was beginning to fit in here in this country. He also liked Cain's partner, dark-haired, dark-eyed Dylan Villard. Even better, he liked the pro-posal Villard made, that if Leif began a trade route and goods become readily available, he should speak to Cain and Villard before dealing with anyone else.

"Continental Shipping is interested in expanding," Villard had said at a meeting in his office at the dock. "We're more than eager for new ports of call."

"That is good. May—perhaps, in time, we will be able to do some business."

As Leif left the meeting, hailed a hansom cab and climbed aboard for his return trip home, he felt relaxed in a way he hadn't in weeks.

He had earned far more money than he required. He had found himself a ship and soon would have a crew.

What he needed was a wife.

He thought of Krista and his groin tightened. He wanted her back in his bed, wanted to make love to her again. He wanted to take her whenever and in whatever manner he wished.

It was time he spoke to Krista's father.

It was late in the afternoon two days later that Leif's opportunity arose. He asked the professor if they might speak, then sat down across from the older man at the round mahogany table in the corner of the professor's study.

Leif wasted no time in presenting his case, and ended with the amount he wished to offer.

"Surely I did not hear you correctly," the professor said, leaning forward in his chair.

"I am sorry, Professor, did I misspeak the words?"

"Perhaps you did. I thought I heard you say you are offering me twenty thousand pounds for Krista."

Leif shoved himself to his feet. "I have insulted you. I knew I should have offered more. Your daughter is worth far more than—"

"Sit down, my boy. You have not insulted me in the least." Leif sank back down in his chair.

"The fact is, twenty thousand pounds is a great deal of money. I'm sure Krista would be flattered, but the truth is I cannot accept your very generous offer. In England, we do not sell our daughters into marriage."

"This you have said before, and yet your women come to a man with a dowry. Is that not the same kind of thing?"

"Well, I suppose in an opposite way it is, but—"

"I am the right man for her. Surely you must see this."

The professor released a breath. "It is clear she cares a great deal for you, Leif, but even if I believed the two of you would suit, it wouldn't matter. The choice is Krista's alone."

"But you are her father. It is your duty to see her suitably wed."

The professor looked away. "I wish I could help you, son, but unless you are willing to stay in England—"

"I must go back. You know this."

"Then I don't believe Krista will marry you."

A bitter taste rose on Leif's tongue. "This is because of her duties to you and her grandfather."

"Perhaps she feels that way. I'm not completely certain. But the truth is Krista's life is here in England. Her family is here and she loves the work she does at the gazette. The magazine has already done a great deal to help pass important reform legislation, and there is far more work to be done."

"She is a woman. She needs a husband, a man to take care of her."

The professor slowly rose from his chair. "I wish that man could be you, Leif, truly I do. But she can't go with you. She simply wouldn't be happy in a place like Draugr Island. And you said yourself you cannot stay here."

Leif rose, as well. "Do you forbid this union?"

"No. As I said, the choice is Krista's. I only want her to be happy."

Leif pushed the heavy box of coins he had brought with him over to the professor. "If you cannot accept a bride price for Krista, take the money as repayment for the debt I owe. I have lived on your generosity for months. You have clothed me, fed me, given me a very fine place to sleep. You have taught me more in these past months than I ever thought to learn. For that I will always be in your debt."

"This is far too great a sum, Leif, and there is really no need for repayment. We made a bargain and you certainly kept your part."

"The money is yours, Professor." Leif said no more, just left the box on the table, turned and walked out of the study.

He didn't go in search of Krista. He already knew what she would say.

Though he believed she well understood that she belonged to him, she was as stubborn as a high mountain goat and her will was as strong as his own. It didn't matter. He knew what was best for her, even if she did not.

Vikings had been capturing their women for years.

When his ship, *Sea Dragon,* sailed for home, Krista Hart would be on it:

Nineteen

The October night was windy and cold, yet the sky was clear and a full moon shone down on the London streets. For the past two days, Krista had been trying to prepare herself for Leif's departure, but now that the time had come, she wasn't prepared at all.

Wasn't it only yesterday that she had discovered him in chains, rattling the iron bars of his pitiful cage? She would never forget her first sight of him without his unkempt, long blond hair, clean-shaven, bare-chested and grinning.

The handsomest man she had ever seen.

It seemed impossible that in the months since his arrival, he had educated himself, won himself a modest fortune and turned the heads of half the females in London.

It seemed impossible that Krista had fallen in love with him.

She moved through the house like a specter, her heart shrouded in sadness.

It seemed impossible that on the morrow, he would leave.

But his final preparations had already been made. With the help of a man named Alexander Cain, an acquaintance Leif had made playing cards, he had acquired a ship and crew. Yesterday, he had proudly taken her and her father to see the vessel he had purchased to carry him home. It was, he had said, a sixty-foot schooner, small enough to be handled by Leif himself, a captain and two crewmen he had hired for the weeklong journey.

He had introduced her to the captain, a burly man named Cyrus Twig, and the two sailors, a leather-skinned, sunbrowned man named Felix Hauser, and another, smaller fellow with a patch over one eye, named Bertie Young. According to Leif, the crewmen, who had no family in England, had signed on for a bit of adventure and the promise of an interest in the trading company he hoped to form.

After the brief introductions, Leif had taken her on a tour of the ship, showing her the crew's quarters aft of the forward mast, and the small but efficient master's cabin in the stern, which would serve as his quarters during the voyage.

"It should do well enough," he said with a smile, "though I would have liked the berth to be bigger."

It wasn't all that small, though it seemed so to Leif. As big as he was, he filled the tiny cabin. Yet it would clearly serve his purpose. Krista had left the ship mired in depression and trying to hold back tears.

Leif seemed not to notice. When they returned to the house, he waited until her father went back to work in his study, then led her into the drawing room.

"Come with me," he said simply. "You have seen my ship. It is a sturdy vessel, not like the one that brought me to your shores. It will carry us safely back to the island."

"I—it's a very fine ship, Leif."

He smiled. "I am glad you are pleased. Now it is time for us to wed. Say you will be my wife."

Her heart squeezed. Leif's simple proposal meant more to

her than all the fancy words Matthew Carlton had ever spoken. She loved Leif so much. Her heart ached with longing and yet she could not accept his offer. "I wish I could marry you, Leif. You will never know how much."

"Then speak the words. Say you will come with me."

She swallowed past the tightness in her throat. "I can't. I cannot go for the same reasons you cannot stay."

"You were meant to be mine. Do you deny it?"

She shook her head, the lump in her throat growing even more painful. "In a way I will always be yours." *I love you,* she wanted to say, but didn't. Losing him was painful enough without making matters worse.

It occurred to her that Leif had never said those words to her, and she wondered if perhaps a Viking didn't equate wanting with love. Perhaps their parting hurt him far less than it was hurting her.

"Is there naught I can say that will change your mind?"

She only shook her head.

Leif said only one thing more. "Then so be it." Jaw set, eyes hard, he strode out of the drawing room. She knew he was angry. How could she make him understand? She watched him disappear down the hall, and fought to keep from crying.

She was in love with him.

And tomorrow he would leave.

The hours ticked past. Supper came, but Leif declined to join them, opting instead to go out for the evening. She and her father ate mostly in silence, both of them mired in gloom. The professor seemed no happier to lose the man who had become a son to him than she was to lose the man she loved.

The hour grew late, but Leif did not return. She waited and waited, then gave up and retired to her room without seeing him. Perhaps saying farewell was harder for him than she had believed.

It was well past midnight when she heard his footfalls on the stairs. He was due to leave at daybreak. Surely he wouldn't go without a final goodbye.

But Leif didn't come, and as she lay there staring at the ceiling, aching with love for him, she knew what she had to do.

Pulling her blue silk wrapper on over her cotton nightrail, she moved toward the door, her feet bare beneath the hem of her robe. Checking to be sure no one saw her, she stepped out into the hall and quietly made her way to his room. When she reached his door, she pressed her ear against the wood and listened for any movement, but there was only silence.

She considered going back to her bedroom, but her feet refused to move in that direction. Instead, she reached for the silver doorknob, found the door unlocked and let herself into his room.

A single candle burned on the bedside table, and in the flickering light she saw that he lay on top of the bedcovers and that he was awake. He wore only his trousers, no shoes or stockings, nothing to cover his heavily muscled chest. His brilliant blue eyes watched her as she approached.

"I—I came to say goodbye."

"I do not like farewells," he said darkly.

"I don't…don't really like them, either, but I—I wanted to see you one last time before you went away."

He came up off the bed like a lion whose sleep had been disturbed, stalking her, his eyes piercing and his jaw hard. "Perhaps there was more that you wanted than just to see me. Perhaps you wanted to feel me inside you one last time."

She shook her head. "No, I…" Warm color rushed into her cheeks. It was the truth and she knew it. She wanted him to make love to her, wanted the memory to carry in her heart once he was gone.

He looked into her face. "Say it. Tell me why you have come."

Krista moistened her lips, which suddenly felt bone-dry. "I needed to see you. I want…I want you to make love to me."

He made no movement, but his gaze turned hot and fierce. "And yet you will not wed with me."

Tears pooled in her eyes. "I cannot."

She thought he might simply ignore her, turn and walk away, but instead he began to unfasten the buttons on the front of his trousers. He pushed them down his long legs and stepped out of them. He was naked underneath and she saw that he was heavily aroused.

"Take off your clothes."

There was something in the way he said the words, something that demanded she obey. She took off her robe with hands that faintly trembled, then pulled the string on her nightgown and let it glide down over her hips.

For long seconds, he simply stood there, his gaze running over her breasts, measuring the width of her waist, the curve of her hips. Suddenly, the lion moved, so swiftly she bit back a startled cry. Krista shivered as he lifted her into his arms, carried her over and settled her atop the bed, then came down beside her.

She thought he would kiss her, but instead he wrapped his hands around her waist and lifted her astride him, spreading her wide, making her feel vulnerable and exposed, yet wicked in a way she had never felt before. She saw the heat in his eyes, felt his powerful erection pulsing beneath her, and a sense of her own female power rose inside her.

"Unbraid your hair."

Her pulse speeded up as she complied, pulling the ribbon at the end, running her fingers through the thick blond strands, letting the silky weight form a curtain around her shoulders. He slid his hand behind her neck and dragged her mouth down to his for a deep, ravaging kiss. He caressed her breasts, molded and shaped them, teased and pinched her nipples until they began to ache and distend.

Heat enveloped her. Desire washed into her stomach and slid out through her limbs. His mouth moved down to her breasts and he suckled her there, and she had never felt such burning pleasure. Her head fell back, giving him better access. She shifted restlessly above him and he groaned.

"I will give you what you came for." His hands tightened around her waist again. He lifted her and she felt his hard length sliding inside until he impaled her completely.

"You will ride me this night," he said. "You will take what you want from me."

And so, greedily, she did, learning how to move, how to shift her body to take him deeper, how to lift herself and then sink down and in doing so gain a rush of pleasure.

Up and then down, the heat building, building. She bit her lip to keep from crying out as he gripped her bottom to hold her in place, and began to thrust hard inside her.

A whimper escaped, then another. The pleasure was too fierce, too sweet, too urgent to bear, but Leif did not stop, just took her and took her, until the tight coil inside her burst free and her body shattered into a thousand pieces. Waves of pleasure washed over her, a medley of sensation so delicious she cried out his name.

Leif followed her to release, lifting her off him at the last minute, spilling his seed outside her body.

She told herself she was grateful. She would bear no fatherless child. But instead of relief, she was overwhelmed with sadness. No golden-haired babe. No son of Leif's to remember him by in the empty days ahead, no one to fill the lonely, loveless future she faced without him.

She started to weep. She simply could not hold back the tears. She felt Leif's lips pressing softly against her forehead.

"Do not be sad, *elsket*. In time, all will be well."

The word meant beloved, and she started weeping again. But she had no right to cry. He had offered her marriage and she had refused. The desolate future ahead of her was of her own making.

They slept for a while, Krista curled in Leif's arms, but she couldn't take the chance someone might discover her in his bed, so she left him sleeping, quietly dressed and returned to her room.

Eventually she cried herself to sleep.

Little by little, Krista awakened. It was still dark, but a sound in her bedroom, a movement somewhere near the door, had roused her. Then she saw the shadow of an intruder next to her bed. She tried to scream, but the instant she opened her mouth, a gag was stuffed between her teeth and her hands quickly bound behind her back so that she could not remove it. For an instant, she was afraid, but as the gag was tied in place and her feet bound at the ankles, she recognized the big, blond brute who wrapped her robe around her and slung her over his shoulder as if she weighed nothing at all.

Fury engulfed her. Krista tried to kick him, tried to scream, but only a muffled croak came out. She wanted to pound on his big, muscular, arrogant back, wanted to rail at him for the unfeeling beast he was, but it was too late. He had her down the back stairs and out the door, had her wrapped in a blanket and tossed into a rented carriage before anyone had the slightest notion she was gone.

He was taking her to Draugr Island.

He was abducting her against her will.

And Krista would never forgive him.

The harbor was quiet this hour of night. A stiff breeze blew over the ocean, driving little ripples across the surface of the water, but the sky was clear, the air cold and clean.

In the owner's cabin, Krista lay beneath the covers on Leif's berth, plenty big enough for two, she realized, no matter what he thought. He hadn't removed the gag. She would be screaming her head off if he had.

He hadn't untied her. She would probably do murder if he did.

She listened to the crewmen moving about the deck above her, tossing off the bowlines, preparing to sail. With a creak and groan, the ship lurched away from the dock and began to move out into the harbor. As the vessel made way, the captain called out an order for one of the crewmen to climb the mast and unfurl the topmost sail, then the rest of the sails were raised. The ship heeled into the wind and began moving rapidly into the open sea.

Krista lay on the berth, fury overwhelming her despair. Through the planking overhead, she listened to Captain Twig continuing to shout his orders. Leif might be a Viking, once the finest seamen in the world, but the people of Draugr had been land-bound for somewhere near three hundred years and he was smart enough to know his limitations.

She had noticed the stacks of books on sailing and navigation that Leif had been poring over in her father's study for the past few weeks. Krista figured that in theory, he probably knew as much as the captain about sailing the *Sea Dragon*.

Dragon. How well the name fit him!

She had likened him to a lion, but dragon suited him better. Heartless, unfeeling, concerned only with his own personal wishes. For the first time, she saw him as the ruthless man he was. A man determined to have his own way no matter the cost.

They were at least three hours out of London before he returned to the cabin. Krista's arms ached from her uncomfortable position on the bunk. She was exhausted from so little sleep and more furious than she had ever been in her life.

In the light of the brass ship's lamp that hung on the wall, she watched Leif enter the room, and wondered if he could read the anger on her face.

"I will remove the gag, but only if you promise not to scream. No one will come in here even if you do."

She would like to scream the house down, but she knew, as he said, it would do her no good. She nodded, waited while he untied the cloth round her head and removed the gag, then clamped down on the shout of fury that rose in her throat.

"How *could* you?" she growled through clenched teeth. "How could you do this when you know the way I feel?"

"You are mine," he said simply. "Did you truly think I would leave what belongs to me behind?"

"I am not *yours!*" she screamed. "I am not a possession to be owned by you or anyone else!"

He held up the gag in warning and she clamped down on another burst of temper. "Please untie me. There is nowhere I can go—aside from jumping overboard—and that, I assure you, I am not going to do."

He didn't hesitate, just strode over, pulled a knife from the top of his black, knee-high boot and cut the strips of cloth he had used to bind her wrists and ankles.

Krista slowly sat up on the bed. "So now I am your prisoner."

"You are my betrothed."

"Funny, but I don't remember agreeing to marry you."

He shrugged the powerful shoulders beneath his full-sleeved shirt. "If you did not intend to wed me, then you should not have given yourself to me."

"But I…but you…you…" She took a deep breath. "What about my father? He is going to be worried sick."

"I left him a note. I told him you would soon be my wife and that there was no need for him to worry. I believe, in his heart, he knows I have done what is best."

"What is *best*? Sailing off to some primitive, godforsaken, sixteenth century island? Forcing me to leave my home? My family? My work? You think that is doing what is best?"

Leif ignored her. Reaching out, he caught her chin in his hand. "Get some sleep, *kaereste*." *Sweetheart*. "Tomorrow you will see things more clearly."

She bit back a reply. Arrogant, domineering, infuriating man! She had to clench her teeth to keep from shouting the words, but if she did, she had no doubt she would find herself trussed up on the bunk again.

Instead, as soon as he was gone, she got up and paced the cabin, trying in vain to vent some of her fury. Leif might be a man who craved adventure, a boy who had spent his life wanting to see far-off places, to experience a new and different world, but Krista wasn't that way.

She liked her life just as it was. She loved London, no matter the sooty air, crowded streets and foggy weather. She loved her family: her father, grandfather and aunt, the cousins who sometimes came to visit.

And she loved running her magazine. *Heart to Heart* meant everything to her. It was her passion, her joy, the challenge that kept her life interesting. Leif didn't understand. He had never understood and now it was too late to make him see.

She took a steadying breath, her anger suddenly deflating. As he had said, she was tired to the bone and the journey had just begun. She lay down on the berth and pulled the covers up to her chin. They had nearly a week before they reached Draugr Island. There was time yet, she told herself. She would think of a way to persuade him to take her back home.

Or perhaps she could persuade the captain and crew. They were Englishmen, not Vikings. Englishmen didn't abduct a woman and force her into marriage. Surely they would help her.

But as she thought of the men, the captain and the others, and tried to imagine what would happen to them should they go against Leif's wishes, uncertainty crept over her. She had seen him fight on two separate occasions. Was it fair to urge the men into that sort of danger?

Her mind spun as she lay beneath the covers. What should she do? How was she to get back home? Eventually, the wash of the waves against the hull soothed her into a restless sleep. As the morning light seeped into the cabin, she dreamed of Leif and home.

Krista didn't hear Leif return to the cabin. It was in the early hours of morning that she awakened and found herself curled against him. She might have allowed herself the comforting heat of his body if she hadn't felt his mouth press against the side of her neck.

Krista leaped out of bed, furious all over again.

"If you think for one minute that you are going to make love to me, you are sorely mistaken. I will fight you with every ounce of my strength. I will not let you touch me, Leif Draugr! Those days are over!"

The edge of his mouth faintly curved. "Come back to bed, sweetheart. I will not touch you, if you do not wish it. But you are a woman of passion, Krista, your needs nearly as great as my own. In time you will seek the pleasure I can give you."

"Go to bloody hell," she said, whirling away from him. It was cold in the cabin, her feet freezing on the icy, wood-planked floor. She heard Leif's muttered curse as he followed her out of bed and padded toward her. She gave only token resistance when he lifted her into his arms and carried her back to bed, jerking the covers up over her shivering body.

"Sleep. It is time I went back to work."

And so he left her there, shivering under the covers, trying to ignore a faint tug of love at his care of her. Then she thought of all she had left behind and the life he meant for her to live. *We aren't there yet*, she thought, and steeled herself for the battle ahead.

Twenty

Logic did no good. Coaxing, cajoling and tantrums did no good. Appealing to the men in the crew did nothing but embarrass her.

"Yer intended says he took yer innocence, miss," said Captain Twig. "And not without yer a'wantin' 'im to. 'E's doin' the right thing by ye. Ye should be grateful."

One-eyed Mr. Young agreed. "You made your bed, miss, if you'll pardon me sayin' so. And Mr. Draugr seems like a nice enough fellow to me."

She couldn't believe Leif had told the men that they had made love. But then, she supposed, being men, it was the one thing they would understand.

Even when she discovered an ally aboard, the result was the same. It was the second day out that she realized the Suthers boy, Jamie, and the little monkey, Alfinn, were also aboard the ship.

"Jamie! God in heaven, surely he didn't abduct you, too!"

The lanky youth, about fourteen, with brown hair and dark eyes, just grinned. "I asked Mr. Draugr if me and Alf could come along, and he said we could if'n we wanted. He said the two of you was to marry. Mr. Draugr…he's promised to take real good care of you." His grin widened. "You just wait and see, miss. It's gonna be a fine adventure."

"I don't want an adventure! I want to go home!"

But the boy just returned to scrubbing the deck as he had been before. A few feet away, she spotted little Alfinn hanging from one of the ratlines above the rail, watching them with eyes even darker than Jamie's. The monkey swung down and ambled across the deck in her direction, and Krista bent to pick him up.

"What about you, little friend? Are you on Leif's side, too?"

Alf chattered a response. Since he was also a male, she figured his allegiance probably fell with that of the rest of the men.

The voyage progressed relatively smoothly. Several brief squalls came up and for a time the seas grew rough, but as long as Krista got enough fresh air, she didn't become ill. Evilly, she hoped Leif would suffer at least a short bout of mal de mer, but when she asked him how he felt, he only smiled.

"My last voyage was far rougher than this. At first I did not fair so well, but I am a Viking. The sea is in our blood."

Perhaps it was. He seemed completely at ease aboard the ship, as if he belonged at the helm as much as Captain Twig. Krista considered that if the sea was in his blood, so must be his desire for her. His passion had not cooled where she was concerned, and in some strange way, she found that reassuring.

Much of his time was spent with the captain, learning all he could about the ship, and the winds, and the vagaries of the sea. He worked even harder than the other members of the crew and took longer shifts at the wheel. But during those times when he returned to the cabin, she could see the heat in his eyes, the need for her that had not lessened.

Krista guarded her own desire. Leif was a strong, virile, incredibly attractive man, but the life she faced with him was completely unappealing. The more intimacy they shared, the more she might fall under his spell, and she refused to let that happen.

For the next five days, *Sea Dragon* sliced through the water toward Draugr Island. Then one morning, as she made her way up on deck, she saw the rugged peaks of a mountainous island peeking through a layer of distant fog. The land itself was shrouded in a grayish mist, almost completely hidden from view.

"You have almost reached your new home, *kaereste*."

"Stop calling me that. I am not your sweetheart. Not anymore."

For a moment he smiled. "Five days and your anger has not cooled?"

"Five years would not be enough."

His smile slid away and his features hardened. "It is time you stop behaving like a child. You will soon be my wife. It is time you learned to accept that."

"I won't marry you, Leif. I have told you that time and again."

Leif simply ignored her, turned and walked away. From what she knew of Viking lore, women weren't forced to marry against their will, but this was Draugr, and of course she couldn't be sure.

A little shiver went through her. As long as she remained unwed, as long as she refused to become Leif's wife, there was a chance she could get back home. Until that time, she was condemned to a life on Draugr Island.

Krista watched with dread as the rocky, uninviting land drew near. It was clear why the place was more legend and myth than real. The coastline was a wall of rock with hundred-foot cliffs guarded by massive boulders whipped by wind and sea.

Wispy fog shrouded the island, making it appear hostile and uninviting. Occasionally the wind blew away the mist, exposing jagged rocks where great plumes of foamy spray shot fifty feet into the air.

She turned as she heard Leif approaching where she stood next to the rail. "How will we reach the island without being torn to bits by the rocks and waves?"

"The harsh exterior is our protection. More than one ship has been destroyed over the years. But there is an entrance through the rocks on the other side of the island. It is impossible to see unless you know where to look. It is the way the men and I were able to sail from here."

Krista shivered. She wasn't certain if it was from the chill or what she would face once they reached Leif's home.

"You are cold," he said. Leaving her there, he disappeared down the ladder to his cabin and returned with a blanket, which he draped around her shoulders. For the first two days, she had worn the same white cotton nightgown she'd had on the night he had taken her from her home, and been forced to stay in his cabin.

At the end of the second day, Leif gave in to her pleading and brought her a set of men's clothes.

"These belong to Mr. Young. You are about his size."

She'd put them on with some trepidation, since she had never worn men's trousers before. But she liked the comfort, she discovered, the ease of movement and the loose fit of the shirt was a joy compared to the confines of her corset. She particularly enjoyed Leif's scowl when he saw her walking around in the clothes up on deck.

"You will stir the men's lust," he said darkly. "The clothes show your pretty behind and your very lovely breasts."

She tried not to feel pleased by his jealousy. "If you don't like the way I look, you should have brought me something of my own to wear."

The edge of his mouth faintly curved. "Oh, I like the way you look. Every time I watch you bend over, it makes me want to take you from behind."

Her face went crimson. "You...you are the most outrageous man!" Still, the image was now fixed in her head—of both of them naked, Leif's broad chest against her back. She wasn't sure exactly how making love that way would work or why the notion seemed so titillating, but it lingered just the same.

"These are good men," Leif continued. "But they are only human. Do not temp them too much."

She said nothing to that. She wasn't sure if she should be angry or flattered. Until Leif came along, she had thought herself plain and too tall to be attractive. Leif thought her a temptress.

Krista almost smiled. It was amazing what that sort of thinking did for one's self-esteem.

By the time *Sea Dragon* inched its way through the rock-lined, narrow channel that led to a protected harbor not visible from the sea, about forty people had gathered on the sandy shore. The last sail was lowered and the anchor tossed over, mooring the ship in a quiet inlet untouched by the violent waves along the coast not far away.

The crew lowered the dinghy over the side and all of them, including little Alfinn, who rode on Jamie's shoulder, climbed aboard. As the boat approached shore, Leif stood up in the bow and began to wave to the waiting throng, and a huge cheer went up. Apparently, they recognized him even in his English clothes.

But then, it wouldn't be difficult, not with his extreme height, powerful build and gleaming blond hair.

Leif's hair had gotten longer, but he still wore no beard. Since beards were the custom of Viking men, Krista had thought that he would grow it back, but so far every morning he had scrupulously shaved with the Sheffield steel straight razor he had learned to use back home.

"Just because I am returning to the island does not mean I intend to forget the things I learned in England," he said. "I like the way my face feels without a beard." He cast her a burning glance. "And I do not wish to make marks on your very soft skin."

Krista ignored a little tremor in her stomach. She wasn't giving up her life for him, no matter how much she might desire him.

She watched him now, standing like a conqueror on the bow of the small boat heading for shore, his heavy iron sword strapped round his narrow waist. The dinghy softly nosed into the sand and came to rest, and Leif jumped into the shallow water. He lifted her into his arms and carried her to shore as the other men climbed out of the boat and pulled it farther up on the sand.

"We will unload the cargo after we are settled," Leif told the others, then began speaking to the group that gathered around him. Though Krista didn't understand every word, she knew he was telling them he had returned and that he meant to stay.

"I have brought friends," he told them. "These men can be trusted. I have brought gifts from the land in which, for a time, I lived. And I have brought the woman who will be my bride."

A roar went up from the crowd, but Krista noticed a cluster of women who didn't look happy at all. One of them rushed forward and threw her arms around Leif's neck. She was as tall as Krista, with hair so pale it gleamed in the sun like strands of silver.

"Leif! You cannot mean it! We are to marry. It is what our fathers wanted. It has always been so!"

Leif eased her arms from around his neck. "The gods have decided otherwise, Hanna. This I cannot change." He looked over to where Krista stood and his brilliant blue eyes came to rest on her face. "Nor do I want to."

Something moved inside her. Something warm and sweet that made her wish with all her heart that she could marry him. She surveyed her surroundings, the barren, rocky island that was Leif's home, the rough, bearded giants in their fur-trimmed tunics and the women in their long, straight, primitive robes, and knew it could never be.

Standing on the sandy shore, Leif stared out over the throng of familiar faces and inhaled a lungful of clean, ocean-scented air. He was home at last, as for a time he'd thought he never would be again.

"Where is my sister?" he asked one of the men, his gaze moving among those gathered around him. He looked up just then and saw her racing toward him down the hill that led from the settlement, her red hair streaming like a banner out behind her. She had known but nineteen summers, and remained as yet unwed. She was the youngest of his siblings and, being the only girl, he had always carried a soft spot in his heart for her.

"Leif! Leif! I cannot believe it is you!"

He opened his arms and she rushed into them, and he held her tightly against him.

"Runa. Little sister, you have grown into a woman since last I saw you."

"I didn't think you were coming back. I thought you must

be dead." She clung to him, and the more fiercely she held on, the more uncertain he became.

He eased her away so he could see her face. "What is it, little one? What has happened while I was away?"

Her pretty gray eyes filled with tears. "Father is dead, Leif. Almost a moon has passed since the day he journeyed to the Otherworld."

His stomach twisted. He should have been here, should never have gone against his father's wishes.

And yet it was difficult to feel regret. How could he regret the incredible knowledge he had gained from the time he had spent in the world away from this one? Regret the woman he had brought home to be his wife?

"How did it happen?" Leif asked.

"Father fell ill. A terrible fever raged within him and even old Astrid could not discover what was wrong. In three days he was gone."

Leif held her tightly again. They had lost their mother many years ago. He could barely remember her. But Ragnaar had always seemed invincible, more than merely a man. Leif had looked up to him as if he were a god himself, and a lump swelled in his throat now as he thought how much he would miss him. "Who has been leading the clan?"

"Olav, since he was next in line to be chieftain after you. Uncle Sigurd has been giving him counsel."

Leif nodded. "That is good, but I am here now. And I promise all will be well."

She gave him a smile, reached up to touch his cheek. "Your beard is gone. You look different—and even more handsome."

He chuckled. "In a way I am different." He took her hand. "Come. There is someone I wish you to meet." He led her over to where Krista stood waiting.

"Runa, this is the woman who is to become my wife. Her name is Krista Hart." He turned. "Krista, this is my sister, Runa. I hope that the two of you will become good friends."

Krista stumbled over several wrong words, then finally murmured, "I am happy to meet you."

Runa frowned at her brother. "What about Hanna? She is your betrothed."

"Hanna and I were never betrothed. The gods have chosen Krista to be my wife instead." He flicked a glance in her direction. For a moment, she looked as if she would argue, but for once she kept silent, and he was grateful.

"It is good you are here," Runa said, still ignoring Krista's greeting. "The Hjalmr clan has been raiding again. They began right after Father died. Mayhap Rikard the Fierce thought us weaker with only Olav to lead us." She smiled. "They will soon learn that Leif the Dragon-hearted has returned. They will think better of mounting a raid against us now that you are here."

Leif looked over at Krista, saw one of her blond eyebrows arch. "Leif the Dragon-hearted?" she repeated.

He shrugged. "It is what my people call me."

"There are several names I'd like to call you," she said to him in English, "but for now I will restrain myself."

He felt the pull of a smile. He liked this woman he intended to make his wife. And he wanted her back in his bed.

"It is better if you speak Norse as much as you can. It will become easier that way. We will speak English when we are alone. I do not wish to forget the language I worked so hard to learn." When she didn't disagree, he took her hand and started leading her toward the road up to his farmstead.

As he passed through the crowd, a group of women came toward him. One he recognized as Elin, the wife of a distant cousin. "You are returned, Leif, but what of the others? Where is my son, Bodil?"

"I am sorry, Elin. The boat was not strong enough to survive the journey. The foreigners who helped us sail it, your son, Bodil, and the others, none of them survived."

"But you are yet alive."

His jaw clenched at the terrible memory of the storm, of dying men and the icy, treacherous sea. "It was the will of the gods."

The woman began to keen for the loss of her son, and several other women joined in. It was sad news he brought this day, and yet the men had understood the danger they faced when they chose to leave.

He started walking again, Krista on one side, Runa on the other. "Krista will need clothing," he said to his sister, "garments suitable for the future wife of a chieftain. I will leave the matter to you."

She didn't look pleased, but she nodded, her gray eyes running over the unusual garments he and Krista wore. "I shall tell Olav of your return and have your quarters prepared." She flicked a dark look at Krista. "Where will the woman sleep?"

"Prepare a room in the longhouse next to mine," he said. "She can stay there until we are wed."

Runa hurried ahead of them up the hill and Krista leaned closer. "Vikings don't force their women to wed against their will—is that not so?"

"Usually, that is so."

"Well, I won't agree to the marriage."

Leif sighed. "You will wed with me. One way or another."

"I won't," she said stubbornly.

And for the first time since he had decided to bring her with him, Leif began to worry.

* * *

Krista made the climb up the steep slope to the Viking settlement. Walking beside her, Leif seemed unusually quiet. Perhaps he was considering her refusal to marry him, but more likely he was thinking of his father.

"I am not certain I understood correctly," she said to him. "Your father is dead?"

He nodded. "He died of a fever nearly a month ago. I should have been here."

She took hold of his arm. "You had to go, Leif. You told me how important it was for you to see what lay beyond the island."

"I know."

"I'm sorry. Truly, I am."

He turned toward her, reached out and gently cupped her cheek. "Always you are caring of others. Even though you are still angry, you are sorry for my pain."

Krista turned away, her heart beating oddly. Of course she cared. She was in love with him. It didn't mean she could live the sort of life he meant for her to live.

They continued up the hill to the summit. The breeze picked up and she shivered against the wind that ruffled the legs of her trousers and blew open the front of her jacket. She drew the coat closer around her. As they topped the rise, she paused. Between the mountainous coastline and another range of mountains rising in the distance, a lush green valley spread out before her. The icy breeze lessened and a warm sun beat down on her face. Surprise must have shown in her eyes, for Leif smiled.

"You thought it would all look as it does along the coast?"

"I thought it might." But instead, a grassy, gently sloping plain appeared, crisscrossed with irrigation channels and dykes. Herds of cattle roamed the grasslands, and great fields, recently harvested of grain, stretched farther than she could see.

"You are pleased."

Krista sighed. "It doesn't matter what it looks like, Leif. Draugr isn't my home and never will be."

"In time you will feel different."

She bit back a reply. The island would be lovely to visit, but she was a city girl, born and raised, and this wasn't a place she could ever be happy living in. They continued along the valley until she glimpsed a cluster of buildings surrounded by low-lying hills.

She had seen drawings in her father's books, the remains of Viking settlements that had been discovered in the Orkneys, the Shetlands, Ireland and Scotland. She knew what such settlements looked like, and this one perfectly fit the image.

"We have ninety farms in our clan. My family's farmstead is the largest. We raise the most cattle and grain and employ the most workers. In past times, we owned slaves, but after the priests convinced the elders that slavery was against the will of the gods, we began to pay our workers, and it has been so ever since."

The farmstead stretched before her, larger than she would have imagined, the buildings spread out around a central longhouse that measured at least a hundred feet. The structures were fashioned of stone and turf, some of them built into the hillsides, all with turf or thatched roofs.

"There is a blacksmith shop over there, and that is the barn where we store hay and the grain we grow for bread and ale. There is a goat shed and a pigsty. A privy sits just north of the house."

Leif pointed to the low-roofed stone building shaped like a rectangular barn, with room after room added on to it. "And that is where we will live."

Krista bit back a groan. Though the surroundings were

lovely, the place looked every bit as primitive as she had feared. She shivered, and Leif draped an arm around her shoulders.

"Come. Let us go inside where it is warm, and I will introduce you to the rest of my family." They would all be living together, she knew. It was the Viking way.

Drawing a breath for courage, she let him guide her into the longhouse, its low thatch ceilings held in place by heavy pieces of driftwood. It was less dismal than she had feared, with an entrance hall, followed by a huge main hall with raised daises running along both sides, probably places for sleeping. Yet it was hardly the sort of accommodations she was used to.

She looked down at the floor beneath her feet, saw hard-packed earth warmed by heavy woolen carpets woven in colorful geometric designs. A massive central fireplace was built into one wall. Flames burned low in the hearth, from driftwood and animal dung, she imagined, since Draugr had no forests. But the fire gave off a good amount of heat, and she quickly warmed enough to remove her coat.

"The kitchen is near the front," Leif said, "and there is a room for weaving off to one side, and also one for storing dairy foods. There is a room we fill with ice and use to store fish and meat." He inclined his head toward the far end of the hall. "Come. I will show you where you will be sleeping."

She followed him, more depressed by the moment. What would she do to keep herself occupied in such a place? Spin wool into thread or weave garments? Churn butter? Cook meals for Leif and the men?

A lump rose in her throat. She had to find a way to make him see that she could not live like this, that her mind would dull with time and that she would simply fade away.

"We will occupy my father's rooms," Leif said, showing her into a large chamber that looked as if it had recently been vacated, a room with its own small fireplace. "Olav and his wife must have been living in here. By rights it now belongs to me—and to my wife."

Krista surveyed the room, which had been freshened with herbs, the huge bed on a raised platform covered by a thick pallet of furs. Whatever possessions Leif had left behind when he sailed from Draugr had been placed in the room. An ornately carved leather shield, a battle-ax and lance were propped against the wall.

"Those are yours?"

"Aye. My favorite weapons I took with me, but now, except for my sword, they lie at the bottom of the sea."

A tunic of deep ruby-red had been spread on the bed, along with a pair of loose-fitting breeches, which were meant to be worn underneath. Fur-lined, knee-high boots of some soft animal skin sat next to the bed on the floor.

"What is in there?" Krista asked, trying not to wonder how he was going to look in true Viking garb.

"You have a bathing room in your house. Through that door lies the pool I once mentioned. It is formed of a natural volcanic spring, heated by the mountain that rises at the center of the island. There are a number of such hot springs in the valley, as well as in the hills."

His gaze ran over the man's shirt and trousers she wore, which outlined her feminine curves. "The night we are wed, I will bathe you and make love to you in the pool."

Krista's breath caught. She fought to block the image of them naked, making love in the heated water. Dear God, no wonder women were so enthralled with him! *A rare manly man,* they had called him, and truly it was so.

"Where…where am I to sleep?" she asked, desperate for a change of subject.

"Until you are my wife, you will sleep in the room joining mine."

She turned toward a door on the opposite side of the chamber. There were no halls in a longhouse, just rooms that connected to other rooms, though the sleeping areas at this end of the house appeared to be very private.

She thought of the days and nights she would spend in the room next to his, thought of his determination to marry her and the battles she would have to fight—not just with him but with herself. She was in love with him, yet even with its minor comforts, this was not a place she could live.

She looked up at him and tears filled her eyes. "I can't do this, Leif. Please take me home."

For long moments his gaze searched her face. Then his jaw went hard. "You are mine. What the gods command cannot be changed."

"What if the gods are wrong?"

"They are gods. They are never wrong."

"Then what if *you* are wrong? You're only a man, Leif. Men are not gods and they are very often wrong. What if you misunderstood and I was not supposed to come with you?"

Fierce blue eyes bored into her. "You belong to me—make no mistake in this. Three days hence, we will wed and you will again warm my bed. Once I am inside you again, you will know the rightness of our union."

Taking her arm, he led her into the room next to his and urged her toward the fur-covered bed. "Rest awhile. I go in search of my brothers. My sister will bring you clothes. You may use the pool to bathe before you change. I will come for you before supper."

Krista swallowed past the lump in her throat and simply nodded.

Twenty-One

Leif left the longhouse, his thoughts in turmoil. He had often imagined his return to the island. Locked in his cage, he had spent endless hours thinking what it would be like, if he lived, to again see his homeland. But nothing had prepared him for the actuality.

Mayhap it was seeing his home through the eyes of a foreigner, a woman of great wealth who had been raised with luxuries he had never imagined until he had arrived in England. Mayhap it was the months he had spent in so different a world, or all he had learned in the days that he had been gone.

He was a different man now than the one who had left, and for the first time he wondered, as Krista did, if he could ever be truly happy in this place that had once been his home.

He thought of the pleading look in her eyes as she had begged him to take her back to England, and his insides knotted. He wanted her to be happy. In his mind, he had pictured her so, seen her laughing as she played with the children he would give her, the sons and daughters he knew she wanted as much as he did.

He told himself in time it would be so. The gods had spared

his life when he should have died along with the others. They had sent Krista to free him from the cruel fate he'd suffered at the hands of his captors. She was tall and strong and beautiful, made exactly to suit him. No other woman had ever fit him more perfectly, had ever made his blood burn with such unrelenting desire.

The gods had sent her to be his. He was as certain of that now as he had been almost from the moment he had first seen her.

And yet…

Leif shook his head. It was only his first day home. There was much to do, much that needed his attention. He thought of how long it had taken him to fit into a life in England, to begin to make a place for himself. Krista was a strong, capable woman. She would make a life here on the island, be the wife he needed, the woman who would warm his bed and give him strong sons.

Taking a deep breath, he crossed the open area in front of the longhouse, his mind moving from Krista to his brothers. Olav and his wife, Magda, lived in the longhouse where their father had lived, as Leif himself had done before he had sailed from the island. But Thorolf and Eirik, his two youngest brothers, had built farmsteads of their own. At the time he left, they had not yet decided to marry. He wondered if, in the year he had been gone, either had taken a wife.

Leif smiled to think of it. Both were big, strapping, lusty men, and handsome, the women seemed to think. He was eager to see them, to learn how they had fared while he was away, and hear more of what was happening with the raiding Hjalmr clan. Tonight at the longhouse, they would feast in celebration of his return, mourn their father and the men who had been lost at sea. And Leif would introduce his brothers to his future wife.

* * *

Krista prowled the room she had been given, then wandered into Leif's room, hoping to discover more about him. On the top of a wooden bureau along one wall, she found a leather belt with an ornately carved oyster shell buckle, a leather headband trimmed with silver and a carved tortoiseshell brooch, the sort used to fasten a man's tunic at the shoulder. There was a leather pouch and several silver armbands, one carved with the head of a dragon. An ivory amulet dangled from a leather thong in the same dragon design.

She had just picked up the amulet when she realized she was no longer alone. Krista turned door to see Runa standing in the open doorway.

"I brought you clothes." Moving past Krista, she carried the garments over to Leif's big bed and spread them out on top of the furs. The wooden shutter on the window was propped open, and in the sunlight, Krista noticed streaks of gold in the girl's flame-red hair, tied back at the nape of her neck with a woven strip of cloth.

"Thank you…Runa."

Like most of the women Krista had seen on the island, Leif's sister was tall and fit. She was extremely pretty, with very fine features and unusual gray eyes that tilted a little at the corners.

"You speak our language," Runa said. "Did my brother teach you?"

"My father taught me."

Curiosity stole into her expression. "They speak our language where you come from?"

"No, but my father is a…a—" she couldn't think of the word "—mentor," she finally said. "He studied your culture and that is how I learned, though I have only a very basic knowledge."

Runa moved around the bed, smoothing the gown she had brought, a long, pale-blue garment of soft-looking wool. Her gaze went over Krista's trousers and shirt. "This is the way women dress where you come from?"

"No. These are the clothes men wear. My clothes were… I borrowed these from one of the men on the boat."

Runa pointed at the blue woolen kirtle and the other items laid out on the bed, including a pair of oval tortoiseshell brooches linked by tiny silver beads, and a shawl of matching blue wool embroidered in patterns along the hem.

"These are for you," Runa said. "Tonight there will be feasting. You may bathe, if you wish, before you put them on."

"Thank you."

Eager to enjoy the heated pool, Krista started for the bathing room, but Runa did not leave.

"My brother says the two of you are to wed."

Krista stopped and turned. "Your brother is wrong."

Runa frowned. "Wrong? How can that be?"

"I won't wed him, Runa. I come from a very different world. I don't belong here. I wish to return to my home."

Runa's gray eyes looked huge. "What foolishness do you speak? Half the women in Draugr wish to wed with my brother. He has chosen you. It is a very great honor."

"If things were different, Leif is the husband I would choose. But my home is not here, it is in England, and I wish to return there."

Runa tossed her a look of disdain. "You are a fool," she said simply, and left the chamber, the heavy leather hinges on the door squeaking softly as she closed it behind her.

With a sigh, Krista went into the bathing room, stripped off her borrowed clothing and descended the narrow rock steps into the water. It was extremely hot, wonderfully so. At home, she never had the luxury of lingering in a bath. In a small bathing tub, the water rapidly grew cold.

Not here. The pool was large enough to hold three or four people, and there were stones beneath the water along the sides to sit on.

She ducked beneath the surface, used a chunk of some sort of soap she found near the edge of the pool to wash her hair, then rested her head back and closed her eyes, allowing the steam and the heat to soak into her bones.

She must have fallen asleep, for she dreamed that Leif was beside her in the water. He was kissing her neck, his big hands cupping her breasts, gently massaging the tips. She made a little whimpering sound as he moved lower, his skillful fingers sliding along her thighs, stroking between her legs.

Pleasure slipped through her and her eyes slowly opened. Krista jerked awake at the sight of Leif's blond head bent over, pressing soft kisses against her bare shoulders, nibbling the side of her neck. She sat up so quickly a surge of water spilled over the rocks lining the pool.

"Wh-what are you doing?"

"I am bathing, just as you are. I have missed this pool a great deal."

"You can't…can't be in here. What will your family think?"

"No one can see us. We will not be disturbed while we are in here."

She swallowed. Steam from the pool rose up in a clinging mist that dampened Leif's golden-blond hair. Water beaded his magnificent chest and powerful arms where they showed above the surface, and in that moment, she had never wanted anything so much as for him to make love to her.

Instead, she moved through the water toward the narrow rock steps and climbed out of the pool, trying to ignore the fact that he was watching and she was naked. A stack of linen cloths sat on a rock at the edge, and she picked up one and hurriedly dried herself.

She flicked a glance at Leif and saw him lounging back against the side of the pool, his blue eyes glinting as he watched her.

"You are mine," he said softly. "Your body knows this, even if you cannot see."

Pleasure still throbbed in her nipples and the place between her legs. Dear God, of all the men on the earth, how could she be so foolish as to fall in love with a man who had the power to ruin her life?

Hurrying out of the bathing room, she snatched the pale-blue woolen garment off his bed, along with a linen undergarment that seemed to go with it, and made her way to the relative safety of the room adjoining his.

It was chilly in the bedchamber. Krista quickly pulled on the thin shift of finely woven linen, much like a chemise, then the loose-fitting blue woolen kirtle. The latter, she found, was actually a two-fold costume, one part of which wrapped under the right arm and came up on the left shoulder, while the other came up the opposite way. Using the pair of tortoiseshell brooches she had found earlier, she secured the kirtle in place.

A brief knock sounded and she turned to see Leif striding into the bedchamber. He was dressed in the knee-length, ruby-red tunic and loose-fitting breeches she had seen earlier, his long legs encased in the fur-trimmed boots. He looked even bigger and more powerful than he usually did, utterly and completely the Viking that he had once been. Nothing at all remained of the man she had fallen in love with, and despair settled deeper inside her.

Leif seemed not to notice. His gaze ran over her embroidered kirtle and appreciation gleamed in his brilliant blue eyes. "Your Viking blood serves you well. You look every bit the Norsewoman, as I knew you would. Come. I have built up the fire in my chamber. You can sit in front of the flames and dry your hair."

She didn't want to go with him. She didn't trust this big blond Viking who stood before her, an entirely different man than the one she had known. For an instant, she closed her eyes, trying to conjure an image of Leif in his fashionable black evening clothes, of him bowing over her aunt Abby's hand, but the image would not come.

Her fingers shook as she picked up the carved antler comb she had found among the items on the bed, and followed him into his bedchamber. Leif seated her on a wooden chair, but when she began to use the comb, he took it from her hand.

"I will do it for you."

Wordlessly, she waited as he sat down on a three-legged stool and carefully pulled the comb through her damp, tangled hair. The act seemed nearly as intimate as the way he had touched her in the pool, and her nipples tightened beneath the simple blue kirtle. But this time, Leif scrupulously avoided any contact other than drawing the comb through her wet locks.

When he had removed all the tangles, he spread the heavy mass around her shoulders, rose from his stool and headed for the door. "I will send the girl, Birgit, to attend you. She will see to your needs from now on."

So Krista was to have a maid, just as she had back home. But then Leif was now the clan chieftain and she was soon to become his wife.

Or so he believed.

She thought of her friends back in England, of her father and how much he needed her, of the business she had worked so hard to build into a successful enterprise, and a lump swelled in her throat. Turning away from the door, she blinked against the sting of tears and fought not to give in to the urge to weep.

Twenty-Two

The longhouse rang with the sounds of shouting and laughter. Vikings were dressed in their finery: women in long flowing robes much like Krista's, some trimmed with intricate embroidery, others with fur; men in tunics and breeches, some with belted waists, most wearing ornate armbands, headbands, brooches and pendants made of silver, beads or shells.

Many of the women were astonishingly beautiful, Leif's sister, Runa, among them—and *tall,* Krista couldn't help but notice. For the first time in her life, she was just a woman, no different than anyone else. The men were tall, as well, big men, heavily built, some extremely handsome even with their long hair and thick beards.

Rows of wooden tables had been set up for the feasting, and a fire blazed in the hearth so the room felt comfortably warm. Seated next to Leif on a raised dais at the far end of the room, Krista thought how much her father would enjoy being here with these people, enjoy the entire adventure that she so completely hated.

The speeches were finally over. Leif had declared this a night of mourning for his father and the men who had died at sea, but also a night of celebration that a new chieftain would take Ragnaar's place as head of the Ulfr clan. It meant *wolf,* she knew, and understood now the silver armband Leif wore above the one with the carved head of a dragon, along with the ivory amulet around his neck.

The hall was full of clansmen from the settlement as well as others who had heard the news of Leif's return and come to join the celebration. Earlier she had met his brother Olav, just a year younger than Leif, and Olav's wife, Magda.

"Welcome home, brother," Olav had greeted Leif, clapping him hard on the shoulder. "We had all given up hope of your return."

"The gods took pity and so I still live." Leif smiled. "It is good to see you, brother. I am sorry to hear about our father. I will always regret I was not here when he died, though I cannot say I regret my journey."

"Was it truly so different?" Olav asked.

"In a lifetime, I could not begin to tell you the wonders I have seen."

Olav shook his head. He was blond and blue-eyed, not as tall as Leif, his features not so well-defined, and yet in a more subtle way, he was attractive. "I am content right here, as always I have been."

Leif turned. "Olav, this is Krista, the woman I have chosen to wed."

"She is a beauty," Olav said, as if Krista weren't there.

"And the woman walking toward us is Olav's wife, Magda," Leif said to Krista, who repeated the only greeting she knew how to say.

"It is good to meet you both."

Olav smiled and nodded, but Magda ignored her. "So you have finally returned," the woman said to Leif. "We had begun to believe you had abandoned us." She appeared to be several years older than Krista, with pale skin, raven-black hair and striking features. With her unusual coloring, Krista wondered if perhaps she was descended from someone who had once been a captive.

"It is good to see you, as well, Magda," Leif said with only a hint of sarcasm.

"You and your foolishness cost the lives of good men."

"They knew the risks."

Magda scoffed. "And what of your duty to your clan? If it hadn't been for your brother, the Hjalmr would have taken everything."

"I am grateful to Olav…and to you, Magda. But as I told Olav, I do not regret my journey. Besides, I am home now and that is what matters."

Magda said no more. It was clear Olav was happy his brother was alive and well, but Magda seemed far less pleased. She had been wife to a chieftain, if only temporarily, and it appeared she still coveted the position.

Two more men arrived at Leif's side, and as he spoke to them, he settled a possessive hand at Krista's waist. "These two rogues are Thorolf and Eirik, my youngest brothers."

"It is good to meet you," Krista said, managing the semblance of a smile. All of the brothers were handsome. Amazingly so. Thorolf had dark hair brightened with faint traces of red that glinted in the light of the fire. He was leaner than Leif, his body long and sleekly muscled, but his shoulders were wide and he was nearly as tall, with the same intense blue eyes.

Eirik looked even more like Leif, with the same muscular build, blond hair a darker golden hue and fine green eyes.

"And this is my uncle, Sigurd. He and my father were brothers."

Sigurd's smile was warm and broad. He was older, perhaps in his fifties, with iron-gray hair and a scar above his left eyebrow that stood out against his pale skin.

"So, at last my nephew has found himself a bride." His pale blue eyes assessed her, taking in the fullness of her lips, her high cheekbones, her softly curling long blond hair, pulled back on the sides with tortoiseshell combs. His gaze moved down her body, measuring her height, her build, the size of her bosom, all of which he seemed to approve. "It appears his wait was worthwhile."

Leif smiled. "Krista is beautiful, but she is also intelligent and strong of heart. She was a gift from the gods and one for which I am truly grateful."

He gazed at her with such warmth she couldn't speak the words that would tell his uncle and the others she had no intention of marrying him. This was Leif's first night home and she didn't want to spoil it for him. Tomorrow would be soon enough for the battle to begin anew.

Instead she gave her usual greeting to his uncle and noticed the way he continued to assess her. As Leif's wife, she would be a powerful member of the community. It was clear he hoped Leif had chosen well.

The evening continued. On the dais, she sat with Leif on one side and his uncle on the other. Next to Sigurd sat the settlement priest, and beyond him, Captain Twig. Below the dais, but in a place reserved for important guests, Jamie Suthers sat next to Felix Hauser and Bertie Young, and perched on Jamie's slim shoulder, little Alfinn chattered merrily at the others in the room.

The small group of Englishmen looked entirely too happy, and Krista sighed, more depressed than she had been when she arrived. There was no way she could convince the men to steal the *Sea Dragon* and return her to London. At least not yet.

The notion gave her a shot of hope. Perhaps in time the men would tire of their primitive environment and agree to take her home.

She was considering the possibility when the growling in her stomach began to distract her. She hadn't realized she was hungry until servants appeared in the hall carrying trays weighed down with food. A wooden trencher was placed on the table between her and Leif, and she remembered it was the way people ate back in medieval times.

The thought depressed her even more and much of her appetite faded.

"You like meat," Leif said, shoving a chunk of beef to her side of the trencher. "There will be mutton and fish and also several kinds of cheese. Our food is simple, but you will never go hungry."

Her stomach rumbled again. She glanced down at the eating utensils beside the trencher, saw a big, antler-handled knife and spoon. The spoon wouldn't help. She picked up the knife, gripping it the way Leif held his, and stabbed it into a big piece of meat. She wasn't quite sure what to do with it now that she had it, and when she looked at him for guidance, she saw that he was frowning.

"It is all right," he said gently. "You can use your fingers. It is proper to do so here." But as he watched her tearing the meat apart and stuffing it into her mouth, his expression seemed to darken and his jaw tensed. "On the morrow, I will show you how to use the knife."

She thought of the lessons she had given him in the elegant dining room of her town house. There was no crystal here, no linens, no gilt-rimmed plates to hold the delicious array of food Cook prepared nightly. Krista was no wilting lily. She was a survivor, and if she had to, she could live as these people did.

A lump swelled in her throat. But dear God, how she wanted to go home.

Leif watched Krista all through the evening. He had introduced her to every person in the hall, and though he knew she was weary, she carried herself like the highborn lady she was. He had never been more proud of her.

Only once had she balked. When he stood to make the announcement of his upcoming marriage, she had clamped her lips together and firmly shaken her head, warning him what would happen if he did.

"By the gods," he said to her softly, "you are a vexing creature, Krista Hart." His words, muffled by the rowdy noise and laughter in the hall, didn't seem to faze her. Furious and strangely depressed, he turned to the revelers, who fell silent as he lifted his drinking horn in a toast to his father instead.

"Let us drink to Ragnaar!" he shouted. "The greatest chieftain ever to rule Ulfrvangr!" Putting the horn to his lips, he emptied the contents, and the hall went up in a cheer.

More toasts were made. One to him as the next great chieftain of the clan, one to the men who had perished in the sea. A toast was made by his brother Eirik, to the Viking with the smooth cheeks of a lad and how pretty he looked, which sent the hall into fits of laughter.

Hoping to dull his anger and disappointment, Leif emptied the horn every time it was filled. His mind grew muddled, his words slurred. He barely noticed when Thorolf escorted Krista from the hall. But as soon as she stepped down from the dais and made her way behind him toward her room, Inga appeared. He remembered the last time he had seen her, the night in the barn when he had taken her in the hay.

"She is gone and you are left alone," Inga said, pressing her lush breasts against him. "It is not right for a man to be alone on his first night home." She smiled, ran her hand along the nape of his neck, sank her fingers into his hair. "I will give you what you need this night, Leif." She cupped his cheek and bent to kiss him, but he turned away.

"I am to wed, Inga. Leave me be."

"She will not wed you. She has said so to your sister." She caressed his clean-shaven jaw. "She does not want you, but I do. Let me give you pleasure. You remember how good it was between us. Take what I freely offer."

He only shook his head.

"Even should you wed, I will come to you. I will live as your concubine. This I will do for you, Leif."

Leif set his empty drinking horn down on the table, suddenly tired to the bone. "The hour grows late, Inga. It is sleep I need this night, not a woman." *At least not this woman,* he thought.

Moving unsteadily, he made his way to his room behind the dais at the end of the longhouse. Sitting down on a bench at the foot of his bed, he removed his fur-trimmed boots, then, with a last glance at the door leading to Krista's room, lay down on the furs and dropped into a heavy sleep.

Krista could not sleep. She had watched Leif drink cup after cup of ale until his senses were dulled and he swayed in the ornately carved, high-backed chair that had once belonged to his father. She had never seen him drink that way before. She was grateful to his brother Thorolf—Thor, he was called—who had come to her rescue, leading her quietly back to her bedchamber.

"It is not like him to drink so much. I have rarely seen my brother drunk." He grinned and she saw that his teeth were white and straight. With his dark hair and brilliant blue eyes, he was incredibly handsome.

"Only once did it happen," he said. "When we were young boys, we wanted to know what it was like to drink like the men. Our father caught us. The next day he ordered us to dig out the pigsty, which, after so much ale, made both of us violently sick. Neither of us ever drank that way again."

"Until tonight," she corrected.

Thor sighed. "You will have to forgive him. He has a great deal on his mind."

Thor left her there, and Krista intended to go to bed, but instead found herself wandering back toward the hall. Careful to stay out of sight in the shadows, she searched for Leif, then froze where she stood as a ripely curved blonde stepped up beside him on the dais. *Inga,* he called her.

Krista remembered the night Leif had called her that, thinking she was the woman he had made love to in the barn. Though the pair stood a little ways away, most of the guests were now sleeping or passed out drunkenly at one of the tables, and she could hear every word.

Hear that the lovely blond Inga intended to become Leif's whore.

Concubine, they were called, and Krista's stomach violently churned. Dear God, how could she have forgotten that Vikings took women into their households other than their wives? Women who serviced their benefactor's needs.

It doesn't matter, she told herself. She wasn't going to marry him. She didn't care how many damnable *concubines* he took to his bed!

But it did matter. It made her sick to even think of sharing him with another woman, perhaps more than one.

As she lay on the pallet of furs, Krista tried to push the thought away, tried to empty her mind so that she could fall asleep. But dawn had begun to purple the sky and still she lay awake, staring at the turf roof overhead.

Eventually, she slept. Olav's wife, Magda, awakened her not long after, telling her it was time she took her place with the other women, either weaving or working in the fields. Krista wondered if Leif had sent her, for the door to his room was open and it was clear he was already gone.

Dressing in the linen shift she had worn last night, and the simple clothes Magda brought her—a loose brown woolen kirtle, along with a double-fold garment that went over it to keep out the chill—she followed the woman out of the room. As they walked through Leif's bedchamber, Krista wondered again where he was.

He hadn't left with Inga last night, she knew, or invited the woman into his bed. But a new day had dawned. Both Hanna with the shining silver hair and his paramour, Inga, desired him. Krista wondered if Leif's lusty appetites would drive him into the arms of either one.

Leif's head was pounding, his stomach rolling and occasionally his hand trembled. Blood of Odin, what had possessed him to drink like a fool last night? He was a man who prided himself on his control. He was the chieftain of the clan, and yet he had given in to the blessed relief of ale-wrought oblivion.

He shook his head, felt the pounding increase, and groaned.

It was Krista, he knew. It was aching with want of her, needing her as he had never needed a woman.

It was fear that in bringing her to Draugr he had done the wrong thing.

His mind swung back to the feasting last night, to the bawdy laughter and drunkenness she had tolerated, though he knew it bothered her. In his mind's eyes, he saw her at supper, her soft, pale fingers wrapped around the heavy staghorn knife instead of a delicate silver fork, and remembered the kick he had felt in his stomach.

She was a lady, a woman who dressed in silk and satin. And though he hated the loathsome corset she wore, he liked the feminine way she looked in her garments. He liked the little flowered garters that held up her stockings, the fragrance of her expensive perfume, the soft kid slippers that encased her slender feet. He liked her just as she was, and seeing her in the hall last night among his drunken clansmen had made his heart feel heavy in his chest.

And yet, deep inside, he believed as he always had that Krista was meant to be his.

His head continued to pound and he ignored a wave of dizziness as he knocked on his uncle Sigurd's door. A few minutes later, the leather hinges creaked and the door swung open.

"Nephew. You are up early, considering last night's festivities. Come in."

Leif moved past him into the house. "I am in need of your counsel, Uncle."

Sigurd nodded. A thin man, pale complexioned, his hair almost completely gray, he was the wisest man in the settlement, Leif knew. If anyone could be of help, Sigurd was the man. He motioned toward the hearth and they moved in that direction, sat down on three-legged stools at a small wooden table.

"You look weary this morning," Sigurd said. "Too much ale last night?"

"Far too much."

"That is not like you." He studied Leif's face. "You did not announce your forthcoming marriage last night and you drank as if the stream had gone dry. Am I wrong to assume your lady is the source of your worry?"

Leif ran a hand over his face, felt the stubble of morning beard he had yet to shave off. "She refuses to marry me, Uncle. I have tried to convince her, but nothing I say seems to change her mind."

"Seeing you together, I would guess you have already taken the girl to your bed."

He nodded.

"And she went willingly?"

Leif's head came up. "I would not force her. Of her own will, she gifted me with her virgin's blood."

"But you have not bedded her since your return."

"How did you know?"

Sigurd smiled. "You do not have the satisfied look of a man who has recently taken a woman."

Leif glanced away. "She needs time to accept things as they are. Since we are not married, I am giving her that time."

"She desires you still. I can see it in her eyes whenever she looks at you."

"I believe that is so and yet she will not wed with me. What am I to do?"

"You cannot force her to marry you. That is not our way. But perhaps there is a way besides words."

"I would be grateful to know what it is."

"Your lady desires you as much as you do her. Use that desire to bring her back to your bed. Once she is there, she will understand the need for marriage. There isn't a woman alive who wouldn't rather be a man's wife than merely his lover."

It made sense. Though in truth, Leif had tried a similar approach before. Still, his uncle was right about one thing—Krista desired him. Leif wasn't a fool. He knew when a woman wanted him, and this one did.

"I will give it some thought." And since his uncle was usually right, he would begin to think what he might do to bring her back to his bed. He smiled as he remembered what he had learned from reading *Miss Boots' Confessions* and *The Pearl of Passion.* Inwardly, he cursed as his body stirred to life, and he was grateful for the loose-fitting clothes.

"There is another matter I came to discuss," he said. "It concerns you and the members of the council. I wish to propose to the elders the opening of trade with the outside world."

Leif leaned forward, his excitement beginning to build. "I have seen such amazing things, Uncle. I have brought some of them with me—lights that burn the oil from the fat of a giant fish, lengths of shimmering cloth woven from the cocoon of a moth. A substance called glass that you can see right through. It can be used for windows, letting in the sun while it keeps out the chill."

"They sound very interesting."

"There is more, Uncle. So much more. I have seen weapons more powerful than any you could imagine. They are called *guns* and they can reach across long distances to kill an enemy. We can arm ourselves with these guns and none will be able to defeat us. And that is only the beginning. With trade, the miracles that could be brought here are endless."

His uncle rose from his chair. "These things you speak of…they are still on your ship?"

"I plan to unload them today."

"Leave them for now. I will meet with the council to discuss this. They will wish to hear what you have to say, but..."

Leif rose as well. "But what, Uncle?"

"But I warn you, Nephew. For three hundred years we have lived in relative peace and safety on this island. Our simple way of life is our protection. There is a chance the elders will not want your gifts, that they will forbid you to bring them ashore. There is even a chance they will demand you destroy your ship so that none of those who came with you can leave and tell what they have seen."

A sliver of alarm went through him. "Once they see what wonders there are—"

"Be forewarned, Nephew. Should you convince them, life here as we know it will never be the same. Change will come to Draugr, not all of it for the best. Be certain that is what you want."

Leif left the house, convinced his uncle was wrong. But Sigurd's words kept rolling around in his head. What if the council was opposed to trading? What if they demanded he destroy his ship, and he could never leave the island again, never take Krista back to see her father, her family, her home?

What if he were trapped in the very life he had fled, with no hope of ever seeing the outside world again?

Leif's stomach rolled, and it had nothing to do with the ale he had consumed last night.

Awaiting a summons to appear before the council, Leif stayed away from Krista for the next several days. He needed to think, needed to decide what to do, and more and more, he worried that his uncle might be right. Once trade with England began, everything on Draugr would change.

He was chieftain now. Was that what he truly wanted for

his people? Was it really in their best interests? Or was his dream motivated by a selfish desire to return to the foreign world he had discovered, to experience more of what he had only begun to learn?

Desperate for answers, he spoke to his sister, asking her to look after Krista until his return. Then he draped a blanket and lightweight saddle over one of the shaggy island horses, tied on his weapons and a sack of food, and prepared to head up to his special place in the hills.

"If there is trouble, you know where to find me," he said to Runa. "Send word if the elders are ready to see me. If I do not hear from you, three days hence I will return."

Swinging up on the back of the horse, Leif whirled the animal and rode away.

Twenty-Three

⮜━━⧆⧆⧆━━⮞

The next day and the next, Krista worked alongside the women. This time of year, they were cutting the reeds that grew along the edge of small ponds in the bottom of the valley. They were tied into bundles, loaded onto carts and hauled back to the compound, where they were cut into shorter lengths and soaked in tallow. The reeds, stuffed into hollow pieces of wood, were called rushlights and were burned to light the inside of the longhouse.

It wasn't so bad, Krista discovered, being out in the fresh air and sunshine, except that the repetitious work soon lulled her into boredom. And the women completely ignored her, even Runa. They laughed and made fun of her clumsy efforts with the scythe, and spoke in whispers whenever she was near.

It didn't matter. She had nothing to say to them and barely understood what they said about her. At least the work kept her busy, though even as she cut reeds alongside the shallow pond, her mind often strayed to Leif. She thought of the woman Inga, and the sort of life he intended for them to live, and despair crushed down on her.

Why hadn't he told her? He wasn't a man to lie, even by omission. Did Leif believe she would already know? Through her father, she had learned a great deal about the Viking culture and she had read more than once about the women in a man's household, including his wife and sometimes his concubines.

How could she have forgotten? But perhaps Leif's attentions had somehow made her forget.

It doesn't matter, she told herself for the hundredth time, and tried to convince herself that if she continued to refuse his offer of marriage he would be forced to wed one of the Viking women instead, perhaps Inga or Hanna, and return Krista home. But she didn't really believe he would, and a pang of homesickness swept through her, followed by an ache in her heart.

She hadn't seen Inga or Leif since the night of the celebration, and it occurred to her that even now they might be together. The thought made her physically ill.

To distract herself, Krista threw herself into her labors. By the end of the second day, her hands were red from wielding the scythe, and blisters had begun to form on her palms. When Runa saw the welts the next morning, she led Krista to the weaving room instead of outside, and set her to work carding wool from the vast basketfuls that were brought into the low, stone-walled chamber.

The work was slow and monotonous, and by the end of the day, Krista was exhausted. She had yet to see Leif, and when she asked Runa about him, the girl merely said that he had gone into the hills. Krista hoped he had not taken Inga with him.

She was sitting in her room, weary to the bone, her hands red and burning, when Leif appeared in the doorway. Krista rose to her feet, her gaze going to his face, so handsome, so impossibly dear that her eyes welled with tears.

"Krista!" He was beside her in an instant, hauling her into

his arms, pressing his cheek to hers. She could feel the rough stubble of his beard and wondered if he had decided to let it grow, to become completely the Viking that he had been before.

"I am sorry I left you," he said in English, whispering against her cheek. "I needed time to think. I do that best in the hills. I should have told you, explained why I had to go. I am sorry, *honning*."

She turned away from him though she didn't really want to, her pulse beating dully, a painful ache in her heart. It was nonsense. Leif was a Viking. He lived as they did and there was no changing that.

He moved behind her, gently rested his hands on her shoulders, very softly caressed them. "Tell me what is wrong."

She swallowed, trembled, forced out a single word. "*Inga*." It came out on a sob, and she hated herself for letting him see how much he had hurt her.

"Inga?" He turned her to face him and his jaw firmed. "What has she done?"

Krista shook her head. "I heard you the night of the feast. I heard her offer herself to you. I know…I know you plan to make her one of your…your women."

His eyes darkened. "If you heard us, then you know I did not accept her offer, nor do I intend to. Whatever Inga and I shared is long past. She holds no appeal for me now. There is only one woman I want in my bed and that is you."

Krista looked away, her heart squeezing painfully. "Even if we were wed, a Viking man often takes other women into his household, his bed. Are you saying…?"

"I am telling you I do not intend to seek out another. My father had one wife and none other. He was true to my mother until the day she died—as I would be true to you." Leif caught

Krista's chin and very gently kissed her. "Say you will wed with me."

The warmth of him surrounded her, the scent of his skin, the strength of his powerful body. Tears welled in Krista's eyes and began to slide down her cheeks.

"I cannot." She brushed away the wetness. "You know in your heart I don't belong here. You know it, Leif, as surely as I do."

He turned away from her and walked to the door, his hands unconsciously fisting. For several long moments, he stood there, his back rigid, his long legs braced apart.

When he turned, his face was an unreadable mask once more. "Runa said you worked with the other women cutting reeds. You did not have to. I should have told you that." He strode toward her. "She said you worked hard, harder than any of the other women. She said it would seem I had chosen well."

Krista hid her surprise, or hoped she did. "That was kind of her to say." During the days since he had left, the women had ignored her or given her extra chores to do. Runa had been no different, but now, hearing his sister's words of praise, Krista couldn't help thinking that perhaps if she stayed on the island long enough, she and Runa might someday be friends.

"I need to bathe," Leif said. "It would please me if you would join me." The heat was back in his eyes, the desire he had kept mostly banked since their arrival.

"I don't…don't think that would be wise."

"To me, it seems very wise." He stared at her for several long moments, his eyes a scorching blue, then he noticed her palms.

"By the gods!" Reaching out, he caught both of her hands in his to examine them. With another soft curse—this one in English—he led her into his bedchamber, to a table that held some of his things, and opened a small soapstone jar filled with salve. Very gently, he spread the ointment over her blistered, work-roughened hands.

"You will stay home on the morrow and every day until your hands are healed. My sister will pay for this."

"It wasn't Runa's fault. I wasn't used to that sort of work, is all. When your sister saw the blisters, she moved me to the weaving room. And they really aren't all that bad."

He scoffed, lifted a sore hand and pressed a kiss against the tips of her fingers. "Tomorrow you will stay abed." He smiled at her softly. "I only wish you would invite me to join you there."

Her heart clenched. She wouldn't, she knew, but dear God, it wasn't because she didn't want to.

Morning came, and with it a stiff breeze that ruffled the valley grasses. Leif left the meeting hall and strode out into a weak autumn sun. His insides were in turmoil, his heart beating dully. Earlier that morning, the council of elders had sent for him, and he had gone to speak with them, to plead his case for the opening of trade with England. To his amazement, he had done so with far more uncertainty than he had thought he'd feel.

Striding from the meeting hall, a small stone building at the far edge of the compound, he made his way toward the barn, intent on saddling one of the shaggy brown horses for a mind-clearing ride into the hills.

"Leif! A moment, please!" It was his uncle, a senior member of the council. Leif waited as Sigurd approached where he stood in the shade of the barn.

"I know you are disappointed, Nephew. I hope you will try to understand."

"They do not want trade. They never have. I should have known it would be hopeless to try to change their minds."

"You must remember our history, Leif. For hundreds of years our culture was assimilated, little by little, into other cultures, until it all but disappeared. Even before we came here, we were the last true Vikings, and only because Greenland was so isolated. It was difficult, nearly impossible to survive in such a hostile world, and so we began to search for another, better place to live, a place where we could remain as we were, as we wished to be."

"I know our history, Uncle. I know the gods blessed us by showing Harald the way to this island."

Sigurd nodded. "We followed him, believing we would be safe, that our culture, our way of life would be protected."

"And so it has been."

"Yes, but only because we have worked so hard to keep others away, to preserve the customs we so value."

Leif sighed. For days he had been thinking that same thing, thinking that it was his duty to keep his people safe, to help them maintain the way of life they had had for hundreds of years.

"I understand, Uncle. And in my heart I believe you and the others may be right. All of my life I have wanted to know the world outside this one. Now that I have done so, it is hard for me not to want to share some of the wonders I have seen, to bring those wonders to my people. And yet I can see how those things would change the very core of our lives."

"It is not what we want."

He glanced away. "I see that now as I should have before."

His uncle clapped him on the back. "You are a strong leader, Leif, and an unselfish one."

Leif just nodded. "I will do my best not to disappoint you or them." He started to walk away, but his uncle's voice stopped him.

"There yet remains one question unanswered."

"What is that?"

"Are you certain your path lies here and not this place you call Eng-land?" Sigurd smiled gently. "When you were a boy, I saw it in your eyes, a thirst for knowledge unlike I had ever seen before. I see it there now, even as you say that you have returned to lead your people."

"It is my duty. I will not dishonor my father by ignoring it."

"Sometimes there are higher duties. Perhaps yours lies elsewhere, Leif."

"I made a vow and I will not break it. And I am needed here."

"And yet, deep inside, you doubt that you now belong here. Do you deny it?"

Leif made no reply.

"Think on my words, Nephew." Sigurd walked away, his shoulders straight as he made his way back to his home at the edge of the compound. Releasing a breath, Leif continued on into the barn.

At least they hadn't asked him to destroy his ship. It was well-hidden in the inlet, out of sight of any passing vessel, and the elders believed it posed no threat. Captain Twig and his men would be allowed to leave whenever they wished, since it would not be possible for them to find their way back to the island in future without Leif's help. At the moment they seemed content in this place, where they were treated as honored guests and popular with the women.

The only threat the ship posed was to Leif's peace of mind. The wonders of England glittered in his memory like stars in the black night sky, calling for his return. And there was Krista to consider. As he saddled his horse and swung up on the animal's back, he tried not to think what the council's decision would mean to her and to her father and the rest of her family. His chest feeling leaden, he urged his horse up into the hills.

* * *

Krista had not seen Leif since early that morning, when he'd checked to see how she fared. During the day, the serving maid, Birgit, attended her, helping her learn new words, sewing new clothes for her and preparing her meals. By afternoon, Krista was bored and wandering aimlessly around the longhouse. Drawn into the weaving room, she sat down at the loom next to Runa.

Viking women did very fine work, she had noticed the first time she was there, spinning wool into threads of various sizes, some incredibly delicate. The fine thread was used to make soft woolen fabrics or for embroidery. Heavier threads were for sewing fur pelts, making rugs or tapestries to warm the floors and walls.

Runa no longer ignored her, and neither did the other women. After her days of working beside them in the fields, they spoke to her almost as an equal. Almost. But the red-haired girl still didn't understand Krista's refusal to marry her brother.

"Do you love another man?" she asked as they sat in front of the loom and Runa showed her again how to work the soapstone spindle, weaving it back and forth across the threads.

"I love your brother, but I do not belong here. I have a life of my own in England, the place I came from. I have duties there, responsibilities, just as Leif has here."

"What sort of duties?"

Krista wasn't sure she could explain about the newspaper and her father and grandfather. Her vocabulary was limited, after all, and describing a world so different from Runa's was nearly an impossible task. But she struggled along, doing the best she could.

When she finished, Runa seemed to ponder her words. "This place you describe…it does not seem real."

"It is very real. You can ask your brother."

"He has yet to say much of his journey. I think it bothers him in some way to speak of it."

Krista bit back a rush of longing. "He was beginning to make a place for himself there. It was amazing how well he fit in."

"His life is here on Draugr. He says you belong here, as well." Runa's gray eyes fixed on Krista's face. "Sometimes the gods decide on a different life than the one we choose. Mayhap that is so with you."

"I don't think so. I think Leif made a mistake in bringing me here. I don't think it was the will of the gods at all."

Runa stiffened. "My brother is chieftain. If he says you were chosen for him as his bride, then it is so."

"What if you were forced to marry a man you did not wish to wed?"

"You love him. You said so."

"Yes, but I am needed at home."

"Mayhap my brother needs you more."

Krista's heart squeezed. What if he did? What if she was wrong and her destiny lay here on Draugr with Leif? Krista almost wished she could make herself believe it.

The women talked awhile longer, speaking of less personal matters, the weather and the tasks to be done in preparation for the colder months ahead. Then Runa rose from her stool and left the weaving room, and Krista took her place at the loom. The simple task of running the soapstone spindle back and forth kept her mind occupied, at least for a while, and she was grateful.

Still, her thoughts strayed to Leif, and she wondered when he would return. Earlier, he had sent Jamie Suthers, who worked now in the barn with the horses, to tell her he had gone into the hills but would be back before nightfall. She knew he had met with the council elders that morning, but no one yet knew the results of the meeting.

Krista prayed they had voted in favor of Leif's proposal, that his ship, the *Sea Dragon*, would be sailing back and forth between Draugr and England, and sooner or later she would be able to persuade him to take her home. As the hours slipped past, she grew more and more anxious to hear, but by the end of the day he had not yet returned to the compound.

Tired more from worry than the monotonous job she had been doing, she left the weaving room and returned to her bedchamber. The soft pallet of furs beckoned and she lay down to nap for a while before supper. Soon she had drifted into a troubled sleep.

Krista was home again. Working with Coralee at the gazette, getting this week's edition ready to be loaded onto wagons on the morrow. Finished sheets of *Heart to Heart* were being lifted off the Stanhope press and carried out to the assembly room to be tied into bundles. Her father was upstairs in his makeshift study, waiting patiently for her to finish so that he could escort her home.

"I love your article this week," Corrie said to her, looking down at the fresh ink printed on the page. "You gave Cutter Harding another well-deserved kick. Perhaps this will give his employees the push they need to rise up and make him listen to their grievances."

"I don't know...the man is extremely unsympathetic. We need more laws to govern working conditions and more people to enforce them."

Her father came down the stairs just then. "Have you two finished solving the world's problems—at least for the night?"

"We're just stacking the last of the bundles."

"Good. I was hoping… I thought that perhaps in the morning before you come to work you might help me with the research paper I've been writing."

She had been so busy lately. Her father was so lonely since her mother died. She knew how much he needed her. She gave him a tender smile. "I'll be happy to read your paper, Father."

"Capital!" He gave her a winning smile in return, and a wave of tenderness washed over her.

They finished their work for the night. Coralee left for home and Krista and her father locked up and climbed into their carriage. She didn't know why, but for some odd reason it felt good just to be sitting on the seat across from him. He looked tired, she realized as she studied the lines etched into his face. He'd been working too hard lately. She would have to see he got a little more rest.

She reached over and took hold of his hand. "I've missed you, Father," she said, but couldn't imagine why, since she saw him every day.

But something was tugging at her memory, something she didn't want to recall….

"Krista! Wake up! They're coming! The raiders are coming!"

Krista blinked as she awoke, groggy for a moment, confused as to where she was. Then she recognized Runa standing at the foot of the bed. Despair washed over her. She wasn't home at all. She was still on Draugr Island.

"Hurry! They're coming!"

"Who is coming?"

Runa caught her hand and hauled her off the pallet of furs. "The Hjalmr!" The girl dragged her toward the window and shoved open the wooden shutter, revealing the darkening landscape that stretched across the valley toward the hills.

"See those torches? Those are Hjalmr raiders riding down off the mountain!"

Krista's pulse kicked up. "Where is Leif?"

"He hasn't yet returned. We've got to find Olav!" Runa started running toward the door, and Krista fell in behind her. She had no idea what the Hjalmr raiders intended to do, but it suddenly occurred to her that she needed to be prepared. Racing back to Leif's room, she grabbed the lance that rested against the wall, then hurried to catch up with Leif's sister.

"Stay here!" Runa ordered when they reached the front door. "I'll go find Olav and be right back!"

"What should I do?"

Runa pointed toward the group of mounted riders advancing down the hill. "Pray they are Hjalmr and not berserkers."

"*Berserkers?* What are—?" But Runa was already rushing away, and in the back of her mind, Krista was recalling what that word meant. They were rogue Vikings, men who disobeyed the law of the land, outcasts who followed no rules and seemed to have no conscience.

Her heart was pounding now and she was, indeed, praying the raiders were Hjalmr, who seemed to be considered less dangerous. Outside the window, men armed with swords and shields, battle-axes and lances, some wearing metal or leather helmets, rushed out of their low stone houses. Krista watched with a combination of awe and horror as the riders thundered across the valley, across the nearby fields, and galloped into the compound. The Ulfr men met their attackers head-on, swinging their own viscous-looking axes and swords.

"Oh, dear God," Krista whispered, just as Runa ran back inside the house.

"Berserkers!" the red-haired girl yelled above the clash of

metal and the wild shouts of the warriors. "And half of our men are off hunting!"

Krista had watched them leave that morning, and seeing how few were left in the compound, her heart sank. "Perhaps…" She swallowed, started again in Norse. "Mayhap the berserkers saw them leave."

"Aye, mayhap they have been waiting for their chance, and saw the men riding out this morning."

Krista trembled as her fingers tightened around the shaft of the lance she had taken from Leif's room. "What…what should we do?"

"Our men will be returning. We can only pray those who are here will be strong enough to hold the compound until the others arrive."

But as she watched the fighting, Krista saw one man fall and then another beneath the brutal blows of the enemy's weapons. The Ulfr men were going to be defeated and, dear God, what would happen to the women once they were no longer able to defend them?

She bit back a sob as a man she recognized from the feast went down, felled by a berserker's battle-ax, a bright red wash of his blood spilling onto the ground as he crumpled to the earth. She recognized Leif's uncle, Sigurd; saw him valiantly fighting two men at once and amazingly holding his own. Olav was there, she saw, wielding his sword with the skill of a master, and still the Ulfr numbers were dwindling.

"Stay here!" Runa shouted. Turning, she disappeared out the door, and Krista realized she was carrying a dagger.

Krista just stood there, frozen. She wasn't a warrior. She had no idea how to fight like one. She watched Runa charge into the fray, saw one of the berserker's fall, saw Captain Twig and the two English crewmen rush forward into the melee of men and horses, each armed with a cutlass.

A berserker whirled his horse and rode straight toward Runa, and for an instant, Krista thought the young girl would surly die. Then the pounding of horse hooves drew her attention across the compound, and her heart nearly stopped beating as Leif rode into the battle.

He sat his horse easily, riding without conscious thought, his huge arms bulging with muscle as he swung his heavy sword, first one way and then another, taking out man after man, then whirling his horse toward Runa and dispatching her attacker.

"Get back in the house!" he commanded, and surprisingly, his sister obeyed, racing back toward the safety of the long-house. Eirik and Thorolf rode up just then, word of the attack apparently having reached their farmsteads. Like their brothers, they were skilled with sword and ax, and soon the tide of battle began to turn.

One berserker after another fell. Other raiders began to scatter, some riding hard back toward the hills. It looked as though the day would be won when a huge, bearded giant of a man set upon Leif. From the start, the battle was even, both men skilled warriors, each masterfully wielding his shield as well as his sword.

Krista's heart thundered in terror. "Dear God, don't let him be hurt," she prayed, her entire body shaking with fear for him. A moment later she saw a second raider moving up behind him. He was out of Leif's sight, on Krista's side of the compound, and though she shouted a warning, in the melee of clashing steel and neighing horses, he did not hear.

There wasn't time to think, no time to be frightened. Leif was going to be killed and she had to do something to stop it.

Gripping the lance, she rushed out of the house, straight toward the man behind Leif. Lifting the weapon, she held it in
front of her and charged forward. At that exact moment, the
warrior turned and saw her, and seeing the rage on his face,
Krista knew she was going to die.

Twenty-Four

"Krista!" Leif's shout was lost in the din around him. His heart was racing, trying to pound its way out of his chest. He could hardly believe the woman who faced his attacker was his bride, and his whole body tightened in fear for her. She looked up at him the instant before she rushed forward, the lance gripped tightly in her hand. The instant before she plunged the vicious iron point into the bearded warrior's chest. The instant before she might have died.

"Krista!" He shouted her name again, but again she seemed not to hear him. Her eyes were huge and fixed on the blood-covered man at her feet, the lance pointing skyward now, protruding through the man's broad chest. Her hair had come loose from the strip of cloth at the nape of her neck, and fell around her shoulders in a cloak of gleaming gold. Tears streamed down her cheeks.

He started toward her a second before he spotted another attacker racing toward her, and the terror he had felt before welled up again so strongly he could taste it in his mouth. His heart seemed to still inside his chest and for an instant, he could not move. Then he whirled his horse, dashing between the two, swinging his sword and neatly removing the raider's head from his body. Spinning the horse again, Leif reached down and swept Krista up in his arms as he and his mount raced past.

He seated her across his lap, his arm tight around her, his body still shaking with a fear that was unlike anything he had ever known. "Krista…" he whispered, pressing his lips against the top of her head. But still she seemed not to hear, just clung to his neck and pressed her face into his shoulder.

"You are safe," he murmured. "I am here now."

The battle was won, he saw, the raiders riding hard for the safety of the hills, some of the Ulfr men swinging up on their mounts to give chase. Leif slowed his horse to a prancing walk and rode back to the compound, reined up in front of the longhouse. The animal danced and snorted, his nostrils flaring, still smelling the blood of battle. Jamie Suthers raced forward, Alfinn clinging tightly to the young boy's neck. He grabbed the horse's reins and Leif slid down to the ground, cradling Krista in his arms.

"Is she all right?" Jamie asked worriedly.

"I think so."

The boy grinned. "She were something, weren't she, gov?"

An odd feeling rose in Leif's chest. "Aye, that she was, lad." And though he believed her unhurt, she was covered in blood and he had to be sure. His own clothing was equally bloody, he noticed as he carried her into the longhouse.

She finally began to stir from her trancelike state. "Did I…did I kill him?" she asked softly.

"Aye, love. You are not injured, are you?"

"No…I don't think so." She looked up at him. "Are they gone?"

He nodded. "They have run like the cowards they are, back into the hills."

She tilted her head to examine him. "You aren't hurt?"

The reminder of the awful chance she had taken and the terrible fear he had suffered began to stir his anger. "I am fine." He carried her into the bathing room and set her on her feet by the edge of the pool, keeping hold of her when she swayed a little. "By Odin, what were you thinking to risk your life that way?"

Some of the color rushed back into her cheeks. "He would have killed you. I couldn't just stand there and let him."

Angrier by the moment, Leif caught her shoulders. "You little fool, you know nothing of fighting. You are a woman. You could have been killed!"

"Your sister fought beside the men."

"My sister is as foolish as you."

Krista jerked out of his hold. "Why, you ungrateful—"

"I am not ungrateful. I will never forget the sight of you racing toward me, risking yourself to save me. I will never forget the wrenching fear I felt for you in that moment—or the pride that you are my woman."

Fresh tears welled in her eyes. "Oh, Leif, I was so frightened…so afraid you would be killed."

He wrapped her tightly in his arms. "Promise me you will never risk yourself that way again. Promise me."

Krista shook her head. "I cannot make such a vow. If your life were in danger, I would do the same again."

Something tightened inside him. Anger and fear and something far stronger all melded together in a blaze of heat and need. "Krista…my brave little Valkyrie." Bending his head, he claimed her mouth in a ravishing kiss. He kissed her until both of them were breathless, their hearts racing frantically.

He might have taken her there against the wall of the

bathing room if he hadn't looked down and seen the blood on her clothes. His own were also streaked crimson, and it reminded him of how close he had come to losing her. Easing a little away, he unfastened the tortoiseshell brooches on her shoulders and began to strip off her bloodstained garments.

"What…what are you doing?"

"You are covered in the blood of our enemies. You need to bathe, as do I."

She looked down at her plain woolen gown, saw the dark patches of blood, and a shudder moved through her. With determined efficiency, Leif stripped off the last of her garments, then his own, lifted her into his arms and carried her into the heated water.

Setting her on her feet in front of him, he used a scrap of linen to carefully bathe her, removing a smear of blood from her forehead, cleansing her hands. Tiny waves lapped at her breasts, and though he was already aroused, his rod grew even harder.

Little by little, she seemed to return to herself, the pain in her eyes beginning to fade. "You never told me about the berserkers."

Leif sighed, regretting the oversight. "They are outcasts and renegades." He used the rag, trailing water over her shoulders, letting it trickle down over her breasts. "Mostly they keep to themselves in the hills. But they are very dangerous men, as you saw this night."

He remembered the chance she had taken and how close he had come to losing her, and grew angry all over again. "I swear to you, Krista, if you ever dare to risk yourself that way, I will take my sword belt to your very pretty behind."

She tipped her head back and stared at him down her nose. "I do not believe you would beat me."

"I would do whatever it takes to protect you—even from

yourself. I warn you, Krista. You are mine and I will not see you harmed."

He caught the glint in her lovely green eyes and knew she meant to argue. Instead, he hauled her against him and crushed his mouth down over hers, kissing her as he had wanted to do all day, as he had ached to do since the moment he had swept her up in front of him out of danger. It was a burning, scorching kiss that said without a doubt she belonged to him.

She didn't fight him as he feared she would, just kissed him back with the same driving need that burned through him. Steam rose from the water as they came together, his rod pressing hotly against her, aching with the need to be inside her.

She had risked her life for him. If he had doubted the wisdom of bringing her here, if he had feared that he might have somehow been mistaken, he didn't now.

She was his and tonight he would claim her, as he should have done long before this.

Krista kissed Leif as she never had before. She could feel him in every pore of her body, feel the heat of his skin against her own, the strength in the powerful muscles of his arms and chest, the heavy weight of his shaft where it rose up hard and hot against her. Desire for him burned like a fire in her blood. Need scorched her feminine core, a need that had never been more powerful.

She had killed a man tonight. It was impossible to believe. She was a lady, a woman gently reared, a civilized young woman who should have fainted at the sight of so much blood. But none of that mattered, not in that moment when she'd realized she was going to lose the man she loved.

Because of what she had done, because of the chance she had taken, Leif was alive and safe, and Krista found it impossible to feel regret. As they stood there naked in the water, she clung to him, tipped her head back as his lips grazed the side of her neck. His big hands cupped her breasts and he gently pinched the tips, turning them diamond-hard, then bent his head and took the fullness into his mouth.

His palm slid over her skin, over the flat spot below her navel. He sifted through the thatch of pale hair at the juncture of her thighs, parted the soft flesh below and began to stroke her. Pleasure, deep and powerful, rose inside her.

For an instant she gave in to her relentless need of him, the love that threatened to overwhelm her. She had never wanted anything so much as to join her body with his, to know the pleasure he had shown her before. Never had she been more vulnerable, more tempted to agree to anything he might wish. Never had she wanted so much to become Leif's wife.

Instead, she pulled away. Casting him a regretful glance, she began to slosh through the water toward the rock steps leading out of the pool. Saying nothing, Leif followed. As she left the water, she reached down for a linen cloth to dry herself, but he took it from her hand.

"I will do it for you."

She didn't protest. She wanted to feel his hands on her, see the heat in his brilliant blue eyes as he ran the towel over her fevered skin. When he finished, he used a second cloth to dry himself, then pulled her into his arms and began to kiss her again.

Desire rolled through her, so strong she barely noticed when he lifted her into his arms and carried her out of the bathing room and into his bedchamber, over to his bed. Not until she felt the warmth of the furs beneath her bare skin did she begin to push him away.

"Please…I beg you, Leif. I cannot do this."

A muscle tightened along his jaw. "You ask me to stop and yet you desire me. Do you deny it?"

She trembled at his slightest touch and she refused to lie. "I cannot deny it, no. I want this as much as you do, but I cannot take the risk. I cannot be your wife, and so—"

"So will you continue to fight me—and yourself."

She felt the sting of tears. "I have to."

Resolve entered his features. "Then I will make this easy for you." Turning away, he crossed the room, returned with something in his hand, and began to kiss her again. She could feel his barely leashed desire and it stirred her own. Dear God, she wanted him so badly. Perhaps just this once…

She had almost convinced herself to give in to her powerful need for him when she felt the soft glide of fabric over her wrist. Her second wrist was secured before she truly realized what was happening.

"What…what are you doing?"

"I am giving you what we both know you want. I learned much in your country. We will see if you like what I learned from the books on lovemaking I found in your library."

Oh, dear God! "Leif, you can't just—"

"Aye, but I can." Using more soft strips of cloth, he bound her ankles to the wooden posts at the foot of the bed, spreading her wide for him. Her body was open, completely exposed, and a soft blush rose over her skin.

She should fight him, she knew. Or beg him to stop, if she had to. Perhaps he would. Perhaps he would simply take what he wanted. After the way she had encouraged him, she could hardly blame him.

But her will to fight was gone, swept away a little more with each of his burning kisses. In truth, she no longer wished to stop him. She wanted to feel him inside her, wanted to be filled with him, to know again the fiery pleasure he had given her before.

Surveying his handiwork, Leif stepped back from the bed. "So beautiful. Like a green-eyed, golden-haired goddess. Before I fill you, I will taste you. We will see if you like it as much as Miss Boots did."

Good Lord! Krista remembered the erotic book he had once mentioned, but had no idea what sort of things might be inside. A little shiver of excitement raced through her, one she knew she should not feel.

Pressing her down in the furs, Leif settled himself above her, his heavy weight propped on his elbows. Nestled between her thighs, he slid his hands into her hair and began to kiss her, gently at first, coaxing her lips apart, tasting the inside of her mouth. The heat of his body burned her skin. Her breasts tingled where his chest hair rubbed against her nipples, and Krista kissed him back, her will to resist completely gone.

Leif nibbled her ear, kissed and nipped her neck, then moved lower, began to suckle her breast. As he teased and sampled, laved her nipple and bit it, she fought not to beg him to take her.

Krista thought that surely he would, that if he wanted her half as much as she wanted him, he would not wait. But instead, he moved lower, trailing kisses over her rib cage, pausing for a moment at her navel, ringing the indentation with his tongue, sending goose bumps over her skin and a deep tug of heat into her belly.

He said he meant to taste her. She gasped as his mouth caressed her most womanly place and his tongue slid over the sensitive nub at her core.

"Leif! You can't…can't possibly…" But she never finished the sentence, and instead began to moan and lift her hips against his persuasive mouth. Pleasure rolled through her. Powerful sensations rocked every part of her body, and her muscles went as taut as bowstrings.

Release hit her hard and she cried out his name, her body shaking all over, pleasure swirling through her like clouds in a storm.

Her wrists were not tightly bound, she realized, and a single tug set her free. Leif moved above her, positioned himself and entered her with a single deep thrust. Krista moaned at a fresh wave of heat and wrapped her arms around his neck.

"You are mine," he said. "This you must see."

He kissed her and she kissed him back, and as they moved together, as he took her with deep, penetrating strokes that seemed to reach her very soul, she thought that perhaps he was right.

That she was the one who was wrong and that her destiny lay not in England but here on the island with Leif.

Twenty-Five

It was late afternoon on a brisk fall day, the wind whipping orange and yellow leaves along the London streets. In the fashionable Mayfair district, Coralee Whitmore's coach drew up in front of Krista's two-story brick town house, and a footman pulled open the carriage door.

"We're arrived, miss."

"So I see." She took the servant's gloved hand and let him help her down the iron stairs, then he followed her up the brick walkway to the door. The footman rapped the lion's-head knocker once, then again, and the carved wooden door swung open.

The butler, Giles, recognized her immediately, and his wrinkled face lit in a smile. "Miss Whitmore. A pleasure to see you. Please do come in."

"I was hoping I might speak to Professor Hart. Is there a chance he is in?"

The butler's bushy silver eyebrows drew together. "He is at home, miss. He has scarcely left the house since the day of Miss Krista's disappearance."

"I was afraid of that. Where is he?"

"In his study, miss. I'll let him know you are here." The butler started down the hall, his posture, as always, perfectly erect, and Coralee fell in behind him. Giles announced her arrival, and at the professor's invitation, she walked into the wood-paneled, book-lined room.

She had thought to find the professor at work behind his desk, as he was nearly every time she saw him. Instead, she was surprised to see him seated in a chair in front of the window, staring out into the garden, a woolen shawl draped over his lap. When he turned toward her, his face looked gaunt, his complexion pale, and she realized how much he had withdrawn into himself since her last visit. Mentally, she made a note to stop by and see him more often.

Pasting on a falsely cheerful smile, Corrie walked toward him. "Professor Hart, it is so good to see you!" He started to rise, but she waved her hand. "Do not trouble yourself. I just popped in for a moment."

"I'm glad you did. Why don't you sit down and I'll ring for some tea."

"I'm afraid I haven't that much time." She sat, though, in a chair just across from him, worried by the slump of his thin shoulders and the pallor of his face.

"I've been meaning to come down to the paper," he said, "but lately I haven't been feeling quite up to snuff."

No, he hadn't been himself at all since he had found the note from Leif Draugr explaining that he had taken Krista away with him to his North Sea island home.

Corrie reached over and clasped the older man's hand. "I know you are worried about her, Professor. But at least you know where she is."

"Do I? I have no idea where Draugr Island might be found, and neither does the rest of the world."

"Leif wouldn't have taken her with him if he didn't care for her greatly. The note said he intended to marry her. He will surely keep her safe."

The professor looked away, but not before Corrie caught the faint sheen of tears in his eyes. "It is all my fault. I should have known what would happen. The man is a Viking, after all. They have been capturing women for centuries. When he pressed for Krista's hand in marriage, I should have known—"

"There is no possible way you could have guessed. She refused his proposal and Leif seemed to accept that she wasn't going to wed him. Perhaps something changed that final night. Perhaps Krista went willingly."

The professor shook his head. "She would never do that, no matter how much she cared for him. Her life is here in London. There is no way she could be happy living such a primitive existence. She knew that, even if Leif refused to believe it."

Corrie rose from her chair and walked over to the window. Fallen leaves formed a thick mat of orange, yellow and red on the gravel pathways winding through the garden.

"Leif is a good man, Professor," she said. "If he weren't, Krista wouldn't have fallen in love with him."

"She never said anything, but I could see it happening. I should have done something. I shouldn't have let them spend so much time together."

Corrie returned to her chair. "Perhaps Leif will realize the mistake he made, and bring her home."

"Perhaps…" But it was clear the professor didn't believe it, that he never thought to see his beloved daughter again.

"I came for another reason besides just a visit," Corrie said, uncertain whether to trouble the poor man further, then thinking that perhaps giving him something to worry about besides his missing child might be good for him. "We are having some problems at *Heart to Heart*."

That caught his attention. "What sort of problems?"

"Well, to start, with Krista away there is no one to write the editorial column. Without it, our subscriptions have begun to fall, and yesterday one of the reformist leaders, a man name Feargus O'Conner, came to see me."

"I know Mr. O'Conner. He is quite outspoken in his support of the factory strikes and such."

"Actually, he came to see Krista, but settled for me in her stead. He came to implore *Heart to Heart* to continue printing articles like the ones we ran on Harding Textiles, the sort of pieces Krista wrote in support of reform."

"What did you tell him?"

"I said I would speak to you."

The professor shoved the woolen shawl off his lap and rose a bit unsteadily to his feet. "What do you propose we do? Surely you aren't thinking that I should write the editorials? I scarcely keep abreast of politics and I know even less about reform. Those were Krista's areas of expertise and I trusted her opinions in those matters."

"I know. I just…I thought that perhaps there was something we could do…until she returns."

But there was no way to know if she would ever return. Krista might already be married to Leif and stuck forever on his godforsaken island.

Since her disappearance, speculation had been rampant, everything from the possibility of murder, to her eloping with the mysterious and wealthy Scandinavian prince she had been seen with so often before she turned up missing.

That, of course, came closest to the truth. The version Corrie and Professor Hart had agreed upon was that Krista had gone to visit her sick aunt Abigail in the country, and there was no word yet when she would be able to return.

But Krista was the soul of *Heart to Heart,* and without her, keeping the magazine running was nearly impossible.

"Perhaps I could try writing the editorials," Corrie said reluctantly. "That is…if you would agree to help me."

His head came up, forcing him to look at her down the length of his prominent nose. "As I said, I know little of politics and reform."

"But you know a great many people. You could visit your gentlemen's club, ask a few questions, see how matters stand. And I could speak to some of the reform leaders, get their opinions on the various bills being put before Parliament."

"I don't know…"

"*Heart to Heart* needs you, Professor."

He let out a weary breath. "Well, I suppose we could give it a try."

Rising out of her chair, Corrie threw her arms around his neck and gave him a daughterly hug. "When Krista comes home, she is going to be ever so proud of you."

His narrow face lit up. "Do you really think she might come back?"

Corrie worked up a smile. "There is always a chance, Professor. Whatever happens, you must believe she is happy. And if that is so, then that is all you could wish for."

The older man nodded. He was sitting back down in his chair when a noise in the hall drew Corrie's attention. Only an instant passed before the study door burst open and a gray-haired man in his seventies stormed into the room. Corrie recognized him immediately as Krista's grandfather, the Earl of Hampton.

"All right, where is she? I demand to see my granddaughter this instant!"

The professor rose again from his chair. "Krista isn't here, my lord. I very much wish she were."

"What has happened to her?" The earl's glance sharpened, then turned shrewd. "Is there a chance the gossips have it right and she has eloped to Gretna Green? Tell me the truth, Paxton."

"I can't tell you where she is, my lord. Only that she is no longer here in London."

Corrie couldn't miss the hope burning in the earl's pale blue eyes. "What about the prince? I've heard the man was quite enamored of her."

The prince, Corrie thought. If Lord Hampton only knew.

For a moment, the professor seemed unable to speak. "As this is a family matter, I trust you will be discreet."

"Of course." The earl flicked an uncertain glance at Corrie.

"Miss Whitmore is my daughter's dearest friend and already apprised of the situation."

"Get to the point, man."

"Krista has been taken, my lord, abducted against her will."

"God's teeth, why haven't you called the authorities? We must find her, bring her back before her reputation is sullied beyond repair."

"There is no way to find her. The man who took her has sailed from the country. Unless he brings Krista home, there is nothing we can do."

"That is ridiculous. I am the Earl of Hampton, an extremely powerful man."

"I'm sorry, Thomas. I know how much you were counting on Krista to marry well and give you an heir."

His watery blue eyes narrowed in speculation. "If she has gone off with a man, there will likely be a child, sooner or later. We will simply force him to wed her. All is not yet lost."

"She may never return," the professor said sadly. "There is no way to know for sure."

The earl suddenly looked older than he had when he walked into the study. "I am not one to show my feelings," he said softly, "but Krista means a great deal to me. Whatever happens, Paxton, I hope you will keep me informed."

The professor simply nodded. As Lord Hampton left the study, he sank back down in his chair and lifted the shawl over his lap.

"Is there anything I can do, Professor?" Corrie asked.

"Pray for her," he said. "Pray for both of them."

Corrie knew that as worried for Krista as he was, the man was also concerned for Leif. He and the big Norseman had become good friends. Whatever happened, it wouldn't be easy for Krista or for Leif.

Corrie bade the professor farewell and left the study. She wasn't sure if he would help with the articles as he had promised, but she hoped he would. She already had her hands full writing the society column and trying to manage the gazette. If Krista didn't return soon, Corrie would have to hire someone to help her.

She sighed. If Krista didn't return soon, there probably wouldn't be a gazette.

Krista awoke to the sound of Leif moving around the bedchamber. It was morning. They had made love twice last night and again before dawn. Any thought of denying him was gone. She wanted him. Whatever else happened, she was tired of fighting the fierce attraction between them.

And yet when she thought of the finality of marriage, of the life she would be forced to live as Leif's wife, her insides tightened into a painful knot. Perhaps Leif sensed her thoughts, for he didn't bring up the subject of marriage, merely began to bundle up some of the furs on his bed, rolling a change of clothes up in the middle.

"Where are you going?" she asked as she watched him.

"Unless you are ready to wed with me, we are going up into the hills." When she made no reply, he continued in the same matter-of-fact tone. "You will need a change of clothes. My sister has brought you a fur-lined cloak to wear over your dress so that you will not be cold, and your boots are warmly lined."

"I don't understand. Why are we leaving?" Tossing back the fur she had slept beneath, she reached out to catch the soft woolen kirtle Leif tossed her.

"My people are not fools. They will know what happened here last night. Since you are not my wife, you are my concubine, and they will treat you as such."

Her face went pale. She hadn't thought of the consequences of last night, but Leif had. He tied a strip of rawhide around the bundle he had made, and turned to face her.

"Is that your wish, Krista? To be my whore instead of my wife?"

Her bottom lip trembled. "I don't…I don't know anymore." Her eyes filled with tears. "I need time, Leif."

He strode toward her, caught her hard against him. "Do not cry, my love. If time is what you need, then time is what you shall have." He eased her away from him. "Go now. Collect what you need for our journey."

She nodded, brushed away the tears on her cheeks. "Is it safe to leave here? What about the raiders?"

"The berserkers will take weeks to lick their wounds, and the Hjalmr will hear the tale of their defeat and stay away, mayhap until spring."

She turned a wistful glance toward the bathing room. "Is there time for me to bathe before we leave?"

Leif gave her a tender smile. "We will bathe at a pool in the hills. Go. I will find us something to eat on our journey."

She left him there and went back to her bedchamber, wondering if she would be sleeping in the room any longer or if she would be sleeping with Leif. She was his concubine now. *His whore.* And all of the villagers knew it.

The notion sat like a rock in her stomach.

Twenty-Six

Krista prepared for her journey with Leif into the hills. Whatever lay ahead, she refused to think of it. If she did, sadness would overwhelm her, and she refused to let that happen. Instead, she was determined to take these few days with Leif and enjoy them.

Riding shaggy brown island horses, they followed a winding trail leading into the rocky hills. When the trail narrowed, Leif rode ahead, showing her the way, pausing here and there so that she could enjoy the spectacular view of towering cliffs and crystal blue ocean below. By the time the sun shone directly overhead, they had reached his private spot high on the mountainside, protected by a wall of granite and warmed by a heated spring.

"We will spread our furs on the ground next to the pool and stay the night. Runa sent food and ale. First we will eat, and then I will show you a little more of my island."

They dined on cold mutton and frothy white curds of cheese. Krista would have traded it all for a bite of fruit or some leafy green vegetable. Still, she enjoyed Leif's company, enjoyed hearing tales of his boyhood and asking him questions about the island.

"Tell me about the Hjalmr," she said. "Who exactly are they?"

"In Norse, *Hjalmr* means *helmet*. It is the shape of the bay where they live. They are Vikings, people not much different than we are, just members of a different clan."

"How did they get here?"

"In the beginning, we were all one people. Many years ago there was a disagreement between the leaders and some of the families moved to the far side of the island. Over time, it was forgotten what the argument was about, but there remained two different clans."

"And they are raiders?"

A corner of Leif's mouth edged up. "Aye, but so are we. Mostly we raid each other's livestock. Occasionally, one of the men will steal a woman belonging to the other clan. It is more a game than a danger."

Her lips tightened. "The clans steal each other's women, just as you stole me."

He shrugged his powerful shoulders. "It is our way."

"It is not my way, Leif."

He didn't reply, just rose from the rock on which he had been sitting, collected the remaining food and set it aside for later. Reaching down, he caught her hand and urged her to her feet.

"Come. I will show you one of my favorite places."

Leading her farther up the mountain, he paused when they reached a sharp granite outcropping. Below, she could see foamy white waves crashing onto rocks just offshore. There were seals on the rocks, warming themselves in the weak autumn sun. Fascinated, she watched the animals diving for fish, so caught up she didn't realize Leif had moved behind her.

"Much is different here," he said softly against her ear. "Some things are better, some worse. Here the sky is clear, the breeze unscented by dirt and soot." He bent his head and kissed the nape of her neck. "And our clothes are more practical. You have discovered how well our women's garments are designed. None of your miserable corsets, no pet-ti-coats. Nothing underneath your clothes but your soft smooth body."

She shivered at the feel of his hands roaming over her breasts, moving down to her hips, stroking her bottom, sliding over her legs.

"All I need do is lift your kirtle and you are mine for the taking."

She gasped as he raised the hem of her woolen dress above her hips and moved closer, till she could feel his hard length pressing against her bottom. She started to turn into his arms, but Leif held her in place where she stood.

"I will take you this way, as a wolf claims its mate." And so she stood with her back to him and trembled as he reached between her thighs and began to stroke her. He nibbled the lobe of her ear and cupped a breast, lightly massaged the tip. All the while, his hand worked its magic, stroking gently, then more deeply, arousing her, making her wet and ready to accept him.

"Did...did you learn this from a book?" she asked breathlessly.

"I did not learn everything from a book." And then he nudged her legs apart and his heavy length probed for entrance. He eased her forward until her palms flattened on the rock in front of her and her hips rose into the air. Krista trembled as he grasped her waist, holding her steady and slid himself deeply inside. She could feel the weight of him, the rigid strength of his arousal, and pleasure seeped through her. Slowly he began to move, thrusting into her again and again.

Leif took her until her body was taut with need, took her until all she could think of was him and the pleasure he gave her. Until she begged him not to stop.

They reached the pinnacle together, Krista sobbing his name into the quiet of the mountains, Leif's deep groan echoing into the hills. He held her close as they spiraled down, and she felt his gentle kiss on her neck.

Lowering her kirtle back over her hips, he caught her hand, turned it over and kissed the palm, then led her back to the private spot where the heated water beckoned. They stripped off their clothes, climbed into the hot, steamy pool and leaned back against the warm rock wall.

As the water lapped at her breasts, Krista thought again of their lovemaking and remembered that once more he had spilled his seed outside her body.

"Does it…does it pain you to withdraw from me as you do when we make love?"

Leif's mouth faintly curved. "It would be more painful not to have you at all."

"You say you wish to marry me. Would it not suit your purpose to get me with child?"

"I do not want a child out of wedlock. I want my son to be born of the woman who is my wife." He raked a hand through his golden-blond hair. "There is a chance it could happen, but I have done my best to protect you."

Always, she thought, he had tried to protect her. She looked into his handsome face and felt a rush of love so poignant it was suddenly hard to breathe. In that instant, she realized she wanted to have Leif's son, wanted to give him children, a houseful of them.

For the first time, Krista realized the extent of the love she felt for him, that the thought of losing him was more painful than the thought of staying forever on Draugr Island.

That she loved him even more than her own life.

She fell silent as she sat in the heated pool, trying to absorb the knowledge, and Leif fell silent, as well. As the afternoon passed, they made love on the mat of furs, and afterward Leif napped beside her for a while. But Krista could not sleep.

She kept thinking of Leif and what it would truly mean to lose him—and the empty life she would live if she were without him.

Tired from a restless night of very little sleep, Krista dressed for the day ahead. Leif had promised to take her to a place where he and his clansmen practiced falconry. The birds were kept at Eirik's farmstead, and first they would travel there. Afterward, they would return to the mountains, and she thought that she would enjoy watching him work the beautiful, predatory birds Vikings used to hunt game.

She watched him now as they prepared to leave camp, Leif filling his satchel with food for the day's short journey, and her heart clenched with love for him. Something shifted inside her, and all of the restless hours she had spent thinking about him, trying to imagine a future without him, seemed to congeal into a single, crystal-clear thought.

A lump began to build in her throat. Leif must have seen something in her face, for he paused in his work and his eyes found hers.

"What is it, *honning?*"

Krista took a steadying breath. "There is something I wish to say, Leif. Something I have known in my heart for some time but was afraid to tell you. I knew it would only make things more difficult for both of us, and so I kept silent."

Leif dropped the satchel and strode toward her, his eyes still fixed on her face. He took hold of her hand and she tried not to tremble.

"Tell me what is wrong, love. Please do not cry."

She didn't know she was weeping until she blinked and

tears slipped down her cheeks. "I can't say it in Norse. I don't even know if there is a word for it in your language. I just want you to know that I love you, Leif. My heart overflows with love for you."

He pulled her into his arms and simply held her. She was surprised to feel a tremor move through his powerful body.

"I don't want to lose you," Krista said against his cheek. "Not ever." She took a shaky breath, determined to finish before her courage faltered. "If you still wish to wed me, then I will marry you."

Leif's hold tightened. She could feel the beat of his heart, the rhythm much faster than her own. "It is my greatest wish, my greatest desire, for you to become my wife."

Krista swallowed, tried not to cry, but more tears rolled down her cheeks. Her heart was aching, beating an odd, painful tattoo, and yet the thought of losing him was even more painful.

He reached up and wiped the moisture from her cheek. "This time is ours, as I have promised. On the morrow, we will go back and I will tell my uncle and the others the news. Three days hence, we will be wed by the priest."

Krista said nothing, just nodded and went back into his arms. *Everything is going to be all right,* she told herself. She would find a way to be happy, to make both of them happy.

All that mattered was being with Leif.

Leif didn't tell his uncle or any of the people in the settlement. He didn't know why, just that something held him back.

Krista had said that she loved him. *Elske* meant love in Norse. His father had loved his mother, but Viking men married more from desire for a woman and the need for a family than love, and Leif had never thought to feel the emotion himself.

But yesterday, when he had looked into Krista's beautiful face, when she had told him she would marry him, that for him she would give up all she held dear, in that moment he had known he loved her beyond all reason.

He had known that he would give his life for her, as she had very nearly given hers for him. He had known that her future happiness was more important than his own, and that although he loved her so much, he would not marry her.

He watched her this morning, seated at the loom in the weaving room at the back of the longhouse, watched her as he had for the past two days. She looked fragile, as she never had before, the inner light gone from her eyes. He had done that to her, destroyed something inside her by bringing her to his island.

He knew that now, knew that he had misunderstood the gods' will, and that she had never been meant to be his.

A terrible ache rose in his heart.

Across the room, Krista got up from her stool and walked toward him, took hold of his hand and raised it to her lips. "Something is wrong," she said. "I can see it in your eyes. Why have you not yet spoken to your uncle and the others? Why have you not spoken to the priest?"

"It is you I need speak to, my love. Come. There is something I must say."

She followed him out of the weaving room, still holding his hand. Her grip tightened a little as he led her across the compound, over to a spot in the sunshine.

"What is it?" She looked up at him, worried now, making his heart beat painfully inside him.

He fought for words, knew he could never find the right ones. "I have made a grave mistake and now I must find a way to right it."

Her worry seemed to heighten. "What...what are you talking about?"

"I was wrong to bring you here. This is not the place for you. I am taking you home."

She swayed a little on her feet. "You can't mean that. You said...you said you wanted to marry me."

He wanted to touch her, but he did not. "There is nothing on this earth I want more."

"Then—"

"Tell me I am wrong. Convince me that this is the place you wish to be, the life you wish to live."

"I want to be with you."

Leif shook his head. Inside his chest, his heart felt as if a dagger had severed it in two. "You were meant for more than this. You tried to tell me, but I would not listen. You tried to make me see, but I was blind to all but my own needs. You must go back, Krista. Before it is too late, before this life destroys you and you come to hate me for it."

"I could never hate you."

"I am not so sure." He reached out and cupped her cheek, and she leaned her face into his palm. "Your place is in England. You have work to do there, people who depend on you. You have known that from the start."

"Yes, but—"

"I have already spoken to Captain Twig and his men. On the morrow, we sail. By the end of the week, you will be back in your home."

Despair moved over her features. He could see pain in her eyes and knew it was there in his own.

"If I return, say you will stay there with me."

He only shook his head. "You know I cannot."

Tears filled her eyes. "I don't want to leave you."

"I have failed you once, my love. I will not fail you again." Bending his head, he very gently kissed her. He lingered a moment longer than he should have, absorbing the softness of her lips, feeling them tremble beneath his. Then he stepped away.

"I will sleep elsewhere this night. In the morning, we will leave." He turned and started walking, a thick lump swelling in his throat.

"Leif!" Krista called after him. "Leif, please!" But he only kept walking.

His decision was made. The truth was clear, as it always had been, if he had not been too blind to see. He would take her home, back to the life she was meant for. No matter the pain in his heart, he would not fail her again.

Krista cried herself to sleep. She dreamed of home and of her father, and in her dream she saw how happy he was to see her. Then she dreamed of Leif, watched him standing next to their small, blond-haired son, saw him beckoning for her to join them, and she raced across the meadow into his arms.

When Runa came to wake her, Krista was smiling, reaching out for Leif, but he was not there.

"My brother awaits you," Runa said. "You must prepare for your journey."

Krista took a deep breath and summoned the will to rise. Her legs felt leaden as she swung them to the side of the bed. "I don't want to go, Runa. I love him too much."

The girl reached out and took her hand. "My brother knows what is best. You must trust him in this."

Krista said no more. For weeks, she had begged Leif to take her home. Now that he was determined to do so, it was the last thing she wanted.

And yet, in a place deep in her heart, she knew, as Leif had come to know, that it was the right thing to do.

She let Runa help her dress in a simple brown woolen kirtle, fastening the ties on the shoulders with tortoiseshell brooches. Rolling another fresh kirtle into a bundle for the journey, she picked up her fur-lined cloak and followed the girl out of the sleeping chamber.

"The men have already gone down to the ship," Runa said. "They are loading food supplies and making sure the vessel is sound for the voyage. I will take you to join them."

Krista walked next to Runa as they made the brief journey along the valley and finally came to the dirt path leading down the slope to the sea. As soon as they left the protection of the mountains at the clifftop, the icy breeze hit her, whipping her cloak and tearing at her hair, tied at the back of her neck with a strip of woven cloth. Krista drew the cloak more tightly around her and continued down the path toward the bottom of the cliff.

The inlet was calm, the cove almost completely hidden by high rock walls. She could see the ship below, Leif working with the captain and his men, and her heart squeezed with love for him.

By the time she and Runa reached the beach, Leif was aboard the dingy, rowing the small boat back to shore. Krista saw that a small group had gathered to watch him depart, Leif's brothers Thor and Eirik, and his uncle Sigurd, among them.

As Leif jumped out of the dinghy and pulled the small boat onto the sand, Thor strode forward to help him. Krista was amazed to see that he had shaved off his thick dark beard, not nearly so skillfully as Leif had learned to do, leaving his handsome face nicked here and there, and a cut or two on his throat.

"I wish to go with you," Thor said. "I have thought on the matter very hard and I wish to see and learn, as you have done."

Leif studied Thor's newly shaved face. "England is a difficult place for foreigners, Brother."

"And yet you wished to return, even spoke to the council about it."

"I was wrong."

"Still, it is my desire to see this new world you have discovered."

Leif looked at Krista. "Do you think your father would teach my brother as he taught me?"

Knowing the professor would be eager for the chance to further his studies, she nodded. "I am sure he would."

"There is nothing for me here," Thor pressed. "I have no woman and, unlike you, no duty that requires me to remain."

Leif glanced away. "No. You are free to go. But this is your home, Thor. Are you sure you truly wish to leave?"

"I am sure."

"The *Sea Dragon* is well-built and seaworthy, not like the vessel we tried to sail before. If you are certain, I will take you."

Thor broke into a grin. Without his beard, he was amazingly handsome, Krista thought, dark where Leif was fair, but tall and masculine and powerfully built.

Sigurd strode forward just then, the wind tugging at his thick gray hair, and Krista saw that he carried a carved wooden box in his hands. "I have something I wish for you to take with you," he said to Leif.

"What is it?"

"Once you are returned to Eng-land, if you still have doubts about returning to Draugr, then I would have you open the box. If you do, you will know why I have given it to you."

"I have a duty, Uncle."

"Take the box," Sigurd said. "Open it only if your doubts remain."

Leif gave a curt nod. As the men prepared to row the dinghy back to the ship, Krista looked at Runa, who reached out and took hold of her.

"Farewell, Sister," Runa said. "I pray the gods will help you find the right path to follow."

Krista's eyes filled with tears. Impulsively, she reached over and hugged the slender, red-haired girl she had come to think of as a friend. "May the gods protect and guide you," she said, then turned and started walking toward the men.

Leif took her small bundle and helped her settle herself in the dinghy. When he looked into her eyes, she saw deep sadness, loss and regret—the same pain she felt. As he began to row the boat back to the *Sea Dragon,* her heart twisted.

It was time to leave. Krista wondered how she would survive when Leif left her in England and returned without her to his home.

Twenty-Seven

Coralee settled back against the velvet seat of the carriage. It was only Tuesday, but as she had done last night and any number of nights the week before, she had worked late at the gazette. Last week's issue of *Heart to Heart* had been distributed on Saturday. True to his word, Professor Hart had helped her put together an editorial in support of Chartist reform, a movement to amend the government to allow more people to vote.

It was a highly controversial and highly volatile notion, mostly unpopular with the upper classes, but she and the professor had advocated using only nonviolent measures to achieve the goal, and she was proud of the job they had done.

Still, with Krista gone, the work of running the magazine seemed endless, and as the coach rolled through the dark, quiet streets toward home, Corrie was exhausted. She had almost fallen asleep when she felt the jolt of the wheels coming to an unexpected halt. An instant later, the door of the carriage flew open and a man clothed entirely in black jerked her out of her seat.

"Let me go!" She struggled as he dragged her down the steps of the carriage, then shoved her against the side of the coach. He was a big man, thick shouldered, with a handkerchief tied over his nose and mouth. Frantically, she glanced around, looking for her coachman, then spotted him on the box with his hands in the air, her footman a few feet away, both of them held at gunpoint by a second assailant, this one mounted, wielding two heavy pistols.

"Wh-what do you want?" She was trembling and hoped he could not tell. There was only a small amount of money in her reticule, and she prayed it would be enough to satisfy both men.

"I want you to stop your damnable articles. Hart's daughter is gone. There's no need for you and that ridiculous female paper to continue interfering in matters that don't concern you." He was well-spoken, she realized, and yet, above the top of the handkerchief, the hard brown eyes that bored into hers had a ruthless quality she could not mistake.

"You don't have to fight someone else's battles, Miss Whitmore. If you try, you're going to get hurt."

"You can't threaten me."

He stepped closer, forcing her to stiffen her spine against the vehicle. "Next time, it won't be a threat. Heed my words, lady. Write your society column and stay out of politics." He said no more, just tipped his head toward the second man, swung up on his horse, and the two men rode away.

Corrie was trembling as her footman rushed forward. "Are you all right, miss?"

She nodded. "Just shaken up a bit." More than a bit, she silently admitted, trying to control her quaking limbs.

"Me and the coachy, we didn't know what to do, miss, what with pistols pointed at us and all."

"It's all right. You did the best you could. I'd like to go home now, Mr. Pots, if you please."

"O' course, miss," said the coachman.

She made her way up the iron stairs and sank back in the deep velvet seat. She wasn't quite sure what to do. If she told her father, or went to the police and he somehow found out, he would forbid her return to the gazette. And yet she couldn't simply let the matter drop.

Tomorrow, she decided, she would go and see the professor. He had hired an investigator before, and for a while, things had been quiet. Now, after a single article, trouble had arisen again.

Corrie released a worried breath. Sweet saints, she wished Krista was here to help her figure out what to do.

It was late afternoon by the time Coralee was finally able to escape her duties at *Heart to Heart* and head for the professor's town house. She had sent a note ahead, informing him she wished to see him, and he had replied that he looked forward to her arrival.

Now, as her carriage rolled to a halt in front of the two-story brick town house, Corrie hoped she was doing the right thing. Professor Hart had not been himself since Krista had left, and Corrie didn't want to upset him any further.

On the other hand, the magazine belonged to him as well as to Krista, and this sort of threat affected all of them greatly. Pulling her fur-trimmed cloak a little closer against the November chill and checking the ribbons holding her curls in place, Corrie hurried up the steps and rapped on the front door.

It was only a moment before Giles pulled it open. "Miss Whitmore, do come in!" He was smiling, as he hadn't been anytime lately, and she was instantly alert.

"What is it, Giles? What's happened?"

"It's Miss Krista. She is returned, miss. Less than an hour ago, she arrived here at the house."

Corrie gave a tiny yelp of glee. "Oh, Giles, that's marvelous! Where is she?"

"In the study, miss. I'll let them know you are here."

He left her for a moment and then returned, beckoning her to follow him down the hall. Grinning, Corrie pushed open the study door, then stopped abruptly at the sight of Leif Draugr in full Viking gear, a sort of belted tunic over loose-fitting breeches and fur-trimmed, soft leather boots that came nearly to his knees. He was standing next to Krista, who wore a smocklike blue woolen gown, her blond hair tied at the nape of her neck.

"Corrie!" Krista turned and raced toward her across the room, and the two of them hugged.

"I am so glad you are home!" Corrie said, never meaning anything more.

"It is good to be back. I've missed you all so much." But Corrie caught the shadows in her friend's green eyes and knew that something wasn't quite as it should be.

Finding out what was wrong would have to wait until they were alone. She flicked a glance at Leif, whose expression looked equally morose, then spotted a third man in the room. He was nearly as tall as Leif, dark-haired and unbelievably handsome, and also dressed in the manner of a Viking.

"This is Leif's brother Thor," Krista said. "He doesn't speak English yet, but my father has agreed to teach him."

Corrie managed a smile, a little unnerved by such a formidable male. "Tell him I am pleased to meet him."

Krista translated, and Thor gave a brief nod of his head.

Corrie fixed her attention on Leif. "So you and your brother will be staying in London?" she asked, hoping for Krista's sake it was true. She could see the love between them every time they looked at each other, and it caused an odd clutch in her heart.

"Leif is chieftain of his clan," Krista said softly. "He is leaving on the morrow and he won't be coming back."

"I see." And suddenly Corrie did see. She saw that Leif had returned Krista home even though it was not his wish, even though he had wanted more than anything to marry her. She saw that Krista, even though she was in love with Leif, would stay here in England because she belonged here and not on Draugr Island.

Corrie's heart ached for both of them.

The group talked for a while, a bit about what life was like on the island. Mostly, Krista was concerned about the gazette. Corrie filled her in on some of the things that had been happening, and in that moment it obviously dawned on Krista that Corrie was there at the house in the middle of a workday.

"Something has happened," she said, drilling Corrie with a glare. "Otherwise you wouldn't be here. What is it?"

Corrie nibbled her lip, hating to worry her friend so soon after her return. "You've just arrived home. In a few days we can talk, and perhaps then you will be—"

"Tell me, Coralee. Why did you come here to see my father?"

Corrie sighed. "A problem has come up and I was hoping the professor could help me."

Leif's piercing blue eyes locked on her face. "What kind of problem?" he asked.

"Last week the professor helped me write an editorial in support of recent reform efforts. It was the first such article written since Krista…left. We printed the piece in Saturday's edition of the gazette."

"And…?" Krista pressed.

"And last night my carriage was attacked."

The muscles in Leif's shoulders went taut. "You were not injured?"

"No, it was merely a warning. The man said that since Krista was gone, there was no need for me or the paper to meddle further in politics."

"Only one man?" Leif asked, taking a step in her direction. He was so big he made her feel even shorter than she usually did.

"There were two, actually, but only one of them spoke to me. He seemed to be the leader."

The professor got up from his chair. "We must send for the police immediately."

"I was rather hoping that we might be able to handle the matter in some other way," Corrie said. "The police are always so busy, and I really haven't much information to give them, at any rate." She didn't have to say more. Both Krista and her father knew how much Corrie's parents hated her involvement with the gazette. If they thought for an instant that she might be in danger…

"Perhaps you are right," the professor said. "Still, I want this man found and dealt with. I shall pen a note to Mr. Petersen. I want this matter put to an end once and for all." Making his way to his desk, he took pen in hand and set about scratching out a message.

Leif said something in Norse to his brother, who nodded. Then Leif fixed his attention on Krista. "I am not leaving as long as you might be in danger."

"There will always be people who disagree with what we print, Leif. It isn't necessary for you to stay."

"Not all who disagree with you are a threat. I am staying until we know more."

Corrie couldn't tell if Krista was relieved or disturbed that he would be staying. Perhaps a little of both…

"Father is sending word to Dolph Petersen," she said to Corrie. "We won't write any more editorials until Mr. Petersen has a chance to look into this. There is no sense taking unnecessary chances."

Corrie was relieved. "That seems reasonable to me."

"On the morrow, I shall return to work." Krista smiled, but there was an empty look in her eyes. "I imagine there is plenty for me to do."

"More than plenty," Corrie agreed, sensing her friend's need to do something—anything—to keep her mind off Leif. "I cannot begin to tell you how happy I am that you are home."

Leif spent the night at the town house, then escorted Krista and Corrie to work the following morning. Dressed once more as a gentleman, in dark gray trousers, a light-gray cashmere waistcoat and dark-blue velvet-collared frock coat, he wouldn't have looked out of place in the most elegant drawing room in London. But Krista would always remember him garbed as a Viking, truly the man he was.

And yet there was another, different side of him that appealed to her just as greatly: his sharp mind and thirst for knowledge, the desire to learn that had first driven him to English shores.

On the journey from Draugr, except when he spoke to Thor, he had conversed only in English, honing his skills, she imagined, for his brief stay in London. He'd spent a good deal of time with his brother, teaching him a few English words and instructing him in some basic customs and manners.

Now that they were in London, Thor had borrowed some of Leif's clothes and spent most of his time in the study with her father, immersed in the first of the many lessons he would need to learn. Like Leif, Thor had been amazed at the sights and sounds of the city and the way people lived here.

He seemed as fascinated as Leif had been, and nearly as determined to learn. Thor and her father had struck up an immediate friendship, and Krista thought there was every chance he would stay in England, as he seemed to wish to do.

As for Krista, she couldn't deny it felt good to be home. And *right* that she be here, no matter how much her heart ached to think that soon Leif would be leaving. She had made the right decision in returning. She knew it deep inside, and yet she would never forget him, never love another man as she loved him.

To bury the pain, she immersed herself in work, going to the office early and staying late into the evening. Leif escorted her and Coralee in the mornings, then returned to pick them up in the carriage each night. After the attack on Coralee's coach, he had decided to stay in the town house, though he could well afford a hotel. He had used only a portion of the money he had won in his gaming endeavors, leaving plenty to take care of him and his brother in excellent style.

Thor was living at the house, as well. Krista imagined once the danger was passed, her father would take him to Heartland to continue his studies, as he had done with Leif. Captain Twig and his small crew remained on Leif's payroll and were living aboard the *Sea Dragon* while they awaited the return sail to the island. Jamie and little Alfinn were rooming once more in the grooms' quarters above the stable. The sweet little monkey reminded her of Leif and all they had been through, and whenever she saw the tiny creature, she sank into hopeless despair.

Determined to keep up her spirits, she kept herself busy. As Coralee had said, there was a great deal to do at *Heart to Heart:* ledgers to review, supplies to be purchased and re-stocked, research to be undertaken for future articles. As the days slipped past and the gazette went to press, she grew more and more anxious to start penning her editorials. She held strong opinions and wanted to do as Feargus O'Conner had asked—continue the support of reform.

Three days after Krista's return, her grandfather arrived at the town house. He had been staying in London, she discovered, worried about her and what terrible fate might have befallen her. She had always believed he loved her, and when he greeted her with tears in his pale old eyes, she could see it was true.

"My dearest girl. I am so relieved that you are home."

"It is good to be back, Grandfather."

He hugged her once, briefly, then set her away from him. "The man who abducted you—I shall have him found, I promise you. I'll see him hang for what he has done!"

She only shook her head. "It wasn't that way, Grandfather. He meant for us to wed. He knew I...I cared for him. He thought he was doing the right thing."

The earl frowned, his bushy gray eyebrows drawing together. "If you care for him and he you, why do the two of you remain unmarried?"

She took a steadying breath, wishing she could avoid the painful subject. "The man lives in another country, a world far from England, and I can't live there with him. Soon he'll be returning and all contact will be over."

The earl seemed to ponder that and she could tell he was disturbed. "You've been compromised, girl. Your reputation has suffered greatly in the time you've been gone. Surely you realize that something must be done."

"I know you had plans for me, Grandfather. I am sorry I failed you."

A shrewd look came into his eyes. "The filly may have fled the barn, but there is always a path for her return."

Krista had no idea what his cryptic words meant, and she didn't really care. Once Leif was gone, she would focus on her work. Her reputation might be ruined, but she had never cared much for society, and that hadn't changed.

The earl left the house soon after their discussion, and Krista hadn't seen him since.

On Thursday, the gazette went to press once more without an editorial and Krista resolved right then that she wasn't going to let it happen again. She wasn't going to let someone—some coward who made threats from behind a mask—stop her from doing the job she had come home to do. She was giving up too much, sacrificing a life with Leif for her beliefs, and she wasn't going to do so for nothing.

When she informed Leif, her father and Coralee of her decision, her father and Corrie were worried. Leif was furious.

"I will not allow it!" he thundered. "I forbid you to put your life in danger!"

Krista only shook her head. "That might have worked on Draugr, Leif, but not here. Here I have a business to run. I have obligations and I won't continue to ignore them. You of all people should understand that."

"If I were your husband—"

"But you *aren't* my husband," she reminded him softly. And he never would be.

Leif turned away, stalking around the drawing room, one of his big hands tightening into a fist. In a burgundy coat and trousers, his snowy cravat perfectly tied, he looked magnificent—and every inch the gentlemen. But Krista wasn't fooled. She knew the man that lay beneath that civilized facade.

She was in love with him.

Though she no longer let her feelings show.

Although it had never been discussed, little by little they had withdrawn from each other. They barely spoke and never about anything personal. It was as if they were merely acquaintances, as if they had never made love, never talked of marriage. Though Leif refused to leave until any threat to her and Coralee had been resolved, Krista rarely saw him. She had no idea what he did when they were apart. She thought that perhaps he was digging around, trying to discover who might be behind this latest threat. Even when he was there in the town house, he kept mostly to himself.

Now, standing across the drawing room, he turned to face her. "Can you not at least wait until you hear from your investigator, Mr. Peter-sen?"

"No. We don't have any idea how long Mr. Petersen's efforts will take. Right now, Parliament is discussing the possibility of new legislation to further improve working conditions in factories and mines. I want to push strongly in support."

As, she had discovered, the *London Beacon* had been doing. They had rebuilt after the fire that had nearly destroyed them, and were pressing more strongly than ever for reform. A handful of other, smaller newspapers were also beginning to make their opinions known. Krista was determined that *Heart to Heart* would take an equally firm position.

She wrote the editorial and it came out in the Saturday edition of the paper. On Monday, Dolph Petersen arrived at the town house.

It was dark by the time the carriage had dropped Corrie off and arrived at Krista's home. As they pulled up in front, Leif, silent as usual, spotted a smaller conveyance parked ahead of them.

"Do you know whose carriage that is?"

"I'm not sure."

He walked her up the brick path to her door, determined to discover who was there.

"It is Mr. Petersen, miss," Giles told them. "He is in the study with your father. They asked if you would join them there as soon as you arrived."

She did so hurriedly, anxious to hear any news the detective might have unearthed, Leif following her progress down the hall. Mr. Peterson and her father stood as she entered the room; Petersen dark-haired and attractive in a rather brutal way, her father thin as always but looking a little less fragile than he had when she'd first returned home.

Krista sat down across from the men on the leather sofa in front of the hearth, and Leif took a seat a few feet away.

"Good evening, Mr. Petersen," she said.

"Miss Hart. Mr. Draugr."

"You are here with news?" she asked.

Petersen nodded. "As I was just telling your father, in the past few days I've managed to come up with several bits of interesting information."

"I should very much like to hear them."

Petersen turned all-business, sitting a little straighter in his chair. "To begin with, two weeks ago, Cutter Harding was found to be in breach of the Collieries Act and fined quite heavily. Rumor has it your articles set matters in motion, and Harding is quite furious about it."

Krista just smiled. "Indeed. Then I must be doing my job and I cannot help but feel pleased."

"The second matter concerns an old friend of yours, Lawrence Burton, the major shareholder of Consolidated Mining. If you recall, it was Mr. Burton's overseer, Harley Jacobs, who went to prison for arranging the assault on you and Mr. Draugr."

"I have hardly forgotten, Mr. Petersen."

"I'm sure you haven't. Now it seems Harley Jacobs has been running off at the mouth to some of his cellmates. He's saying the attack that night was Burton's doing, not his. He's been bragging about how well he fared in the matter, how well he and his family are being taken care of."

Krista leaned forward in her chair. "Are you saying that Harley Jacobs was merely a scapegoat who took the blame for Lawrence Burton in exchange for money?"

"I'm saying Burton, not his overseer, may have hired the men who attacked you and Draugr that night."

"I see."

"What about the threat Miss Whitmore received?" Leif asked.

"I haven't uncovered anything in that regard yet. The description of Miss Whitmore's assailant fits several different people. Until I've got more to go on, I'm not ready to make accusations."

Krista wished that Petersen had made more progress, but it had only been a matter of days. He answered whatever questions they had, then left the town house. As soon as he was gone, Leif turned to Krista and her father.

"I will speak to my brother, tell him this latest news and ask him to keep an eye out for trouble when I am not here." He paced away, his broad back rigid, then turned again, his gaze locked on her face. "Do you know how hard this is for me? Thinking you might be in danger but knowing that my presence here only makes this harder for us both?"

Her heart squeezed. "Leif..."

"Say you will be careful. Say you will not do anything foolish that might put you in even more danger."

"I'll be careful," she said softly, unable to look away from those worried blue eyes.

She would be careful—as she promised—but already she was thinking of the ball Coralee had mentioned, a lavish affair being given by a man named Miles Stoddard, head of one of London's most wealthy industrialist families. Gossip had it Stoddard was angling for a title for his eldest daughter and willing to spend any amount to secure one.

Corrie's family had been invited, of course, and though her father, Viscount Selkirk, had declined, Corrie's aunt, Lady Maybrook, had agreed to act as Corrie's chaperone. It was reputed the ball would be an outrageously expensive affair, one of the most extravagant parties of the year, and Corrie planned to write a feature about it for the society page of the gazette.

There was no way to know if Cutter Harding would be in attendance, but every chance Lawrence Burton would be there. It was well known that his wife, Cecilia, was extremely society conscious, always pushing to climb higher on the ladder of influence. She was years younger than her husband, an attractive woman Lawrence Burton doted upon. She enjoyed lavish parties, and of course, there were her two marriageable daughters to consider.

If Krista went with Corrie, perhaps she would have a chance to speak to Mr. Burton, get some clue as to whether he might be the man behind the threats being made against *Heart to Heart*.

"Krista…" She felt Leif's hands on her shoulders, forcing her attention back to him. "I do not like that look on your face."

Krista merely smiled. "Do not worry. I said I would be careful."

"Aye…that is what you *said*."

But Krista knew him well enough to know he wasn't convinced.

Twenty-Eight

—❧❧❧—

Light shone through every window of Miles Stoddard's huge stone mansion in the Shrewhaven district of London. It was one of the more recently developed areas, the houses here mostly owned by the newer wealthy elite. There were no dukes or earls in residence, and yet each of the brick or stone mansions was palatial, a testament, Krista thought angrily, to the money the owners earned off the backs of the poor working classes.

The thought was a bit unfair, she conceded. Over the centuries, there had always been misuses of power. That had only begun to change very recently, with the efforts at working class reform. Aside from that, many of the people who lived in Shrewhaven treated their employees no less fairly than anyone else.

Walking next to Corrie and her aunt, Lady Maybrook, Krista made her way up the wide stone steps to the ornately carved double front doors. She had waited until Leif went out for the evening, then dressed and left the house, leaving a brief note for her father, who was working with Thor in his study.

She shouldn't have come, she knew. Gossip about her had been rampant since the day she had disappeared, and now that she was returned, the rumors had grown tenfold. Even though her father, grandfather and Aunt Abby had all used their influence to put the matter to rest, she was fairly certain her reception tonight would not be golden.

Clamping down on a sudden bout of nerves, she pasted a smile on her face, lifted her chin and walked through the door, passing a pair of liveried footman along the way. In a gown of sapphire silk with an overskirt of silver-shot tulle, she couldn't help thinking of the simple gowns she had worn on Draugr Island. Tonight, above the sweeping neckline of the gown, the tops of her breasts were exposed, drawing the occasional glance of a well-dressed gentlemen, plus a few stray glances from gossipy matrons who, no doubt, wondered which of the tales about her were true.

Krista steeled herself. She had known what would happen when she came here tonight, but she was determined to seek out her adversary, should she be lucky enough to find him. She was back in London, gowned once more in a tight-fitting corset and petticoats, and she had a job to do.

As they walked across the majestic entry beneath a massive stained-glass dome, Corrie leaned closer. "Are you certain this is a good idea, Krista?"

"It is a dreadful idea. The gossips are having a field day speculating as to where I have been these past weeks, and as the publisher of *Heart to Heart,* I am already highly unpopular with a number of the guests."

"Well, we cannot leave now or it will only make matters worse." Corrie glanced around, seeing, as Krista did, a number of people staring in their direction.

"I have no intention of leaving," Krista said firmly, though her legs felt shaky beneath her skirt.

"What should I say if I am asked about your return?"

"Father and Grandfather are telling people I was staying with my aunt in the country. Aunt Abby fell ill, you see, but is now, thanks to my selfless efforts, back on her feet."

"That sounds credible."

"Perhaps. I think mostly no one wishes to incur the Earl of Hampton's wrath—or Aunt Abby's."

Corrie stifled a laugh. "She is a rather formidable creature, your aunt."

"As is yours," Krista said, casting a look at the regal, silver-haired matron. Lady Maybrook, not the least intimidated by people she referred to as "working class," led the girls into the ballroom and headed straight for the punch bowl. But instead of punch, both Krista and Corrie picked up glasses of champagne.

"To steady my nerves," Krista explained.

"Indeed," Corrie agreed, taking a rather large sip.

The ballroom had been decorated even more lavishly than the rest of the house, with thousands of candles in gilt candelabrum and huge sprays of fresh camellias and gardenias. An eight-piece orchestra liveried in bright blue satin played on a curtained stage at the end of the ballroom.

Sticking to the tale that her father and grandfather had created, Krista replied to inquiries about her recent sojourn to the country.

"It was completely unexpected," she said to Mrs. Clivesdale, the rotund mother of a wealthy railroad entrepreneur. "My aunt is usually quite robust."

"Is she here?" the woman asked, lifting her quizzing glass to peer down the length of her short, broad nose.

"I'm afraid not. Aunt Abby is still recovering, you see."

"Of course, I understand."

The woman understood nothing at all, which suited Krista perfectly.

The evening progressed, not quite as painfully as she had imagined, since several friends of her grandfather's were also in attendance. She recognized Lord and Lady Paisley, as well as the Earl and Countess of Elgin, all of whom were extremely loyal to her grandfather. Matthew Carlton's father, the Earl of Lisemore, was there, standing next to his son Phillip, Baron Argyll. Then she spotted Matthew.

With his light-brown hair and refined features, he was as attractive as ever, and she thought that her life would have been so much easier, so much less painful, if she could have fallen in love with him instead of Leif. He saw her in that moment and his head came up. Long strides carried him in her direction.

"Krista, you are home. Your grandfather told me. For a time, I did not think to see you again."

"Did you not? I have merely been away in the country. Aunt Abby became ill and I went to tend her."

"Yes…that is what the earl said."

"But you do not believe him."

"It doesn't matter. All that matters is that you are returned." There was something in his expression, a familiar interest she had thought long dead. He took her gloved hand and brought it to his lips. "I am hoping that in time, now that you are home, we will be able to renew our… friendship."

Surely he held no hope he might resume his courtship? He had known her feelings for Leif. Surely he had guessed that she had been with him these past weeks.

Before she had time to respond, Corrie returned from her brief conversation with a friend. "Good evening, Matthew."

"Miss Whitmore."

There was something in Corrie's face that put Krista on alert.

"I'm sorry to interrupt," Corrie said, casting her an urgent glance. "But I need to speak to Krista on a matter of some importance."

Krista turned to him. "I'm sorry, Matthew. If you will excuse us…"

He made a slight bow. "Of course."

Corrie tugged Krista a few feet away, over to the side of the ballroom. "We need to hurry!"

"Good heavens, Coralee, what on earth is going on?"

"I saw him, Krista! The man who waylaid my carriage, the one who threatened me!"

"Are you certain?"

"I saw him, I tell you. He is right here in the ballroom."

"How can you be sure it is he? You said he was wearing a mask."

"Not a mask, a handkerchief tied over his nose and mouth. I recognized his eyes. They are very distinct, you see. A hard, dark-brown, nearly black, and there is a ruthless quality in them that is impossible to mistake."

"That is all? You think you know his eyes?"

"There is also the matter of his build. The man is large, with very thick shoulders, just like the man I saw. But more important, I recognized his ring."

Krista frowned. "You never mentioned a ring."

"I didn't think of it, not at the time. Not until I saw it again tonight. It was a bloodred garnet inset with a pair of crossed sabers. It was very unique. I don't know how I could have forgotten."

"Where is this man now?"

Corrie took Krista's hand and led her toward the rear of the ballroom. "There, that man talking to Mr. Stoddard."

He was the man hosting the ball.

"Stoddard is as rich as Croesus!" Krista hissed. "Surely he wouldn't be hanging about with the sort of ruffian you describe."

"I tell you it is he!" She looked completely convinced, her green eyes wide, her small, finely formed features taut.

"All right, if you are that certain, we need to find out his name."

"Why don't we ask Matthew? He knows a lot of people. He'll probably know who it is."

Matthew stood not far away, in conversation with Diana Cormack and her husband, Viscount Wimby. Though Krista was reluctant to speak to Matthew again, if she asked Lady Maybrook it might arouse the woman's suspicions, and she didn't want that. Which left her no other choice.

They waited impatiently for Lord and Lady Wimby to walk away, then made their way toward Matthew.

"Sorry to bother you, Matthew," Corrie said, "but we were wondering if you might be able to help us. Do you happen to know who that rather large gentleman is? The one standing near the doors leading out to the terrace."

Tall as he was, Matthew could see over the heads of most of the people in the ballroom. "Standing beside the door, you say?"

"Yes."

"That man is Porter Burton. Why do you ask?"

Krista's eyes widened. "Is he related to Lawrence Burton of Consolidated Mining?"

"He's Burton's eldest son."

"Are you sure? He seems too old. Lawrence Burton has daughters half that man's age."

"Porter is Burton's son by his first wife, Maryann. She died in childbirth, and it was some years later before he remarried. You seem unduly interested. Why do you ask?"

Krista managed a smile. "No particular reason...

ust…Corrie is writing about the party and she is trying to cat-log a few of the guests in attendance."

Corrie smiled brightly. "For my article— Yes, that's right. Thank you, Matthew, ever so much."

They left him standing there staring after them, Krista tug-ing Corrie through the crowd, eager to speak to Porter Burton.

"It was Burton's own son who threatened me!" Corrie prac-tically hissed. "Of all the nerve!"

"Harley Jacobs said Burton was the man actually respon-sible for the assault on me and Leif. It seems it wasn't the fa-ther, but the son who paid the overseer to take the blame."

Corrie stopped in her tracks, jerking Krista to a halt. "You don't think he is also the man responsible for the fire at *Heart to Heart?*"

"I am thinking that he probably is. And perhaps he ordered the *London Beacon* destroyed, as well." Krista tugged her friend forward. "Come on. I want to talk to him."

Corrie dug in her heels. "That is what you are planning? Are you insane?"

"There are four hundred guests at this ball. I am perfectly safe and I want to hear what the man has to say." Krista ignored whatever reply Corrie made and simply kept walking. She had almost reached her destination when Porter Burton strode out through the French doors and disappeared onto the terrace.

"You can't go out there," Corrie whispered. "Your reputa-tion is already hanging by a thread, and besides, it might not be safe."

"The man is hardly going to attack me in front of all these people!"

"But—"

"Don't worry, I'll slip out another door so no one will see me." Krista took a steadying breath and stepped into the crush

of people, emerging a few minutes later out on the terrace. She
spotted Burton immediately, leaning against the wall, his features partly in shadow, partly lit by the flickering light of the
lanterns burning along the balustrade. He was elegantly
dressed, his clothes perfectly fitted to his large-boned frame
and yet somehow he did, indeed, look like the ruffian Coralee
believed him to be. He was smoking a cigar, the tip glowing
in the darkness. He tossed it away as she walked toward him.

"Good evening, Mr. Burton. My name is—"

"I know your name." He came away from the wall, his eyes
hidden in the darkness, and yet she could feel them burning
into her. "You're Krista Hart. I heard you'd left London. I'd
hoped we'd seen the last of you."

"You and your father would like that, wouldn't you? Unfortunately, I am returned and your threats and bullying won't
keep us from printing the truth."

"The truth? Or your opinion of the truth?"

"It doesn't matter. It is our right to print what we believe."

Far bigger than she, he took a step toward her. It surprised
her to feel a moment of trepidation, even here among so many
people.

"I don't care what you believe," he said, "you and the rest of
the bleeding hearts. You're going to stop printing all of your
drivel or suffer the consequences." His mouth curved in a ruthless smile. "The *Beacon* is barely hanging on. One more problem and they'll be out of business. Unless you want the same to
happen to your little magazine, you had better stop meddling."

"I'll go to the authorities. They'll have you arrested, just like
Harley Jacobs."

He straightened, no longer amused. "Try it and you'll only
look like a fool. You can spout your accusations, but you
haven't got a shred of proof. Jacobs won't talk and neither will

anyone else. It's only a matter of time until all of this nonsense comes to an end, and once it does, we'll still be running our business." He took another step toward her, forcing her to move back until a big potted cypress blocked her way.

"There's a lot of money involved in the mining business," he said, "and we aren't going to let you do-gooders keep us from getting our share."

She tried to edge away, but Burton stood in her path. "Let me pass," she stated.

He made no move, just kept those hard eyes fixed on her face and a half smile on his lips.

She heard a faint sound, then a big hand settled on Burton's shoulder. "Do as the lady says."

Krista wished she didn't feel so relieved to see Leif standing behind her opponent. Burton turned, seemed surprised to discover that Leif was even larger than he, and gave a brief nod of his head.

"Enjoy your evening." His voice held a hint of sarcasm that Krista ignored as she watched him stroll back toward the ballroom.

No such luck with Leif. She steeled herself against the fury she read in his face.

"How…how did you know I was here?"

"I heard about the ball tonight. And I know you well, lady."

Her cheeks colored at the memory of exactly how well he did know her.

"You promised to be careful," he continued. "If that is so, what are you doing here in your enemy's camp?" Dressed in elegant black evening clothes, his blond hair freshly trimmed and brushed till it glistened, he looked magnificent. The mysterious Scandinavian prince had returned and his presence would not go unnoticed.

Inwardly, Krista groaned. There was bound to be more gossip, more problems for her and her family.

"I hoped to speak to Lawrence Burton," she said. "Instead, I talked to his son. Coralee says Porter Burton is the man who threatened her."

Leif's whole body went tense. "*He* is the man you were talking to out here?"

She nodded and Leif swore in Norse. Turning away, he started striding toward the French doors, and Krista had to run to catch up with him.

"You mustn't confront him, Leif! Not here!"

He seemed to realize the trouble that would cause, and visibly clamped down on his temper. "How can I protect you if you continue to stir up trouble?"

"It isn't your job to protect me."

"No? If that is what you think, then you are wrong. I cannot leave England until I know you are safe."

She tried not to be pleased that he cared so much, tried to ignore the possessive look on his face. She reached up and gently cupped his cheek. "Then perhaps you will have to stay."

For a moment their eyes met and held. Leif caught her hand, drew it to his lips and kissed the palm. He said nothing. They both knew he could not.

"Will you tell the police about Porter Burton?" he asked.

"We don't have any proof, just Corrie's word that she recognized her assailant's eyes and his ring. I doubt that would hold up in court. I'll speak to Father and also to Mr. Petersen. Perhaps they will know what to do."

Leif glanced back toward the ballroom, where ladies gowned in silk and satin whirled to the music of a waltz in their escorts' arms. Krista wondered if he was thinking of Draugr Island and how different life was here.

"It is cold," he said. "Get your wrap. I am taking you home."

Krista shook her head. "This isn't Draugr, Leif. I can't possibly leave with you. I shouldn't even be out here alone with you."

A muscle tightened in his cheek. With a sigh of resignation, he nodded. "I will let you go back to Coralee and your friends. When you are ready to leave, I will follow you home in my carriage."

"I don't think you need to—"

He stopped her with a glare.

"All right, I'll plead a headache. Corrie will never forgive me, but that is beside the point. And at any rate, on the morrow, there is work I need to do."

Krista and her party left within the hour, Corrie's departure, as usual, grudging.

"I hate to leave," she said as they gathered their wraps and Lady Maybrook went to summon her carriage. "It is such a lovely party."

"Except for Porter Burton."

"Well, yes, except for Porter Burton."

But Burton *was* there, watching them as they left the house, and Krista was suddenly glad that Leif would be following them home.

"We'll bring in the law," the professor said, outraged.

"It won't do any good," Dolph Petersen argued. "Porter Burton is right—you don't have any proof."

"What about the ring?" Krista asked. They were seated in the study, Leif and her father in chairs across from her and Mr. Petersen. Since Thor was only beginning to learn English and this was a family matter, he was upstairs studying in his room. "Father says a pair of crossed sabers is the symbol for Consolidated Mining."

Petersen didn't look impressed. "It's not enough. All you have is Miss Whitmore's word against the son of one of the wealthiest men in England."

"Coralee is the daughter of a peer."

He shrugged his shoulders. "It's still just her word against his." He leaned back in his chair. "We can't involve the police—at least not yet—but there might be another way to stop Porter Burton from posing any more of a threat."

Leif sat a little straighter in his chair. "How?" he asked in that straightforward manner of his.

Krista hadn't seen him since the party. She tried not to wonder where he spent his time when they were not together. Perhaps he had returned to the gaming tables, though she didn't think so. He had never particularly liked the idea of making money off another man's vice, and had done so only to achieve his end.

"The police can't help us," the investigator continued, "but maybe someone else can."

"Go on," Leif urged.

"Porter Burton is Lawrence Burton's heir. His father keeps him in royal style, and once the elder Burton is dead, Porter will be hugely wealthy. Put pressure on the old man to stop his son's allowance and threaten to cut him out of the will, and Porter will have no choice but to fall in line. He'll be forced to stop his attacks."

"I'm afraid I don't understand," the professor said. "Why would the elder Burton agree to such a thing?"

"I have a very strong feeling the old man knows nothing about his son's nefarious activities," Petersen explained. "Lawrence Burton has a young wife he adores and two daughters who'll need to find husbands. If his son's activities came to light, it would be ruinous for all of them."

"It won't work," Leif said. "As you say, we have no proof."

"You don't need proof. You need someone powerful enough to force Burton senior to take action against his son—or at least threaten to do so. Miss Hart, your grandfather, the Earl of Hampton, is a man with that kind of power."

Krista pondered the investigator's words. Her grandfather was an extremely powerful man and, where his family was concerned, extremely protective. If she went to him and explained what they had discovered about Porter Burton, he would help her, she was sure.

"You are worth every farthing, Mr. Petersen," she declared.

He rose from his chair and smiled. "Let me know how it goes, will you?"

"Certainly."

Petersen left the house and the three of them discussed how they should proceed.

"I am the one who must speak to the earl," Krista said.

The professor nodded. "Lord Hampton adores you, even if he doesn't want you to know it. He has been extremely worried ever since you began to receive those threatening notes."

"He knew about the messages I received?"

"There is little the Earl of Hampton does not know."

Krista wondered if he knew about Leif and her journey to Draugr Island. A blush rose in her cheeks. Surely, after what she had told him after her return, he had guessed that she and her abductor had been lovers.

Still, he had done his best to help salvage her ruined reputation, and she was certain he would help her with this.

Twenty-Nine

Leif refused to let Krista travel to her grandfather's house alone, though he grudgingly agreed to wait for her in the carriage.

"After the ball and your talk with Burton, the danger to you is greater than ever before."

It was true, she knew, and so she gave only token resistance. The carriage pulled up in front of the earl's town mansion, a three-story Georgian residence at the edge of the city that had belonged to the family for more than a hundred years. A young blond footman helped Krista down the carriage steps and followed her to the door, then waited on the front porch for her to return. She could see Leif though the windows of the carriage, his jaw set, his eyes watchful.

Ignoring a sudden stab of pain that he would soon be gone, she made her way inside the house and was shown into one of the earl's elegant drawing rooms.

Her grandfather joined her there, seating himself on one end of the pale blue brocade sofa while she sat on the other.

"I am glad you have come, Granddaughter," he said. "I planned to call on you later in the week."

"You did?"

"There is a matter we need to discuss, but for now, tell me why you wished to see me."

Krista wasn't quite sure where to begin, so she started with the threatening letters she had received some months back and the fire at *Heart to Heart,* which he was already aware of. Then she told him about the assault on her Leif had thwarted, which he wasn't.

"These men are entirely disreputable," she said. "If it hadn't been for…my protector, I believe they would have forced themselves upon me."

A flush rose in his wrinkled cheeks. "You should have come to me! You're the granddaughter of the Earl of Hampton!"

"We hired an investigator, Grandfather, a man named Dolph Petersen."

He nodded, some of his temper receding. "Petersen. Good man. Couldn't have chosen better myself."

She went on to explain about Harley Jacobs, the man who'd pleaded guilty to hiring the brutes who assaulted them, an overseer at Consolidated Mining. "We thought the matter was ended. Then Coralee Whitmore was threatened at gunpoint on her way home from the gazette. We are certain the events are related."

"You said Jacobs is now in prison?"

"That is correct. But you see, as it turns out, Jacobs wasn't truly the villain." She went on to reveal how Porter Burton, son of wealthy mine owner Lawrence Burton, was actually responsible for hiring her attackers. "It is likely he set the fire at *Heart to Heart,* as well. He practically boasted that he destroyed the *London Beacon.*"

The earl leaned back against the sofa, propping his gnarled fingers over his chest. "So finally you have come to me for help. What is it, girl, that you wish me to do?"

She explained her reasoning to him, asking him if he would be willing to speak to the elder Burton, to use his power and influence to get the man to control his ruthless son.

The earl sat forward again. "I'm your grandfather. I will do whatever it takes to protect you. But there is something I want in return. It is the matter I was coming to discuss."

Wariness settled over her. "What is it?"

"In exchange for my protection, I want you to marry. I want you to wed Matthew Carlton."

"What!"

"Listen to me, Krista. Your reputation is in tatters. The only way to salvage what little remains is for you to marry, and you need to do it soon."

"But…but surely Matthew is no longer interested in wedding me. Why…why would he wish to marry a ruined woman?" But she kept seeing the look on Matthew's face when last she had spoken to him. Even with her tarnished reputation, he had made it clear he was interested.

"Why is not important. The fact is, I've already spoken to the man and he is willing to overlook your…*transgressions,* whatever they may be."

Her dowry. It was quite large, and no doubt her grandfather had promised a good deal more if Matthew would still agree to wed her.

"What say you, girl? With Matthew as your husband, you will be free to continue printing your gazette. I'll take care of Burton and his son and any other problems that might come up. There'll be no more threats, no more danger—on that you have my word."

Her insides tightened into a painful knot and Krista found it suddenly hard to breathe.

"You have always wanted a family," the earl added, speaking a little more gently. "That isn't going to happen now, not unless you heed my words and do what is necessary."

She bit her lip to keep it from trembling.

"Matthew is a fine man," he continued, "and he has always held feelings for you. I believe he will treat you well, and in time, perhaps you may even come to feel a certain amount of affection for him."

Perhaps she could. She would never love him. She could never love any man the way she loved Leif. But she and Matthew had been friends. Perhaps they could be again. And deep down, she knew her grandfather was right. If she didn't marry Matthew, she would be left a spinster. After the weeks she had shared with Leif, she knew how good it felt to be held by a man, to enjoy a man's company, to feel cared for and protected.

And there was the matter of children. She had always wanted a family. She would never have Leif's child, but she would have Matthew's children to love, the children they would share together.

Her heart twisted hard inside her. As soon as it was clear that she was no longer in danger, Leif would leave.

If she couldn't marry him, what did it matter whom she wed?

And there was her family to consider. Her grandfather needed an heir. It was her duty to provide one.

"I—I would need some time to… Some time before we…before we…"

"If you are worried about your duties in the marriage bed, Matthew has agreed to give you whatever time you need before he claims his husbandly rights."

Krista swallowed. She would need as much time as he would grant her to get used to the idea of sharing her body with a man besides Leif.

She looked into the earl's dear, wrinkled face and the lump

in her throat became a thick knot of tears. "If Matthew still wishes to wed me, I will agree."

Relief and pleasure glinted in the old man's cloudy blue eyes. "You're a good girl, Krista. You always have been. On the morrow, I shall speak to Burton Lawrence. Once the matter of his son is dealt with, you and Matthew can be married by special license. We'll have the wedding right here at Hampton House, just a few close friends and family. I'll send word to your aunt Abby. The two of us will take care of everything."

Krista rose a bit shakily from the sofa and the earl rose, as well. "You will let me know what happens with Burton?"

"You may expect to see me no later than day after the morrow." His jaw hardened in a manner she had rarely seen, and Krista thought that even in his declining years, the Earl of Hampton was an extremely formidable man. "Rest assured, by the time I am finished, Porter Burton will no longer be a danger to you or anyone else."

Krista made no reply. She believed him, utterly and completely.

She started walking on legs that felt wooden. Leif waited for her in the carriage, and seeing him, knowing she would soon be forced to marry another man, sent a sharp jolt of pain into her heart.

She said nothing of her decision on the way back to the town house, merely told him her grandfather had agreed to help and she firmly believed that in a day, two at most, the matter would be put to an end.

Leif turned away from her to stare out the window. "The weather worsens each day. Captain Twig worries for our safety, should we postpone our voyage much longer."

She knew little of sailing, but she had been concerned about the weather, as well.

"As soon as word comes from your grandfather and I am satisfied you will be safe, the *Sea Dragon* will prepare to leave."

She wanted to beg him to stay. Wanted to tell him that if he left, she would never be the same, never again know the kind of happiness she had with him. But asking him to stay wouldn't be any more fair to Leif than staying on Draugr had been to her.

On the short ride home, Krista kept silent, saying nothing of her upcoming marriage.

Unwilling to say the words that would sever their relationship forever.

As promised, two days later, the Earl of Hampton arrived at the town house. Leif had gone out to check on his ship and crew, but Thor remained, a man capable of handling whatever threat might arise. Krista led her father and grandfather into the study, where the earl related the news of his meeting with Lawrence Burton and the subsequent encounter between Burton and his son, at which the earl had also been present.

"Petersen, as usual, was correct," her grandfather said. "The elder Burton knew nothing of his son's criminal activities, and he was positively livid. He was terrified to think what his wife would do should she and their daughters lose their coveted social position and become pariahs in society. When he spoke to his son, he told the man in no uncertain terms that if there was a single incident against any of the reform papers—whether Porter was responsible or not—his funds would be permanently cut off. He would be chopped from the will as if he had never existed, and banished forever from the family."

"Good heavens," Krista exclaimed.

"Well done!" said the professor.

Her grandfather smiled, his pale eyes crinkling at the corners. "It is over, my dear. You and your friends—and your blasted ladies' gazette—are out of harm's way. Porter Burton has been banished to the country where, I imagine, at least for some time, he will remain."

Krista rose from her chair, walked over and kissed the old man's wrinkled cheek. "Thank you, Grandfather."

"You are the granddaughter of an earl. Never forget that. The next time you need help, come to me."

"I will, I promise. Thank you."

"Now on to a more pleasant topic—the matter of your upcoming nuptials."

Krista had told her father the news, and though he was saddened that the man could not be Leif, he had always liked Matthew and was delighted at the prospect of having him for a son-in-law.

"I've spoken to the vicar and also your aunt Abby," the earl announced. "The wedding is scheduled to take place a week from this Saturday at Hampton House. I thought we might use the conservatory, since it is too cold out in the garden."

She nodded, feeling strangely light-headed. None of this seemed real and yet she knew that it was, that soon she would be a married woman.

"Perhaps…" She swallowed. "Perhaps Matthew and I should speak. It seems strange to wed a man I haven't spent time with in weeks."

Her grandfather reached over and took her hand. "You and your husband will have plenty of time to know each other after you are wed. Until then, why don't you ask your friend Miss Whitmore to help you choose a wedding gown and whatever else you might need for your trousseau?"

Dear God, she hadn't even considered a wedding dress.

Even as she imagined the sort of gown she might wear, an image of Leif appeared, so tall and handsome, standing next to her in the spot that belonged to the groom.

She swallowed again, the lump in her throat growing bigger. It wasn't going to happen. "I'll speak to Coralee. And thank you again, Grandfather, for everything you have done."

Krista had to resign herself to the life that stretched ahead of her, and get on with it.

Thirty

❧❧❧

It was time for Leif to leave. On the morrow, he would sail from England, back to his island home. Krista's heart felt frozen inside her chest.

Though she had risen early, she hadn't seen Leif that morning. At first she had been terrified that he had decided to slip away without saying goodbye. But her father assured her he had only gone down to his ship to see to last minute preparations for departure, and that he meant to return.

It was a workday. Krista needed to keep busy, distract her mind and heart from painful thoughts of Leif. She was working behind her desk when he appeared in the doorway, striding into *Heart to Heart* just after luncheon, tall and blond and incredibly handsome. Her heart lifted at the sight of him.

She rose as he walked toward her, reached out and caught both of her hands.

"I could not stop thinking of you," he said. His eyes, that brilliant shade of blue, were filled with such sadness a lump rose in her throat.

"I am so very glad you came."

"I know you have work to do. I thought... I wondered if

mayhap… If perhaps there is something I could do to help." For an instant he had slipped into Norse, which happened only rarely, and she realized he was hurting as badly as she. She wanted to lead him off somewhere so that they could be alone, take him to a place where she could lie in his arms one last time.

But she would soon be married. It wouldn't be fair to any of them.

She managed a smile. "I imagine I could find something for you to do."

Leif smiled in return. He wanted to be with her this final day and she wanted more than anything to be with him.

She put him to work sorting and carrying stacks of freshly printed magazines, a job that came easily for a man of his strength. They worked together all day, their eyes constantly seeking and finding each other, speaking the words neither of them dared to say.

She was tired by the end of the day and yet she didn't want to leave, didn't want these last few precious hours to end.

One by one, the staff departed, until only Coralee remained.

"I may as well go home, too," Corrie said, and Krista could read the sympathy in her friend's green eyes. Corrie turned to Leif. "I am sorry things worked out the way they did, Leif. I will say a prayer for your safe journey home."

"Thank you," he said, with a faint inclination of his head.

Corrie left and the building was empty except for the two of them. Krista lingered, desperate for this last bit of time with him.

"There is a book Father needs from upstairs," she said before he could announce it was time for them to leave. "It is on the desk in his study. I'll just go up and get it."

"I will go," he said. "What is the name of the book?"

"*The Saga of Grettir the Strong,* I believe he said."

Leif nodded. His gaze held hers for several long moments before he turned and headed up the stairs. He had just disappeared from sight when she heard glass breaking in the door at the rear of the office, then footsteps on the wooden floor in the back room.

A chill went down her spine. *Dear God!* She started to shout for Leif, but the cocking of a pistol, pointed in her direction, froze her where she stood.

"I'd keep my mouth shut if I were you." The intruder hadn't bothered donning a mask. Dressed completely in black, Porter Burton looked even more threatening than he had the night she had confronted him at the Stoddards' ball. She prayed Leif would hear them talking and realize the danger.

"What are you doing here?" she said loudly. "Get out immediately!"

His lips twisted into the ruthless half smile she remembered from their encounter on the terrace. "Did you really think my old man was going to frighten me into doing his bidding? *I* run Consolidated Mining, not my spineless, social-climbing father. Lawrence Burton is nothing but a puppet, a front man. There was a time he was in charge, but the fact is, things have changed. I'm the one running the company now. Without me, Consolidated Mining is nothing, and no one knows it better than he does."

Krista steeled herself against those cold dark eyes. "If you don't leave immediately, I'm going to summon the police. I'll press charges against you—and it won't just be my friend's word against yours, it will be my word, as well."

"Is that so?" He turned slightly, called out over his shoulder, "Reynolds, Higgins, get in here!"

Two men stepped out of the back room. Krista remembered Corrie's somewhat sketchy description of the other man who had accosted her carriage on her way home from work—a lean man with a scar on his chin. She saw him now as he walked into the room. Leif hadn't yet returned downstairs, and she prayed that meant he had heard her arguing with Burton, and realized there was trouble.

"Hop to it, boys," Burton ordered his henchmen. "Let's get this done and get out of here."

Krista's eyes widened as the two men picked up cans of lamp oil they had carried into the room, and began to spill the liquid around the perimeter.

"Stop this at once!"

"I didn't think you would be here, but I'm glad you are. It saves me a whole lot of trouble."

"Wh-what do you mean?"

Burton smiled, and she fought to control a shiver.

"Terrible about the fire at *Heart to Heart*," he said with a sad shake of his head. "Too bad the owner got caught in the blaze."

"You're insane!"

"Not in the least. I'm a businessman, Miss Hart. Your articles are stirring up trouble with my employees and that is costing me money."

Krista didn't know if he was crazy or just ruthless and greedy. Whatever the truth, he meant for her to die, and she wasn't about to let that happen. Turning, she bolted across the room, but Porter Burton caught her before she could reach the door. He dragged her back toward the rear of the printing room, past the big Stanhope press, and slammed her down in the wooden chair next to Coralee's desk.

"Reynolds—get some of that twine they use to tie the bundles," Burton called to the man with the scar and the narrow-set eyes of a predator.

Reynolds disappeared into the back room. Long seconds passed, but the man didn't reappear.

"See what's keeping him," Burton commanded the second man, and he, too, disappeared through the door.

Krista held her breath, praying Leif had gone down the back stairs to lie in wait for the men. But if he had, he might be in danger. A faint, muffled noise drifted into the printing room, then all fell silent again.

The clock ticking on the wall sounded like a bass drum. Krista's heart pounded nearly as loudly, her nerves strung taut as she perched on the edge of the chair, waiting for a chance to escape.

Burton's hard eyes swung away from the rear of the building and bored into her. Krista gasped as he jerked her out of the chair and his thick arm tightened around her neck. The cold metal of the pistol barrel pressed against the side of her head.

"I take it your *friend* is here with you," he said, clearly remembering how Leif had appeared out of the darkness to protect her the night of the ball. "You may as well come out!" he shouted. "If you don't, I'm going to pull the trigger and your lady friend is going to be very dead."

"Leif, don't do it!" she cried.

"Shut up!" Burton tightened his hold around her neck until she was gasping for breath and clawing at his arm in an effort to free herself. Her assailant eased his hold, but only a little.

"It's your choice, my friend." He cocked the pistol, and Krista's heart thundered. She bit back a sob as Leif stepped out of the back room, making himself an easy target for Porter Burton.

"Raise your hands," Burton commanded, and Leif slowly lifted his arms. "Get over here with your woman."

But Leif was already moving, his mouth set in a grim, determined line. Krista recognized that expression. It was the same one he had worn the night he had fought Burton's henchmen, severing one of the men's fingers with his sword. The expression he had worn on Draugr when the berserkers attacked.

Leif had been in a killing rage that night.

For an instant, she felt sorry for Porter Burton.

"Stop right where you are," her captor commanded.

Leif stopped, but his hard eyes remained on Burton's face. "Let her go. Before I have to kill you."

The man laughed, a deep, grating sound. "I hate to point this out, but I'm the one holding the pistol."

"Let her go," Leif repeated, and the words, so quietly spoken, had a deadly ring that seemed to make even a ruthless man like Porter Burton wary.

"What did you do to my men?"

"I didn't kill them. But I am going to kill you if you do not let her go."

Burton took a step backward, hauling Krista with him. A wastebasket sat at the edge of the typesetter's desk, and one of his legs clipped it as he moved past. He stumbled, and Krista saw her chance. Kicking backward with all her strength, she shoved his gun arm upward, pushing the pistol away from her head. At the same instant, Leif swept in like a Valhalla wind, pulling out the knife he carried in his boot so quickly she almost didn't catch the motion.

Burton fired his pistol at the same instant Leif's knife buried itself in her captor's heart.

Krista screamed as the man fell backward away from her and crumpled in a heap on the floor. A pool of blood spread across his chest and his eyes stared sightlessly upward. She was trembling, swaying unsteadily on her feet when she saw Leif striding toward her. He hauled her into his arms, cupped the back of her head and pressed her cheek into his shoulder. Krista clung to him, shaking all over, her eyes filled with tears.

Leif's hold tightened. "He will trouble you no more. It is over, *honning*. Now you will be safe."

She swallowed. Sliding her arms around his neck, she simply held on to him. For long moments, they just stood there. Finally, the tremors running through her body began to ease.

Krista took a steadying breath and drew a little away. "What…what about the other two men?"

"They are…resting. Your carriage is parked at the end of the street. I will tie the men up and send the coachman to bring the police."

She went back into his arms for a last brief hug, then let him go. Porter Burton was dead. There would be questions—lots of them. The Burtons were a powerful, wealthy family. But the lamp oil spread around the office and Burton's attack on her tonight would make what had happened perfectly clear. And with three men against one, Leif's actions would be deemed self-defense, which meant he would be exonerated completely.

It was over at last.

Krista's heart sank.

At last Leif could go home.

It was late when they got back to the town house. A constable had arrived at the office with a half-dozen policemen. They had spent a good deal of time asking questions, as she had known they would. The authorities had to be certain, beyond doubt, of the truth of what had happened at *Heart to Heart.*

Krista had sent a message to her father so that he would not worry, but though it was well after midnight when they arrived, he and Thor were waiting when she and Leif walked in.

Her father hurried toward her and Krista went into his arms.

"My dear girl. I am so very sorry. Your grandfather and I had been so certain…" He held her out to look at her. "Are you sure you're all right?"

"I'm all right, Father." She clamped down on a shiver and tried not to think of Porter Burton and how close she had come to dying. "Leif was there and…and… It is over, Father. It was Porter Burton all along."

The professor ran a hand through his graying hair and released a weary breath. "And now he is dead. The wages of sin, I suppose."

Leif's brother came forward just then, big and dark, and even in civilized clothing clearly a man to be feared.

"And you, Brother?" Thor asked in Norse, his handsome face lined with worry.

"I am well," Leif said. "And my friends' enemies are vanquished."

"The police cleared Leif of any possible charges," Krista told them, "since it was obviously self-defense." She went on to briefly explain that it was Porter Burton who actually ran Consolidated Mining. She told them what he had planned to do that night, and how they had stopped him and his two hired henchmen.

"You were both very brave," the professor said, squeezing Krista's hand. He looked over at Leif. "So much has happened. Perhaps you will wish to postpone your journey for a day or two, give yourself a chance to recover from all of this."

Leif just shook his head. "Now that Krista is safe, it is time for me to leave." He spoke to Thor. "Are you certain, Brother, that you wish to stay in England?"

"You were right, Leif. There is much to learn in this new world. The professor has been teaching me and soon we will leave for Heart-land, where he has offered to teach me much more."

Leif gave a faint nod. "Then so be it. Mayhap one day our paths will cross again."

Thor reached out and caught his brother's arm. "Are you certain of this path you have chosen, Leif? It is clear you have deep feelings for Krista. Are you certain your destiny lies in Draugr and not here?"

Tears burned Krista's eyes. She found herself praying that Leif would change his mind, that he would stay in England and they could be together, but in her heart she knew that he would not.

He only shook his head. "I have a duty to our people. I made a vow to Father and I will not break it."

The professor touched Krista's cheek as if he knew her thoughts, knew how badly she wanted Leif to remain, knew that it took all her willpower not to throw herself into his arms and beg him to stay.

"The hour grows late and Leif will have to be up early," the professor said. "I suggest we all retire and try to get some sleep."

Krista looked up at Leif and found his incredible blue eyes on her face. The time had come. Ignoring the lump of tears in her throat, she merely nodded, turned and began to climb the stairs. As the group reached the top, her father and Thor continued down the hall to their bedrooms, but Krista paused and turned to Leif.

"Will I see you in the morning before you leave?"

"I will be gone before sunup. It is best we say our farewells now."

"Yes… I—I suppose that would be best." But she didn't want to say goodbye. She didn't want to lose him, now or ever. Krista made no move to leave and neither did Leif.

"I will never forget you," she said, the ache in her throat so painful she could barely speak. "I will never love another man the way I love you. No matter what happens, no matter what the future might bring, you will always be the husband of my heart."

His gaze grew fierce. "You are mine. It has always been so and always will be." Gently, he cupped her face in his hands and very softly kissed her. It was the first time he had touched her so intimately since they had returned to England, and Krista's eyes welled with tears. For an instant she kissed him back, melting against him, sliding her arms around his neck. She was trembling, aching inside. She felt as if she was dying— and that if she were, she would welcome it.

She kissed him and kissed him and could not seem to stop. It took every ounce of her willpower to let him pull away.

"I am leaving and you must stay," he said to her softly. "If we do not stop now, I will take you, as I ache to do."

She reached out and touched his cheek, realizing that was exactly what she wanted. For an instant she thought of Matthew, but she owed him nothing—not yet. It was a marriage of convenience, a matter of money and gaining an heir, and he had agreed to wait to claim his husbandly rights until she was ready.

She would do her duty, be a good wife to Matthew. But if she couldn't have the man she loved, at least she could have these last few precious hours with him.

"I want you to make love to me. I have never wanted anything so badly."

But he only shook his head. "This I cannot do." Bending toward her, he gently kissed her one last time. "Have a good life, Krista Hart."

Then he turned and started walking, went into his room without looking back and quietly closed the door.

Krista leaned against the wall for support. On legs that felt wooden, she moved down the hall, entered her own room and closed the door.

Her maid had retired for the night and Krista did not wake her. Instead, she managed to remove her bloodstained day dress, wash her face and pull on a fresh cotton nightrail. She unpinned the thick blond curls that rested on her shoulders, sat down on the bench in front of her mirror and pulled the silver-backed brush through her hair.

Tonight was the last time she would ever see Leif.

He wanted her, she knew. Just as she wanted him.

If she went to him, would he refuse her?

He was a strong man, and principled, and he would worry he might leave her with child. But if he did, she would rejoice, be grateful for the part of him that he had left behind.

Krista rested the hairbrush on the dresser and rose from the bench. Ignoring the cold wooden floors, she walked to the door, pulled it open and stepped out into the hall. It was windy outside and she could hear the rustle of branches against the windowpanes. If the weather held, tomorrow would be a good day for sailing.

Her heart ached dully. Krista opened Leif's door and prayed he would not send her away.

Leif stripped off his clothes, noticing the rusty stains on his coat and waistcoat that reminded him of his encounter with Porter Burton this night. His hands unconsciously fisted. Burton had meant to harm Krista. If Leif hadn't been there—

He shoved the thought away. It was over. Krista was safe. He had to believe that. If he didn't he would not be able to leave.

The clock on the mantel chimed. It was two in the morning and yet he had no wish to sleep. In a few hours he would leave for the docks and prepare to sail just after dawn. He pulled on a clean pair of trousers, set out his boots and a clean shirt to put on before he left, then went about packing the tunic, breeches and fur-lined Viking footwear he had worn on his arrival. He would leave the rest of his English clothes behind for Thor. Leif no longer had a use for them.

He wondered if he would return one day for a visit, if the elders would even permit it. He told himself it wasn't Krista he already yearned to see, that it wasn't the woman he loved who called to him even now, before he had left her here on these foreign shores. In his mind's eye, he could see her in the simple white nightgown she had worn the night he had stolen her from this house, the night he had claimed her as the woman he would wed.

He looked up just then and it was as if his memory had come to life, as if the creature walking toward him in her simple white nightgown, her golden curls floating around her shoulders, had stepped out of his dream.

But this creature was real. A flesh-and-blood woman come to him as he had longed for her to do.

"Krista…"

"I had to come, Leif. Please don't send me away."

He walked toward her, drew her into his arms, held her against his heart. "I could not send you away. I no longer have the will."

She looked up at him and the love in her eyes made his chest ache.

"Make love to me," she said.

He knew he shouldn't, that as careful as he always was, a child might result. "What will you do if there is a babe?"

"I will love it. Just as I love you."

He couldn't deny her; he would do anything for her. And he could no longer deny himself. Capturing her face, he kissed her deeply, kissed her with all the feelings he held for her.

"I never thought to love you," he said gruffly. "I wanted you. I thought that would be enough."

But it wasn't enough, he now knew. He wanted her heart as well as her body.

"We only have this one night," she said. "Somehow it will have to be enough."

He tipped her chin up with his fingers. "One night will never be enough, but I will try to make it so." And then he kissed her again, and his tongue found its way into her mouth and hers into his. Her hands ran over his naked chest and she pressed her soft body against the hardness of his own.

Leif kissed her thoroughly and fiercely, then pulled the string at the neck of her nightgown and slid it off her smooth, pale shoulders. He eased the fabric down over her breasts, over her narrow waist, over the gentle swell of her hips. She stood before him naked, and the sight of her heated his blood.

He drew her back into his arms for another burning kiss, felt her breasts pressing into his chest, and filled his hands with their fullness. He took each one into his mouth, heard her soft moan of pleasure, and his rod grew stiff and heavy, aching with his need of her, his fierce desire to be inside her.

Not yet, he told himself. He would pleasure her this night, give to her all he had to give. He would love her so fiercely she would never forget him. If she took another man into her bed, still she would think of him and remember this time together.

Lifting her into his arms, he carried her across the room and drew back the covers, then settled her on the deep feather mattress. Leif unfastened his trousers, shoved them down his legs, then joined her naked on the bed. For a moment he lay beside her, admiring the way the moonlight revealed her softly curving flesh, the beauty of her face, the paleness of her hair. The wind blew outside the window and he could hear it keening through the leafless, frost-covered branches of the tree behind the house.

It was a sound that whispered through his soul, a bone-deep sadness he knew would never leave him. The gods had played a cruel and bitter trick and he wondered if he would ever forgive them.

Still, they had given him this one last night, and he meant to make the most of it. When Krista reached for him, he went into her arms, kissing her deeply, taking what he wanted, what she wanted, heating her desire and his own. His mouth moved down her body, worshipping each of her lush, womanly breasts, kissing the soft skin over her belly, then moving lower. Settling himself between her legs, he pleasured her with his mouth and his hands, laving and fondling, until she reached release. He watched as her body arched upward in fulfillment, her eyes closing, her teeth sinking into her full bottom lip.

His need for her grew nearly unbearable. Absorbing her cries of passion, he slid his tongue into the sweet cavern of her mouth even as he thrust his hard length inside her. He filled her completely, taking what he so desperately wanted. Krista arched once more, urging him deeper still, and Leif groaned. He thrust into her again and again, branding her as his, filling her and filling her until she cried out his name and slipped over the edge into a shuddering release.

Still he did not stop, not until he had stirred her desire once more, her hips lifting toward him, meeting each of his deep strokes and silently demanding completion. She was his equal in passion, giving and taking with the same fierce need for him that he felt for her, and together they climbed the pinnacle and soared into the heavens.

They lay together for a time before he took her again, their mating fierce and yet gentle, at times almost reverent. When they had finished and she slept deeply, he wrapped her in her nightgown and carried her back to her room. She didn't awaken as he stooped to build up the fire in the hearth, didn't stir when he kissed her one last time.

By the time she awakened, he would be gone.

It was morning. Krista reached for Leif, but the bed was cold where he should have lain, and she realized the room she slept in was her own. A sob swelled in her throat. She reached for him again though she knew he was not there, her hand trembling as she touched the pillow next to hers.

Something lay atop it. Her fingers curled around the object and she sat up to see what it was.

There in her palm was a small, intricately carved ivory ring. It was the ring Leif had meant for her to wear as his wife.

She could not bear it.

By now the tide would have gone out. The *Sea Dragon* would have sailed, carrying Leif away from her forever. Clutching the ring in her hand, Krista turned her face into her pillow and began to weep.

Thirty-One

Krista moved through the following days as if in a trance. Coralee helped her select a wedding gown, a lovely pale blue lace-and-tulle concoction with a full skirt and lacy train that made her look like a fairy princess—a very tall fairy princess, but still, the gown was lovely.

Though her heart wasn't in it, Krista ordered ball gowns, day dresses and traveling suits she might need in her new life with Matthew Carlton.

Krista had yet to see him. She thought that her grandfather was afraid she might change her mind about the wedding, and so no chance for a meeting arose.

She didn't care. In truth, she cared nothing for the wedding she had agreed to, nothing for the future that loomed so bleakly ahead of her. She tried to keep her mind on work, to focus her thoughts on upcoming issues of *Heart to Heart*, but it was difficult to concentrate. She knew her family and friends were worried about her, but there was nothing she could do to escape the lethargy that weighed her down like a lead-lined cloak.

It was three days before the wedding when Coralee came into her office and quietly closed the door. "I wish to speak to you."

Krista looked up from the article she was trying to pen with very little success. "What is it? Has something happened?"

"I'm worried about you, Krista. Are you certain you are all right? I have never seen you this way. You're not eating enough. You're skin is pale and you can't seem to concentrate on the simplest of tasks."

"I'm all right. I am just…just a little nervous, I suppose. Surely that is normal for a woman about to be married."

"You are still in love with Leif and scarcely ready to wed another man."

"I will always be in love with Leif. But he is gone, so what does it matter? Matthew is willing to marry me and I am in need of a husband."

"Surely you can wait, postpone the wedding for a couple of months, give yourself a bit more time to heal."

Krista shook her head. "Time won't change anything. It is my duty to marry and give my family an heir. Grandfather has made all the arrangements and I am not going to disappoint him again."

"Krista…"

"Please, Coralee. My mind is made up. Leif is gone and he isn't coming back. If I cannot marry him, it doesn't matter whom I wed."

Corrie released a sigh. "I suppose you aren't the first woman who has married for reasons other than love."

"No, I am not. This is a marriage of convenience and both parties are well aware of it."

"You make it sound so cold. Is there a chance that someday you might develop feelings for Matthew?"

Krista glanced toward the window. The wind still blew, carrying Leif farther and farther away. "Perhaps it will hapen…in time. If I am lucky and we have children, then perhaps certain feelings will grow."

Corrie rounded the desk, leaned over and hugged her. "The wedding is only three days away. If you need anything—anything at all—just let me know."

"I need your friendship, Coralee. I have never needed it so badly."

Corrie reached out and caught her hand. "You have always had my friendship, and it has never been stronger than right now."

"Then with your help I will get through this. I will marry Matthew and get on with my life."

A stiff wind filled the sails of the *Sea Dragon,* propelling the schooner through the heavy swells. The ship heeled over, cutting through the frothy whitecaps stretching to the horizon. The tall masts creaked as Leif stood on deck behind the big teakwood wheel.

He was more than three days out of England, nearly halfway to Draugr Island. For each of those days, he had felt the pull of England like a great magnet calling him back. He had never felt anything like it, a power so strong he could almost believe he was beckoned by the gods themselves.

But he had a duty, he reminded himself. His people needed him and he had made a vow to his father. And the gods had never meant Krista to be his.

For three days he told himself this. For three days, he tried to convince himself. It was only moments ago, after another long, sleepless night, that he'd remembered the box.

The carved wooden box his uncle Sigurd had given him the morning he had sailed from Draugr Island.

"Once you are in Eng-land," his uncle had said, *"if still you*

*have doubts about returning to Draugr, then I would have you
open this…."*

"I have a duty, Uncle."

"Take the box," Sigurd had said. *"Open it only if your doubts
remain."*

Leif had taken it and placed it beneath the berth in his cabin.
He had never thought to open it. But each day, his doubts had
grown, and now he was driven to see what lay inside. Giving
the wheel over to Captain Twig, he strode toward the ladder
leading down to his quarters in the stern of the ship. It took only
moments to find the box and pull it from beneath his berth. He
set it on his bunk, lifted the rusty iron latch and opened the lid.

Inside, on a cloth of finely spun wool, lay an amulet carved
from the tusk of a walrus, suspended from a leather thong. He
recognized the object at once. It had been worn by his father
and his father's father before him. In the center of the ancient
amulet was a small silver hammer, the thunderbolt of Thor,
the god who protected men from evil.

Next to it rested a scrolled parchment fashioned from the
skin of a sheep.

Leif's hand shook as he reached for the paper and unrolled
it. He recognized the writing as his uncle's.

> *If you are reading this, then you have opened the box
> and it is clear that your future no longer lies on Draugr.
> Before his death, your father freed you from your vow, but
> only if it was certain your destiny lay elsewhere. He be-
> lieved until the end that you would return, and he asked
> me to give you his amulet to protect you on your life's jour-
> ney. Fear not for your people. Olav will rule wisely in your
> stead. He belongs here as you never did. Follow your heart,
> Nephew, and the path the gods have chosen for you.*
> *Sigurd*

Leif's heart beat oddly as he set the note aside and picked up the amulet. For as long as he could remember, his father had worn the hammer of Thor around his neck, as protection from whatever perils might lie in his path through life.

Ragnaar had given the necklace to him, his eldest son. Even after Leif had gone against his wishes, his father had loved him. And mayhap, in the end, he had understood why Leif had been compelled to leave.

Holding up the leather thong, Leif lifted it over his head and settled the amulet against his chest. It was as if he could feel his father's presence there beside him in the cabin.

"Thank you, Father," he said solemnly, his hand closing over the intricately carved ivory. Turning, he walked out of the cabin, filled with a sense of freedom and joy unlike anything he had known. The gods had been right all along. His heart and his destiny lay in England, and at last he was free to claim them.

As he strode across the deck, he shouted, "Make ready, Captain Twig! There's been a change of plans. We are returning to England!"

Leif smiled to think that in going back to a land that had once been so foreign—returning to Krista—he would at last be going home.

It was Saturday, Krista's wedding day. She rose early to prepare for it. Her trunks had been sent to her grandfather's town mansion, Hampton House, at the edge of the city. It was a bit of a carriage ride, and the wedding was set for noon. She and her father needed to get under way so they would not be late.

Though Thor had been invited, he had declined, and she thought he must have understood that though he was dark where Leif was fair, just looking at him reminded her of the husband she could not have.

He walked Krista and her father to the door, bent and kissed her cheek. "Be...happy, Krista," he said in English, and when her eyes widened at his effort and she smiled, he actually grinned, a rare occurrence for Thor.

"Thank you," she replied, and he nodded and seemed pleased to have understood.

Even before they left the house, her smile began to fade. She wasn't looking forward to a future with Matthew, as a new bride should have been. She wondered if it was truly fair to marry him when she was in love with another man.

She was lost in thought as she and her father rode through the crowded London streets.

"You look beautiful, my dear." The professor's voice reached her from the opposite side of the carriage, drawing her back to the present. She wasn't yet wearing her wedding dress; Coralee would help her change once she reached Hampton House. But her hair had been coiffed into thick golden curls that rested on her shoulders, and her maid, Priscilla, had pinned fresh gardenias into each cluster.

"Thank you, Father."

"You are going to make a beautiful bride."

Krista didn't reply. She only prayed that Matthew would keep his word and give her time to adjust to being his wife. She wasn't ready for any sort of intimacy between them. She needed a chance to get to know him, to come to terms with the future that lay ahead of them.

In time it will all work out, she told herself.

And she prayed that it would be true.

Once the *Sea Dragon* reached the London docks, it didn't take long for Leif and his men to make fast the lines and secure the boat. As soon as the task was completed, he leaped from the deck onto the wooden pier that led to the quay along the waterfront.

He rubbed his week's growth of beard, wishing he had taken time to shave before he left the ship, but he had been too eager to see Krista. He couldn't help thinking how different he looked from the civilized gentleman he had appeared when he had left England a week ago. His first day on the water, he had shed his English clothes and tossed them into the sea, hoping some of his painful memories would go with them.

It hadn't worked. He had dressed as a Viking, but the memories remained. He had been haunted by visions of a golden-haired goddess, as no man should have to endure.

But that was in the past and today it did not matter.

Leif found himself smiling. He was back in England, back in the land he intended to make his home.

Waving to Twig and his men, he strode along the quay in search of a hansom cab. It was a dark day, overcast and windy, the air damp with the promise of rain. His fur cloak whipped in the breeze as he hailed a cab and climbed in, eager to reach Krista's town house.

The journey seemed to take forever, though he knew it was less than half an hour. Leaping down from the cab, he flipped a coin to the driver, grateful he hadn't tossed the few he had taken with him into the sea with his clothes. Long strides carried him up the front porch steps. He pounded several times before the butler pulled it open.

"Good morning, Giles. I am here to see Krista. Where is she?"

For a moment, the old man didn't seem to recognize him. Then his aging face broke into a smile.

"Mr. Draugr! Do come in!"

"I need to see Krista, Giles. I will tell her myself I am here."

The butler's smile instantly faded. "Good Lord! Miss Krista…oh, dear me…"

The old man suddenly looked pale as death, and Leif's chest tightened. He took a threatening step in his direction. "Where the bloody hell is she?"

"She is…she is—"

"Getting married," Thor said in Norse, striding into the entry, followed by the lad, Jamie Suthers, and the little monkey, Alfinn, who rode on Jamie's shoulder.

"Married! Blood of Odin, what are you talking about?"

"Her grandfather arranged it," Thor told him. "She had to have a husband, he said. Something about a duty to her family. The professor tried to explain, but I did not catch it all."

Leif's hands unconsciously fisted. He understood exactly why Krista felt she had to marry. She had a duty, she had told him, and Leif understood that above all things. "What is the man's name?"

"Mat-thew Carlton."

Leif held in a wave of fury. "She is marrying that cold-hearted bastard today?"

Thor nodded.

"Where?"

"A place called Ham-ton House."

"I know the place. I was once there with Krista."

"Lord Hampton's estate is well known," Giles said. "Any cabbie will know how to get there. But you had better hurry. It is almost time for the wedding."

"Good luck to ye, sir!" Jamie hollered as Leif started running for the door. Thor's footfalls pounded behind him, the two men racing out to the street to wave down a cab. In minutes they were tearing through London, Leif's heart pounding in rhythm with the horse's hooves.

"How much farther is it?" he asked the driver after what seemed hours.

"Just a bit more, gov'nor."

"I'll pay you extra to get us there as fast as you can!"

The driver whipped the horse into a faster trot, and the carriage careened wildly through the streets toward the outskirts of the city. Finally, some ways up ahead, Leif caught a glimpse of open fields, then a huge three-story mansion on a hill in the distance.

"There she be, gov'nor."

Unconsciously, Leif reached for the amulet around his neck. Silently, he prayed that the gods would grant him this one last wish and he would get to the house in time.

Thirty-Two

It was a dismal, dreary day, with flat gray clouds hanging over the landscape. Wind rattled the trees, causing barren branches to scrape against the glass panes of the copper-roofed conservatory. Inside, lush green foliage formed the backdrop for the wedding about to take place.

Krista had to admit Aunt Abby and the earl had done an amazing job of making the greenhouse look like a welcoming garden. Along with the plants and miniature orange trees there were huge white urns overflowing with camellias and gardenias. A white latticework arbor decorated with the same pink and white flowers had been set up at one end, and rows of white garden chairs flanked it, each row trimmed with a large bow made of pale blue ribbon.

Krista was dressed in a gown of the same pale blue, the bodice fashioned of lace, the waist cut into a deep vee in front. The full gathered skirt was of lace as well, with a shorter, silver-shot overskirt, and her feet were encased in pale blue satin slippers.

The music of an organ began and she took a breath.

"Are you ready, my dear?" her father asked.

Krista simply nodded. She would never be ready, but she

could hardly tell him that. Her hand trembled as she took his arm and they made their way down the aisle between the rows of garden chairs toward the altar in front of the arbor. Organ music accompanied the march, the notes drifting above the plants and flowers in the conservatory.

Matthew waited for her at the altar. Tall and attractive, he was dressed immaculately in black and gray, his trousers, jacket and silver waistcoat fitting perfectly. He wore his thick, light brown hair short and parted stylishly in the middle.

His family was there—his father, the Earl of Lisemore; his brother, Phillip, Baron Argyle; and Phillip's plump little wife, Gretchen. Several of Matthew's friends, some Krista didn't yet know, were among the small gathering, and she recognized Lord and Lady Wimby.

On Krista's side of the aisle, Coralee looked oddly stoic, sitting next to her parents, Lord and Lady Selkirk. A number of Krista's grandfather's friends were present, including the Marquess and Marchioness of Lindorf, Lord and Lady Paisley. The archbishop was a close friend of the family, and though he wasn't conducting the ceremony, he sat among the guests, in the front row next to the earl.

Aunt Abby sat to the earl's left. Looking elegant and attractive in a gown of lavender silk, she occasionally dabbed a handkerchief discreetly beneath her eyes. In the last row sat *Heart to Heart*'s small staff: Bessie Briggs, Gerald Bonner and young Freddie Wilkes. Standing at the back of the conservatory, Krista's maid, Priscilla Dobbs, and several of the upper staff watched as she made her way down the aisle.

Most of Krista's friends were there, all but Thor, Jamie and little Alfinn, who waited back at the town house. They wished her well, she knew, and though she prayed it would be so, her heart did not believe it.

When she reached Matthew's side, his smile was soft and warm and yet did nothing to reassure her. She tried to return the smile as her father gave her into Matthew's care and the two of them turned toward the vicar, a small man with silver hair and wise, kindly eyes.

Vicar Jensen surveyed the crowd, then began the ceremony, glancing only briefly at the white, leather-bound bible resting open on the altar in front of him.

"Dearly beloved. We are gathered together today, in the sight of God and these witnesses, to join this man and this woman in the bonds of holy matrimony according to the ordinance of God."

Krista took a breath, fighting to control the trembling inside her.

"Marriage is an honorable and holy estate instituted by God and is, therefore, not to be entered into lightly, but thoughtfully and reverently, and in the fear of God. Therefore, if any man can show cause why these two people should not be lawfully wed, let him speak now or forever hold his peace."

A long silence ensued. Krista found herself praying that someone would speak up, shout from the rafters that this wedding was a travesty and that it should be stopped before it was too late.

But no sound came.

Her chest felt leaden. Her insides were quaking as the vicar began speaking again, intoning the words that would make her Matthew's wife.

Leif paid the cabbie, leaped out of the carriage before it rolled to a stop in front of the mansion, and raced for the massive front doors. He lifted the heavy brass knocker and began a furious pounding that didn't stop until one of the doors swung open and a thin, black-clad butler appeared.

He studied Leif through a pair of silver-rimmed spectacles. "What the devil…?"

"We're here for the wedding," Leif said. "Where is it?"

The butler surveyed him head to toe, taking in his woolen tunic, heavy fur cloak and soft leather boots, his slightly long hair and week's growth of beard. "I find that highly unlikely, sir." He solidly slammed the door.

Leif swore foully and started pounding again, but the heavy door did not open.

"We will have to go around to the back," Thor said, and both of them started moving toward the high stone wall that surrounded the estate. They scaled it without much effort and dropped down into the garden on the opposite side.

"We can go in through the servants' entrance," Leif said, heading in that direction, but Thor caught his arm.

"Do you hear that?"

Someone was singing a very solemn song accompanied by the music of an organ. Leif spun toward the sound, and a copper-roofed building at the back of the garden caught his eye. "In there," he said.

As they hurried forward, through the tiny paned windows he could see a number of well-dressed people seated in rows inside.

And then he saw Krista.

"There she is!" Thor said excitedly.

Leif nodded. "We must hurry." He began running toward the vision in blue who belonged to him and no other man, yanking open the door and racing inside. When he reached the entrance to the area where the wedding was being held, he stopped, terrified for a moment that he was too late.

Krista stood next to Matthew Carlton and a priest was speaking, saying the wedding vows, Leif knew. But all he could see was Krista and how pale she looked.

And how beautiful.

He strode down the aisle, unmindful of the gasps of the women and the outrage of the men who shot to their feet as he moved past, his eyes fixed on the woman who belonged to him, the woman he had come to claim at last.

The vicar began reciting the words that would bind her forever to Matthew. It was time to commit, time to repeat the vows that would make her Matthew's wife.

"Do you, Krista Chapman Hart, take this man—"

It was her father shouting Leif's name that stopped the vicar's words and had her spinning toward the door of the conservatory, spotting the towering blond giant who strode toward her down the aisle.

Her breath caught. For an instant, she thought she must be dreaming. She blinked but he was still there, coming closer, his jaw set in a fierce, determined line. He was dressed as a Viking, and she imagined that he must have changed his mind and come to take her home with him to Draugr, after all.

If he had, she would go and gladly. She had no heart for this marriage, this life that stretched ahead of her. It was no longer important. Only Leif mattered. Only Leif.

Her eyes filled with tears as he strode the last few paces and stopped in front her, reached out and gently touched her cheek.

"Krista…"

Matthew stepped between them. "What the devil do you think you're doing, Draugr?"

Leif straightened to his full height. "I have come for my woman. I intend to make her mine by English law as well as in the eyes of the gods who live in the place I come from."

Matthew whirled toward the guests in the conservatory, who were staring in awe at the spectacle playing out before them. "I want his man thrown out of here! He has no right to be here! I want him out—now!"

Her grandfather was standing now, as astonished as the rest of the crowd. He hurriedly made his way to where the small group stood before the altar, his bushy eyebrows drawn nearly together.

"See here, young man—you are interrupting my granddaughter's wedding!"

"She cannot marry this man," Leif said. "Krista belongs to me and I am here to claim her." For an instant, his eyes touched hers and there was so much love in them that fresh tears welled in her own.

"Take me with you, Leif. I don't care where we go as long as we can be together."

He turned to her grandfather. "Krista is mine. Ask her if you do not believe me."

"This is ridiculous!" Matthew's face turned red with rage.

"My son is right." The Earl of Lisemore left his seat and started down the aisle. "Matthew is engaged to this woman. The marriage settlement has already been paid. Have this man removed, immediately!"

Her grandfather drilled Krista with a glare. "I want an explanation, girl, and I want it now!"

She opened her mouth to reply, but Aunt Abby spoke up in her stead, carefully making her way toward them down the aisle. "I'll explain it to you, Thomas," she said. "This fellow is Leif Draugr. Mr. Draugr is the man Krista loves. He has come for her—and far past time, indeed—and it is clear she wishes to marry him."

Krista silently thanked her aunt. "Grandfather, Leif is the man I told you about…the man I love. He is the only man I wish to marry." She turned to her groom. "I'm sorry, Matthew. I never meant to hurt you in any way."

Matthew's face darkened, his mouth thinning into a bitter, ugly line. "Hurt me? You stupid bitch. I needed the money. It was always about the money. You're costing me a bloody fortune!"

Leif's powerful muscles tensed and his jaw went iron hard. Grabbing the lapel of Matthew's immaculate black coat, he spun him around, doubled up a fist and punched him in the face. Several women screamed as Matthew crashed into the latticework arbor, tumbling it backward, sending camellias and gardenias flying into the air.

Matthew's brother, Phillip, raced up, ready to enter the fray, and Krista saw Thor making his way down the aisle to his own brother's side. Dressed in English clothes, Thor looked far more the gentleman than Leif, and yet she could feel the power, the warrior in the man that was so deeply a part of him.

It was Lord Lisemore who broke the tension, so thick it seemed to sizzle around them. "Enough of this! My son has made matters more than clear. I believe it is time for us to leave. Help me get your brother on his feet."

Phillip looked shocked. "But, Father—"

"Your brother has an obsession with gambling," the earl told his son. "He is deeply in debt, which I have pretended not to know. I thought marrying Miss Hart would help him straighten out his life."

Matthew groaned just then, but made no move to rise from his place among the fallen flowers. His father and brother moved toward him, lifted him onto his feet and began to propel him unsteadily down the aisle toward the door.

"My word," Vicar Jensen said as the men disappeared from view.

"Indeed," said the professor, who had also joined the group.

Leif fixed his piercing blue eyes on the earl. "Krista says you need grandsons. My blood runs hot and strong and I will give her sturdy sons who will make you proud."

The earl's shrewd gaze traveled from the top of Leif's blond head, over his muscular neck, powerful chest and shoulders. "Yes…I can see you have very good bloodlines." He scratched his chin. "If you marry my granddaughter, will you agree to live here in England?"

"I once made a vow to my father that forced me to leave. But I am now free of that vow, and England is the home of my choice. I will stay, if Krista agrees to become my wife."

The tears in Krista's eyes spilled over onto her cheeks. Leif was staying. It was her heart's greatest wish.

The earl looked at the professor, who was grinning in a way Krista had never seen him do. "Well, Paxton, what do you think?"

Her father looked at Leif and she could see the affection and relief in his eyes. "I think we shall have to postpone the wedding for a day or two, until we can obtain a special license."

"Nonsense," said the earl. Turning, he walked over to his friend the archbishop, a lean, elegant-looking, white-haired man who sat in what seemed an amused yet fascinated silence in the front row.

"What say you, William? We've a license here, but it appears to have been issued in the wrong name. Can you correct that error?"

The archbishop smiled and rose to his feet. "I believe I can. Though it is highly irregular and I imagine some…adjustments will have to be made once I return to Canterbury." Moving along the row of seats, he joined the group in front of the altar. "Vicar Jensen, the license, if you please."

"Of course, Your Grace."

There was a brief flurry of activity as pen and ink were located and the necessary changes made. "As I said, this is highly irregular. I shall expect a sizable donation, Thomas, as a gesture of your good faith."

"That goes without saying, Your Grace." Her grandfather turned to Vicar Jensen. "I believe, sir, it is time we got on with the wedding."

"Capital!" said the professor. "Only this time my daughter will have a far more suitable groom."

Leif looked at Krista. Taking her hands, he carried them to his lips. "Today you will wed with a Viking, but on the morrow your husband will become a gentleman once more."

"However you dress, in your heart you are still a Viking. It is both sides of you that I love, and neither would I change."

Leif smiled softly and Krista smiled back.

"Get on with it, man," said the earl to the vicar, tossing Leif a look no man could mistake. "The sooner these two are wed, the sooner my new grandson-in-law will be carting his lady wife off to bed." He turned to Krista, whose cheeks began to turn red. "I'll have a chamber prepared in the east wing of the house. On the morrow, I am returning to the country. The two of you are welcome to stay as long as you wish."

Krista smiled shyly at Leif. "I believe my grandfather intends to hold you to your promise of grandsons."

Leif's eyes turned a scorching shade of blue. "I mean to keep my vow. I can think of nothing I would rather do."

Krista's blush deepened and her grandfather cackled with glee. In minutes, the ceremony was over and they were pronounced man and wife. Perhaps Leif's gods had been right. Perhaps from the start, she was destined to be his.

"You may kiss your bride," the vicar said, and Leif drew her into his arms. Whatever the truth, her heart belonged to him, just as his belonged to her.

And by the time Leif had finished his ravaging kiss, there wasn't a soul at the wedding who didn't believe it was true.

Epilogue

Six Months Later

Leif lay next to Krista in their bedroom in the town house her grandfather had given them as a wedding gift. They had just made love and were resting contentedly in the huge four-poster bed.

The room was warm. Lying next to him, Krista drowsed peacefully in the crook of his arm. It was May. Moonlight brightened the flowers in the garden at the rear of the house. A thin ray glinted between the curtains, lighting the gold of Krista's hair. His wife was so beautiful. Each day she seemed more so.

Sometimes Leif's breath caught when he looked at her, just knowing that she was his wife. At other times, he thought how close he had come to losing her. He had his uncle Sigurd to thank for the gift of his freedom and the life that now stretched ahead of him, and he would be forever in his debt.

Absently, he stroked Krista's silky hair, thinking how much had happened in the months since his return to England. He had never been a man to sit idle, and the first thing he had done was visit the friends he had made, Alexander Cain and Dylan Villard, the owners of Continental Shipping. Leif had a natural gift for sailing, he had discovered, and he enjoyed the sea, a legacy, perhaps, of his Viking heritage.

He had proposed to the men a shipping venture that included his brother, and had offered to put up both his and Thor's share of the capital. He wanted to start a packet line that carried goods to and from small, out-of-the way North Sea islands. He hoped to include village ports in England and Scotland, and eventually, Ireland and Wales, perhaps even more distant countries.

Cain and Villard had readily agreed, and so they had formed a company called Valhalla Shipping.

The *Sea Dragon* had been their first vessel, but already they had added four more. The money had begun to pour in, and it appeared the venture was going to be successful.

Leif found himself smiling. Thor's English was improving rapidly, and these days he rarely conversed in Norse, except when he was frustrated or nervous. There was plenty for him to do in their rapidly expanding company, and Thor seemed to thrive on the challenge.

In the big, deep bed, Leif felt Krista stir, then her soft lips pressed against his chest. "You are not sleeping," she said. "I thought you would be tired after…"

She let the sentence go unfinished, and even in the dark, he knew that she was blushing.

He kissed the top of her head. "I was thinking what a lucky man I am."

She shifted onto her side and propped herself on her elbow, drawing the sheet up to cover her lovely breasts. "We are both of us lucky." She leaned over and kissed him, and his body began to stir. "You've given me everything I ever wanted. I have my freedom, the independence I always valued so highly. I am married to a man I love more than my own life, and…"

"And…?" he pressed, raising one eyebrow.

"And soon I will have something even more precious."

His gaze sharpened on her face. "What is this you speak of?"

"I—I was going to wait a little longer to tell you. I wanted the time to be exactly right."

Leif shifted, came up over her, drew her down beneath him in the bed. He could feel her heart beating against his own. "Say it. Say the words I wish to hear."

Krista smiled at him, reached up and touched his cheek. "I carry your child, my love. It is the greatest gift you have ever given me."

Leif's gaze turned fierce. "It is only the first of many such gifts I mean to give you."

Then he kissed her and Krista kissed him back, looping her arms around his neck. It was the sweetest kiss she could remember, a gentle, yearning one that turned deep and hot and wild. Leif came into her again, claiming her and yet making her feel cherished.

Once, she had fought for her independence. In marrying Leif, she had given her future, her soul, into the care of a man unlike any she had known.

A unique and special man, Krista now knew.

A man with a heart of honor.

Author's Note

I hope you enjoyed HEART OF HONOR, the first book in the Heart Trilogy that continues with Coralee's story, HEART OF FIRE. HEART OF COURAGE is the third book in the series set around Krista's London ladies' gazette, *Heart to Heart*. Since you've met Krista and Leif, I hope you'll want to visit them and their friends again. Until then, best wishes and happy reading.

Kat

Turn the page for a preview of

SUMMIT OF ANGELS

the next thrilling paranormal romance
by
Kat Martin

Coming in July 2007
from MIRA Books

One

Autumn Sommers tossed and turned, an icy fear creeping over her. Gooseflesh rose over her skin and moisture popped out on her forehead at the vivid, frightening images expanding into the corners of her mind.

A little girl raced across the freshly mown front lawn of her suburban home, laughing as she played kickball with her friends, a child of five or six years old with delicate features, big blue eyes and softly curling long blond hair.

"Get the ball, Molly!" a little boy shouted, red-haired, all of the children around the same age.

But Molly's curious blue eyes were fixed on the man standing on the sidewalk holding a fuzzy black-and-white puppy. Ignoring the ball, which rolled past her short legs into the shrubs at the edge of the yard, she hurried toward the man.

"Molly!" Angry, the little boy raced after the ball, picked it up and gave it a sturdy kick back toward the other children, who squealed with delight and chased after it.

Molly saw only the adorable little puppy.

"You like Cuffy?" the man asked as she reached up to pet the dog with gentle, adoring strokes. "I have another puppy just like him. His name is Nicky, but somehow he got lost. I was hoping you might help me find him."

Lying in bed, Autumn shifted restlessly beneath the covers. "No..." she muttered, but the little girl couldn't hear her. She moved her head from side to side, trying to warn the child not to go with the man, but little Molly was already walking away, the puppy held snugly in her arms.

"Don't...go..." Autumn whispered, but the little girl just kept walking. Still clutching the puppy, the child climbed into the car and the man closed the door. He made his way to the driver's side, slid behind the wheel and started the engine. An instant later, the vehicle rolled quietly off down the street.

"Molly!" shouted the red-haired boy, running toward the disappearing auto. "You aren't supposed to go off with strangers!"

"Molly!" One of the other girls clamped small hands on her hips. "You're not supposed to leave the yard!" She turned to the red-haired boy. "She's really gonna be in trouble."

Worried now, the boy stared down the empty, tree-lined street. "Come on! We've got to go tell her mom!" The children started running toward the pathway leading to the house.

When the boy reached up and slammed the knocker down on the door, Autumn awakened from the dream.

Her heart was beating, thundering in her chest. Staring up at the ceiling, she blinked several times as the dream slipped away, then dragged in a couple of calming breaths. The dream was over and yet she remembered it clearly. She was still unnerved by what she had seen.

With a sigh, she glanced at the glowing red numbers on the digital clock beside her bed. It was almost 6:00 a.m., her usual time to get up. She was a fifth-grade schoolteacher at Lewis and Clark Elementary, though the summer break had just started and she was off work until the first of September. She punched off the alarm before it buzzed and swung her legs to the side of the bed.

Grabbing her quilted pink robe off the foot of the bed, she raked back her short auburn hair. It was naturally wavy. She only had to shower and towel herself dry and her hair fell into soft russet curls around her face. For her busy, athletic lifestyle it suited her perfectly.

Autumn thought of the dream as she headed for the bathroom of her twelfth-floor condo-apartment. Were the images she had seen a result of something she had watched on TV? Maybe something she had read in the newspapers? And if they were, why had she experienced the same dream three nights in a row?

The shower beckoned, the steam rising tantalizingly up inside the glass doors of the shower. She climbed beneath the soothing spray, then spent several minutes soaping and washing her hair, indulging herself in the warm, caressing water.

A few more minutes spent in front of the mirror applying a light touch of makeup and fluffing out her hair and she headed back into the bedroom to dress for the day. In jeans and a T-shirt, she went into the living room, a cozy, sunny area with sliding glass doors at one end leading out onto a balcony overlooking downtown Seattle.

With her father's help, she had purchased the apartment five years ago, just before real estate values had gone completely out of sight. She would have preferred one of the small Victorian homes near the Old Town district, but the condo was all she could really afford.

As a compromise to living a high-rise lifestyle, she had furnished the interior with antiques and hung lacy curtains at the windows. She had pulled up the carpet in the living room and replaced it with hardwood floors, then covered them with floral rugs and painted one of the walls a soft shade of rose. The bedroom was done in a floral print and she had bought a canopy bed.

The apartment was homey, nothing like the house in her dream, which, she had noticed last night, appeared to be a large custom-built, beige stucco-tract home with fancy brick trim. She had only gotten a glimpse, or at least remembered only enough to get the feeling the area was fairly exclusive, the children nicely dressed and obviously well cared for.

Autumn sighed as she grabbed her purse and headed for the elevator out in the hall. She was meeting her best friend, Terri Markham, at Starbucks for coffee before she headed over to her summer job at Pike's Gym. One of the things she liked best about living in the city was that everything was in walking distance: museums, theaters, libraries, and dozens of restaurants and cafés.

The grammar school where she taught was only a few blocks away, the gym was just up the hill, and Starbucks—her favorite—sat just down on the corner.

Terri was waiting when she arrived, twenty-seven years old, the same age as Autumn, a brunette who was slightly taller and more voluptuously built than her own petite, five-foot-three-inch frame. Both women were single, both career women. Terri was a legal secretary at one of the big law firms in town. They had met five years ago, introduced by mutual acquaintances. They say opposites attract and maybe that explained the friendship that had grown between them.

Autumn pushed open the glass door leading into Starbucks and seated at the back of the room, Terri shot to her feet and waved.

"Over here!" she called out.

Autumn wove her way through the tables packed with morning coffee drinkers and sat down in one of the small wrought-iron chairs, gratefully accepting the double-shot, nonfat latte that Terri shoved toward her.

"Thanks. Next time it's my turn." Autumn took a sip of the hot foamy brew that was her favorite morning drink and saw her friend frown above the rim of her paper cup.

"I thought you were staying home last night," Terri said.

"I did." Autumn sighed, catching the concern in Terri's glance. "But I didn't sleep very well, if that's what you're getting at."

"Honey, those dark circles are a dead giveaway." She grinned. "I didn't get a whole lot of sleep, myself, but I bet I had a lot more fun."

Autumn rolled her eyes. Everything about the two women was different. Where Autumn was interested in sports and loved being out-of-doors, Terri was obsessed with shopping and the latest fashions. And when it came to men, they couldn't have been more opposite.

"I thought you stopped seeing Ray." Autumn took a sip of her coffee. "You said he was dull and boring."

"I wasn't with Ray. I'm through with Ray. Last night at O'Shaunessy's I met this really hot guy named Tom. We really clicked, you know. We had this, like, incredible karma or something."

Autumn shook her head. "As I recall, you said you were going to reform. No more one-night stands. You said from now on you were going to get to know the guy, make sure he wasn't just some deadbeat."

"Tom's not a deadbeat—he's a lawyer. And the guy is terrific in bed."

Terri always thought the guys were great in bed the first time they made love. It was after she got to know them that the problems began. Autumn's emotions were too fragile to handle casual sex, but Terri was far more outgoing and spontaneous. She dated as many men as she could fit into her busy schedule and slept with whomever she pleased.

Autumn rarely dated. Except for her two teaching jobs, one at the grammar school and the other at exclusive Pike's Gym where she gave classes in rock climbing—her passion in life— she was kind of shy.

"So I know why *I* didn't get any sleep," Terri said. "What about you? You didn't have that weird dream again, did you?" Autumn ran a short, French-manicured nail around the rim of her paper cup. "Actually, I did."

After the second time it happened, she had told Terri about the dream, hoping her friend might have seen or read something that explained the occurrence.

"Was it the same? A little girl named Molly gets into a car and the guy drives away?"

"Unfortunately, yes."

"That's weird. Most people have recurring dreams about falling off a cliff or drowning or something."

"I know." She looked up, a tight feeling moving through her chest. "There's something I've never told you, Terri. I hoped I wouldn't have the dream again then I wouldn't have to worry about it."

Her friend leaned across the table, shoulder-length dark brown hair swinging forward with the movement. "So what haven't you told me?"

"This same thing happened to me once before—when I was a sophomore in high school. I began having this nightmare about a car wreck. My two best friends were in the car, and another kid, a new kid at school. I dreamed the new guy got drunk at a party and drove the car into a tree. It killed all three of them."

Terri's blue eyes widened. "Wow, that really was a nightmare."

"Back then I didn't say anything. I mean, it was a dream, right? I was only fifteen. I thought if I mentioned it, everyone would make fun of me. I knew they wouldn't believe me. I didn't believe it myself."

"Please don't tell me your dream came true."

Autumn's chest squeezed. She never talked about the nightmare. She felt too guilty. She should have done something, said something, and she had never forgiven herself for it.

"It happened exactly the way I dreamed. The new guy, Tim Wiseman, invited my friends, Jeff and Jolie, to a party. He was a year older and apparently there was liquor there. I guess they all got a little drunk, which Jeff and Jolie had never done before. On the way home, Tim was driving. It was raining and the streets were wet and slick. Tim took a curve too fast and the car slid into tree. He and Jeff both died instantly. Jolie lived a couple of days, but in the end, she died, too."

Terri stared at her in horror. "Oh, my God…"

Autumn glanced away, remembering the devastation and overwhelming grief she had felt back then. "I should have said something, done something before it was too late. If I had, my friends might still be alive."

Terri reached over and captured Autumn's hand. "It wasn't your fault. Like you said, you were only fifteen and even if you'd said something, no one would have believed you."

"That's what I tell myself."

"Has it happened again anytime since then?"

"Not until now. The first time, my mom had died two years earlier in a car wreck, so I figured maybe that's why I dreamed the dream, but now I don't think that was it. I keep hoping this isn't the same, but what if it is? What if there's a little girl out there somewhere who's about to be kidnapped?"

"Even if there is, this isn't like before. You knew those kids. You don't have any idea who this little girl might be. Even if she exists, you have no idea where to find her."

"Maybe. But if I knew the people in the dream before, maybe this little girl is someone else I know. I'm going to check school records, take a look at student photos. Maybe the face or the name will click."

"I suppose it's worth a try."

"That's what I figure."

"You know I'll help in any way I can."

"Thanks, Terri."

"Maybe you won't dream it again."

Autumn just nodded, hoping it was true.

The Crystal Rose

New York Times bestselling author

REBECCA BRANDEWYNE

London, England, 1850: Rose Windermere is nearly knocked to the ground by a man who whispers a dire warning…and presses a letter into her hands before fleeing. The mark with which the letter is sealed recalls Rose's idyllic childhood in India and a world that was destroyed when an uprising left her friend Hugo dead.

Pulled back into the exotic land of her youth, Rose must now unravel the strange machinations of a man whose lust for power will threaten a monarchy—and Rose's own heart.

"Intriguing tale (à la Dickens) that will captivate gothic fans."
—*Romantic Times BOOKreviews*
on *The Ninefold Key*

www.MIRABooks.com

MRB2296

REQUEST YOUR FREE BOOKS!

2 FREE NOVELS
FROM THE ROMANCE/SUSPENSE
COLLECTION PLUS 2 FREE GIFTS!

YES! Please send me 2 FREE novels from the Romance/Suspense Collection and my 2 FREE gifts. After receiving them, if I don't wish to receive any more books, I can return the shipping statement marked "cancel." If I don't cancel, I will receive 4 brand-new novels every month and be billed just $5.49 per book in the U.S., or $5.99 per book in Canada, plus 25¢ shipping and handling per book plus applicable taxes, if any*. That's a savings of at least 20% off the cover price! I understand that accepting the 2 free books and gifts places me under no obligation to buy anything. I can always return a shipment and cancel at any time. Even if I never buy another book from the Reader Service, the two free books and gifts are mine to keep forever.

185 MDN EF5Y   385 MDN EF6C

Name	(PLEASE PRINT)

Address	Apt. #

City	State/Prov.	Zip/Postal Code

Signature (if under 18, a parent or guardian must sign)

Mail to **The Reader Service:**
IN U.S.A.: P.O. Box 1867, Buffalo, NY 14240-1867
IN CANADA: P.O. Box 609, Fort Erie, Ontario L2A 5X3

Not valid to current subscribers to the Romance Collection,
the Suspense Collection or the Romance/Suspense Collection.

Want to try two free books from another line?
Call 1-800-873-8635 or visit www.morefreebooks.com.

* Terms and prices subject to change without notice. NY residents add applicable sales tax. Canadian residents will be charged applicable provincial taxes and GST. This offer is limited to one order per household. All orders subject to approval. Credit or debit balances in a customer's account(s) may be offset by any other outstanding balance owed by or to the customer. Please allow 4 to 6 weeks for delivery.

Your Privacy: Harlequin is committed to protecting your privacy. Our Privacy Policy is available online at www.eHarlequin.com or upon request from the Reader Service. From time to time we make our lists of customers available to reputable firms who may have a product or service of interest to you. If you would prefer we not share your name and address, please check here. ☐

BOB07

Kat Martin

32326 SCENT OF ROSES	__ $7.99 U.S.	__ $9.50 CAN.
32207 THE HANDMAIDEN'S NECKLACE	__ $7.99 U.S.	__ $9.50 CAN.
32199 THE DEVIL'S NECKLACE	__ $7.50 U.S.	__ $8.99 CAN.
32125 THE BRIDE'S NECKLACE	__ $7.50 U.S.	__ $8.99 CAN.

(limited quantities available)

TOTAL AMOUNT $_____
POSTAGE & HANDLING $_____
($1.00 FOR 1 BOOK, 50¢ for each additional)
APPLICABLE TAXES* $_____
TOTAL PAYABLE $_____

(check or money order—please do not send cash)

To order, complete this form and send it, along with a check or money order for the total above, payable to MIRA Books, to: **In the U.S.:** 3010 Walden Avenue, P.O. Box 9077, Buffalo, NY 14269-9077; **In Canada:** P.O. Box 636, Fort Erie, Ontario, L2A 5X3.

Name: _____
Address: _____ City: _____
State/Prov.: _____ Zip/Postal Code: _____
Account Number (if applicable): _____

075 CSAS

*New York residents remit applicable sales taxes.
*Canadian residents remit applicable GST and provincial taxes.

MIRA®